Relevé

By Kate L. Hart

Relevé

Library of Congress

Control Number: 2024909423

979-8-9853974-4-4

Printed in the United States of America

Books by Kate L. Hart

The Reality Show series

The Reality Show

The Whole Package

RelevÉ

Voices of Victorian Women series

The Lark

High Bred Rose

The Basra Pearls

Tattered Silk

Contents

Chapter 1

My hard plastic brace rode up under my armpit and rubbed in a weary, overbearing way. I bled where it chafed my torso raw. Not to mention the agony as the brace contorted my body forcing my spine to stay in line.

It would eventually make me crazy.

On top of all this, Mom expected me to go into public. She expected me to vacation as if nothing was wrong. As if.

"Erin, come on," Mom said, jumping out of the car. She moved quickly as if I should just be able to follow. But I sat in the car fidgeting in the heavy plastic back brace I wore day and night, refusing to get out. I hated the way people looked at me. One kid asked his mom if I were a robot because I couldn't move without jerky stiff motions. Adults took one glance, then turned their heads pretending not to notice me at all.

At ten years old, I knew how to play this game.

Mom knocked obnoxiously on my window, making her finger into to the curling 'come on' sign. When I didn't move, she opened the door.

"Let's go," she said impatiently.

I exited the vehicle breathing in the hot wet Hawaiian air that bathed me in perspiration. I moved slowly, and not just to be obnoxious; that was just a bonus. My stiff body ached after sitting so long. My hips were on fire. I stretched the way the physical therapist taught me but stopped when it forced the tears out of my eyes. I gingerly hobbled toward the spot where Mom stood on a bridge looking out at a waterfall. Dad and Drew already climbed down toward the waterfall, but I could barely move. I tried not to be queasy from the long, twisting road we drove to get to the one specific waterfall in Maui.

"Isn't this bewitching?" Mom asked, watching me while pulling her puffy blonde hair up off her neck. My whole family had sunkissed golden blond hair, but Mom's came from a bottle. She'd been a ballet dancer earlier in life and it showed the way she held her body – her shoulders back, her long neck moving her head gracefully in every direction, keeping her hyper aware.

I rolled my eyes. She noticed. She noticed everything. She was the first to notice when I couldn't stand up straight. She jumped all over the diagnosis. Scoliosis. She quit selling houses and went all in to help me. Every time I grew discouraged or wanted to give up, Mom pushed harder.

Everything my mother did made me stand out further. She forced me, not only to continue dance lessons but made me take more. I couldn't do half of what the other girls were doing without excruciating pain, but she didn't care. She made me continue anyway. I looked ridiculous, like at our yearly holiday party where dad's exceptionally large partner rolled his long limbs all over the place without moving any other part of his body and calling it dancing. When I pointed this out to her, she told me at least he let himself have a little fun. Apparently, I am more fastidious than an old man.

To try and force me to be normal, she often invited neighborhood girls over for movie nights and pool parties. They came. Their mothers made them come. They gawked at me in my brace. And to make matters worse, they saw what Mom did to the house. The week after she gave up being a real estate agent to take care of me, she redecorated the house. It gave me vindictive pleasure to tell her that all the neighbors, as indicated through their daughters, thought her color schemes for the entryway and sitting room outrageous and loud.

Our next-door neighbor, a particularly mean girl who was physically perfect in every way, let me know that her mother was petitioning the neighborhood association to write a bylaw stating that houses must be decorated in earth tones. I informed my mother of this hoping to see her positive smile fade, but it didn't.

Instead, she planned a family vacation. She took us to Maui – that's Hawaii. She forced me to snorkel. I forced myself to hate every moment of it. Even when a huge sea turtle came up and nudged me like an old friend. I moped like any self-respecting ten-year-old whose mother took her summer vacation captive.

She retaliated and took me on a car ride to purgatory. The road twisted for hours as we traced the outline of the coast. Perfect aqua tropical ocean bordered by lush emerald palms and underbrush. Every time I shifted in my seat, I moaned so she knew how badly I hurt. My dad almost ran off the road. He always asked what I needed. He would get me anything to make it better. Mom didn't say a thing to me. So, I ignored him. Then he would get annoyed with her.

When we finally stopped at the waterfall, I wanted to puke but wouldn't give her the satisfaction. I stood next to Mom and vocally agonized over the pain in my back and hips so she knew how bad such a long drive hurt. She watched the waterfall and not me.

"Come on," Mom said moving toward the path Dad and his perfect child Drew trod down to a pool beneath the waterfall.

"I can't climb down there," I growled, looking around, embarrassed, tugging at my back brace that rubbed unbearably, with only a thin tank top as a barrier against my moist, hot skin.

"Of course, you can," Mom said taking my hand, so I didn't slip in the mud. I pulled away and almost fell. Mom caught me. I hobbled down the path until I came to a large boulder in my way.

"If you hold on here," Mom said, showing me how to climb over.

"I can just wait here," I said. I looked at the boulder as an insurmountable task.

"Come on, right here."

"Fine," I snapped. I grabbed a hold of the rock and slowly maneuvered the body brace I wore. I heard people come up behind me, but I couldn't go any faster. My face burned hot as I inched my way over the boulder. Relief spread through me as I slid down and my feet touch the muddy path.

I might have felt a little victory, but a man in his twenties with extremely strong looking calves jumped over the stone and huffed as he pushed past us. He let us know he was annoyed. Mom, a very pretty woman even in her mid-thirties, gave him a small wave. His expression thawed. He gave her a congenial head nod as she pleasantly pulled me out of his way. I glared at that man with everything, I was worth. He didn't notice. A few others following him passed us. Though they were more polite about it, they all glanced at me uncomfortably.

I hobbled faster down the little path trying to move more quickly, but my center of balance was off, and I slid into the mud.

"For heaven's sake, Erin, you have to move at your own speed," Mom said helping me up. "Nobody else can dictate how fast you are capable of walking. Even if you move a little slower you will still make it to the same place. It's not a race."

I said nothing but continued to move quickly. I stumbled twice. If Mom hadn't been there, I would have tumbled into a sharp rock and cracked my head open. By the time I climbed down into the mist of the waterfall, the man with the calves already headed back to his car. I sat down over-heated and mortified, trying not to cry over being so slow. The dropping water fell like crystal teardrops from above, cooling me. Mom sat next to me.

"Do you see that moss growing up the rocks?" she asked.

"My back isn't impairing my vision," I said.

"It is almost the same color as the new growth on all these trees, isn't it?" she asked. I looked up. Lush green trees surrounded the cove that held the cool water runoff. Each tree grew two or three inches of new green, an almost florescent color compared with the lime green of the older parts of the branches.

"How many colors of green do you see here?" Mom asked.

I looked around and started to count but couldn't really tell.

"There's a lot."

"Erin, do you suppose that man who tripped over you on the trail noticed just how many colors of green there are in this gorgeous cove?"

"No."

"No, because he didn't bother to stop and really look."

"No, I guess not."

"Wasn't he a little childish letting us know how annoyed he was?" she asked, looking at me. Something in her tone felt accusatory. I bit my lip but did not respond.

"So, I ask you, should you feel sorry for yourself for going a little slower or for him for not appreciating this glorious, heavenly spot?"

"Or us both for having to drive on that road?"

Mom smiled but said nothing.

"I guess him. This feels…good," I said breathing in the mist of the waterfall speckling my face and cooling me down.

"Why did he bother coming this whole way and not enjoying it for a while?"

"I don't know. There are people in this life who look, but never see. Sweetie, there is a well inside each of us.

When you pull from it, you use up your precious energy. Will you waste your energy to be angry at a stranger you'll likely never see again because they put you out for a minute or two, or use the space in your head to see this beautiful place?"

I nodded. I never knew what to say when Mom brought out her hippy dippy side.

"You are being given an opportunity to see. I will not feel sorry for you because of it. It is time you stop feeling sorry for yourself as well," she added. I nodded. I didn't want to be like that man who would push past a ten-year-old in a back brace and have the nerve to act annoyed. I never wanted to be that man.

"Can you smell the wet earth and the tang of the plants?" Mom asked.

"Yeah," I said realizing I could distinguish each smell if I tried to find its source. I sat looking around and enjoying the water flecks on my face. I realized the exertion I made hiking down to the waterfall warmed up my muscles and I didn't feel as stiff and uncomfortable.

"Mom, is the moss the color of your couch?"

"It is," she said smiling, "a very natural color if you know where to look."

"And the red curtains are the color of those flowers?"

"Magenta," she said. I looked around. Our sitting room looked like the little cove we were in. The dark purple-brown rock I sat on was the color of the wood carvings and end tables in the room.

"My second year selling homes I won a trip here," Mom said. "It was the first time I'd ever felt like I earned something. I drove to this exact waterfall and I sat here feeling the peace of the island and this place. I fell in love with everything about it."

"You were trying to turn our living room into this place?"

"It helps me when I get stressed out."

This statement hit me in the chest. I tried to blink away the tears. I stressed her out. I knew this because I caught her crying a few times when she didn't think I was watching. My tender little heart broke knowing this. I sobbed out loud.

"I'm… I'm sorry you quit your job for me. I … I'm sorry I can't be the daughter you always wanted."

"I'm your mother, and you are still my Erin. You are mine. Nothing has changed inside; it is just your shell that's a little curvy. I love you no matter what."

"Then why are you forcing me to act like nothing's wrong?"

"That is not what I'm doing, Erin. I'm using my well of energy to help you. I've done a lot of research. I need you to accept what is happening to your body."

"I've accepted it more than you," I said. "You want me to be normal, but I'm not."

"No Honey, you want to sulk. You want to give into the idea your life is ruined. I want you to turn your attention, your energy, to fight. Everything I've read says you can't heal scoliosis," she said. "You have to fight it."

"It hurts," I whispered.

"All wars worth waging do," she whispered back.

"Okay, but how?"

"Move into relevé, sweetheart."

"What?"

"It means to rise up."

I said nothing to this.

"Erin, you have to work hard. It's the only way. Especially in your dance classes."

"I'm slower and older than everyone since I had to start over," I complained, hating how embarrassing it was to go in classes with the seven-year-old students.

"Then work harder and move up," she said, grinning at me.

"How? I'm so slow?"

"It doesn't matter how fast you go as long as you are moving forward. Never, never give up an experience that comes your way unless you have to."

"Like hiking to the waterfall?"

"Yep."

"But you made me."

"Yes, and I will continue to. You are my child, and I will be sure you live life to the fullest. I can push you, and ruin our relationship, or you can help push yourself and we will always be best friends, but either way, you have to fight this."

"Okay," I leaned against her. I was more afraid of losing her than fighting scoliosis. She kissed my head.

"Do me a favor, Sweetie."

"What?"

"Be kinder to Drew. He is trying too hard to be kind to you."

"Always defending Drew," I said rolling my eyes.

"I didn't stop being his mom because your back curves." Before I could respond, she said, "Come on, let's go bathe in the waterfall."

"Can I?"

"Trust me, together we can do this."

I trusted her. She helped me out of my back brace. I slid into the cool pool. The heat rash all over my back and torso stung and then soothed. My dad swam over to me, and, glancing at Mom, he gave me his hands. He pulled me further into the water. I frog paddled to where the water dropped down into the pool and a mist rose. I was able to stretch out in the water. My muscles relaxed.

If I hadn't gone swimming, I may not have made it back down the never-ending twisty road.

We stopped at every small shop on the road. I knew Mom did it so I could get out and stretch. Dad kissed me and hugged me every time we stopped. I didn't push him away like I had been. Every time we stopped, he claimed we had a duty to support the local economy.

Drew did not complain about the extra four hours it took us to make it down the road. Scoliosis wasn't happening to just me. My family endured it as well, though they did it with a touch more grace than I had been.

I developed a new tendency to look for colors. It distracted me long enough so I didn't go crazy trying to tolerate the constant pain.

The next day we went to a dock to rent a sailboat. I sat down waiting for my dad to come back. I stuck my feet in the ocean, which looked like blue ink when the clouds came out. I pulled my foot out hoping it turned color, but it didn't.

The white and red sailboat we rented looked majestic against the sky-filled puffy white clouds. It cut through the waves creating a white frothy wake that grew into purples and blues until it moved on and gave the ocean back to the blue of the sky.

I couldn't man the sails with the captain like Drew did. Nor could I pull in the huge yellowfin tuna my brother caught. I had to stay sitting so I didn't further injure my back. However, I could be happy for Drew. Drew had happy mischievous blue eyes and blond hair, and strangers would comment on how adorable he was. Often it was hard to look at his adorableness when I felt like Quasimodo.

It took some effort. It took a few tries to pull enough energy from Mom's well, but instead of pouting because he could still do things that I could not, I cheered for Drew when he caught his fish. The strangest thing happened. Because I was happy for him, instead of spewing my wrath at him, he stayed around me instead of running away. He spent the rest of the ride sneaking me juice pouches.

Mom told him not to take anymore or it would ruin my appetite for lunch. She pretended not to notice when he did it again. Something about us working together made her smile bigger than she had since my back started to curve.

We found a spot on the beach with a grill, and I helped cook the fish over the coals with fresh pineapple and mangos. Drew, being an eight-year-old boy, stuck a long dry leaf into the coals. It ignited. I screamed.

"Get some water!"

"Dad's going to kill me," Drew said. Dad ran toward us with a shovel.

"It's okay, I'll take it!" I watched the leaf burn.

"Drew," Dad started as he buried the leaf in dirt, "how many times--"

"It was my fault sorry Dad," I said. "I didn't think it would catch fire on the coals."

"Oh, Erin honey, yeah, those coals are red hot. Be more careful, okay, Sweetie," he said kissing my forehead. He took the leaf and carried it down into the surf to be sure it was out.

"Thanks Erin," Drew said, grinning.

"That's okay. Just don't do it again."

"Okay."

Over the next few years my parents suspected I was taking Drew's blunders upon myself, but never said anything.

When we came home from Maui, I still looked for colors. Mom's island sitting room became my favorite place to stretch. I complained sometimes, but not nearly as much. Instead, I pushed myself. I found ways to fight through the pain. I cried; the tears could not always be restrained but I never stopped fighting.

At the end of the summer Mom threw a back-to-school party. The neighborhood girls came. This time when my mother's sitting room was brought up as loud, I suggested they only thought so because they had never been to Maui. All the colors were very natural there. Each girl made an excuse as to why their parents hadn't taken them. I suggested they go before they pass judgement on my sitting room. That is the summer I started growing taller despite the S curve in my back.

Chapter 2

How I went from that beginning onto a reality show followed a very distinct path. A path, though hard, I would not undo for anything. It took me exactly where I am supposed to be. Not directly. No path can be traversed without avoiding boulders and sliding in the mud. I endured faltering, only to slip and then find my footing several times along the way.

The first steps on my path were the seven years of imprisonment in my back brace. With hard work and patience, I learned to dance again while fighting scoliosis. The only time I gained freedom from my brace was when I danced. I don't know if I loved dancing, or hated the brace, but after a while, ballet became my solace.

My curved spine started to sink into the muscles in my back. Eventually I scarred where the brace rubbed until it bled, healed, then bled again. A heat rash often covered my torso all summer from the brace. The leo I wore when I took it off Mom ordered from a special Italian yarn, was near heaven to put on and soothed it for a time.

I endured while dancing and learning the name of every color. I never made many real friends. At first, I was disabled and only those who took on charity cases talked to me in the most downward fashion, and for some reason very loudly. Then, after fighting long enough, I became the competition. Except I became capable of moving and spinning in ways the other dancers couldn't, inhibited by their spines. I found a life in the light of the stage and started to crave it.

From fourteen to seventeen, I lived in dorms in New York and danced while going to school.

By age seventeen, I finished growing. My spine never twisted worse from ten to seventeen because I wore the brace. By seventeen the S shape in my back wasn't even detectable to most people.

I endured an operation to straighten a disc which significantly helped the lower half of my back.

In ballet, I advanced enough to go directly into the New York Dance Company, but my parents insisted I get a college degree. Nobody said it was because I had to have something to fall back on, in case dancing professionally didn't work out, but we all knew that was the reason.

I went to Barnard University and pulled good grades while I participated in The American Ballet's summer intensives on top of getting a double major in Dance and Economics. After graduation, I joined the American Ballet. I was much older in terms of professional dancing starting at twenty-three, but I worked hard and promoted into the corps de ballet quickly. After two more years, I was promoted to a soloist but still fell behind in terms of where I wanted to be in my dance career. My parents and I started to find ways to distinguish me from the other soloists.

I started blogging. I was very open about my scoliosis and my journey to become a professional dancer. I ended up with hundreds of thousands of followers.

One day, my dad, who also acted as my manager, received a phone call from one Julian Morrows, producer of *The Whole Package,* a very popular television reality show. And since I needed the publicity, I agreed to meet with him. It had nothing to do with the fact that *The Whole Package* was my favorite show. Really, nothing.

My parents and I went to the studio building in New York. We dressed in black suits and looked as if we could battle aliens. I pulled my blonde, waist-length hair into a braided bun and buttoned up my tight suit jacket so I looked professional. Mom wore her suit a little looser, and her shoulder-length hair down, but we still looked more like sisters than mother and daughter.

Dad always jelled his short blond hair, streaked with butterscotch, to the side. He was scraping his head on six feet tall and kept himself in good shape for a man in his early fifties.

We rode an impressively fast elevator to the top floor. Exiting the elevator, we walked to a series of glass doors.

"Erin, welcome," said a woman wearing short-sleeve blouse and trousers, opening one of the glass doors. I nodded at her but didn't have time to say anything

"Erin thanks so much for coming," said a man in his 40s with a silver-grey hair and beard. He walked toward me, his wide smile like a warm, fuzzy blanket pulling me in.

"I am Julian Morrows."

He turned his head and introduced the other two men and a woman in the room. I couldn't hear what he said, as his face wasn't turned toward me, but toward my father. After I shook hands with everyone, I shifted in time to hear Julian say:

"We were meant for each other, my show and your story. You are an inspiration to every little girl with a dream who has health problems."

"Thank you." He seemed genuinely impressed by me.

"Have you seen my show?" he asked, motioning for me and my parents to sit in armchairs across from him.

"Every season," I replied. "Is Dr. Corbon coming to this meeting?"

The woman who developed The Whole Package was one of my personal heroes. I couldn't wait to meet her.

"Oh, she isn't involved in this part of the show," Julian said. This time his smile faltered. "I'm glad you've seen the show. It's always best to know what to expect."

"I love *The Whole Package*."

"I loved reading your blog. Do you know I spent hours reading about how you…"

Julian Morrows gushed about my blog and my accomplishments for fifteen minutes. His warm brown eyes danced and my self-worth tripled from his estimations. The slender, stuffy looking man, who must have been in charge, spoke rarely, but listened carefully and received almost as much praise from Julian as I did. Julian talked for a long time about how much time commitment the show entailed. Finally, after explaining what it took to come on the show, Julian gave me a contract to sign. My father, an attorney, said: "I'll read that and get back to you."

"I need to know in the next few days, but I doubt you'll need that long. Erin is the whole package. I see her as being extremely competitive," Julian said, He winked at me in his very friendly way.

"Okay, thanks," I said, knowing my grin stretched ridiculously big as I left the office. I was going on my favorite reality show ever.

Though I did not need convincing, my parents encouraged me to put my career on hold for a few months and go on *The Whole Package*. A little bit of fame goes a long way in the dance world. I didn't hesitate. Instead, I embraced the idea of becoming a Top Principal dancer for the American Ballet, pushing me toward the lifetime achievement of being declared one of only a few Prima Ballerina Assoluta.

A little over a year later I packed my bag for northern California, ecstatic.

My mother was a be-prepared-for-anything, and then expect-the-best-to happen-to-you kind of lady. I did not question when she brought down her huge, black, be-prepared-for-anything suitcase.

"Here Sis, look what I got you," Mom said holding up a gorgeous navy-blue cocktail dress. It was off the shoulders with beading across an A-Line bodice, and an airy chiffon skirt. I loved skirts that swirled around me like I danced instead of walked. Mom always wanted me to try other looks, but I knew what I liked, and I wouldn't wear what I didn't.

"Wow, thanks Mom."

"Of course."

"What happened to the other dress we chose?"

"You can only bring one suitcase. That dress would wrinkle. This dress will travel well." She fidgeted over the dress. When Mom got nervous, she shopped and fidgeted.

"Is something wrong?" I asked.

"I... I don't want to worry you."

"What happened?"

"I read that Julian Marrows and Dr. Corbon are having creative differences and Dr. Corbon won't be as involved this season." Her hand began to play with my long hair.

"Ah, man," I said. "I really wanted to meet her."

"I know sweetheart, but I think we can trust Mr. Marrows to look out for your best interest. Besides, we don't know what that means, anyway. We have no idea how much she did with the show before. She might have just come up with the concept of a show about a resilient person being rewarded with a million dollars. Then made a few guest appearances. Mr. Marrows may always have done everything."

"That's true." I stopped my mother's hand. "Do you really think I'm going to need my blow-dryer? You don't think they'll have one?"

"Do you want to be caught without it? Hoping that mane of yours will air dry?" She laughed, twisting the end of my waist-length ivory blonde hair trying to get it to curl.

"No."

"Besides, even if they do have one, it won't be this one," she said holding up the professional grade dryer.

"True." I settled it into the mesh casing of the bag with my curling iron, straightener, styling glove, clips and the five bottles of product I used to clean and style my hair.

We over-filled the bag with every little thing I might need. Mom talked, mostly about what an amazing opportunity I would have to make a name for myself, win a million dollars, and come back to take the top spot in my dance company.

"I don't know, Mom. That seems a little optimistic." I pushed down on the huge suitcase to zip it closed.

"Come on, Erin. Who wouldn't come to see the winner of *The Whole Package* dance live?"

"Yeah, hopefully," I said, trying to manage my anticipation.

"Just don't fall too hard for the judge," she said, nudging me.

"Oh, come on. The romance is just something they cooked up in the last few seasons."

I shook my head, knowing my face was bright red. Secretly I knew there was a chance I could fall in love with the judge. I welcomed the idea. I received a folder a week earlier introducing the judge, Ethan. A hot pediatrician topped my list of someone I'd date. I wanted to be a little in love. There was never a real lasting love that came from the show, simply good chemistry, and a little romance. It all sounded divine to me.

Chapter 3

I flew to California, my blonde hair hanging down to my waist, my smile contagious, and my life experience whispering I could accomplish anything I tried.

The first hint things were not as I expected came when I walked into the hotel lobby and noticed Julian Marrows. It almost appeared he was waiting for me. I waved to him with the friendly mannerisms we shared. He looked at me twice in a way that made me sure I smelled like airplane. He said nothing to me but turned to a stylist standing next to him and said, "She looks like a child. Cut her hair."

"Oh, I have to keep it past my shoulder blades," I said, "I'll be kicked out of American if I don't."

"It'll grow back. I need you to appear less… juvenile. It helps the audience see you've grown up. Unless you've changed your mind about coming on the show," Julian said. He leaned forward and arched his eyebrows. He examined me as I examined him. His whiskers were pewter streaked with steel, iron-cladding his strangely altered will over mine. His sharp nut-brown, eagle eyes zeroed in on me, and I knew he threatened me. I had to make a choice.

My dad had watched Julian closely. Dad assured me I would win and become a principal dancer. My dad was like a human lie detector.

He swore Julian was telling the truth when he said I had a good chance of winning.

"I guess cut it," I said, knowing it was an awful sort of gamble. The stylist took me back to the hotel spa. I couldn't watch as long creamy locks spilled to the ground and were swept away.

My indigo eyes didn't seem fairy-like with the blonde bob. Instead, all I saw was the haircut of my seventh-grade math teacher. I hadn't liked her. In this moment of self-defeat, I did not hold my core straight, and my right shoulder rose slightly higher than my left. My spinal cord shaped my body. I took a deep breath, I squared my body, and determined to make the best of the situation.

"Oh, that look is…very flattering," Julian said squinting at me when he came back into the room. If I didn't know better, I would think he was upset that I looked presentable.

"Thanks," I said looking more at the stylist than Julian.

After I checked in, I showered all the excess hair off. The prop master came up to my room and quickly approved my perfect beaded navy cocktail dress for the next day. I tried to lay down and rest but couldn't relax. It was an anxious night, which was unusual for me. I performed for thousands of people on a regular basis and rarely felt nervous.

The next morning, I put on my dress, but had no idea what to do with my hair so I just left it to hang down. I didn't even need my diffuser; all the curls were cut out. At the time specified in my packet, I walked alone to the hotel conference room for a welcome brunch. Julian didn't seem to even notice me. Considering he got a little too handsy with the girls he did notice, I started to think I wanted to be ignored by him. I wasn't disappointed.

The brunch was held in a room that felt too small for the twenty-five or so people assembled.

Carrie, a charismatic woman with Spanish red-brick hair and matching eyes, came in and Julian followed her around spewing his charm on her, as he once had on me. Her posture was particularly good, her cocktail dress looked vintage lace and expensive silk, and her eyes were quick to see.

I stood at a tall table nibbling a muffin and watched her. I felt annoyed – I was used to being the dazzling one.

After a short presentation about how to look good on camera, an extremely thin woman with strawberry blonde hair and sky-blue eyes set her plate next to mine.

"You figure that's our competition," she said nodding at Carrie and Julian with no other introduction.

"Probably," I said holding a hand to her. "I'm Erin."

"Serena," the woman said, batting her long coppery eye lashes, like she had to impulsively flutter when she introduced herself.

"Should we try to befriend Carrie?" I asked.

"No, she'll submarine us. We definitely don't trust her," Serena said. Her light strawberry blonde hair swung when she assured me, and I wondered why she was allowed to keep hers past her shoulder blades.

"I doubt she can submarine us," I said with a laugh.

"Come on. Don't be so naïve, Erin," she said. "They always have a spy who causes trouble for the contestants. She is clearly working for Julian. If you get close to her, she will find ways to undermine you."

"I've seen every episode of this show. I've never seen that," I said.

"Not in the first two seasons, but Lena in season three," Serena said.

"Oh, right," I said remembering the woman who could turn any situation catty.

"She was less obvious, but I definitely think last season it was Harley."

"Yeah," I agreed. "She made it for a long time without being kicked off. I thought she'd go every time, but she just kept making it into the next rounds."

"Because she was the plant," Serena said. "Trust me, if you stick with me, everything will work out."

I trusted my new friend, treasuring the experience of camaraderie with another woman. Julian glanced at us, catching our attention and smiled warmly. Serena even waved a little. I felt better about everything. We chatted over brunch about past seasons. Serena was a little mean about some of the other contestants, but I couldn't help noticing everyone was extremely typecast.

"Okay, the busty, slutty one," Serena said. She nodded toward a woman. I looked and saw a gorgeous woman in a short spaghetti strap dress. She had a blunt bang across her forehead and short, wheat-colored hair. She had a shapely body and could model swimsuits. She was what I thought of as beautiful.

Being content with my body was hard. On some level I knew it wasn't fair to my poor body. It carried me through every day, always complied when I forced it to keep dancing. But the shapely woman who could model swimsuits – she was my ideal.

I wished at that moment I defended her, but I felt like I was making a friend. I wanted a friend so badly I did not. Serena finished: "Her name is Tess. She'll keep the show in sarcasm. Like Oliva last season."

"Yeah, and the smoky blonde woman, the really pretty one, is going to be the drama queen but no one will care because she's so pretty," I said, annoyed at the sight of her curly blonde hair down past her shoulder blades. Her impeccable beauty, her perfect shape made her seem a fantasy.

"Her name is Sandra, and you are totally right," Serena said laughing with a huge toothy grin.

"What about that woman there?" I said looking with a nod at a woman curled over her table. She had olive skin, her dark hair spilling over her shoulders as she seemed to be creating mental lists of a study sheets, or a chore chart. We both watched her look to the ceiling and then chant to herself.

"I doubt she'll even make it on the show," Serena whispered, "I think her name is Veronica."

"Yeah, probably not," I responded.

I wondered where I stood in that. I felt the new sensation of the tips of my hair on the back of my neck and tried to figure out who I was from the previous season. I didn't really seem to fit any role. When I asked my new friend, Serena just said:

"We are both Christy, of course. We're the winners."

"Well, of course we are," I said with a laugh.

Chapter 4

We were bused out to a lonely spot on the cliffs overlooking the ocean. I was contestant number nineteen of twenty. I sat waiting forever to meet the judge. Then it was over in less than a minute. Meeting Ethan, the hot pediatrician, was short and very anticlimactic. I told him of the path I trod, but he was preoccupied, and perhaps overwhelmed. The encounter was a letdown.

On the other hand, opening the door and peeking into the manor house excited me in a way I had not expected. The house was so familiar to me. It was much smaller in real life than on TV. The rooms that seemed separate on TV were a part of the huge open living space but were decorated as if they were distinct.

The most important room, the elimination room, was the empty space at the bottom of the staircase. Next came the sitting room, a set of sofas, and two love seats. The dining room table finished the open space. It had twelve place settings; an indicator half of the twenty contestants would be cut before the night ended. At this point I did not doubt I had a seat at the table.

Surreal didn't even begin to describe what it felt like to see it all in person. I stared so long into the house that I didn't have the momentum to pull my suitcase up the lip of the doorway. My strength could not be so stunted with warm muscles, but cold, I struggled. I couldn't lift the wheel high enough to get it unstuck and hold the door open at the same time.

Serena, who appeared to be looking for me, made eye contact. I thought she would come help me, but she ducked into a back-room area under the bend of the stairs. Carrie, Julian's submariner, of all people, came over and said, "Here, Erin. Let's lift it up."

"Oh yeah, it's stuck," I said feeling the blood rush to my face. We pulled, and it finally lurched through the door.

"Here, Erin, come do your interview," Serena said. She sat on the sectional set up in front of a TV screen to which the cameraman could send his live feed.

A tall cameraman with the lean muscles of a dancer, wavy toffee-colored hair, and sparkling cocoa eyes, looked out of his camera surprised to find me already situated.

"Erin, the ballet dancer with scoliosis," he said welcoming me into his space. He watched me, like he found me intriguing. This man showed more interest in me than Ethan. He asked me all about the path I trod to get there.

He'd done all sorts of research to know me. We talked for a long time, and I could see out of the corner of my eye Serena wanted to leave. There was something to be said for being prepared. I killed every question with perfect clarity and knew exactly what to say until the cameraman leaned in and said, "Do you think it further injured your back when you fell on stage at seventeen? Is that the real reason you had to get a disk in your back fixed?"

I stared at him, stunned. I felt myself start to shake. How did he even know about that? It happened in practice.

"I… we couldn't be sure," I said feeling off balance.

"But can you really recommend parents put their children into ballet if they are suffering from scoliosis?"

"Absolutely," I said fired up, "I mean, yeah, research on scoliosis comes out all the time saying yea or nay, but ballet saved me. Overcoming scoliosis is about getting back up. Every time I fell, I got back up and I am stronger physically and mentally for it. Isn't that what this show is about, resilience? You can't really pick yourself up resiliently unless you've fallen first, right?"

The cameraman looked up. His face broke into a grin.

"You are right," he said. He beamed at me like he was proud of me. I relaxed and grinned back feeling proud of myself for standing my ground. It felt like I passed the first test.

Then it hit me like a flash. Julian Marrows was acting so distant as a test. He couldn't look like he favored me, it was too obvious. I decided Serena was right. Carrie was the plant. The other women were already sucking up to her. I smiled more brightly sure I had this all figured out.

We finished the interview and the cameraman moved out from behind his tripod. He wore a plain black t-shirt and black jeans with clunky black boots. He reached out his hand to me and took mine in both of his caressing it slowly. His eyes smiled into mine. He said, "Thanks for the interview, Erin."

"My pleasure," I said, regretting the way my hand felt so cold when he let go.

Everyone pretended to mingle, but Ethan stood in the center of a funnel. We all gravitated toward him. He broke free from the woman after a while and went to find the other contestant. As he passed by us, Serena stood up and grabbed my arm. She shoved me in front of him, so it looked like I cut him off, and she was holding me back.

"What the…?" I stammered, embarrassed. Ethan looked surprised. Serena nodded at me, like, duh, talk to him.

"Hey," I said, looking at Serena unsurely.

"Hey, Erin, the dancer with scoliosis," he said.

"Yeah," I stammered, unable to move past the embarrassment of knocking into him.

"I was going to tell you before I have a friend whose curvature wasn't as bad as yours, but she played tennis in order to strengthen her muscles," he said.

"Really?" I asked, "that's so--"

"I have a patient with scoliosis," Serena cut in. "It doesn't limit your life expectancy."

I looked at her. Ethan squinted a little.

"It can be very painful," he said, glancing at Serena.

"No, yeah, I know, but there is hope," she said. Turning to me she said sweetly, "You know it doesn't necessarily inhibit your life expectancy."

"No. Right," I said.

"When my parents died, I thought I would die too, but I had to stay strong for my little sister," Serena said.

"You are amazing," I said, feeling so sorry for her. I couldn't imagine not having my parents. She told Ethan a lot about living in a group home with her sister. She made sure she kept them both up on her homework. They put such an emphasis on school she ended up graduating magna cum laude from nursing school.

Ethan nodded at her a lot. He glanced at me. I nodded and smiled. Though Serena told her sad tale well, she felt rehearsed and sounded more like bragging than grieving. After a while Ethan shifted the conversation.

"Erin, did you have to wear back brace quite a bit?" he asked.

"Eighteen hours a day, I only took it off the six hours I danced. I slept in it," I said.

"That's dedication. I have a patient with scoliosis. She refuses to wear her brace and isn't showing up for her physical therapy sessions. I'd love for you to come talk to her after the show ends," he said.

"I'd love that. I taught ballet to underprivileged kids for a while. I love working with kids."

"That's awesome. How old were you when you finally took your brace off for good?" he asked. I laughed. "I think you may only be interested in me as a patient," I said squinting at him.

"No, no, I … well it really is intriguing that you were able to go without fusing your back at all."

"Keeping all your range of motion as a dancer is so important," I said. "It is imperative." I bent to the right, brushing my hand across the floor gracefully. "Not all dancers can bend like I can. It can be a gift if your patient looks at it the right way."

"Yeah, not like losing your parents at an incredibly young age," Serena cut in again. "There is no way to look at that like it's a gift."

"Ethan, we need you to mingle," Lance said pulling him away.

"Bye, Erin, Serena," he said moving away.

I looked after him, but Serena said, "You looked so dumb. Don't be so obsessed with dancing; you make a fool of yourself again."

Then she bent over making sure I knew how awkward I had looked in front of Ethan. She laughed like it was so funny. I disregarded her when the cameraman I liked came up and offered me a plate of cheese and crackers.

"Hey, you double as a waiter," I said, mirroring his grin.

"Yeah, the main camera operator is following Ethan around. Our room cameras fill in the extra screen time. Despite my degree in digital media, I'm passing out refreshments," he said.

I laughed.

"I'm Colby, also known as camera operator Number Two," he said reaching a hand from under the tray.

"Erin," I said shaking with him again. This time the action felt more professional as he only had access to one hand.

"Right," he said with a laugh.

"Do we get to meet Dr. Corbon? Or is she not doing this season at all?" I asked.

"Uh, she's more into her talk show now. This is Julian's baby," Colby said quietly.

"Oh," I said, disappointed.

"Yeah, Julian is awesome, though. He's going to get me in touch with the powers that be so one day I can work with the network directly," Colby said, excited.

"Your degree is in camera operating," I said.

"I've got a bachelor's in digital media, but I'm getting a master's in journalism. I'm going to be the next Steve Kroft," he said.

"Is that..."

"Sixty Minutes, they sniff out stories and report on them," he said.

"That's cool," I said.

"Thanks," he said grinning. He was good looking enough to go on air, and he couldn't be much older than my twenty-five. He caught me examining him and I blushed, looking away.

"What do we do now?" I asked.

"Duh. We get Ethan's attention. The more we interact with him, the more he remembers us," Serena said, scowling at Colby.

"Or you relax and recognize that each of you have great stories of resilience and trust the process," Colby said.

"That makes sense. This is meant to be a way for women to showcase each other, not compete, not really," I said, but stopped.

Ethan had sidled up to us while camera operator Number One went to the bathroom. He was listening to me.

"Hey," I said surprised Ethan came over to me of his own free will, and not Serena's badgering.

"I wanted to ask you," he said. "Oh sorry. Am I interrupting?"

"No, no," I said, standing up uncomfortably, brushing cracker crumbs from my lap. "What's up?"

"I wanted to know if you'd come to Boston this Fall. I would love for you to run a clinic on how to keep your chin up while battling scoliosis," he said. "Is that something you'd be interested in?"

"I'd love to. I have tricks on how to keep the back brace from chafing as well," I said.

"Yeah, let's set this up for sure," he said warmly. The way he smiled at me, searched me even, I thought we may be having a connection, a bit of a spark. His silver blue eyes were almost unreal, alien-like, and put me on edge like he was probing me. I preferred Colby's light brown comfortable eyes that encouraged me to speak.

"You should read her blog," Colby said touching my arm, so I turned to looked at him, his grin turning his face into a perfect shape. "She could also teach them some stretching techniques."

"That's true," I said nodding at Colby.

"That'd be great," Ethan said. Turning to Colby, he said, "What's that blog address? I'd really like to read it."

"Hopefully, you didn't spell anything wrong," Serena said, walking up behind me and bumping my shoulder. "Ethan minored in English,"

"I have nightmares about that," I said laughing,

but moving away from her. That was the second time she bumped into me. I was hyperaware when anyone came into my space. I couldn't be caught by surprise. If I was jarred too badly, and I didn't flex my core, I'd have a painful flare up when I laid down at night. Ethan's cameraman came back, and he went outside. Most of the contestants followed.

Serena seriously would not let the man out of her sight. It was a long afternoon. I mingled, flirting with Colby when he wasn't busy. I started to memorize where all the cameras were to fight off the jet lag of losing three hours. We finally made it to the eliminations.

I was not surprised when Ethan gave me a key to the safe containing one million dollars.

Julian would not have invited me onto his show just to kick me off the first night. I was sure I had a real shot at the title.

Chapter 5

The next morning, I woke stiff and uncomfortable. The elimination room, a bare room with wood-like floors, was emptied of risers. The space had to be emptied so equipment could be hauled with ease through the front door.

Nobody was in there in the morning, so I used the space. By my estimates and counting steps, it had to be a good 18 x 22 ft, plenty of space for one person to dance in. I slipped into to the kitchen to get my workout clothes. I was able to get in a fairly good workout, short as it was, and committed to waking earlier the next morning.

How my suitcase ended up in the kitchen I would never know. When I went into the kitchen to get my showering stuff, Carrie, of all people, offered to help me haul my stupid, huge suitcase up the stairs. Serena, now my roommate, who was in the kitchen, didn't even acknowledge my need to get my suitcase upstairs, nor, since she was my friend, indicate she may want to help me.

The gap in our friendship grew even more apparent during that day's filming.

Our second day of filming turned out to be a game of dodgeball. My positive attitude and the very spell *The Whole Package* held over me shattered.

The first competition was always active and a test of cooperation. Ten thousand dollars was always the prize won in the first show. The winner of the money and the last person out on the winner's team also won more time with the judge.

Dr. Corbon, in an interview, once said she opened the show like this because it forced the contestants to work together but it also showed people's real character when money was on the line. And it did. The competition was aggressive and some of the women, especially Sandra, the beauty queen, went crazy competitive. None of this is why the show's credibility sunk.

The longer we shot and reshot play after play, everyone was placed and prompted over and over. Nothing was spontaneous. Then, the strangest thing happened.

Carrie's roommate, the beautiful dark-haired and emerald eyed but shy girl named Veronica was incredibly good at dodgeball. She threw hard and Carrie ran fast, switching directions like a football player. Unfortunately, they weren't on the same team because the game would have wrapped up much sooner. Julian must have thought the same thing.

Just when Carrie was set up to throw Veronica out, and finally win the stupid game, she stopped. She pretended to trip and sent the ball back to Veronica. She refused to throw the ball at Veronica.

The game hit a stalemate because then Veronica would not get Carrie out. Carrie and

Veronica were friends. Real friends. Not just the kind of friend you have so you don't have to eat lunch alone, but real true friends. Or they were drunk. There was a lot of light beer and wine coolers at the location by the beach where we filmed.

Astounded, I watched as Lance, the host, rearranged the game so Carrie and Veronica were on the same team. Then we started the game entirely over again. I was proud, and even slightly jealous of the friends who clearly had each other's backs.

"This is so ridiculous," Serena complained to me after we were both out again. I shrugged. This was not enough of a complaint because Serena said, "Aren't you pissed?"

"Yeah, I mean I get they've both played really well. But to rearrange the game to pretty much fix the first competition… I don't know – it feels unfair," I answered, annoyance growing in my chest. I watched as Carrie retrieved the ball, but tossed it to Veronica to get Sandra out, again. I glanced at Serena. I suspected she would have hit me in the head with the dodgeball if it meant she won.

"You know this means Carrie is going to win the whole show, right?" Serena said as she looked at my annoyance and adding to it frustration against the contestants still in the game.

"Maybe," I said, remembering Julian swore I had a real chance with my story of resilience. Although Julian didn't seem to remember. He couldn't really show Carrie so much preference, though. It was all a trick, right?

"Don't be so naive," Serena snapped, "It's like when you dated that guy you were competing with for a spot in that dance. He was manipulating you then, just like Julian is now. How many followers does your blog have?"

I clenched my jaw. Serena asked me about the guys I dated the night before. Instead of guarding my confidences, she used it against me.

"Seriously, how many?" she asked when I didn't answer.

"A few hundred thousand," I said, jiggling my leg and glaring out over the ocean.

"And you announced several times you were coming on the show," she said.

"Yeah," I said.

"Right, Sweetie. He's after your following," Serena said. She flipped her long strawberry-blonde ponytail in my face like he'd duped her and not me.

"Oh, Ethan's looking at us," she said, and in a startling way she put a smile on her face and waved at Ethan. I wanted to cry. Ethan looked twice at me. I tried for a smile and wave. It must not have been convincing because he glanced at me again just to be sure I was okay. I couldn't even look at him.

Serena took his interest as an invitation to go over and talk to him. I sat in my cheap folding camp chair; afraid it would give out if I shifted to get comfortable. What was I doing? I should have been finishing the last few performances of the season and getting ready to vacation somewhere amazing with my family.

"Hey, you okay?" Colby asked, settling in Serena's seat.

"I don't know. I'm not even sure why I'm here," I said. "Clearly everything is being skewed to Carrie's advantage. I didn't realize the show was so… you know, scripted."

"It's not necessarily. Just wait. Carrie isn't playing by the rules. Julian needs to splice this episode together sooner than you would think. This dodgeball game will be the first segment so he can't really afford to wait for Carrie and Veronica's nice contest to play out," Colby said.

"I guess," I said as I watched Serena kissing up to Ethan.

"Come on, chin up, get into the game." He grinned at me.

"Okay," I said with a little laugh.

"Hey, can I ask a favor?" he asked.

"Sure," I said, surprised.

"Julian is letting me use his equipment to do a project for my videography class. I have to do it on my own time, but I was just wondering if… Well, you were dancing this morning," he said.

"Yeah."

"Can I tape you sometimes?"

"I don't see why not; do I need to come down in full make up or –"

"No, nothing like that," he said, "If you wear the same color, like you were in all black today, that's fine and do your hair the same way every time we film, that would be perfect."

"Not like I have much choice," I said flopping the half ponytail that kept my hair out of my face.

"That's adorable," he said. I rolled my eyes at him but couldn't help smiling.

My smile only lasted a little while. By the time, the dodgeball game finally ended, I felt like a hard piece of plastic rubbing my skin raw, annoyed, and wanted to go to bed. I watched *The Whole Package* so often thinking the contestants were overreacting to every situation. I didn't realize how far they were pushed before they reacted. Keeping my calm was going to be much harder than I thought.

Chapter 6

Back in the house, we met the clothing designers who would be outfitting us for many of the challenges and rewards. They competed against each other for an opportunity to launch their careers. The top designer usually created the winning contestant's final gown. How well I did would impact how long my designer kept creating outfits for me.

In an interview Dr. Corbon once said it tested the contestant's interactions and cooperation with another person. She loved the vulnerability of the symbiotic relationship.

I liked the idea of getting my style updated. I didn't have much time for fashion, so I was pretty much my mom's mini me. Since it was in my designer's best interest to make me look good, I felt confident. I had tried to follow some of my favorite designers after past shows ended. They never really did much if they didn't win.

I went into the back room filled with mirrors and tables, certain to find an ally.

"Erin, this is your designer, Von," Lance, the host, introduced.

"It is so nice to meet you," I said holding my hand out to him.

"I don't do germs, honey," he said looking at my hand.

"Sure. No, I get that," I said pulling back.

"Since you didn't win the first challenge, I'm going to start on your elimination dress. I have to use this," he said. He held up an eight-layer fluffy slip and rolled his eyes.

"Okay," I said. I cleared my throat because I didn't know what else to say.

I tried to chat with him while he took my measurements, but he didn't seem interested. Instead, I stayed as still as possible and listened to Serena instruct her very friendly designer as to the best looks for her body type.

The next morning dawned clear and resplendent. We drove back up the coast in the bus until we reached civilization. We waited in a small outdoor sitting area on the grounds of a large Veteran's Home.

Julian's production assistant, Patrick took me to an area that lost a little of its antiseptic look and became more like a hotel. The doorways had something like a neck to it, so someone passing by couldn't just look into every room even with the doors open. This made it hard for the occupant to see who was at the door and invite them in.

At the mouth of a hallway, we stopped in front of a door propped open. Patrick nodded at it, then scurried away to place the next contestant with no further instruction. I watched him turn quickly back into the main vein of the building. I stepped slowly into the room, unsure what I was supposed to do.

Feeling like an intruder I knocked on the open door.

“Enter,” called a stern sounding high pitched voice. I stepped in. On the far side of the room a desk under a window held shadow boxes of medals. That was it, there were no other decorations, no pictures. It was stark, cold. I took one more step to fully enter the room. Against the opposite wall, monitoring equipment surrounded a hospital bed. Next to the bed a woman leaned back in a recliner. She pulled herself up a little when I fully entered the room

I stopped moving when I saw her.

Her head almost sat on her shoulder to the right. Her shoulders and upper back lumped into a hunched back which must have been fused many times. She wore a greyish blue wig with pale blue slacks to match it. Her eyes were small, and she had to lift her head uncomfortably to look at me. Her twisted form petrified me to my very core.

“Hello,” I said when the breath re-entered my chest, “My name is Erin.”

“I know who you are,” the woman snapped. Taken back I asked, “You must be Dorothy?”

“Dot. The boys all call me Dot,” she snapped.

“Do you watch the show?” I asked.

“I do, and I know you are a fraud,” Dot said angrily. She shifted her eyes away from me, huffing.

“I… I don’t know what you’re talking about,” I said, startled.

"You never had scoliosis, or at least not bad enough that you could tell," she said.

"I have type-two scoliosis. My primary thoracic is at a 34-degree curve and the secondary curve in my lumbar was at a 22-degrees before I had surgery. I was ten when it developed in less than a year. I wore a back brace 18 to 20 hours a day for seven years," I said, feeling defensive.

"Oh, please. They would have made you get fused," she said.

"Not anymore. There are other methods than just fusing. My mom researched and found other ways to help me," I said.

"Well, my mom knew I'd never catch a man and made me attend to my studies. I learned four languages and when all the other girls were getting married, I served my country as an interpreter," she said.

"Wow, that really is a remarkable accomplishment." I tried to soften her.

"Yes, but you dance," she stated, making my accomplishments small.

"I do," I said fiercely. She sounded just like my aunt, an extremely well-paid attorney, similar to my father.

"I want to see your back," Dot said.

"Are you serious?"

"Yeah, to see if you really have the cursed curvies."

I did not know what to do. I didn't love exposing my back to anyone, let alone this cranky old woman who clearly meant to punish me for her life with scoliosis. Even on my blog and

Instagram, I preferred to show pictures of my x-rays, or my dancing. I didn't like the long scar or strange lumping of muscles around my spine.

"I don't have anything to prove to you," I said crossing my arms and sitting down in an uncomfortable, creaking wooden chair near the door.

"I knew you were faking."

I clenched my jaw and looked out the window. She did the same and we sat in silence until Colby came in to set up his camera.

"Ethan will be in here next; we will have fifteen minutes to film you then I'll take you to a woman named Edith."

"Oh Edith, she's a la-te-dah," Dot said moving her hand up and down, "if you know what I mean."

"I don't," I said. I glanced at Colby.

"She's a princess type, like you. All the boys following you around, acting like you're something special because you're a dancer," Dot said lifting her head back so I could see she rolled her eyes. I glanced at Colby to see what he thought of that.

He gave me a smirk, like he found the feisty old woman amusing, then he said, "You're right, I've always found blonde women who can dance something like the Pied Piper. I don't know what happens to me. It's magnetic, I just can't stop myself from..."

Colby moved like he had no control and bumped into my chair. I gasped, startled. He did it again. Worried the chair might break, I stood.

He turned but acted like we were magnetically connected, coming back too quickly putting his large hand on my waist. He played like he couldn't quite pull himself away from me and I felt defended.

"All right, that's enough of that," Dot said. She rolled her head along her shoulder, "You are a charmer." Looking to me she said, "You have to look out for the charmers. They don't want you; they want something from you."

I squinted looking to Colby to see if he was offended. He laughed and said, "Come on now. I just admitted one of my darkest secrets about dancers and…" He stuck his head on my shoulder and looked up at me with the most endearing golden eyes. I laughed. We all stopped at a knock on the door. Colby quickly found his position behind the camera.

"Hey, it sounds like you guys are having fun in here," Ethan said coming in.

"No, we are not," Dot snapped, "I want Erin to show me her back and she won't. I don't believe she even has scoliosis."

"I'm sure that's a personal decision for her," Ethan said.

"Are you kidding? She wears it like a badge," Colby said.

"It's a hard to feel so vul –" Ethan started.

"Like a Rockstar," Colby interrupted, "Erin you don't feel shy about showing off your back, do you? All that you've overcome, I would think you would dance in open-backed leotards."

"I don't really," I said. A shiver ran through me for feeling embarrassed. I had thousands of scoliosis followers whom I always encouraged to be bold. I couldn't get filmed looking ashamed of my back.

"I don't care about showing my back. I just don't think she has the right to demand I do," I stammered, then pulled up the back of my shirt and bent down so Dot could see. Colby disappeared behind the camera to get a better angle.

Ethan lightly touched my spine showing Dot the curve and how I'd done specialized exercises to build up my back muscles. Ethan asked me to bend forward further and showed her my rib hump.

"See? This is where she had a disc repaired," he explained, touching the scar on my back. "Erin, did they deflate a lung to get to it?"

"Yeah, the surgery was about ten hours long," I said. I closed my eyes remembering how long it took to get my lungs back to full capacity.

"It's still a relatively break-through surgery, but they are treating scoliosis in so many different ways," Ethan said. I held my breath praying he didn't mention the enormous amount of money it took to reshape the disc in my spine instead of getting fused.

"Well, I'll be," Dot said, snuggling up to Ethan. Ethan put a hand on her shoulder that was more of a hump really and told her some of the other new ways people with scoliosis were being treated. Dot soaked up Ethan's touchy-feely bedside manner and I started to feel cold, so I put my shirt down. Colby smiled at me. I nodded, trying to be okay about exposing my back to the world.

After fifteen minutes, Colby said, "Sorry Dot, we really need to get to Edith's room."

I quickly waved and said, "It's nice to meet you, Dot."

I was the first to walk out of the room. Ethan still spoke to Dot, but Colby quickly gathered his equipment and followed me.

"Sorry about her," Colby said. "Sometimes these older folks don't have much else to do but analyze all we younger folks do wrong."

I grinned at him but realized Ethan hadn't followed us into the hall. I turned back to see where he was. I had so little time alone with him I should use it wisely. I started to go back into Dot's room, but Colby asked:

"Hey, can you get this for me Erin?" nodding to a wire slipping out from under his arm.

"Sure, here," I said, grabbing it and tucking it around his shoulders.

"Oh, thanks," he said. He glanced surprised at the coil on his shoulder. Julian's assistant, Patrick, opened a door all the way down at the end of the hall and waved to us. Colby hurried toward it. When he was almost there, he turned and realized I wasn't with him. I tried not to notice the disappointed look on his face. I couldn't help but wonder if he was crushing on me. We had a fun little flirtation happening. Still, he couldn't blame me for stopping to wait for Ethan to come out of Dot's room. I had so little time alone with him.

"Hey, you okay?" Ethan asked, waving to Patrick calling for us to hurry.

"I think so," I said but shivered a little.

"Erin, be yourself. Don't push beyond what you're comfortable with. I like Colby, but he's…. I don't know. Just don't forget he works for Julian. You have to take care of your back no matter what, okay?"

"Thanks, Ethan," I said taking the arm he offered to escort me down the hall. We took on the appearance an old timey couple in promenade, the spirit of the place forcing the manners of an older generation upon us.

Chapter 7

"Let's hope this woman is a little happier to see us," I said, looking over at Ethan.

"I got your back if not," he teased

"Maybe you can use a pointer next time," I said. He laughed a little, but we said nothing else. I'd never been a chatty person, and Ethan didn't seem to mind.

We approached the open door, and the smell of grandma perfume wafted into the hall. My first glimpse into the room I saw Colby setting up his camera. I glanced at him and felt guilty for taking Ethan's arm. Especially, when Colby ducked back behind the tripod as we entered the room.

It felt a little like he was mad at me, but that didn't make sense. I came onto a reality show. I wanted to win. He had to understand that, but jealousy wasn't always rational. Was he jealous of Ethan?

This room bloomed with roses. A dozen pink roses sat in a vase on the desk covered by a bubblegum pink tablecloth and crowded with trinkets and figurines. The woman sitting on the edge of her recliner wore all black with a pink shrug. She had dark bobbed hair, drawn-in eyebrows and a broad theatrical smile. She held a rose-pink manicured hand out to me.

"Erin darling, come in, come in," she said pulling my hand to her bosom, and lurching my body into her personal space.

"Hello," I said. I leaned away.

She pulled my hand to her chest again and said, "There are so few real women in this place. I just need to soak you up."

I didn't bother mentioning Dot. I could see she meant for me to. I did not want to know what she thought of the linguist. Instead, I pointed to her arrangement of figurines on the table nearest her.

"You were a ballerina?" I asked.

"I am a ballerina. Such things never leave us Erin, darling. You will see, even when you are my age, how horribly cursed we are to always need the stage."

As she said this, she shook her head adamantly and reached out in ballet first position with her arms.

"I get that," I said trying to engage in the conversation when I wanted to tap her shoulders down into the correct posture.

She did all the positions with her arms. I nodded, acting impressed, unsure what to say. Finally, she finished. Ethan and I clapped. When we reached an awkward silence, I asked, "Did you serve in the military?"

"Oh, heavens no. My husband was a doctor in the army. They paid for his schooling." She reached over to a silver framed picture of a handsome young man in uniform.

"He's been gone for some time now," she said. "Don't live to be so old you're a burden, Erin darling."

"There is so much you can offer," I corrected her. "You just shared your wisdom about dancing with me. I'm sure your children and grandchildren are lucky to have you in their lives."

She made a face and did a hand movement I couldn't understand. Then she whispered.

"They're all just waiting for me to die so I don't spend all my money on this place."

"That can't be true."

"Oh, you are too sweet for your own good, darling. Now I would like to see you dance so I can tell if you have what it takes to really make it."

I looked at her. My mouth dropped open. I looked to Colby and Ethan. They both started moving tables, and the bed to the other side of the room until there was a five-foot square for me to dance. I did a few turns; my leather bottom Mary Jane flats were very like ballet slippers. I really was a ballerina through and through like Serena said. Glancing at Edith, I wondered if I should try to be a touch more well-rounded.

To my great surprise, Edith started giving me instruction.

"Chin up, tummy in, drop that buttocks Darling, drop it."

For the next fifteen minutes I took a dance lesson from a woman who must have been a high school dance teacher at best. She didn't understand how I moved differently because I was molded differently. I became a ten-year-old girl trying uselessly to please a dance instructor, who didn't understand my body looked slightly different when I balanced.

Her dramatized claps, as if they could force my body to comply with her instructions, only made it worse. At the end she graciously told the camera I would go far in the professional dance world if I could figure out how to stop flaring my ribs. Between Edith and Dot, I left hating my body. I loathed this tired old fight. My insecurity longing for another body, and my having to force it to accept my body as it was. My spine wasn't going to suddenly straighten because I hated how it contorted my body.

I found it was harder convincing myself without my long hair to shield my back and make me feel fairy-like.

Thankfully, when Julian edited it with his own special perspective, I looked like I was dancing in a music box, stuck to one spot on the floor, and she just looked enthusiastic. He also showed Ethan and Dot examining my back, but somehow Dot looked proud of all I accomplished, instead of being bitter about what she couldn't do. Julian's editing rivaled that of any political candidate's image created on the road to office.

When we came back to the bus, I looked at the other contestants. Veronica's, huge emerald eyes were dull like she'd been crying.

Her beautiful symmetrical face tilted downward obscured by her cranberry hair. Carrie's velvety cinnamon eyes were trained out the window of the bus but looked as though they didn't see anything.

Even Tess, the woman cast to be the sarcastic comic relief, had no words left. She ran her red fingernail melancholy across the carpeted pattern on the back of the seat in front of her. I wondered if they all felt a little more vulnerable to mortality than when they awoke that morning.

I contemplated my life, and how I'd really isolated myself in the dance world. At the end of my life would I be so wrapped up in the dance world that I had no room for my family and any other accomplishments? At least I had my education.

Serena came back on the bus last, looking smug and self-important. She sat next to me, but I wished she wouldn't.

"I take it that all went well for you?" I asked, when she couldn't stop bouncing, and looked at me like I was supposed to ask.

"I rocked that competition," she whispered, her icy blue eyes scanning the bus to be sure nobody looked as happy as she did. "Ethan watched as I pretty much revolutionized their eating schedule."

"I thought you had a resident," I said.

"Who hadn't eaten yet. The orderly tried to pass it off like Byron didn't want to eat, but I had his number. I asked to look at the schedule, and my patient was skipped due to sloppy scheduling. I fixed it, showing the orderly a few little tricks that I've picked up along the way. I made this place better; it's going to be way more efficient now."

"That's great," I said. I wondered if there were an orderly inside cursing her name, or if he truly didn't know how he'd ever gotten along before he met her. She used her beauty like a siren to an unsuspecting sailor, but some guys could see through it.

I thought Ethan was starting to. Colby didn't even seem to notice Serena. She was pretty and all, but then he did have a magnetic connection to blonde dancers. As for the orderly, I had no idea. Serena's filter was just as impressive as Julian's.

Chapter 8

By the time eliminations came, I was silent and taciturn. Every time I spoke Serena spoke over me or one of the other women made me feel small. Filming all day, while being metaphorically elbowed out of the competition, reminded me of my dance company.

Natalia, the current top principal dancer, often gave me pointers or advice. She did it in the same way Serena did. Pulling me down just when I needed my courage most. I idolized Natalia and always thought she wanted to help me but watching Serena I realized she didn't. Not really.

I made it through the elimination. As Serena pointed out, I wouldn't get kicked off in the first half of the season, not until my loyal fans were rooting for Carrie. Sometimes when Ethan zeroed in on me, I almost thought maybe I had a chance of winning. At times, he really did seem interested in me. I would try to impress him, and he acted impressed. Only too soon, Serena would assure me Carrie was going to win, and I would agree as I watched Carrie and Ethan.

But if Carrie was going to win, why was Serena still trying so hard?

My days on the show blurred. Filming, stretching, feeling humiliated, dancing every morning to somehow endure the next long segment of filming. I slept half of what I was used to, and occasionally, I received attention that somehow smothered me while making me feel alone at the same time. I spent my days fighting to keep my head above it all while taking every chance I could to get Ethan's attention. Colby was the only one interested in me. When I saw him walking toward me to give me a word of encouragement, I felt like I could endure a little bit longer.

On the Fourth of July, Julian did the humiliation episode. Early that morning, Colby filmed me dancing for over two hours. Just to prove I wasn't ashamed of the scarring on my back, I wore a black racerback sports bra and black leggings without the black tank top I usually donned. I sat stretching to stay limber before the long day of filming.

"We have ten minutes before we're filming," Carrie called coming into the house. Lance seemed a bit infatuated with her, so I didn't doubt he was trying to help her. In turn she tried to help us.

"You've got to be kidding me!" Serena said.

She barreled up the staircase pushing Carrie into the railing. Heaven help anyone who got in her way. I didn't bother following her. I couldn't handle being around Serena. After Serena's great exodus up the stairs, Carrie and Tess headed in that direction. I would have asked Carrie for more details, but she was having some sort of debate with Tess, so I went in to eat breakfast – I once left for the day without eating and it was miserable.

I ate quickly before Serena could come in and examine the label of my Greek yogurt and granola to let me know how it wasn't a healthy breakfast and I needed to watch it since my face was getting pudgy. I sat alone. Since no one else opted to eat, I basked in my solitude and lost track of time. When I finally snapped out of it, I realized it had been longer than ten minutes. I hadn't even been noticed as missing. I went into the main area of the house. Serena had not dressed, but rather undressed. She stood there in her underwear.

"I just have to be comfortable when I sleep," she said to Ethan who had come in with Julian and the camera crew. I laughed a little. Serena was always cold and wore flannel pjs to get comfortable in the cool of the coastal climate. I watched her, wondering why she'd changed into her underwear.

I realized we were about to be humiliated.

Every season, the episode I hated the most was the humiliation one. Grace under pressure is what they called it. I watched Serena. Not only did she know what was coming, she chose to do it in her underwear. I couldn't be sure what her strategy was.

We were ushered onto the bus without the opportunity to change our clothes or grab anything. I spared a glance at the coastal fog climbing the mountains around us. Shivering, I hoped the sun would manage to cut through it as the morning progressed. I sank into a seat across the aisle from Carrie and Veronica. I wanted to try and be around them when we were humiliated. Only then did I notice Carrie had dressed. She wore a sundress. She looked nice.

Did Julian help her? Did he mean for her to win this competition? Was she, as Serena suspected, about to submarine us?

I glanced over at Carrie's face, she looked dismal. I glanced over at Serena. She was bouncing – excited, or freezing, I couldn't be sure.

I took a deep breath. What was really happening? Dad always told me to look beyond what was being presented to see what hid beneath the surface. Serena claimed to help me, but never did. Carrie, on the other hand, called out and warned us to get going. Why did Carrie look so upset then?

I chose to eat, not realizing I was choosing between clothes and food. I shivered, rubbing my arms hoping the friction would create heat. Serena chose to put on her underwear. We both did this to ourselves, but for some reason Carrie looked like she was taking responsibility for our poor choices.

Veronica seemed to be the only one who didn't get any warning, her ponytail still dripped down her back, and her damp towel and wet swimsuit had to be uncomfortable. Carrie couldn't be blamed for that, either.

I wondered why some people like Serena thought everyone owed her something, while other people like Carrie thought they had to be everything to everyone. Where did I fit in that? I tried my best to be nice to people, but I didn't tend to take much interest in other people's lives. I didn't ask for anything from anyone. Is this why I don't have real friends? I kept to myself?

I stopped myself from worrying about this. I was about to be humiliated; it wasn't exactly time to go soul-searching. None of this supposition warmed me and I wished I had dressed.

I regretted my choice even more when we arrived at a small-town breakfast with the mayor where I was fed everything from scones to eggs. I tried to smile. I tried to harness Mom and her ability to stay calm, but I felt on edge and ornery.

When Serena smiled, it was almost serpentine, like she may swallow a bird's egg at any moment. She made the saliva in my mouth coat my throat like I may throw up.

"May I please have another blueberry scone," Serena asked, holding the arm of the waiter, a young handsome man, who liked being touched by a half-naked woman.

"I'll be right back," he said.

"Thank you so much," she said trying not to make the chattering of her teeth so obvious. I wanted to point out each scone had at least 400 calories, but she didn't seem to care this morning.

Everything about her was fake. Her smile, her simper, the way she acted like her request was a request when really it was a demand. Serena submarined me. Serena was the plant. She was the Lena from season three and I hadn't even noticed. Did Julian tell Serena to submarine me or is that how she thought she had to play this game?

She knew about my blog, my followers. She knew I grew up in affluence, though we never talked about me anymore. I thought the way I spoke or dressed gave me away, but what if she was on the show to submarine me? That didn't make sense though. I clearly wasn't a threat. Carrie was the center of the storm, the eye of Ethan's affection, the star of Julian's show. So why did Serena submarine me?

An older woman wearing a flag on her knitted sweater hobbled over to our table and told Carrie how nice she looked. Carrie looked like she might turn green. Instead of being her bright happy self, she seemed so defeated. It dawned on me that Julian went out of his way to humiliate her by making her look like she'd been underhanded and put herself above us all.

She dressed. She looked so guilty for getting dressed.

I looked at the situation realistically. I had no chance of winning. The effort Julian made to humiliate Carrie – I'd seen the same pattern the last season. There was always a contestant who stood out, who danced En Avant, to the front of the stage. The contestant getting personal twists on the challenges –that person won. Was Carrie chosen from the first, or did she fight her way into center stage while Serena pulled me under?

Betrayal bathed me in anger. Did Julian Marrows lie to me when he said I had a chance? If so, he also lied to my father. That was not easy to do. I felt so lost, so confused in the commotion. I'd never been an untrusting person. All the people in my life were trustworthy, but now, I felt…exposed…wary.

I stopped myself from thinking, as Mom called them, the negative thoughts – and took a deep breath. I could do nothing about that right now. Instead of moping, I started to look around me. I noticed the patriotic red, white and blue balloons twisted in a huge strand over the top of us. I looked at the decorations and found myself being caught up in it. Who went to so much effort to celebrate their home? How many hours had it taken for this breakfast to be set up? Whoever did all the work must not like our table much.

Allowing my mind to wander away from our group of misfits, I overheard the conversation at the table next to us. I was placed at the end of the table nearest the next table. The cameraman set up next to me and I wasn't in his shots. However, it put me closer to the table behind us. I grew interested in their grumblings, as they were about us.

Tickets for the brunch must have been expensive, because I heard a woman at the next table over complain about the price she paid for an entire table, and something about a dress code. She wore a bright cherry red dress, her white hair was curled and molded with hair spray to hold up a red, white and blue jester's hat. The woman next to her wore a large pumpkin hat. What exactly would a dress code include or exclude, I wondered?

The woman with the pumpkin on her hat noticed me examining her. I glanced at the hat and smiled, strangely caught up with the urge to laugh. The woman gave me a prim little smile, but she seemed to mellow out in just that interaction.

When her friend opened her mouth to complain louder, the pumpkin lady said, "Come on, Shorty. Your granddaughter wears less than that on a daily basis."

The woman in the jester hat glared but said nothing else. The woman in the pumpkin hat winked at me. I grinned at her.

We went straight to the parade after breakfast. Many flags flew along the parade route. I stood with the audience and put my hand over my heart as the veterans passed with the flag. I'd never been to a small-town celebration of Independence Day before.

"That was nice, wasn't it," Serena asked as we all sat down.

"Yeah," I said but my voice was swallowed up in brass instruments that started playing patriotic songs.

"You knew this was coming. Why are you in your underwear?" I asked Serena over the noise.

"The winner of this competition is always the one who is the most humiliated but is able to overcome it. I need to win this competition."

"Why, I thought you said Carrie is going to win," I said.

"Not if I can help it," Serena grinned.

"Yeah but –"

"Hush, the camera's coming," Serena snapped, grinning.

I turned away from her, annoyed. Instead, I watched the parade. Lots of pumpkins decorated the stand, obviously important to the local community.

While all the other contestants drowned in their humiliation or tread water to prove they weren't capable of the emotion, I lost myself. I wasn't a focal point for the show. Colby filmed me clapping for some children who danced in brightly colored skirts, but moved on to Sandra, who found ways to make her annoyance heard.

Julian didn't even notice me when he pointed at who should be filmed. Ethan was beside himself trying to make Carrie feel better. I easily melted into the background at the town BBQ. I started talking to the locals, and really enjoyed the day. A woman even took pity on me and gave me one of her company tee shirts. It made me feel better. I remembered most people tried their best. It was only the few loud ones, like Serena, who would submarine a person.

The fireworks over the ocean were my favorite, palm trees in chartreuse that reflected in the dark waves beneath. The loud booming reverberated through my chest, just as a bunch of azure flowers with taffy pink centers exploded in the sky, each finding their own place on the ocean's surface before they faded away into a smoky shadow, and were gone. Streaks of fireballs shot through the murky shadows of retreating fireworks and exploded into strings of fire falling onto the ocean. Enamored in the experience, I felt at peace.

My peace did not last.

Chapter 9

That night, Serena accused Carrie of sleeping with Lance to get information. Carrie was so defeated. I tried to point out all she did was get dressed, but Serena pushed her until Carrie looked like she may cry. Serena took on a whole new life. She dug and cut at Carrie until her face turned bright red and her spirit crumpled under the pressure.

I wanted to say something, but couldn't because watching Serena work Carrie over, I realized, she'd done the same to me. She'd crushed me. I couldn't even pretend to be positive; I wasn't even trying to play this game. Serena submarined me. I didn't want her to do it to Carrie, but how could I help her? Carrie was drooping. But why? Because she had enough sense to get dressed when she told all of us there was only ten minutes until Julian came. Why didn't Carrie point out it was Serena who had chosen to get undressed?

It was only a sundress for heaven's sake.

I couldn't stand the commotion. I walked out toward the kitchen to get a drink. I heard two low voices talking, Patrick, Julian's assistant, and Colby. I would have said something, but my vocal cords seized up when I heard my name.

"Erin won that competition hands down," Colby said.

"Julian can't let her win, but you're right. She naturally came out of the humiliation really fast. She found ways to have fun."

"Julian didn't think she'd come out of it that fast. He got so mad when I tried to film her. I don't know why," Colby said.

"He doesn't want Dr. Corbon to see when she reviews the tapes, is my guess," Patrick said.

"I wonder why he didn't switch to a different competition altogether. He had to know Erin would do well," Colby said.

"Yeah, but Carrie had the sundress, and he didn't really know how else to embarrass her with it."

"I think Erin is more of the whole package than Carrie is," Colby said.

"You have crush on Erin," Patrick teased.

"I just think she's more positive about life than Carrie. Carrie seems so put upon, almost depressed, this week," Colby said.

"Yeah, but Serena is being really mean to her," Patrick defended.

"She was mean to Erin as well," Colby said.

"Carrie has a lot more on her shoulders than Erin. I don't think it's fair to compare them. Erin has support, and her scoliosis is under control. You know Carrie is still trying to figure things out. She's pretty much on her own."

"The show is about resilience," Colby said. "Not just who has a hard life, or everyone would qualify."

"I guess, but it doesn't matter what we think. Just between us, I think Julian has some sort of arrangement with that guy who nominated Carrie," Patrick said.

"That's probably true, but not fair, not at all fair to Erin," Colby said. I heard them coming toward me, so I stepped back toward the other contestants who were still fighting. Serena already told me I had no chance of winning but hearing it out loud broke my heart.

The contention in the house exploded over the next week. We started to do less out of the Manor House, and instead were thrown together and stirred until Julian caught us all in some act of disgrace or other. The only other outside filming we did that week was a trip to an amusement park with foster kids. Serena easily took over as leader of that pack.

Chapter 10

I'd never been to amusement parks as a child. Doctors, my parents, Dance Masters and Mistresses – all forbade it, along with skiing, and anything else that could be considered jarring. It was unfortunate the first amusement park turnstile I pushed through happened just after my dreams felt crushed.

After a few rides Serena was called to do an interview since she'd grown up in a group home like the kids we were hanging out with.

"Here, you save my place by Ethan," she whispered to me as she swung herself under a metal bar. My mouth opened slightly. When had I become her placeholder? I'd given up, but clearly, she hadn't. Did she honestly think she could beat Carrie?

I looked around. Where was Carrie?

The foster kids proved to be much more of a handful than anticipated. They had no desire to stay together, and Patrick had to keep at least two contestants with each group of kids. If one kid had to go to the bathroom, two contestants had to go with her.

After an hour at the park, Ethan and I were alone in line with most of the foster kids. Patrick looked extremely frazzled.

"Erin, have you always wanted to be a dancer?" Ethan asked when the foster kids didn't want much to do with us adults.

"After I was diagnosed…" I stopped. He looked distracted.

"Are you sick of hearing about this?" I asked.

"No, no sorry. I feel like you're the only one who hasn't really told me your story," he said refocusing on me.

"Oh, I figured you were getting sick of me harping on it," I said, realizing it was Serena who didn't want me to talk about it.

"Not at all, I find it intriguing. Please tell me about how you overcame your diagnosis," he said smiling at me.

"Okay, after I was diagnosed, Mom made me set wellness goals. Most of them revolved around stretching and dancing. I fell in love with the self-expression and after a while it became the goal for my life." My heart dropped, and a sadness washed over me. I worked so hard. Nope, I refocused, I could think of that later.

"…only works if you engage," he was saying.

"Dancing opened a world for me, gave me something to fight for. During college, I did these Summer Intensives – they're like really extreme ballet classes and that's when I set my final goal."

"What?" he asked, genuinely interested.

"I want to be a Prima Ballerina. I studied only classical ballet from then on with American Ballet."

"Oh, that's cool," Ethan said, his alien silver eyes squinting at me.

"You have no clue what that means do you?" I asked.

He laughed.

"I've only ever heard the term in a derogatory way, like you're such a Prima Ballerina."

"Yeah, it's a common misconception among those who aren't into ballet. See, there are different levels of dancers. I'm a soloist, so I've moved up to a certain point, but I'm not a principal; those are main roles. The top role, say Odette in Swan Lake, goes to the top principal dancer at the audition. The female dancer who consistently gets main roles, in many different countries, would eventually be considered the prima ballerina assoluta of this era."

"Oh, okay. I hope you make it to Prima someday."

"Thanks," I said feeling that old fire light inside my chest. I wanted it so bad. I started to feel feisty. I wasn't past my prime. I had a gift. I worked hard. Yes, I cut my hair without talking to the ballet mistress, or the wig master and yes, I was literally wasting away on a reality show, but that didn't count me out. I'd started over twice in my career. I could do it again.

As polite as Ethan tried to be, he wasn't interested in me. We stood together quietly. He seemed to need the repose, and when I had nothing to say, I tended not to talk. It made me quiet at times, and I often heard and saw more listening and observing.

I leaned my back against the bar and tried not to be overwhelmed with the idea I was losing my dream. How could I not believe in the hope I'd held fast to since becoming an adult? I noted the pale green and blue that colored gum became when freshly deposited on the ground as opposed to the off-black it became after a few days.

Serena came, Colby in her wake filming all the at-risk kids. All the girls were exceptionally interested in the hot cameraman. Serena quietly pushed her way through them. When she reached me, she pushed me a little to indicate I should move so she could stand by Ethan.

I tightened my core and said, "Hey, how did your interview go?" pretending like I didn't know what she wanted.

"Really, really good," she said nodding at me with a wink. I assumed this meant she did something to keep Carrie away.

"That's good," I said. I turned to Ethan like I didn't understand her hints to move.

She bumped me again, this time indicating with her eyes I should move out of her way so she could stand by Ethan between the two steel rails guiding the line. Irritation grew inside me. I wanted her to stop acting like I had to do everything she said. She had a gift for making everyone look foolish on camera, and I couldn't go down that path with her.

Instead, I stood my ground despite her nudging. I waited until Ethan looked up. Then when she jammed me again, I exaggerated my body movement to her push and said:

"Ow," and looked at her like she was a lunatic.

"You have got to stop shoving her," Ethan said irritated. "You do it all the time. Being a nurse, you know she can't be jolted like that."

"Sorry, Erin, I lost my balance," she said, "Geeze, Ethan, calm down."

Ethan rolled his eyes. He did not believe her. Did he see how she treated me? He seemed to really resent her, no matter how big her fake smile spread.

Ethan asked me, "Are you sure you should be riding this roller coaster, Erin?"

"I don't know," I said. "Julian said I can't avoid the challenges because of my back, but no one ever films me, so I don't really know what to do most of the time."

"Well, just jump out of line. I'm sure Julian won't even notice," Serena said trying to get into the spot next to Ethan. I grew angry. Instead of any rational response I said,

"I read all the restrictions. It should be all right," I said giving her an unconvincing fake smile. I was not moving for anything.

"Okay, well, come sit by me," Ethan said taking me by the arm. We climbed up the stairs to the platform to load the coaster car. He turned his back on Serena. I turned back and realized Colby was filming us. How much of that interaction had he caught?

I won something. Not on the show, but within myself. I was soaring – until I was literally soaring. The choppy wooden coaster climbed plank by plank slowly into the sky. The air caught in my chest and I took Ethan's hand terrified. What was I doing?

"It's going to be okay," Ethan said. "Really watch the track and try to move with the car. Hold your core with those dancer abs I know you have."

"Yes, I do," I said taking a deep breath. Which made it possible for me to scream all the way down the steep hill we jolted over. My back jerked badly once when I didn't anticipate which direction we were turning. Then when we stopped, it whiplashed me like I'd been in a car crash. I stepped off the ride and my hips ached. It was a painful night after I went to bed. The feeling I bested Serena did not last long and the anger inside me spread as I tried to sleep with my body on fire.

What was I thinking? I did it so Julian would not get mad at me. Why did I care what he thought? I lost. Ethan was very polite to me, but nobody would be fool enough to recommend I lose my heart to the man.

I wasn't doing anything so stupid again. Especially not for Julian Marrows.

Chapter 11

"Hey, you okay this morning?" Colby asked after filming my barely-a-workout the morning after I survived another elimination.

"I'm just sore. I've got to ice and grab some Ibuprofen…" I stopped rambling. I felt so frustrated, captive in my own skin. I wanted nothing more than to go home and start the summer over.

"I wish I hadn't cut my hair is all," I said finally as I waved and walked up the stairs.

"It looks really nice framing your face," Colby called after me. His compliment only enhanced my fear of facing the corps de ballet, all vying for the soloist spot I left open to go on this stupid show. I wanted my life, my dream back on track. After I took an ice-cold shower, I dressed and left our room just after Serena. At the stairs Serena saw Carrie down below and called to taunt her.

I hated Serena.

Like a burning unquenchable fire, it consumed me. I hated her. Why did she have to take my self-esteem? Maybe if I'd been able to compete from the beginning, I would still have a chance of winning. Especially if Dr. Corbon still had some control over the show.

Serena took my chance away. Or did I give it to her?

Loathing for her swelled from my heart and spread all over my body. I stood behind Serena at the top of the stairs. She didn't see me. I clenched my jaw and thought about pushing her down the stairs. Just one strong shove. I wanted to hurt her, make her feel like she made me. I'd never hated anyone like I hated Serena.

Carrie glanced at me and smiled. I mimed pushing Serena down the stairs, mostly because I stood there too long for any natural interaction. Carrie grinned at me, like I was just joking.

I crossed my arms tightly, astounded with myself. I almost hurt Serena. I'd never physically assaulted anyone.

I followed Serena down to breakfast shaking, too afraid to be alone. Carrie noticed something was wrong with me. She talked to me. She asked me about growing up with scoliosis. Instead of sitting quietly and eating normally, I told my story. I needed to syphon back some of the power I'd always had in my youth. Carrie was so kind I wondered if Ethan said something to her. She was kind and considerate to me.

How had I ever thought Serena right about her? And why did Serena target me in the first place? Clearly Carrie was meant to be her competition. Why, only after she sufficiently sank me, would she start in on Carrie? If I'd competed from the beginning, would I have had a chance? Maybe, but probably not. Especially after of what Colby and Patrick said about Julian not letting me win a competition.

None of it made sense.

As we ate breakfast, Carrie talked to me like a human being. I was overcome with a desire to help her. If she could make it out of Serena's trap that would mean at least Serena didn't win.

That day we went shopping in San Francisco. I sat on the bus across the aisle from Carrie and Veronica trying to focus on anything but my rage. Something about a story Carrie shared, where she openly flung her wealth in Serena's face, then rejected its influence made me feel better. It might just have been the sour grapes it brought out in Serena, but something shifted in Carrie on that bus ride.

I offered Carrie some licorice. She looked deep in thought and almost startled at my offering. Then she took the licorice and smiled at me. Not the fake halfway-to-hell smile, but a real happy smile.

When the bus stopped, I stepped out into the aisle. Serena was behind me. She shifted to push around me. She wanted to be the first one off the bus. I was so annoyed that instead of letting her by, I planted my dancer thighs in her way.

"Erin, move," she snapped in my ear.

"I have to get my stuff," I snapped back, then I stepped back, making Serena's toothpick body back up.

"Erin!" she snapped.

"Tess is getting out," I said calmly.

"Seriously," she said.

"Veronica," I said indicating she should get out of her seat. I let everyone go before Serena.

"What is your problem?" Serena asked. She shoved her knuckles painfully into my ribs.

"Just calm down. You're like a yappy little puppy," I said, not reacting furiously like she deserved, like I knew she wanted me to. Tess found this most amusing, and Carrie smiled at me. We were together in this new fight against Serena and I liked it.

Colby didn't get to the mall until a few hours into filming. His deep announcer voice echoed across the food court and caught my attention. He was explaining he had to turn in his dissertation that morning while we were in the city. I turned hoping to congratulate him but stopped short. Tess handed him half of her sandwich. She grinned at him pulling on his shirt in a way that felt too intimate. He smiled back at her, then took a huge bite.

I squinted my heavy painted eyelids complete with fake lashes and stared at them. I couldn't look away. Colby… he… he acted like… maybe we were just friends. He remembered me. He was the only one who ever remembered me. Did Tess, who was extremely good at getting attention from every man on set, really need his as well? He glanced over at me and caught my eye just as Tess leaned over to wipe something off his mouth. I looked away trying not to feel jealous.

Unable to control my eyes I glanced back. Colby lifted what was left of the half sandwich, she gave him and nodded while looking appreciatively at Tess. Tess watched the back of his very fit form walk away. Colby carefully didn't look at me. He shoved the rest of the sandwich in his mouth quickly. Colby chewed fast and nodded to the other cameraman who'd come back with Ethan.

"Erin, you're next," Colby called, jogging toward me, covering his mouth and trying to swallow. Once his mouth was empty, he smiled at me in a way that brought out the perfect V shape in his face. I leaned away from him. What was that?

The first cameraman, the one who always went with Ethan, stepped back and Colby said:

"I'm ready. Let's go."

Ethan must have found this peculiar because he looked to his normal cameraman. The middle-aged man was already searching the food court for lunch. Ethan shrugged and, moving toward me, he said, "All right. Erin, let me guess. The leggings store."

I laughed. I stepped in to walk with him, and ignore Colby.

"Nope," I said.

"All right. Do you want to just tell me?" Ethan asked. We came to the main lobby of the mall where we had to choose a direction. I realized if his cameraman was eating, he likely hadn't so I pulled out a protein shake I'd been hoarding.

“You’re a life saver,” he said. He chugged it, and I had a chance to consult a mall map.

“First floor,” I said as we headed for the escalator. Ethan and Colby followed me.

“Hang on, I have to be sure we have permission,” Colby said grinning at me.

“Sure,” I said refusing to look him in the eyes and turning coldly away. Why did seeing him flirt with Tess hurt me? No, I had to focus. This challenge was a way for me to show my spending habits, and what I deemed a part of my success. I had two minutes to figure out how I could do that in an electronics store.

“I thought for sure we would get to see some of your dancing,” Ethan said. He looked disappointed.

“In the mall?”

“San Franscisco is known for their street performers.”

“Street performers are a moment of smiles. Ballet is for those who can slow down, those who are willing to give way to the ground and live in a dream for a time,” I said. I felt homesick.

“But if you perform for me then I could claim to have seen the Prima Ballerina of our era before the world knew her,” he said, sounding happier.

“It is my favorite thing to do every morning while you are out jogging, Ethan,” Colby said significantly, covering the mouth of the phone. I glanced at Ethan who blushed a little. He seemed…I sat up straighter. Carrie went jogging every morning. Did they meet up? Was Colby reminding Ethan he'd already chosen? The way Colby stood in front of me a little it felt like he was claiming me.

"…It's your loss," Colby finished saying too seriously. "Anyway, we are going to cut out the store's name. Let's go."

He tromped in front of us hauling his camera. We looked around the store, and I used the time to talk about economics. I told Ethan how some companies thrived because they were always in the lead with emerging technology, but they also knew how to get it out to the public. Ethan asked questions and tried to be interested in me and show the viewer all my strengths. He wasn't nearly as engaged as he was when I talked about my dancing.

Ethan left halfway through to find the bathroom. I worked on giving Colby the cold shoulder, but he said:

"Did Tess's antics actually make you jealous?"

"You wish," I said.

"I do," he said, too seriously, squatting to see my hidden blushing face.

I rolled my eyes but couldn't help smiling.

"No matter what anyone says, you are the whole package, Erin. Don't let Serena make you feel lesser, okay?" he said, cuffing a warm large hand around my arm.

"I'm trying," I said leaning into him.

"You are my favorite contestant. You know that, right?"

"I guess," I said, blushing because whatever else was happening, I'd overheard Colby tell Patrick as much. Colby kept flirting and I needed his attention so badly I ate it up.

I was much happier by the time Ethan came back. Ethan seemed to relax over our time together. Though he didn't have any romantic affection for me, Ethan liked me. It seemed he found solace in my presence, and I liked being the person he was comfortable to be around.

I had no idea what else to do so I picked out a laptop because a person should never stop learning. Especially if they go on a reality show, because if scoliosis can't kill *The Dream*s of a professional dancer, trust this: a reality show producer can.

Chapter 12

The challenge for the next week was rock climbing. We went out to a cliff on the beach. Two days in a row. The first day we learned how to climb the cliffs. I climbed a little way up, but the second I felt uncomfortable, I stopped and came down. By the end of that first day, we knew who would win the competition, anyway. We still had to go back and film the next day. I refused to climb. Why bother? It seemed so pointless. Veronica and Sandra would win. They were both exceptionally good at climbing. Colby filmed me saying:

"I am finished dancing if anything happens to me."

They didn't even bother harnessing me.

Carrie, on the other hand, climbed like she was being chased and she had to keep going. Julian came out of his equipment van and watched her. Serena didn't bother climbing far up the cliff. She came down quickly, uncomfortable with the challenge. Serena stepped down to the damp sand after her climb. Julian walked up to her.

He glanced at me and I moved away knowing he wanted me gone. I stopped. I didn't have to leave. What was he doing to Serena? I listened hard and heard him say:

"Looks like Carrie doesn't know when she's lost."

"No kidding," Serena said taking a big step out of a harness.

"I wonder why she keeps climbing," Julian said, dripping every word with annoyance.

"Maybe she's having fun," I said, biting my lip, and scooting back in his space. Julian started in surprise when he found me still there.

"It's one of those situations where she holds us up to mess around. She's so inconsiderate," Julian said defending himself to me, while shaking his head.

Serena winked at him and said:

"I'm on it."

He grinned. Walking away he gave her butt a pat. She swallowed hard but nodded to herself like she was doing the right thing. I felt the creepy sensation of spiders crawling up my neck. How long had this been going on? I thought back to remember any other interactions between them. Serena was the only one who ever spoke up when Julian was around. She seemed to know a lot of little details that no other contestant knew. She knew Sandra had to get her nails done once a week because Ethan insisted on checking her nails for dehydration to be sure she wasn't forcing herself to throw up.

I remembered the way Julian smiled at us – no not us, at Serena – at the welcome brunch. He had… she knew everyone's names. She knew everything before the show even started. No, no, certainly they hadn't been… my stomach lurched, and I had to swallow bile.

Once she was free of her climbing equipment, Serena walked to the bottom of the cliff, right below Carrie. She put her hands to her mouth and yelled up. Her grating voice bounced off every rock that jutted out: "Carrie you lost. Why are you still climbing?"

After Serena cat-called a few more times, I lost it. I walked up behind her, flattened my hand and swung my arm with all my might smacking her right in the back of the head.

"Hey what the…" She turned, holding her head, more startled than hurt.

"Are you kidding me!" I hissed.

"What," she said glaring at me and rubbing the back of her head.

"Are you being paid to submarine her or did Julian just manipulate you into doing it?"

"What are you talking about?" she asked.

"You're making a fool out of yourself and I can't figure out why," I said.

"It's just annoying. Carrie always making us wait. It's cold and stinky out here."

"Maybe so, but Colby is catching everything. Every time you yell, he's filming it. You are submarining yourself now."

"I am not that stupid – not as stupid as you."

"You are playing right into Julian's hand. If you're not the submariner, then why?"

"Do you want to know who the real submariner is?" she asked turning on me like she may hit me.

"Who?"

"Colby," Serena said. I looked over at Colby. I thought it was funny, but the look on his face told me everything. His mouth opened but nothing came out. His eyes were apologetic and horrified all at once. The breath caught in my chest. I wanted to die of humiliation. All his flirting, all the attention he slathered on me. The way he coaxed me to focus on him. He was distracting me from what I really wanted. He was keeping me from being the whole package. I had been so sure he was the only one helping me.

"Julian told me about the dancer with a blog," Serena continued. "He said you were the one to beat. No matter how hard I tried I couldn't keep you from talking to Ethan. Colby did."

I stammered.

"Why?" I asked Colby, horrified.

"It's… it's my job. I know it doesn't seem fair, but it's all a game. You're supposed to –"

"It's not like you're special to Colby. He's been messing around with Tess as well," Serena said snidely, "but then what member of the crew hasn't been messing around with Tess, really?"

"Look Tess was just…" Colby stammered like an attractive man shouldn't have to show self-restraint. "She's in your face and you can't put her off…"

"It's none of my business," I said, taking deep breaths to keep from crying.

"You're just his meal ticket," Serena said sneering.

"You really are a horrible person," Colby said to Serena who looked shocked to hear this. He continued: "You have done way more damage than everyone else combined."

"I am playing the game. Everyone else is getting sucked in."

"Serena, are you… in a relationship with Julian?" I asked, as if my eyes had been opened and I was extremely worried that she had been sucked in further than the rest of us.

She didn't respond.

I finished, "Because, he's not going to spare you when the time –"

"Oh, Carrie needs medical attention. I better help," Serena interrupted, turning from us and jogging away. Her face was bright red, and I couldn't help noticing her blinking hard.

"Erin, you weren't just…" Colby stammered.

"Don't bother, it's fine," I said walking away from him. He followed me and said:

"When I graduate, I'll have the experience and education to write my own ticket. I know that's not an excuse, but as distasteful as this job is, it's the experience that will lead to a whole new world for me."

"Sure, I get that. I do. Now I want to be alone, and I need you to get that!" I said, still trying not to cry as I turned away from him to walk toward the ocean. Colby kicked the sand. He took his camera, and I noticed he caught every desperate thing Serena did. I wondered if Serena would regret enraging the cameraman.

I blamed Serena for submarining me, but she was playing the game the way she thought she had to. Julian did that to her. He made Colby do that to me. And all that was left was realizing, no matter how badly Serena treated me, Julian pulled the strings. He called me into his office and made me believe I couldn't lose. He talked me into coming on his show. Then he made Serena follow me, letting me know I had no chance of winning. That's how he got his contestants to fight for something he knew they would never get.

But then I must have had a chance. He wouldn't have bothered if I didn't have a chance. My dad even believed him.

The ocean was a slow melancholy dance, helping me mourn the mistakes I made. I watched the way the clouds made the water dull and wished the sun would come out to make it shine like it did in Maui. I stood watching it for a long time.

I was done letting things happen to me. I was not the sort who let things happen. I made things happen.

At this point, all I could do was control my rage and find my way off the show without exposing myself. I did not edit this show. How I reacted on camera would follow me, and my career, for the rest of my life. I was on a stage. I plastered my ballerina smile on my face until I figured out how to leave.

I took a deep breath and watched the ocean. The calm serenity of the scene before me took hold and I drew in the peace it offered me. I could only go forward. I would have to find another way to become a principal dancer.

I came back after having my lung deflated and became a soloist in the most prestigious dance company in the world. I could get on stage without the nerves of the other dancers. I could spring from demi-plie` and hold myself en pointe on one leg longer than Natalia, the top principal dancer at the American Ballet. My talent would not be ignored. I would push forward, despite this show and its producer. Serena eventually came back; she didn't look as confident as when she left.

"You didn't need to help. Ethan's a doctor," I said, this time not angry or even aggressive.

"Julian is manipulating you into exposing yourself. Colby did it to me, I get that. I'm not trying to hurt you or one-up you. I'm being your friend when I tell you hope I'd can't honestly believe Julian needs you to smother Carrie. He's making a fool out of you and if I were you, I'd stop."

I didn't wait for a response. Something that happened to her a long time ago made it impossible for her to respond kindly. It had nothing to do with me. Not really.

I couldn't be sure Serena heard me; she was so stubborn, but I'd been her friend in telling her. If I'd noticed sooner, I believe I would have said something. I would be that kind of friend and maybe one day I would have a friend who would do the same for me.

Serena watched the ocean until the bus loaded. It looked like she may have been crying.

Over the next few days, Serena tried more desperately to submarine Carrie, but Carrie was immune to her. Serena no longer had a purpose, and her time on the show closed over her as if she were drowning, and the harder she thrashed, the faster she sank.

Up until the moment Ethan eliminated her, Julian pushed her until she cried and stomped off his show. I did not judge her. Her emotions were raw and she was broken. Julian broke her. I would not suffer her fate. I had to go on the defense. I would not be broken on camera.

Chapter 13

When there were only five of us left in the house, I knew my time was coming to an end. Tess drove Carrie crazy flirting with Ethan. The three created the same love triangle that emerged in the last couple seasons, likely in the time frame when Julian took over from Dr. Corbon.

Veronica kept winning every competition per Dr. Corbon's ground rules, no one could justify kicking her off. Sandra or I was next. I couldn't imagine being torn down and humiliated just so my followers would accept my leaving. I woke earlier the morning after Serena left. I danced harder, knowing I needed my calm more than ever.

Colby had the nerve to tape me every morning still. I didn't ask him not to, but I didn't sit and talk to him when I took water breaks. I ignored him. When I finished, I turned to him tersely and said, "I need to see Julian, now."

"Oh um…" He searched my face, and I did not flinch. He put something in his ear and pulled out his walkie and said, "nineteen is on camera seven."

We waited for a minute and then he said, "You can go out to the studio."

"Thanks," I said throwing on my boots over my slippers and walking toward the door.

"Erin," Colby called.

"Yeah?" I asked waiting for him to justify himself as all the guilt-ridden must.

"It's just a job, it's just a game you know. Please try not to take it personally," he said.

"Oh, trust me. I don't believe there is anything personal between us," I said, turning away from him. I walked down the long driveway toward the little house that Julian used as his studio. The coastal morning air cooled me after my hard workout, making me comfortable.

Patrick met me at the door and walked me down a hallway. He glanced at me with pity. I glared at him, refusing his pity. Patrick flinched like I frightened him. He took me into a room with a long table full of monitors, and one large screen up on the wall. This screen showed me paused in relevé, my leg behind me in arabesque. I stopped for just a moment and looked at my form. It was perfect. I would find my way back into professional ballet. I had to.

Julian stood from his place at the desk strewn in takeout wrappers. Which accounted for the smell of onion and bacon.

"What can I do for you, Erin?" Julian said.

"I am not a fool. I see what's happening here. I can see you mean for Carrie to win and Tess to be the runner up. I want to be eliminated next. I do not want to be humiliated. And you could do me the courtesy of a competition I might actually do well on."

"You knew before you came on the show that it was designed to test you and your resilience."

"I also thought I actually had a chance of winning. You made it sound very much like that when you recruited me and my 300,000 followers."

He said nothing. I knew I had to get him into a corner or he'd ignore me entirely.

"In return for letting me go I will not blog about how you patted Serena's butt last week, nor will I imply the entirely inappropriate relationship between the two of you."

"You can't –"

"I can't say anything about the show. Your touchy-feely hands, and cruelly targeting unprotected vulnerable women are not safeguarded by the studio's contract. You met my father, the corporate attorney. He explained my contract to me fully," I said folding my arms and glaring.

Julian watched me. Fear registered behind his eyes. He could not afford an attorney of the caliber it would take to beat my father in any legal field. The studio would abandon Julian the second sexual harassment charges were filed.

"Fine, you can leave, and I'll even make sure you look good, but you have to be gracious in your blog about your time on the show and me."

"I'll be gracious about the show and never mention you. And that is only if you don't make me look ridiculous between now and then,"

I snapped feeling the blog was no longer mine anyway.

That day we were all measured for ballroom dancing gowns.

For the competition, we went to a local hotel. The ballroom was carpeted, but since only myself and my partner moved swiftly, it didn't matter much. My partner was a professional dancer in the theater. We moved so well in sync on the show that for the first time I had fun. He tried to convince me to give up ballet and be his partner on the ballroom dancing circuit. I laughed along with him but didn't discount the idea. When had I become open to new career paths?

On a break while Sandra complained loudly that some people didn't dance their whole lives, I hydrated. Carrie sat next to me and said:

"I've been coming back from my run and watching you dance in the morning while I stretch," she said.

"Creepy," I said, and grinned.

"I just mean to say, I can tell you really love it."

"I do," I said.

"Sometimes…it's just, lately sometimes you seem a little embarrassed about your dancing," Carrie said, glancing at me.

"I… since I've been here it feels like something I should have grown out of when I grew up. Not something I should have stuck with until I made it my career, you know?"

"No, do you know how many people follow through on a one-in-a-million dream?"

"I can't say I followed through," I said.

"You are like a living painting, it's art… it's beautiful. You are more than the rest of us. You have something special in you. You are a ballet dancer. Don't deny that," she said, bumping my shoulder.

"Yeah, no. I know you're right," I said, realizing I'd been ashamed of my dancing. It was like being ashamed of a child or something else that grew roots in my soul and then sprang out of me. I danced, I breathed and my heartbeat – these were all things that kept me alive.

"I'll always be a ballerina," I said. I wanted to tell Carrie about cutting my hair, but becoming vulnerable anywhere near Julian was so unsafe.

"I… I thought I had to have a backup plan, you know."

"Stop it, just go for it. You are so young, you have so much life. Don't worry about a backup plan," she said.

"I…" I looked at her. She was serious.

"You're right. I'm going to make it as a dancer. I have to. There is nothing else that makes me feel alive," I whispered, afraid someone might hear and use it against me.

"Loving what you do is a gift. You have no idea. Just do me a favor, if dancing is who you are, don't be ashamed of it—go after it," Carrie said.

"What if I never get to the level I want to reach," I asked, terrified of saying it out loud.

"Will that change the fact that you go to work every day and get to dance?"

"It's all I want to do. It's part of who I am," I said.

"Then be proud of that, be yourself."

I thought about this. I was strong. I had a gift. Carrie was right. I would not dismiss that because people like Serena and Dot didn't think it was enough. They had no idea the work I put into being a professional ballet dancer.

"Look at Julian," Carrie said. I looked over.

"Yeah," I said.

"No. Really look at his outfit; it's like he's an actor in his own life. His sweater vest, his white-collar button-up shirt open at the neck, and his sleeves rolled over his biceps. All with dress pants…dress pants. Do you recognize that look?"

"Um…he's going on a yacht later?" I asked, laughing.

"I think today he's dressed as Fred Astaire. He always kind of dresses like he's an extra in his own show. Sometimes at night Veronica and I try to decide who Julian is play acting," she said.

"Gene Kelly sported that look; my grandma had a crush on him. He wore his shirt like that because he had the biceps for it," I said snorting a little. Julian's fashion sense was all over the place.

"Next time he messes with you, remember that you are an amazing ballet dancer, and you know that, and he is a man playing dress-up like a child because he has no clue who he is," she whispered and winked at me. I laughed.

"Carrie, Erin, the batteries on your mic packs are dead," Julian snapped at us. I looked up and realized the cameras were trained on us.

"Oh, are they?" Carrie feigned innocence. She had been reminded to change her batteries so often we all knew Julian took breaks based on when her mic died. I, on the other hand, had never been reminded to change the battery pack on my mic.

"You are very astute," I said as we stood up. I wondered if Carrie noticed every little detail about me.

"It's a curse," she said. "Come on, let's get a new battery pack before Julian hyperventilates."

It was no surprise Carrie and I won the ballroom dancing competition. I remembered vaguely watching *The Whole Package* before I knew what happened behind the scenes. I had always been on the edge of my seat wondering who would win. I couldn't even comprehend how Julian made the competitions look tense to the viewer. Maybe he really was the talented artist he claimed to be. He certainly had a gift for distorting reality.

Chapter 14

I learned our reward for winning the ball room dancing competition was to take a cancer patient parasailing. Carrie was excited; she had no impediment that could keep her from flying behind a boat.

We drove with Patrick to pick up a very pale young man with the short sprouting of hair to prove his return to health. Only when I saw Jonah did I believe he was recovering from cancer.

Carrie focused entirely on the young man while we drove all the way up to Emeryville. She quickly bonded with the cancer patient; her dad having died from the illness. They were sweet together and I wondered if Julian set up this reward just for Carrie. He surely didn't do it for me. The closer we drew to Emeryville, the more my body involuntarily shook.

A little after nine, we pulled into a parking lot at what looked like a private marina filled with sailboats. I sat in the car after everyone else climbed out. They headed down a lovely path lined with shrubs and ice plant to the wooden dock. I finally climbed out of the car and followed.

I quickly saw how they knew what direction to go. Julian stood on the marina yelling instructions at Colby. Colby looked to be yelling back at Julian over the wind coming up off the bay. Carrie and the cancer patient stopped to talk by a well-kept boat shop. I walked toward Julian, trying to hear what he argued with Colby about.

"Fine, do it your way," Julian said, and Colby nodded. Colby looked at me like he wanted to say something.

"Go, before I change my mind," Julian snapped, turning toward us. Colby turned away hauling his gear to set up.

"Okay, let's go," Julian said to us.

"I don't think so," I said. I was done playing this game.

"Erin, you have to," Julian said, but his tone was more cautious than demanding.

"Not with my spine," I said.

"Ethan and I have been arguing all morning," Julian sounded more like he was fine fighting with Ethan but didn't want to anger me, though. He put his hands out to me cautiously and said, "I went to the trouble of hiring, at my own expense, a specialist. He cleared you, so go get…ur if you could please get in the boat, we have a schedule to keep."

Ethan came out of the boat shop. He looked irritated. He jogged over to me.

"Erin, I don't think it will hurt to just take the boat ride," he said. "You don't have to parasail."

Julian interrupted. "This is not your area of expertise, Ethan." He turned to me. " I've gotten a specialist who says you will be perfectly safe, Erin." He pulled out his phone and scrolled to a number.

Julian handed me the phone. The screen was greasy right in the middle where his beard stopped, and his cheek started. I held it an inch away from my ear not wanting it to touch my face.

"Hello," I said.

"Hey Erin, this is Dr. Brown. I am a spine surgeon," he said. "Since you have not had surgery in the last two years, I officially clear you to go parasailing. Have fun."

"Are you a neurosurgeon?" I asked.

"Orthapedic," he answered.

"Orthopedic," I said.

"Yeah, that's what I said," he responded, "The boat is in the bay. It'll be a nice ride. Parasailing isn't even considered an extreme sport. Just relax and have fun. Now I have a patient. I've got to go."

I handed Julian back his greasy phone.

"Okay let's go," Julian said walking down the dock toward a motorboat. The motorboat looked small to me and had no logo on it. As we didn't sign any company waivers, I couldn't figure out if Julian just knew someone with a boat or what.

"It was probably a chiropractor on the phone," Ethan complained.

"Or an actor who didn't learn his lines correctly," I laughed. "He said he was an Orthapedic surgeon."

He grew even more concerned.

"Erin, don't do this," he said.

"I'm sure it'll be fine. It's not even considered an extreme sport anymore," I said imitating the nasal in Julian's voice. Ethan broke out laughing like he couldn't help it, and put a hand on my back to make his point again. Before he said anything, Carrie walked quickly to catch up to us.

"Hey guys, what's so funny?" Carrie asked. She glared at me. I started, what did I do? Was she jealous? Of me? I glanced at Julian and wondered how he accomplished that, because that is the only way Carrie would be intimidated by my friendship with Ethan. I leaned over to her and said, "A character from Gilligan's Island."

She glanced at me, then to Julian in his dark blue jacket with gold buttons and white pants. Carrie relaxed and started to laugh. Ethan also seemed to understand what I said because he laughed as well.

"It's a pity his prop closet didn't have an ascot," I said. "It would have finished the look nicely."

Carrie laughed harder and hooked her arm into mine. I was a little proud of myself. I think I was making a friend. I felt stupid and immature for admitting it, but I'd never really made the effort before.

The boat's captain called out then threw me a life jacket. Ethan put a foot on the dock and one on the boat to help Carrie and me climb into the side of the boat.

The so-called doctor's assurances I'd be fine did not comfort me. I'm sure the viewer at home was pacified. I didn't know what to do but play along so I did.

"You don't have to do this, Erin," Ethan said again.

"No, it's fine," I said, gritting my teeth. I always wanted to try things like this. Why not?

"Here, let's at least strap you in really well," Ethan said.

Ethan pulled the straps so tight on my life vest, I couldn't breathe. Ethan made sure the main part of my body that curved was braced.

The captain, a muscled man in his mid-forties with no shirt or life vest on, clearly felt only his eyes required protection and wore mirrored aviator sunglasses. A trimmer version of the man in his early twenties, his son, stood on the back of the boat as his first mate. They both looked cold, despite it was in the high seventies, a pretty nice temperature for the northern coastline.

Instead of thinking too much, I examined the bumpy, mountainous shoreline as we jostled around in the water moving out of the marina. We didn't ride far into the bay. We stayed close to the shore for filming.

The main cameraman rode in the front of the boat with us. Colby set up on the marina that reached out into the bay like fingers resting on the top of the water. Julian stood next to him, on the middle finger that stretched out the furthest.

The first mate unfolded a huge swatch of cloth with tangerine and cobalt squares that billowed out into a parachute. My teeth chattered, but I wasn't especially cold in my blackboard shorts and rash guard.

"Here, Carrie will go first so you can see and make sure it's something you want to do," Ethan said.

"Just a hundred feet," the cameraman called to the captain who nodded. Carrie and the cancer patient were harnessed to a bar creating a swing that attached to the parachute. The first mate let out the rope and they gently floated a hundred feet upward in the air. The cancer patient whooped, and Carrie laughed. She looked at home flying.

Watching her fly made me want to try it. Until it was my turn. After Julian came over the walkie saying he got what he wanted, the boat reeled them in as though it had snagged a huge, colorful fish from the sky. Carrie lifted her legs and sat back down on the back of the boat. Her long turquoise board shorts rubbed against the platform, but it didn't look painful.

"How was it?" I asked Carrie when she came back into the boat.

"So fun. It was like floating and not really rough," she said looking at Ethan to confirm.

"I want to try," I admitted.

"Yeah. I think you'll be fine," Ethan said helping me sit up onto the platform.

"I promise I'll give you a nice ride," the captain said as his son grabbed the clips on my harness and attached me to the parachute so I could swing next to the young man.

"I'll make sure he gives you a good ride," Ethan said, and he sounded like he was threatening the man. I nodded, unable to stop my teeth from chattering. The young patient, whose name I couldn't remember because I was so anxious, took my hand.

"It's a blast," he said grinning at me, and kissing my hand.

"I've got this," I said, smiling back at him.

All too soon we lifted off from the boat. The ride seemed so much calmer when Carrie did it. Granted this time I ascended to three hundred feet instead of her hundred. We flew up into the sky, the reel of line releasing us into the atmosphere. I clawed the young man's hand. I hated that I couldn't remember his name, since I was likely maiming him. The rope slacked, then jerked a few times. I watched the young man carefully to see if it worried him. He smiled at me.

Then I smiled. It was actually quite peaceful. Parasailing was much smoother than the roller coaster. Sometimes I wondered if my parents overacted about my back so often in my youth that it had given me a warped sense of protecting it now. But then, I couldn't be comfortable considering how tightly Doctor Ethan put me into my life jacket, so maybe not.

"Open your eyes, Erin," the young man next to me said.

I squinted against the wind. For just a minute I forgot everything and looked out at the bay. I took a deep breath of thin air. It felt foreign to my lungs. The water was a color I did not know. It was green and grey. Not quite olive green, and not exactly graphite grey. The water ate the coastline, and the buildings along the wharf looked like they may eventually be swallowed. I felt both overwhelmed and enamored with the view.

I may have relaxed and enjoyed it if a huge gust of wind hadn't started batting the parachute around like huge cat paws playing with a massive ball of yarn. I felt a tugging sensation and realized we were already being pulled in. This relieved me and I released the cancer patient's hand, grasping the tethers of my swing.

When we were within twenty feet of the landing pad the boat jerked, turning directions. The rope went slack, just as a powerful gust of wind came up and the parachute folded. We dropped straight down instead of at an angle.

I screamed like the reaper was coming for me. The scream had been sitting on my chest for weeks. It was the vocalization of everything wrapped up in this sharp plummeting to the water. It was loud, long and ridiculously hard to rein back in.

"Whoa, Erin. You're okay, we're okay," the young patient yelled, pulling my arm upward like he could lift me back into the air. I only stopped screaming because I had to draw breath. My companion dropped my arm. He pulled himself up on the tethers and grabbed the bar above us. He swung a little as he contorted his body, kicking the tow line in front of us. The offending panel of the parachute ballooned out again. It slowed our descent.

"Okay… okay… sorry," I said wiping my tears.

"We are going to be fine," he said. I believed him. He had done this before. He knew how to straighten the parachute. I looked down to see what happened. A kite surfer cut us off and couldn't seem to get out of the way. The boat skipper overcorrected. The tug of the boat on the parachute line stopped supporting our weight. Our descent slowed, but we floated toward the water instead of the boat.

My toes dragged through the water before the line went taut and we moved forward again.

"It's just a little dip, Erin," the young man next to me called. "People pay extra for those."

"I might throw up," I said seriously feeling woozy.

"It'll just feed the fish," he said with a laugh.

The captain drove and yelled while his son scrambled on the landing platform. I glanced over at the marina and saw Julian screaming at the boat but couldn't hear anything he said. I hoped he was very afraid.

"You okay, Erin?" the young man asked.

"You must think I'm such a baby," I called, remembering his name was Jonah.

"I think that was about more than the dip," he yelled watching me. "I saw Mr. Marrows bully you into this harness."

I nodded feeling the shake in my body while wiping more tears. He took my hand and kissed it again with old soul eyes.

As we came close to the boat, we were still a little low.

"Lift up your legs! Do not put your feet down!" the son and captain both yelled at me several times as the winch pulled us in.

Being reeled in so quickly pulled up my board shorts and scraped my thighs on the landing platform. The captain, who looked like he hadn't a care in the world before, now watched me to be sure I was all right. His son took my hand and helped me step down into the boat.

I couldn't believe my idiocy. What if we'd crashed hard into the water? What if... Why was I being so stupid reckless?

A dancer sacrificed many things for her craft. It was like I was trading my whole life for this one month.

The captain and his son moved fast after I was safely in the boat to stow the parachute. As they worked, the kite surfer they almost hit came back yelling at them. All I heard was something about going back to Monterey to parasail, it was too windy in the bay. The captain waved and peeled away. I couldn't imagine the effort Julian went through to set up this reward.

Carrie loved parasailing. She was disappointed she couldn't go again because of the high winds. In fact, throw a cancer patient into the reward, and this was … it was Carrie's experience. Did Julian do all this to make her moldable in his hands?

It worked.

Julian stood on the dock when the boat motored in. Carrie didn't scowl at him as before. She even smiled at Julian instead of analyzing him with distrust. She let her guard down, gushing over her flight to Ethan and Jonah. He put me – my personal health – at risk so Carrie would be more susceptible to him. That couldn't be right? Could it?

Chapter 15

I rarely interacted with my designer, Von. He took my measurements the first day, then laid out on my bed what he wanted me to wear. His designs were all run-of-the-mill. Nothing stood out. Except for his sad, sad attempt in the challenge to use plaid, I never looked better or worse than anyone else. Carrie always looked better than the rest of us. And Veronica's dresses always fell apart.

Still, I took the effort to whisper to him this was likely my last week. He nodded and held fabric swatches up to my face. Whatever he was doing, it wasn't for the next eliminations where he had to use the bold primary colors.

Screaming out all my frustrations left me empty. I went through the next few days quietly, making no effort whatsoever. Thankfully Veronica found ways to help me. She was a true friend to me in those last days, especially when I was expected to groom a dog for an adoption fair, and my allergies were out of control.

"Come on, we've got to start filming," Lance called when my final elimination ceremony arrived.

I walked down the stairs with a feeling of nostalgia. It was over. I would get on a plane and go home. I didn't love my dress, but at least I didn't look like Snow White. Veronica's dress was blue on top with a yellow skirt, and red puffed sleeves. For all her kindness to me, she deserved better. With great relief I stepped up on the single riser where all five of us were displayed.

I watched Ethan, wondering if he even cared about sending me back into the real world with nothing.

"Veronica," Ethan called.

I smiled, so glad my friend made it another week. She however hesitated. My heart beat too hard in my chest. Something was wrong with her. She moved off the riser too slowly. She seemed sad, or angry. I had gotten the impression a few times that she was falling hard for Ethan but disregarded it. She and Carrie talked all the time. Of course, she knew how much Carrie…

Looking at Veronica I could see she hadn't known. She must have finally seen how enamored Ethan and Carrie were with each other.

Veronica finally reached him. Ethan offered her a key. Again, she hesitated. I couldn't breathe. What if she… No. No one ever rejected the key. It just wasn't done. Veronica watched Ethan, and my heart stopped. I needed to leave. I had to get out. What if she didn't accept the key?

Finally, Veronica took the key he offered and moved over to the chosen side.

Didn't she know it was my turn to leave? I was not *The Whole Package*.

I was not The Chosen.

When I finally stood alone on the riser, emptied of the women Ethan had chosen, and all the keys to the safety deposit box were handed out, I wanted to crawl under my covers like I had when I was first diagnosed with scoliosis.

"I'm sorry Erin, I really feel like you deserve this. I think all of you deserve this. Each of you is so competitive at this point. You just haven't won enough competitions," Ethan said as he bid me farewell for the sake of the camera.

I nodded to him. "I understand, and thank you for this opportunity."

Then the camera shut off. It was over.

Everyone hugged me to say goodbye. The strange warmth from Tess and Sandra after all the catty back and forth felt ridiculous. But it only amplified Veronica's hug. Sweet Veronica who'd been something real seeped into me and I broke.

I cut my hair. I didn't get enough airtime. I only won once. I gambled on my career, and I lost. Would I be given my spot back at the American Ballet? There were certain unwritten rules you did not break.

The tears rushed my cheeks before I could stop them. Carrie was last to hug me. Carrie who was supposedly meant to submarine me, saw my tears, and pushed me toward the door. She made it seem like she was helping me with my enormous suitcase, but instead, she was making sure the cameraman didn't get a clear shot of my tears. Ethan saw them. He looked heart-sore for me, but Carrie moved me quickly out the door and I loved her for it.

"What, what is it?" Carrie asked once we were outside and the driver hauled my colossal be-prepared-for-anything suitcase into the trunk.

"After I flew to California, Julian insisted I cut my hair to get on the show. I told him… Anyway, he insisted. I'm not sure I can get back into my dance company with short hair," I said trying to gain some control over myself.

"Oh Erin, I'm so sorry," Carrie said squeezing me again.

"I wish we'd been friends this whole time," I said. "I'm sorry I let Serena in."

"She had a gift; you can't worry about it," Carrie said.

I laughed contemptuously. Serena's ability to take away my self-worth was a gift to Julian. How ridiculous since both she and I were now eliminated from his show. Wiping my eyes, I said, "She did."

"You ready?" the driver asked as Carrie wiped my face with a tissue and dabbed it, smoothing some of the extra makeup on my neck to cover the red spots expertly, like she'd been mopping up all the other contestant's tears as well.

"No," I said, "but I guess it's time to face real life."

I wasn't ready for any of this. I may not have pulled it together, but Colby walked past us and climbed into the limo with his camera. I set my face, determined not to let him see inside me.

The way he glanced at me, his eyes drawn in concern, I knew he'd seen me crying. Thankfully, there was a barrier between us and he was no longer being paid to comfort me.

A makeup artist touched up my face in the limo. Colby ducked into his camera while I answered the list of questions he asked. He had never seen me; there was always a barrier between us. I took a deep, sustaining breath. If nothing else, it was over.

Chapter 16

The next morning, I woke early to the sounds of Manhattan out the window of the hotel and someone beating on my door. I opened my door.

"Come along, fame doesn't wait," said a blonde woman with puffy hair. "Julian sent me to be sure you get to your interview at the morning show on time."

"'Kay," I said disoriented. I'd gotten in so late; I hadn't done anything but grab my jogging pants and a tank top to sleep in.

I rummaged around trying to put my stuff in my suitcase while she tapped her foot.

"Don't bother changing. You'll get dressed there," she said pointing to the bag Von sent with me.

It was tradition for the eliminated contestant to dress in her designer's final creation on the morning show. When I pulled it out at the studio, the blonde lady said, "Oh, that's not too bad. You should be in good hands here."

I put on the tight periwinkle dress with a ruffle down the thigh. It was possibly the best thing Von ever made me. Perhaps he was talented when he didn't have to conform to Julian's guidelines, but then weren't we all?

After I was dressed, I waited in the green room long enough to wonder why I'd been awakened so early. Finally, I was brought down to the set, like it was time for my interview on the morning show, but again I just stood there on the sidelines.

The bustling studio moved. Every member of the team knew what to do. The lights and sounds kept a palpable beat that brought life – movement – to dart, to jump, to turn in dramatic tension. Then it stopped. Everything went quiet. The lights fell off everywhere except center stage. I held my breath. The host paused, like a teacher, waiting for everyone's attention. Then she spoke and the dance was off again.

"Welcome back. We are watching the storm over Hawaii with meteorologist Barb Wright. Barb, do you think this storm will be categorized as a tropical storm, or a cyclone?"

I listened carefully, hoping Mom's favorite spot in the world would be safe from the storm. The women chatted over what it would take to upgrade the storm to a cyclone. One of the co-hosts was extremely worried about his vacation home staying in one piece.

I pulled at my dress, feeling awkward. As a dancer I usually wore skirts that flowed. The tight dress Von made for me inhibited my movement. My segment as the newest cast member of *The Whole Package* to be eliminated had been pushed back twice since the tropical storm loomed over the big island of Hawaii.

At the next commercial, the host of the morning show, Samantha Prowers, apologized for the delay. She invited me to go outside before my interview. I walked out, a cameraman in front of me. It was hot. Way hotter than the coast of Northern California. The mask of makeup I wore started to sag. The cameraman filmed me waving for a minute, but the crowd assembled seemed more interested in getting the camera operator's attention. I stood smiling, trying to get my dress to stop sticking to me while Samantha joked with a few of her viewers.

"Erin, Erin," a lone voice called. A man, about my age, in his mid-twenties, waved to me. I looked at Samantha to see what I should do. She eagerly watched the studio producer sprinting toward her. They whispered urgently. I took a deep breath and walked over to the man calling my name. He waved to me with a huge grin. His sandy hair and tanned skin made his white teeth gleam. He was muscled, not the lean muscles of a dancer, but the bulkier frame.

"Hey, thanks for coming out," I said. I pulled on the tips of my blonde hair willing it to grow.

"Of course, you were robbed. You are The Whole Package," he said, looking charming.

"Thanks," I said with a fake laugh, "What's your name?"

"Jaxon. Jaxon Giles," he said. "Now that we've been introduced let me buy you dinner tonight."

I laughed my fake laugh again, then said, "I am exhausted. Thanks though."

"Tomorrow night," he said.

I squinted.

"What… what do you do for a living?" I asked.

"Making sure I rake in the dough?"

"No… I'm making sure you're not a serial killer," I said.

"I am in sports medicine, but serial killers could be too," he said.

"You are not making your invitation very inviting," I said.

"Okay. You're from Baltimore, right?"

"Yes. Again I have to wonder if this is creepy."

"No, it's not. You went on television. A lot of people know you're from Baltimore, but you tour with your ballet company."

"Yeah," I said looking away. He didn't notice me blinking hard.

"I figure since you aren't on tour, you'll go back to Maryland, right?"

"Okay," I said.

"I'm from Philly, and tomorrow night, I am going to drive all the way to The Oyster House in downtown Baltimore at seven. Do you know it?"

"Of course," I said.

"If you show up tomorrow night with friends and your mace, I will buy you and your friends dinner."

"I have a lot of friends," I lied.

"I will buy a few of your friend's dinner," he amended. He looked at me waiting. His white V-neck tee shirt and ripped black skinny jeans with pricy shoes made him look like a pretty boy.

His groomed face scruff, hair jelled into the perfect messy spikes, screamed a personal groomer.

I usually dated polished traditional men. I'd never dated a man in skinny jeans. And yet, he was literally the only person in New York City who remembered me. It was kind of sweet, and if I decided not to show up, he couldn't really blame me.

"Okay, I'll come, but only because I really love The Oyster House, and if you turn out to be creepy, you can't sit by us."

"Fair enough," he said as Samantha called me to come over to her and an important looking man.

"See yah," I said, unsure if I'd show up.

"You won't regret it," he said.

"Okay," I said. I waved over my shoulder.

"Erin, good," the important man said. "I'm so sorry there is officially a cyclone heading for Hawaii. I'm afraid we're going to have to cancel your appearance."

"Oh, okay," I said unsure if I should feel let down or relieved.

"Here, this is my assistant. He can take you back to the green room."

"Thanks," I said walking away. I turned back and found Jaxon still watching me, so I waved and then followed the assistant back to where I'd come from.

This could describe my whole reality show experience – a total letdown. I changed back into my joggers and a tank top, the coolest things I had, and left the studio as quickly as possible. Unwilling to call my parents I decided to find my own way home.

Chapter 17

I dragged the be-prepared-for-anything suitcase down to a cab, then through Penn Station, took a train with no air conditioning to Baltimore, and finally another cab to the upscale neighborhood where my folks lived. The cabbie parked behind a black Audi, and I wondered who my parents were entertaining. It was business, no doubt.

The cabbie, an excessively hairy man – so much so, his scruff crawled all the way up and out from his arm pits and over his tank top – ran my credit card. I sat in the cab facing my parents' gorgeous three-story red brick home. It looked out over the bay and had the perfect New England feel to it. The wrap-around porch was strewn with white wicker furniture placed in every spot that boasted a view. Some nights my parents drank lattes there gossiping about the neighbors driving by in golf carts after their games.

I tipped the man using my credit card, but apparently, he felt no need to help me with my luggage. He popped his trunk but did not exit the cab. I clambered out disgruntled. Pulling the suitcase free of the cab's trunk, I wished I had tossed the thing into a dumpster at the studio.

I turned to find my little brother, Drew, jogging up the street toward me as the cab drove away. He was by far the untidiest member of my family. He didn't care if his basketball shorts were off-brand. A few inches taller than me, he had a trim frame and could run for miles without getting tired. His blond hair had darkened since we were kids and he let it grow out until his girlfriend made him cut it. His picotee blue eyes held sunshine in them. Sincere and comfortable, he was by far one of my favorite people in the world. He grinned when he realized it was me pulling the equivalent of my weight in the form of a suitcase.

"Hey, you need help with that?"

"This thing is seriously ridiculous. It's not even how heavy it is. I can't seem to get the right leverage on it," I said trying to pull the huge suitcase over the curb.

"All right, I got it," he said, lifting it easily. I felt something catch in my chest seeing my little brother's warm smile. I wanted to sob. I pushed it away and smiled back. He didn't believe my smile, so I stopped.

"We don't pretend with each other," he reminded.

I nodded and stopped trying to smile.

He took the suitcase by the handle and pulled it up the walkway.

"Who's here," I asked by way of distraction.

"I don't know. Probably business," Drew said.

"Oh right," I said quietly.

"You okay?" he asked before he opened the door.

"I don't know," I answered honestly.

"Well, put on a smile for the folks and whoever's here," he said. "We'll get ice cream later."

"Thanks, Drew," I said pressing my forehead into his arm. He grabbed the back of my head and squeezed, finishing the awkward hug we'd done since we were little, and our parents made us apologize to one another after a fight. I walked through the door he held open. He dropped my suitcase at the foot of the stairs.

"Let's say hi to the folks, then I'll take it up," he said. He saw that I looked inclined to climb the stairs and duck off to my part of the house.

"Of course," I said.

I would usually call out to my parents, but they were in the backyard grilling for clients, as was their Friday night tradition in the summer. We wound our way to the back of the house. The kitchen was immaculate, which meant Lucia had been here until the guests arrived. I walked to the screen door, but stopped abruptly when my parent's voices came into focus and I realized they were talking about me.

"Erin is talented, you can't pretend she isn't one of your best dancers," Mom said.

"That waist-length hair was her best asset. Why she cut it I don't know," said a voice I knew as well as my parents. It was an old friend of the family, Noel Landry, the director of the American Ballet.

"Come on Noel, it'll grow back," Dad said.

"Andrew, it was a long shot, anyway. Her height makes it hard to find her male counterpart. She's cut her hair, she hasn't been training for over a month and she has her issue," Noel said delicately.

"She is not the first professional dancer with scoliosis," Dad snapped back.

"No, but she will never have the longevity, careerwise, to build the audience Natalia has. She just isn't capable of it with her back. What she's done is amazing. I mean maybe if she'd won *The Whole Package*, you'd have some footing, but she was barely on it. I doubt she's even gained more followers for her blog from it."

"Yeah, that producer made it sound like she was going to win. He and I need to have a little chat," Dad said.

"Come on, Andrew, just try to be realistic about this," Mom cut in, sounding feisty "It's time we tell her the truth. No amount of finagling is going to get her center stage now."

"Well, I wouldn't destroy her dream," Noel said, taken back.

"We just have to find another angle. There is always another angle to come at the thing," Dad said, encouraged.

I snuck a peek out the door. Dad sat at the patio table, concentrating across the table from Noel. Genetically, Dad looked like Drew, but the way he carried himself was as different as night and day. He kept his dark blond hair tapered at the sides and combed back in a classic polished style. He never wore anything that didn't prepare the opposition for how good he was, based simply on how much his clothes cost. He was easily the smartest person I knew. His shrewd blue eyes were trained on Noel, daring her to disagree with him.

He was possibly the only person in the world who intimidated Noel. Her gaze darted here and there, like she couldn't afford to be caught. Her dark hair tied in a tight knot at her neck contrasted the loose, billowy black silk shirt she wore. Her slightly plump, liver-spotted hand always tapped out a beat whether the music played or not. Now it worked a particularly fast tune on the table.

Mom stood with her back to me, but I could feel her impatience by the hand balled at her waist. Her long thin dancer's body had no glitch to it like mine did, and she looked immaculate in her cap sleeve boat-neck dress with a summery floral pattern on it. Mom's buttery blonde shoulder-length hair curled at the ends, and her sharp eyes saw what she wanted to see.

Drew made to open the door and alert them of our presence, but I stopped his hand and put my finger to my mouth. I peeked back out the door when I heard Noel clear her throat.

"She has enough discipline. Maybe she could help train. You know I only let my most talented principals do that."

"Just keep an open mind," Dad said.

"Andrew, I think Noel means for her to find a niche as a teacher in a local studio," Mom said. She sounded sarcastic, but I couldn't be sure.

I backed up as Mom picked up a pitcher off the table and headed for the door. I pushed Drew back and we ran out of the kitchen. I pushed him all the way to the stairs. He picked up my suitcase. We hurried up the staircase to my sitting room. My brother looked lost trying help me. He stammered:

"Do you…? Can I…?"

I shuddered, the tears already starting in my eyes.

"Please, cover for me, just give me a few minutes alone," I said.

"You know I can't keep a secret," he said.

"Go for another run," I said hopefully.

"I… I'm meeting my study group in a half hour, but when I get back you will have to face them."

"Okay. Thanks, Drew," I said.

He patted my arm and gave me my privacy. I felt the tears roll through my body as I shut the door behind him. I walked through the outer room to my bedroom. Mom had been in her ivory phase when she decorated it. I liked it well enough, but it was my bathroom I missed the most over the last month. When I used the Jack and Jill community-style bathroom on the reality show, I told myself I'd have a bubble bath in my huge jet tub as soon as I got home.

I passed it now without a backwards glance and sat at the chair in front of my huge mirror. I pulled on the tips of my hair as if it may somehow grow back instantly. I opened a drawer and found one of my many detangler brushes. It moved way too fast through my hair and collided with my shoulder. I threw the brush at the mirror and it cracked instantly. I ran out of the bathroom and curled up under the puffy ivory duvet, hiding my head in my arms, sobbing.

I had moved away from home at fourteen to attend a school of dance. Alone I endured the stares and taunts as the freak in a back brace. I shut everyone out and spent hours perfecting every movement required of me. When the other dancers went to dinner, I built up the muscles in my back. I fought to be the top of every class I attended. Hours upon hours of my life I gave to one day dance center stage. My feet were deformed from dancing on pointe for so many years. Couldn't the universe see how hard I worked and give me a break? But no. I would never be the top principal dancer.

I tried to disbelieve Noel's words, but I knew they were true. Only a handful of people really understood the world of dance and all it took to succeed, on and off the dance floor. Sadly, those were the people who could keep me from my dream. I wanted to dance. I didn't want to teach dance. I wanted to be the star. Growing up in my studio productions I was Sleeping Beauty, the Sugar Plum Fairy, Odette, and I was alive. Nothing else in my life made me feel like that.

I wanted to tour the world as a Prima Ballerina Assoluta. I understood why Dad wanted me to go on *The Whole Package*. I needed the fame that would sell tickets. My ability to sell tickets was the only way Noel could convince the other board members to give me a chance. I wept into my bed consumed with the anguish of a wasted life. I put an arm over my face and cried hard and long. I finally tired out and fell asleep.

Chapter 18

"Erin, sweetie, when did you get home?" I heard my mother ask from somewhere outside of my dream.

"I just laid down and…" my head dropped back on the pillow.

"Okay, just sleep dearest, we can catch up tomorrow."

I closed my heavy eyes and opened them again. Mom asked, "Erin, do you intend to sleep away the entire day?"

"Yes."

"Come on, you've been asleep for hours," she said. "Come eat something."

I sat up and rubbed my eyes against the glare of sunshine from the blind she opened. Mom sat next to me on the bed and examined my face. She looked worried.

"You're right. I'm starving," I said, afraid of what her examination would find.

I stood and Mom followed me down the stairs and into the kitchen. Drew sat in there eating lunch. Mom fixed me a sandwich and Drew watched me. He gave me a head nod a few times and I couldn't be sure what he wanted. Everything was foggy. Finally, he said:

"Mom, you had company last night?"

Oh, right. Mom stiffened up and wiped her hands on a hand towel before answering.

"Yes, Noel came over. We were talking about hair pieces, Erin. You don't have to –"

"I heard her tell you she won't take me back," I said before she could put her positive spin, also known as an outright lie, on the thing.

"Oh, well, Noel is just –"

"The director of the American Ballet. She knows what she's talking about when she says I have no chance."

"More is happening here than you know, Erin. Besides, she doesn't have the last word."

"Deep down I knew if I didn't win *The Whole Package,* I'd never be made a principal dancer, but it hurt to hear it."

"That's overly dramatic. Come now dear, we'll talk about this when your father gets home. I promise you he is not giving up."

"Maybe he should," I said bitterly.

"Erin, please be reasonable," she said. She sounded much more serious now.

"Why didn't you tell me she didn't see me ever becoming the top principal dancer?" I asked.

"Erin, sweetie, the world of Ballet doesn't work like that. You know it doesn't. If you want something you fight for it – I expect you to fight tooth and nail for your dream, sweetheart," she said, her eyes concerned.

"I did. I fought to be The Whole Package. I cut my hair, I went parasailing, and this, this is all I have to show for it," I cried pulling on my bob of a haircut.

"Come on. Your dad has some other ideas. There are more ways to make a name for yourself. He's golfing with some clients, then we have a dinner. After that we will sit down and talk. You will see the situation is not as dark as it seems," she said.

"I can't tonight. I'm meeting some friends at The Oyster House," I said, knowing I had to assert my own schedule, or my mom would try to plan out my life until I moved back to New York out of frustration.

"What friends?" Mom asked.

"Some people I met on the show. We agreed to meet tonight," I said.

"Is that safe?" Drew asked.

"You and Phoebe can come too," I said. I saw Mom nod out of the corner of my vision.

"That would be fun. I need a break from studying," Drew said, texting his girlfriend.

"Your father's only looking out for you," Mom said.

"I know," I said. "Noel was right about one thing. I haven't had a proper workout in a while. I think I'll go do some Barre work after lunch."

"That's the spirit," Mom said. I finished up and changed into a leo and boy shorts. As a corporate attorney, my dad let Mom, a real estate agent, design her perfect home. She had done it four times. Every time she sold the home after a few years, and it appreciated significantly in value.

Our current home was sixty-five hundred square feet, the basement was a dance studio, weightlifting area, with other fitness equipment. Mom still danced for her workout, but it was no secret this house had everything I needed to succeed. Mom often hinted when I married, she and my dad would move out of the house and give it to me and my husband. I laughed before, because I was on the road so often, I generally lived in short-term sub-lets. I never bothered to get my own place, let alone take theirs. Now I wondered if she designed this home knowing I would end up giving dance lessons out of the basement for the rest of my life.

I turned my music on way too loudly and warmed up. I danced for two hours, just pushing my body back into shape. Usually, I felt beautiful when I danced, but all I could do was watch the wall of mirrors as my half ponytail flopped around, loosening hair that stuck to the sweat on my neck.

I couldn't face my father, not when my dream felt dead. He didn't let dreams die. Even when I was little, he wouldn't let me stop believing in Santa; he left me little notes from him. When all the other girls started to notice boys, I still said he would always be my fellow. But I couldn't pretend now, not even for his sake. After I worked out, I showered and dressed, hurrying my brother out of the house before Dad got home.

Chapter 19

The Oyster House, a ritzy restaurant in downtown Baltimore, overlooked the Patapsco River. We parked on the street about a block away. Drew helped Phoebe out of his huge, four-door truck, then let me out. My sore feet slammed to the ground tingling.

"Here, I got you these," Drew said grinning and extending his hand toward me. I took the small bag he held out and opened it. It was the perfect pair of dangly sterling silver earrings.

"The way they spiral, the lady who sold them said they would always keep spinning…kinda like you when you're dancing," Drew said.

"I could never wear dangly earrings before," I said examining them, while feeling the last of the air conditioning in the truck on my neck and the heat of the night warming my front.

"Right, they ended up caught in your hair. I remember it drove you nuts, so I figured you could try again."

"Thanks, Drew," I said thinking I may possibly have the coolest little brother in the world.

"Come on," Phoebe called, annoyed.

Drew and I started. We had been raised to be polite, and not keep people waiting. He slammed the door to the truck. His girlfriend stood and waited on the curb across the street tapping her high-heeled foot at us. Despite my rigorous upbringing to be polite, I slowed down. The sight of her impatience annoyed me.

Phoebe hadn't changed physically in the four years since I met her, yet her attitude had drastically altered. She wore her light brown hair highlighted blonde in layers, flat-ironed around her face, down to her shoulder blades. Her hazel eyes were different colors depending on what she wore, and she always wore something to show off her perfect abs. Tonight, she wore a turquoise strapless top, but her matching chunky necklace almost looked a part of the shirt. Her low-riding jean skirt showed off the muscles around her belly.

Though she looked the same as when I met her, her personality changed dramatically.

When we first met, Phoebe acted nicer. She pretended to be humble, even proud to be with Drew. After a year or two she acted … different. Now, everything about her put me off.

My whole look, a tunic-style summer dress with Converse sneakers made me a little girl next to Phoebe. I may have believed this brewing annoyance toward her lay in my insecurities. Bu then Phoebe stopped Drew and took a deep irritated breath as she said, "Here, let me fix your collar. You are such a child, Drew."

My brother preferred jeans and superhero t-shirts, but Phoebe insisted he wear button-down shirts when they go out. Drew didn't look like himself; he looked like the cover of a magazine.

After experiencing *The Whole Package*, I was tired of playing a role, not being in control of my own life. But it made me angry to see my brother forced to play dress up. What's more, what right did she have to get annoyed because we made her wait a minute or two? Phoebe always expected politeness out of Drew and me. Yet she never returned the courtesy.

An idea popped into my head. Carrie forced Serena to wait for her, and it drove Serena nuts. I decided to do an experiment. Instead of going along with everything Phoebe wanted, I would do my own thing and see what happened.

"Here, guys hold up, I really want to try these on," I said stopping in front of a store window. I took off the little pearls I always wore and put on Drew's earrings.

"Erin, the bathroom is right in there," Phoebe said looking around to see who watched us. She had grown very aware of the way people looked at her as an extension of us. Mom said it was an insecurity, but that didn't make sense. Phoebe seemed overly confident.

"I know. Just give me a sec," I said fixing the part in my hair and pretending to ignore her annoyance. The earrings looked cute, and my hair didn't get all tangled in them when I shook my head.

"These are gorgeous. Thanks, Drew," I said.

"Those are gorgeous. Where's mine?" Phoebe asked, glaring at Drew.

"I ordered you those diamond ones you wanted," he said looking sheepish.

"Where are they?" she asked playfully.

"They've shipped," he said taking the hand she offered him.

She tried to pull him away, so he would move forward without me. Drew stood his ground.

Phoebe huffed and folded her arms. She jiggled watching me look at my reflection in the window. When this didn't hurry me up, she snapped:

"Erin, your friend is waiting for us. Let's go," and pushed forward toward the restaurant. I took one more look at myself. I smoothed my part again and pushed my hair behind my ears making the earrings the focal point. I liked that better.

"Sorry," I said catching up to Drew who trailed behind Phoebe like he was trying to decide if he should wait for me or catch up to her.

"It's fine. Her earrings will come. I ordered them from –" he started.

"I'm not sorry you bought me earrings," I said taking his arm, "I really appreciate it. I forgot I always wanted to wear danglers but couldn't. I'm sorry your girlfriend overreacted about you doing something nice for your sister."

"Come on. She's stressed out," he said.

"Why?" I asked.

"Her rent went up."

"Let me guess. She wants you to pass the bar, move in and pay for it?"

"You know Mom and Dad will cut me off if I move out," he said.

"You've got your law degree. They aren't doing much for you these days, anyway," I said.

"I don't suppose you've forgotten after I pass the bar, Dad is going to get me an office in his practice. Then I'll move out."

"Then you'll marry Phoebe and live happily ever after?" I asked, glancing up at his face.

"She… well she wants to…" He looked at the back of his girlfriend's head, "She wants to elope once I pass the bar," he said.

"Seriously, she'd do that to Mom?" I whispered because she was slowing down so Drew could open the door for her.

"I won't I swear. I'll figure it out," he nodded. I said nothing else. We were at the door of The Oyster House.

My parents offered to pay Drew's way through Georgetown Law if he lived at home and wasn't married. They said this two years ago, after Phoebe started talking about marriage. Though none of us said it aloud, we were all terrified for Drew to get a high-paying job and not need my parent's support anymore. I almost thought Drew dragged his feet, like on some level he knew she was wrong for him.

Drew held the door of glass and wood to the restaurant open for me. It made me want my manners. I nodded my thanks.

Chapter 20

Jaxon sat in the entryway, playing on his phone. He looked up as I walked in. He waved and stood. I took a few steps toward him.

"Yummy," Phoebe whispered in my ear as he walked toward us. He wore a white button-up shirt rolled at the sleeves and open at the neck with slacks. His tie hung loose. To me, he looked like an eighth grader who didn't want to wear a suit to middle school graduation. Phoebe appeared pleased with the look because she crowded in behind me to get introduced.

"Erin, I'm so glad you came," he said, kissing my cheek.

"Thanks," I said twitching where his whiskers hit my face.

"Hi, I'm Phoebe," she said not waiting for me to remember her but holding her hand out to him.

"Hey, good to meet yah," he said, looking to Drew who stood on the other side of me, almost trying to decide if he and Phoebe were together.

"This is my little brother, Drew, and you already met his girlfriend, Phoebe," I said.

"Hey," Jaxon said giving Drew his hand. Phoebe shot me a dirty look.

"Hey," Drew said, clenching his jaw. He hated when Phoebe flirted with other guys.

“Is this your party?” the hostess asked, smiling her biggest smile at Jaxon.

“Yeah, come on Erin,” he said putting a hand on my back and pulling me in front of him.

“I’m so glad you came,” he said over my shoulder.

“I needed to get out,” I said bluntly.

We were seated at a window with a view of the river. I wasn’t in the mood to be social, but it didn’t matter. Phoebe wanted to know everything about Jaxon, apparently the two or three details I gave on the ride over weren’t enough.

“Erin says you’re in sports medicine?” she asked.

“I’m a physical therapist,” he said.

“Do you work in a practice or clinic?” She squinted unsure what he even did.

“My brother and I own a practice together. We inherited the office from our uncle when he passed away last year…” he trailed off like he hadn’t meant to say that.

“What is your specialty?” I asked to refocus him on something else.

“I specialize in injured athletes, but also work with car crash victims and stroke patients. Anyone who needs physical rehabilitation, really.”

“That was decent of your uncle. Some people luck out in the family department,” Phoebe as she looked out the window. She had not lucked out in the family department.

"Well, it was conditional. He left us the practice as long as we take care of our cousin," Jaxon said.

"He left you a child?" Phoebe asked, snapping back to Jaxon, looking appalled.

"No, she's twenty-four, she's special needs. She lives in a home, we just have to look out for her," he said.

"Good for you. Family should stick together," I said.

"Thanks," he said warmly. Phoebe did not like him looking at me.

"Have you always lived in Philadelphia?" she asked.

"Nah, I grew up in Buffalo. I moved here after my uncle became sick and needed a physical therapist to take his place at the practice. Since I was going to school for it, it made sense."

"Your brother and you majored in the same thing?" I asked.

"No, he's more of the –" Jaxon started to say.

"Have you ever worked with anyone famous?" Phoebe interrupted.

Jaxon dropped the name of some professional athletes, then he looked at me again to praise him. I nodded, impressed, but Phoebe quickly said, "I love Buffalo wings. Do you just eat them all the time?"

"Not as much as I used to," he said with a laugh.

"I'll bet you eat them spicy," she said. "Drew won't eat anything too spicy."

"You don't like spicy food," Drew said.

"But I'm a girl."

She laughed and looked at Jaxon to laugh as well. He smiled, amused at the very pretty woman flirting with him.

After a few minutes, Jaxon asked which of the local night clubs we frequented.

"Erin is always out of town, and when she's home, she goes to bed early," Phoebe said.

"That is true," I said agreeing as if she wasn't trying to insult me.

"I, on the other hand, love The Zone. Have you been there?" she asked.

"When did you go there?" Drew asked.

"Oh," she said growing red, "the girls and I went. Just to hang out."

"We should go after this," Jaxon said.

"That would be awesome," Phoebe said.

"Might be fun," I said, looking at Drew.

"Sure," he said, through gritted teeth.

I barely listened. Instead, I started to watch the way Phoebe flirted with Jaxon. I couldn't help wondering what if she left Drew for Jaxon. I looked at my brother. His annoyance flared the longer Phoebe flirted. How much more painful would it be after they married?

We all suspected she cheated. A guy in her building always lurked around her. When Drew tried to take out student loans a year ago so they could move in together, she refused. She told him how lucky he was to have a family that would support him. When he tried to drop by, she would get angry and tell him to call first.

What if… I watched Jaxon. He wasn't my type at all. He was her type, stylish, confident. He ate spicy foods. He talked about all the clubs he'd been to.

I wasn't a schemer. I felt guilty for even thinking these thoughts. Mom always said we support each other no matter what. She and Dad supported my dream to be a professional dancer to the point of ridiculousness. I wanted to support Drew, but did support mean help him out of a bad relationship or let him continue down the path of self-destruction? At a certain point what should a sister to do?

Chapter 21

After we ate, we left The Oyster House and went to the club. I'd never really been a part of the club scene. I spent so much time and effort in my dancing. I couldn't do anything to my body that might ruin my hard work. The club was dark enough that a laser show could be seen on the upper floor. The music was loud, and still, I could only distinguish the beat. The dancing looked more like a trampoline fitness class. We were quickly sucked into the jumping.

Phoebe didn't show any preference for Drew. She danced with him, Jaxon and any other guy in the room. If guys got in too close to her, she pushed them away from her with an anger that surprised me. I didn't know how to do this, and every guy in the room acted like he had permission to touch me. After a while Drew stayed by me to keep the more aggressive men away.

Phoebe said something about the bathroom, so I followed as she pushed a path through the crowd.

"Isn't this a blast?" Phoebe asked when we were both washing our hands in front of the bathroom mirror.

"It's kind of a workout," I said using a paper towel to blot my forehead. I glanced at Phoebe through the mirror. Trying to decide how often she went clubbing I asked:

"Is it always this crazy?"

"Nah, it's a Saturday night," she said.

"That makes sense," I said. We were silent for a minute. Finally, I asked politely:

"So how is clerking for Judge Carson going?"

"Oh, he's a total pig," she answered. "He thinks we all want to sit and listen to him talk. He flirts with me and I have to sit there and smile."

"You don't have to," I said.

"I do if I want to keep my job."

"He couldn't fire you for not flirting with him," I said.

"Nope, he can't, so he'd find another reason. He's done it twice to other women," she said. "Trust me, you are so lucky to be in a field where you aren't constantly hounded."

"That sounds terrible," I said, unsure what else to say.

"Yeah, but Drew is almost done," she said. She glared at the tube of lipstick she applied like she had every right to be frustrated with him. This statement supercharged my sisterly outrage, and my self-respect. I went on the defensive.

"Oh yeah, Drew said you guys might elope."

She started a little, surprised he'd shared their secret. I took out my lipstick and said, "It's probably a good idea, then you don't have to mess with the pre-nup."

I turned to fix my lipstick, like I hadn't just dropped a bomb on her. Through the mirror I saw her flinch.

"What pre-nup?" she asked.

"Oh, I don't think I'm supposed to say anything, sorry," I said, "Do you think I'd look cute with side bangs? This cut makes me look like my seventh-grade math teacher."

"Yeah, you'd look better with side bangs," she said snidely. "So come on, Erin, what about the prenup?'

"Oh, it's nothing. I think my dad said something about insisting on a prenup before he puts Drew on the path of partnership in his law firm. It'll be better if you guys elope. Drew doesn't want to work for our dad his whole life. It'd be better if he finds his own groove, you know," I said. I smiled at her through the mirror.

"He really wants to go into corporate law," she said.

"Oh yeah, but there are plenty of law firms. In fact, I bet you could vet lawyers just watching them."

"I'm in criminal court. He doesn't want to go into criminal. He'd have to go court-appointed," she said, cringing.

"Oh well I'm sure you two will figure it out," I said, "I am for sure going to get side bangs."

"Yeah," she said. I could see her swirling the saliva around in her mouth like she was getting ready to spit. She was so mad. I smiled and politely held the bathroom door open for her. She nodded with her face set, and fierce.

She pushed the crowd to create a path. She fumed and people quickly moved for her ire like a line of fire burning through paper. I felt very guilty. That was probably the first time I'd ever actively manipulated another human being. I thought a lot about the reality show, and how Serena had manipulated me so effectively.

She would drop her bomb while pretending to be interested in something else, like her hair or a bug bite. It made it seem like she wasn't invested in the conversation at all. I didn't like Serena. I hated that I was taking her lead, but this was my little brother. And his happiness would never be with Phoebe.

From that point on Phoebe was all over Jaxon and completely ignored Drew. Jaxon tried to continue to flirt with me, but Phoebe wouldn't stop. I felt so bad for my little brother. By the end of the night, I wished I hadn't interfered.

"Hey, let me walk you to your car," Jaxon said following us out of the club.

"Thanks," Phoebe cooed walking with him. He couldn't put her off, so he put an arm around both of us, despite Drew being on the other side of her. Phoebe snuggled in. I noticed he wore his cologne too strong. I folded my arms leaning away. He had to lean toward me not to lose contact. Phoebe almost tripped over his legs.

My suspicion Jaxon wanted something from me was finally confirmed. After a night of ridiculous subterfuge, buying me dinner, and paying for my entry into a club Jaxon felt he could impose on me however he wanted.

"Erin, my cousin, Mia, is really into *The Whole Package.* It would mean so much to her if you came over and watched it with us Thursday night."

"Of course, we will, that would be so nice," Phoebe said.

"I can't. I need to study," Drew said shortly.

"Oh well, that doesn't mean Erin and I can't go," she said. I shrugged off the weight of Jaxon's arm to look at Drew. I was humiliated for him, but how else did I get Phoebe to be with someone else? Jaxon saw my hesitation. Taking his arm off Phoebe's shoulder, he focused on me: "Please, Mia has no friends except her television buddies. I know she would appreciate it so much."

I closed my eyes feeling like the biggest betrayer in the world.

"Okay, maybe just for the show," I said. Drew glanced around Jaxon and Phoebe at me. I couldn't look at him.

"I'll get the truck," he said and stomped away.

I stopped with Phoebe and Jaxon. Jaxon texted me, then took a picture of himself so I'd know who was calling. Phoebe took his phone and acted like it was the most natural thing in the world for her to take a selfie and program herself into Jaxon's phone. She went so far as to call herself, so she had his number.

I watched all this hating myself. Drew was my brother. We always looked out for each other. But what did it mean to look out for him at this point? If Phoebe really loved him, she wouldn't desert him when she found out her access to Dad's money diminished, right?

I nodded goodbye to Jaxon as Drew drove up. I climbed into the innards of the truck cab while Phoebe continued to say goodbye.

Chapter 22

"Seriously, Erin," Drew said.

"You know I can't handle letting down a little developed disabled girl. I'll figure out how to go alone," I said, seeing his anguish.

"That's not safe. He's clearly a player," Drew said.

"I'll take someone else," I said.

"No, just take Phoebe. Maybe they're better together," he said watching his girlfriend lean against his truck, touching Jaxon's arm and laughing.

"She's…" I stopped. Once, when they were on a break, I said some not so flattering things about Phoebe. When they got back together Drew ended up telling her and I had to grovel for weeks until she finally forgave me."

After Phoebe gave her flamboyant goodbye, she climbed into the truck. She closed the door and Drew sped away.

"What was that?" Drew asked.

"What's the matter with you?" Phoebe asked.

"""You encouraged that guy like you don't even have a boyfriend," Drew snapped. "What is the matter with you?"

"Why didn't you tell me your dad is talking about pre-nups?" Phoebe asked turning the conversation on him. I swallowed hard.

"Who said that" Drew said looking at me in the rear view.

"I didn't… I thought you both knew," I said lying out my teeth.

"He only said it once, and then he took it back," Drew said.

I tried to hide my surprise.

"Then why does Erin think he won't get you a place in his practice if I don't sign one?" she asked.

Drew looked at me again. I bit my top lip, certain my face was red.

"Would it matter? I've always thought about going into criminal law."

"What is the matter with you? You can't make money at that until you build up a bunch of bums as clients. Unless you're going to defend gangbangers or spoiled private school brats who get caught with drugs, there isn't money in it," she said.

"Actually, I thought I'd be a prosecutor."

"What?" she snapped. "I have not wasted four years of my life on a public servant. Seriously, do you have any idea how fast they burn out and become professors, or how often they're threatened? No! I forbid it."

"You forbid it?" he asked astounded, "Then I forbid you going to nightclubs and flirting with other men."

"Excuse me?"

"Well, if we can forbid each other," he said quieter.

"Me wanting you to be successful is not the same as you trying to stunt me actually living through my twenties. I am only twenty-seven. I have every right to live and enjoy this time in my life. But for you to ruin your future, capping your income at a hundred grand if you're lucky. No. that is ridiculous. Your dad is pulling in a few million a year. Don't you want to help our children out the way he helps you?" she asked.

"Of course," he stammered.

"While on the show, I got so much flack for how our parents helped me," I interrupted.

"Really," Drew said, but I wasn't sure if it was because I interrupted, or if he was interested.

"Yeah, the other contestants acted like we shouldn't use our parents' help," I said, trying to defuse the fight.

"There are plenty of guys at Georgetown who resented me for finishing my degree and having a job waiting for me," Drew said.

"They're just jealous. If your dad wants to give you a leg up in life, what's the big deal?" Phoebe asked.

"Sometimes I feel like I should give back," Drew said.

"Maybe you should; you're very fair. A few years as a public prosecutor and then go into dad's business might be a good way to give back," I said, not just to taunt Phoebe. Drew craved being a hero. He'd be amazing as the victim's advocate.

"Come on! Who do you give to except your kids?" Phoebe said. She sounded scared.

"Plus, Erin, you would never have made it as a dancer without your parents' help. Don't your shoes alone cost a grundle? You wouldn't think of giving up performing to teach underprivileged kids."

"I did in college," I said. I wished wish I'd kept it up, but touring with American left me no time for anything else.

"Yeah, plus, my dad sponsored plenty of dancers for Noel. Half of them don't make it because they aren't willing to put in the work Erin does," Drew said.

He was right. I did work hard. Most times even harder than the top principal dancers. I couldn't think about it. Drew and I were on the defense together.

"Drew," I said, "there are plenty of people who don't make it through law school. They drop out, and even those who graduate didn't pull your perfect grades. At a certain point you have to fend for yourself, no matter what your family can do for you."

"Yeah, but at the end of the day, people like me who have to take out student loans and work their way through college can't pull Drew's grades because we have a lot more on our plates," Phoebe said.

"Serena, my…a… from *The Reality Show*, she graduated Magna Cum Laude from nursing school on scholarships and student loans, all while raising her younger sister from the age of eighteen," I said.

"Well, she's got to be one of those doesn't even have to study to pull good grades, natural intelligence type. That doesn't count," Phoebe said.

I did not correct her, though I knew Serena had scrambled and scraped her way through. She was scrappy. Like I'd been scrappy, pushing my way up the ranks of my dance teams. I won competitions on this side of the pond and the other. Didn't that mean I deserved my success?

"Should I have turned my parents down when they offered to pay for my education? Should I have worked my way through?" Drew asked.

"Why? That doesn't even make sense," Phoebe said as we pulled up to her building, "Look Drew, let's talk about this later, okay? I can't even talk to you right now. I can't stand it when you try to tell me who to be."

"Well, I don't like watching you flirt with other guys when you're supposed to be my girlfriend, unless that's not who you want to be," he said.

She stopped. She looked taken back. Drew had never been the one to break up with her. She recovered and rolled her eyes at him. She quickly jumped out of Drew's truck before he said anymore. She slammed the door. She ran into her building.

I never in my life saw someone in the very act of flight.

I crawled up to the front seat and Drew drove away. He was quiet. He waited for me to talk. I couldn't stand him being mad at me.

"I'm so sorry. Watching her with Jaxon made me so mad. I just … I lost it. I knew it would hurt her feelings if I mentioned the pre-nup. I'm sorry," I said.

"She's like another person when we're in public. She flirts, and I can't stand to be around her. Then when it's just us, she's my best friend. I … which one is she?" he asked.

"She's both, and if you marry her, you get both of her sides."

"If I marry her. You don't think she'll marry me?"

"I don't know. I'm not used to seeing her like this, I guess. It surprised me," I said, annoyed I had to tiptoe around what I wanted to say.

"You're a lot more… you never used to speak up when we fight. It surprised me."

"Serena would pummel me. She'd emotionally just pummel me. One day, out of nowhere, Carrie started giving it back. It felt… braver than staying quiet."

"Do you like Carrie?"

"Oh, it didn't seem like it on the show," he said.

"No, the show was creating drama. Turns out, I don't like drama. I really can't stand being bullied. It makes me a little girl again; you know the one who all the girls were mean to because I walked weird with a brace."

"Sorry, Erin."

"No, I'm sorry. It's your life, and you know what you're doing. I will not interfere again." I vowed in my heart not to try manipulating Pheobe again.

We were quiet for a few minutes. My stomach gurgled uncomfortably at the idea of leaving Phoebe alone to manipulate my brother. Drew was smart. He knew what he was doing. I bit my cheek not to say anything. Drew looked over at me, I smiled and then looked out the window.

"Just say it. We don't play games with each other," he said.

I nodded. I would be brave enough to say out loud what I thought, no backhanded manipulations. Just my truth.

"I don't get it. You're amazing. Why do you put up with her?"

"I love her. You sacrifice for the one you love."

"But don't you want someone willing to sacrifice for you?"

"She does. Look at her waiting four years for me to finish law school."

"As opposed to what? Going out clubbing every night? Flirting with men she finds attractive? I mean, come on, how is she waiting for you?"

He glanced at me, annoyed.

"Okay, I'm done. I love you. I want you to be happy. Just think about it, okay?"

"Okay."

"So, turnabout's fair play. So how did my date go tonight?" I asked.

"He's a total player; stay away from him."

"I can't disappoint the special needs girl waiting to meet me. I don't think he even likes me. I think he made all this effort to meet me so I would meet his cousin."

"Yeah, maybe. Be safe. Don't go alone. Take Phoebe with you."

"Are you sure?"

"She's flirty, but she's not as innocent as you."

"Are you sure?"

"Yes."

"You are an awesome brother."

"I really am," he said, laughing.

He parked in the garage and left me with a discouraged, "Good night."

Chapter 23

I slept most of Sunday, trying to get back into a good head space. I cried and gave up, and then refused to give up, and mentally exhausted myself. By Monday morning, I decided I would start over. I did it when I was ten. I did it at seventeen. I would do it again.

A dancer must dance. I could either let go of my identity, or start over again.

So, I worked hard. My feet bled, my body ached, and by the end of the day, I could barely force my legs to keep me up. I didn't stop. When I stopped my dream dissolved in front of me like a castle made of sand hit by waves. I didn't know how to fight for it except to force my body back into shape.

My dad swore Noel didn't kick me out. Apparently, we'd revisit my place in the company in three weeks. That's when they started training for the Fall Season. The way he said we'd approach them again told me he meant to use his substantial means to get me back in. Again and again, he assured me I didn't understand the politics of the dance world.

His bribing Noel wasn't that hard to understand.

I smiled for him and went back to my studio and danced. I focused on nothing and everything. I did not remember Noel's voice saying I could never be the top principal dancer.

I focused on forcing my sore leg muscles into a deeper plie. I did not remember humiliating myself on television. My world turned, and when I stopped spinning, I went back to leaping. En pointe, I continued choreographing the dance I'd started working on the show. It gave me a problem to fix. It gave me direction when I had no map back to where I wanted to be.

Jaxon texted a lot. He wanted my opinion on his outfits. He sent reels on social media and his favorite playlists. It felt like he was barraging me with content, as if that would make us good friends without the bother of knowing each other for a long time.

When I stopped for a meal, or to go to sleep, I texted back how busy I was. Finally, he came to my house and brought me dinner Tuesday night. My parents were at a business function for one of the corporations Dad represented. Drew was with his study group.

We ate out on the patio by the infinity pool. When it was just the two of us, I struggled to say anything to him.

"Are you a musician?" I finally asked when he couldn't stop talking about a record that just dropped.

"Nah. I DJ'd through college. It was a blast, but it's not a grown-up job. Got me through school, though," he said.

"That's great. If you could get into a club or get enough wedding receptions or what not, you could really get going."

"Nah, I'm pretty invested in my practice. I work with my brother. Without me, he'd be sunk."

"You guys must be close."

"Nah, we can't stand each other."

"Really? You work together?"

"I was close with my Uncle Brian. He meant to leave the practice to me, but Chris ended up in sports medicine so he felt obligated to leave it to both of us."

"Oh, that's weird. Your brother didn't always want to go into sports medicine?"

"No, we both played football for University of Buffalo. I always meant to be a physical therapist like my uncle. But with college football, Chris got into sports medicine. Uncle Brian became sick, and didn't want to play favorites, so he gave the practice to both of us. It's annoying. Now I'm kind of stuck with this holier-than-thou brother."

I watched Jaxon. His lips pursed with exaggeration when he talked about his brother.

"You must always have been athletic."

"Yeah, I guess."

"Do you enjoy physical therapy?" I asked, confused he didn't want to talk about his real life, just things he liked on his phone.

"It's fine. It'd be better without Chris. Today he told me I needed to be more professional. He's a wet rag and can't handle anybody who's personable." The more he spoke, the more Jaxon grew aggravated.

"You don't have to work with your brother. Sell your half of the practice and find another," I said.

"Oh," he stammered. "Nah, I make good money. I think if my cousin Mia weren't so dependent on me, I would try to get out of the practice. I can't leave her. Chris and I share the condo my uncle owned next to her care center so we can be close to her."

"You can't stand your brother, but you live with him?" I asked, feeling like his stories had a few holes in it.

"Yeah, it's a gorgeous condo, view of the Philly skyline. Anyway, I can see by the way you're walking you've been working on pointe," he said changing the subject.

"Yes, I have," I said. "I already missed half the summer season. In three weeks, American comes off break for Fall season. I have to be ready."

"Do you want me to stretch you out?" he asked winking.

"Naw, "Naw," I said, pretending I didn't understand his innuendo. "I'm working on my flexibility. I spent about two hours stretching. I'm loose. My calluses are raw and I've got blisters."

As I said this, I took off my slipper to show him.

"Ouch," he said.

"It's okay," I said. I thought maybe he'd have some advice for taking care of my feet, but he didn't say anything. We both sat quietly looking out at the bay.

"I told Mia you're coming Thursday night. That's okay, right?" he finally said.

"Sure, it'll be fun," I said trying not to be annoyed. "Phoebe keeps texting to remind me."

"Yeah, me too."

'Really?"

"Yeah, I'm kind of surprised she's in a steady relationship. She doesn't act like it."

"Poor Drew," I said looking out at the pool.

"Your brother seems like a nice guy."

"He is".

Jaxon then asked how they got together. He tried not to seem interested in Phoebe, but he kept probing about their relationship. I couldn't help thinking he'd only come over to find out how serious Drew and Phoebe were.

I tried my best to be honest, but they really could be described as off again on again. I did not discourage him from admiring her. I knew it was wrong, but I couldn't help it. Jaxon and Phoebe seemed the same and would probably be happy together.

Chapter 24

By Thursday night I was finally growing stronger. My endurance started to come back, and I could dance for six hours with only water breaks. I went into a haze of fury and desperation choreographing. If Phoebe hadn't come to get me, I wouldn't have remembered my obligation to Jaxon.

Thankfully, Drew was already gone when Phoebe showed up mid-afternoon. She wore a black see-through mesh top that showed her black cropped cami underneath and a high-waisted short red skirt.

I had just showered and had on my pajamas. My feet were in an ice bath and looked bad.

"Come on, Erin," she said.

"I look like crap; I don't want to go. Seriously, Phoebe, I can't even see why you need me there. Clearly, you've decided to leave Drew and go for Jaxon. It seems like I'm only in the way," I said, tired of it all.

"That's not true," she said but her lips had to suppress a smile. She finished, "Besides, his cousin wants to meet you. She's an outcast in her home and only has her cousins as friends."

"Fine," I said. I put on Yoga pants and a threw on a tank top that said, "It didn't kill me."

I did a half ponytail in my stupid short hair and put on my support socks and tennis shoes.

"You look like you're going to the gym," Phoebe complained. "What if we want to go out after?"

"I'm not going out after," I said.

"Fine," she glared, "but if we decide to, you'll feel left out."

"I'll be all right," I said, climbing down the stairs.

My parents kept a car for me, but I didn't drive often. What with being at boarding school and then college in New York, I never learned to drive until a few years earlier. I usually caught rides to wherever I was going when I was home. That is why I didn't even offer to drive until we both stopped in the doorway. She headed toward our garage and I moved toward her car on the curb.

"Come on, we're driving all the way to Philly," she complained.

"Fine," I said. We went to the garage and my choices were the Tesla my parents bought for me to use, and Mom's new Mercedes convertible.

"Come on. Take your mom's car," she said. I texted Mom and asked. She was delighted I was leaving the house and told me to grab her emergency credit card if I needed anything. I did not relay this to Phoebe, certain we would need something if she knew.

As I adjusted the seat to my legs, I felt my mother's presence in the way the savory leather smell mixed with her perfume, and the mints she sucked on. Mom wanted so badly for me to be open with her. After she helped me with my scoliosis, we never had any kind of wedge between us. I felt so dreary hearing Noel kill my dream. I felt defeated. I couldn't let my mom into my inner self until I could overcome the feelings. She would give me perpetual pep talks until I forced myself to pretend to be okay just to get her to stop.

Which brought me to my biggest problem: I had no idea how to fix anything. I usually worked hard, harder than anyone else. That was enough. No matter how hard I worked it wouldn't get me an audience. It was a helpless feeling, being so alone, and yet surrounded by people who would do anything for me. There was nothing anyone could do.

I drove the two hours to Jaxon's house like an old lady according to Phoebe who insisted she would drive home.

"Finally, that was the longest drive ever. Here, park over there," Phoebe said pointing out the visitor parking at the assisted living home.

"Oh, good call. Then, I don't have to park on the street," I said thinking Phoebe had an incredibly good eye seeing the parking from so far away. After I parked, I opened my door and then locked the car. I buried the keys in my purse as I climbed out so Phoebe couldn't ask for them.

Jaxon lived in a nice complex next to an even nicer assisted living home.

The assisted living home was surrounded by gardens that isolated it from the city. It featured a huge weeping tree, with long hanging ropes of golden branches. The tenants could sit at tables and get fresh air while the branches of the great tree would tickle their faces. I would have admired it more, but I had to run from the air-conditioned car into the air-conditioned assisted living home on this record-breaking hot day.

The frosted glass doors slid open as we approached. The lobby looked like a posh hotel entrance, with only the slight scent of decaying life, nothing like the stench Dot and Edith lived with.

We went to the front desk and signed into the home. The receptionist, a large woman with an unfortunate facial hair issue, glared at us a little and then directed us to Jaxon's cousin, Mia's room. Phoebe started walking down a hall while I still listened to the receptionist's instructions. I barely caught up to her as she knocked on a door covered in kitten stickers. It swung open and there stood a young woman with Down syndrome.

"Erin," she called enthusiastically, shoving Phoebe out of the way. She tackle-hugged me, knocking me back. I smiled. I think it was the first time I smiled in days.

"Hey guys! Come in," Jaxon called from the kitchen behind her. As Mia squeezed me, I looked over her shoulder at her suite. It had a small fridge, sink, and microwave, but no stove.

Her living area had a couch and television. A large doorway showed her bedroom.

"Come, come," Mia cried, shoving Phoebe out of the way again.

"What the…" Phoebe stammered. She waited at the doorway to be sure it was safe.

"Sorry, she doesn't know her own strength," Jaxon said, coming toward us with popcorn.

"Careful, Mia," he said putting a hand on my back trying to pull me past Mia and not dump the popcorn.

"I don't want her. I only want Erin," Mia said, nodding at Phoebe.

"I don't care, she's coming, too," he snapped putting the popcorn down on a side table. That is when Mia burst forth in a string of profanities. Jaxon laughed so hard I thought he would fall over. I could see why Mia didn't have many friends in the home mainly filled with older folks.

"Mia," I said sternly, "Phoebe is my brother's girlfriend. If she can't come in, then I can't come in."

Mia thought about this for a minute then said:

"Okay. Come in, Erin."

I moved through the door, and Mia put her arms around me. She swung us through the room and managed to hit Phoebe's light frame with her substantial rump. Phoebe cursed as Jaxon closed the door behind her. Mia was so enamored with me I thought maybe I could help her.

I said, “Can you please be nice to Phoebe?”

“I don’t need to be nice to Jaxon’s girlfriend. She is mean to me.”

“No, sweetie, that’s not Jaxon’s girlfriend it’s…” I stopped midsentence. Jaxon and Phoebe glanced at each other, then looked away.

Had Phoebe already met Mia?

“Come, sit, we will watch your show together.”

Mia grabbed my wrist and pulled me toward the sofa.

“Okay Mia,” I said looking from Phoebe to Jaxon, neither of whom would look at me or each other.

Mia turned on the TV and we watched the intro to *The Whole Package*. It was so interesting to know what actually happened versus what the television showed. It looked like Ethan flirted with everyone, but it hadn’t been like that. He hovered around Carrie all the time.

“I am sorry you didn’t win,” Mia said, laying her head on my shoulder.

“It’s okay. It was a mean show anyway. See how they make it look like Tess is fighting with Veronica?”

“Yeah,” Mia said.

“Veronica doesn’t fight. She’s too shy.”

“I fight, I am a good fighter,” Mia said.

“Mia, you can’t hit your neighbors,” Jaxon snapped.

"I didn't today. I promised not to since you brought me Erin," she moped.

"Mia, you are so strong, you could really hurt someone if you hit them," I said concerned for the fragile patients housed near Mia, especially after experiencing her hug.

"They start it," she said knitting her brows.

"How?"

"They take my stuff," she said.

"What did they take?"

She glanced at Jaxon and Phoebe. They were small talking, like relative strangers should, so Mia pulled a little figurine out of the couch cushion.

"Oh, that is a lovely fairy," I said.

"There's the fairy!" Jaxon said. He lunged for it out of nowhere.

"What are you doing?" I asked, blocking him.

"That is not hers. They are threatening to kick her out if she doesn't give it back," he said.

"You just mad because Chris is going to let me live with you guys," she said holding the fairy tightly.

"Mia, can you please," I started to ask, startled at the venom Jaxon was seething toward his handicapped cousin.

"Give it now," he shouted, leaning over the top of me to wrestle the toy away from Mia.

"NO, NO NO!" she shrieked.

"What is going on here," a male voice called from the doorway.

"I found the stupid fairy," Jaxon shouted, still climbing over the top of me.

"What are you… Get off," I snapped. I felt Jaxon being pulled off me and Mia.

"Chris, Chris, Jaxon stealing my stuff," she said identifying the newcomer as Jaxon's older brother.

"Jaxon, what are you –" He stopped speaking abruptly. He looked at me ruffled. He tried to stand up except Mia clung to me like I could save her.

Chris looked at Jaxon. His eyes flared, livid. He looked back at me being smashed under Mia, her fairy imprinting her wings into my arm.

"What is going on?" Chris said, still glaring at me. I stopped struggling and went limp. What did I do?

"I found the stupid fairy," Jaxon said, ripping it away from Mia.

She started screaming right in my ear.

"Just give her back her fairy," I said clapping my hand over my ear next to her mouth. No one heard me over Mia's wailing. Jaxon disappeared with the toy.

Mia finally let go of me and ran after him. Chris caught Mia and said something that was drowned out. Mia sobbed and sobbed while Chris tried to comfort her.

Chris, Jaxon's older brother, was good looking. He was clean shaven, with a high forehead, high cheek bones and a perfect triangle nose. He wore slacks, a white dress shirt and his tie was knotted at his throat like an adult. His coconut brown hair was impeccable, and his raging eyes were an aqua color.

I stood up straightening myself and moved toward Phoebe.

"Should we go?" I mouthed, watching Chris trying to calm Mia

"Jaxon will figure it out," she said.

"They said she has to apologize," Jaxon said as he came back into the room.

"No," Mia said defiantly.

"You little pain in the –"

"Jaxon," Chris and I yelled together.

"Oh, right," Jaxon said looking at me. "I haven't introduced you." His face turned into a smug smirk.

Chris gave him the most venomous glare I'd ever seen as Jaxon put an arm around me and said, "Chris, this is my friend Erin. She's going to be my girlfriend. I'm going to for-sure convince her."

I felt my white face turn red. I glanced confused at Phoebe, whose perfectly tan face turned ashen white. Her eyes turned to slits and she looked just as irate as Mia.

I stammered as I looked from Jaxon back to Phoebe. Finally, my eyes rested on the brother. My first traitorous thought was that I would date him. My stammer turned flirtatious as I said toward Chris:

"I don't know about –"

Chris glared and my comment dropped. Wow, he was ornery. On the outside he was perfect, but I'd never been looked at with so much contempt. I wanted to leave. And why not? I wasn't anything to these people.

"Mia, sweetheart," Chris said taking a deep breath and softening, "I need you to apologize to Ms. Duchene."

"No," she said.

"Look I can see you guys have your hands full," I started. "Phoebe, maybe we should…"

"Nooooo, Erin, noooo," Mia cried. I looked at Mia who had lost her figurine and seemed so downcast.

"You can come over to our place and finish watching your show if you apologize," Chris said glancing at me like she was watching some sleazy soap opera and I was the star. Clearly, he would never be caught dead watching reality TV.

"Erin too?" she asked.

"Sure," he said. He glanced sardonically at Jaxon and then at me with disdain.

"Come on, Erin, let's apologize," Mia said. She took me by the wrist again and pulled. She was so rough; I couldn't imagine her pulling on any of the elderly patients like that. I had to run to keep up with her.

"Mia, refined young ladies do not run down the hall," I said, simply because my legs burned, and she bruised my wrist where she held on.

"Do they walk like this," Mia asked her eyeballs straining down toward her feet so she could be sure she was walking right. I pulled her grasp from my wrist and took her hand.

"I am a ballerina, and ballerina's walk like this," I said going up on my toes in releve'.

"Like this," she said as we walked.

"Well done," I said looking back. Chris was right behind us glaring at the doors we passed. Jaxon and Phoebe walked behind him arguing quietly.

We stopped at a door down the hall. The door had a wreath of purple and pink silk flowers. I looked around and noticed every door had been personalized with wreaths, and placards or pictures. A frail old woman with see-through skin, trembling hands and short curly hair finally opened the door before us.

"Hello Ms. Duchene," Chris said. "Mia has something to say to you."

Mia pursed her lips and closed tightly.

"Come on Mia," I coaxed. "We are missing my show."

She threw her hands in the air like she just remembered that.

"I am sorry I took your fairy toy," Mia said, but she didn't seem sorry.

"It is a collector's figurine, the set is worth over a hundred dollars complete," the woman said in a shaky voice holding up the fairy. "It is worthless, incomplete."

"Mia is really sorry and swears she won't come into your room and take your… fairy again," Jaxon said coming in close behind me. He pushed an arm between us to nudge away

Mia's pudgy hand that reached out for the fairy. "Right Mia?"

She said nothing.

"If she touches it again, I will see to it she is kicked out. Stealing is against the by-laws," the woman said. She slammed her door.

"Old hag," Mia said.

"Mia, that is not a ladylike statement," I said.

"That's what Jaxon calls her," Mia said, glancing back at him.

"Seriously?" I asked looking at Jaxon, who had come in too close to my face. He laughed, and I looked to the brother on the other side of Mia for help. He stared at me with a disappointed look. He couldn't possibly think I was wrong, so why did he condemn me with his glare?

"Come on, Chris. You go check her out, and I'll take them over," Jaxon said.

Chris grunted some kind of agreement and left. The rest of us followed Jaxon next door to the high-rise they lived in. Mia held my hand and skipped across the courtyard as we went. She jumped as the elevator went up and landed hard. Phoebe grabbed the metal rail to steady herself.

Jaxon took great pleasure in showing us around the elegant three-bedroom condo. As Jaxon showed us the open kitchen-dining room area, he paused and waited with a weird sort of pride about the place for us to feel the same. He seemed almost…sentimental. He pointed out two closed doors, on one side of the condo, that were assigned as Chris's room and office. A set of stairs went up to another door, that Jaxon said was his room and he nudged me. Phoebe's eyes narrowed.

The setting sun reflected light through huge windows onto hardwood floors in the main area of the condo. The black leather furniture somehow absorbed the light and trapped it so it didn't gleam off the black stainless-steel appliances.

"Isn't this so nice?" Phoebe said quietly as I took in the view. The Philadelphia skyline and the Delaware River were like a backdrop to Mia's building and the courtyard.

"Erin, come on," Mia complained so I walked back into the condo and sat near the arm of the leather couch. Mia scooted in.

By the time we found the remote that turned on the obscenely huge TV, the show was almost over. Chris came in looking grim as ever, and I did my best to ignore him. Feeling the tension between the brothers made everything uncomfortable.

"Can I see you in the office please," Chris snapped at his brother, who had sat on the edge of the couch. They glared at each other. Chris looked mad. Not just mad, irate. Jaxon rolled his eyes like a teenager, and I watched him stomp off into the other room. I'd never seen two brothers at such odds before. Since the show was at commercial, I asked Mia, "Is everything all right?"

"I come here instead of staying home because I get in trouble at night. It makes Jaxon mad 'cause he wants to be alone with his girlfriend," she answered smiling at me and then glancing at Phoebe.

Phoebe wasn't listening. She moved to a kitchen chair close to the room where the brothers disappeared. She didn't look interested in the show, but seemed to be playing on her phone and listening in.

"Is Chris mad at Jaxon?" I asked quietly.

"He was not supposed to go meet you, Mia answered. "Chris said it was creepy. Jaxon didn't listen. Jaxon never listens. He's mean."

"Jaxon loves you," I said.

"No, Jaxon loves Jaxon," Mia insisted, scowling. Then she smiled and pointed to the television, "Look. There's Ethan. I love Ethan."

I watched as Ethan walked onto the screen. He wore a tux because the elimination process was starting.

"We wanted you to win. Who do we want to win now?" Mia asked me.

"Carrie or Veronica. They're the nicest ones left," I said.

"Okay," she said.

We watched the show. Ethan called Carrie forward to receive a key to the million-dollar prize money.

Carrie stood silently for a moment. Then, looking hard at Ethan, out of nowhere, she refused the key and turned away.

No one ever refused the key. Especially not the person winning the show.

"What happened?" I asked.

"I don't know. Do we want Veronica to win now?" Mia asked looking at me innocently.

"I suppose so," I said, confused. I quickly pulled out my phone. Tweets were out of control.

"It looks like Ethan was… um kissing Tess, and Carrie caught them," I said. "She walked off."

"That was stupid. She should have stayed on," Mia complained.

"No, she… Carrie is so awesome," I said.

"She seems a little self-righteous," Chris said from behind us. I jumped a little. I hadn't heard the door open. Phoebe may have also been caught unaware because she was bright red and staring at her phone.

"Nah, Carrie's really nice. Serena was the worst," I said.

"Weren't you and Serena friends?" Chris asked, looking disappointed in me. I stopped. Was the cranky brother into reality shows after all?

"Serena was seriously mean. She knew how to look sweet on camera, but she… anyway I didn't like her," I said standing up. I wasn't going to sit around and defend myself to the crankiest man alive. "I have a long day of dancing tomorrow, so I'd better go. Mia, it was such a pleasure to meet you."

"Will you come back?" Mia asked.

“I’ll tell you what. If you leave Ms. Duchene’s figurines alone, I will get you some of your own. I have ballerinas,” I said.

“I want ballerinas,” she agreed.

“Promise to leave hers alone?”

“I promise,” she said.

“If Jaxon tells me you took them again, I’m not going to bring you ballerinas,” I said.

“Okay,” she said, and she gave me a huge hug that pushed the air out of me. She let go. I moved out of her arm span quickly.

“Bye,” I said waving to Jaxon. Chris glanced at me, so I extended the wave to him. He graced me with a clipped head nod. That is when I decided I had no intention of coming back. I had her address. I would buy the toys online and have them shipped directly to Mia. These people had way too much drama for me. I used to love the thrill of a little reality show drama, but now it just felt immature.

To my surprise, Phoebe made no protest at our early departure. She barely acknowledged Jaxon to say goodbye. I wondered if he offended her when he announced I was going to be his girlfriend. She couldn’t be too pissed. Considering she had a boyfriend.

“You okay?” I asked her on the elevator ride down.

“I’m great,” she said in a way that sounded not so great.

“You don’t mind that we are leaving.”

“Nope.”

I let the quiet sit between us as we walked to the car.

"Chris seemed pissed, didn't he?" I asked once we were heading south on the 95. That was all the invitation she needed to spill what she overheard.

"Yeah, when Chris went to check Mia out, the manager lady said Mia was growing hostile to many of the other residents. They're afraid she may hurt someone. Chris blamed Jaxon and said if Mia has to move out of the assisted living home, she's taking his room."

"He wouldn't give up his office for her?" I asked.

"I don't know, but Jaxon talked like the place is theirs, but from the way his brother is ready to kick him out, I'm quite sure the Condo belongs to Chris. Jaxon is a total fake. You should stay away from him."

"He's not my type."

"He's no one's type. He's a liar. Jaxon said the Condo came with the practice of his uncle, so it should be both of theirs. But while you fiddled with the TV remotes, I investigated their practice," she said conspiratorially.

"Does it have a bunch of stars on Yelp?" I asked sarcastically.

"Yeah, they have some really high-profile clients too," she said seriously. "I mean Jaxon really has the DPT, that means he got his doctorate, but that's the only thing he didn't lie about. The practice, like the apartment, belongs to Chris."

"Are you sure? Jaxon is always talking about his practice."

"I don't know, but I think so. Jaxon really hates Chris. He…" she stopped abruptly realizing she went too far.

"How do you know that?"

"We're friends," she said. "He's that guy who talks way too much right up front."

"Are you a little in love with him?"

"No, no. Drew is my man," she said sounding more resolved than she had on our way to the City of Brotherly Love.

"Then how do you know Jaxon hates his brother? He didn't say anything about it when we went out."

"Jaxon was at The Zone Tuesday night and we talked."

"He went clubbing after we had dinner?"

"He took you on a date Tuesday night." She glared at me as if I had done something wrong.

"He bought me dinner, then he partied with you?"

"He is a total player," she said. "You should stay away from him."

"I'm not at all into him so it's not me who should stay away from him," I said. She nodded and looked out the window.

We were quiet for a minute, but my curiosity got the better of me.

"Why doesn't he get along with his brother?"

"Are you into the brother?" she asked.

"He's a prick. He glared at me all night," I said. "I'm trying to understand why."

"He's hot, I mean hotter than Jaxon, but he's a total control freak. Guys like that are more trouble than they're worth."

"But why does he hate me?"

"Chris was mad Jaxon went to meet you. He said it was creepy, and they have an image to keep up."

"I should have maced Jaxon when I had the chance," I said laughing it off.

"What doesn't make sense," Pheobe said, still ranting, "according to Jaxon, Chris only got into Sports Medicine to one-up him, as always, and then his uncle left his practice to both of them."

"So, it is both of their practice," I said.

"Jaxon isn't listed as a co-director; it's just Chris," she said looking into the glow of her phone.

"Humm. So maybe the uncle saw how irresponsible Jaxon is and gave it all to Chris. Maybe that's why he dislikes him so much," I said.

"Jaxon is only listed as one of two Physical Therapists, and he's taking new patients. If he's part owner, then why is the other guy full and he's not?"

We both paused. I couldn't think of any reason he wouldn't be given the title of co-something or other on the web site. Phoebe strained her mind asking the question a few times, hoping against hope to find a way for

Jaxon to be part owner, but couldn't. Jaxon must not be making as much as she hoped.

I could see her finding her resolve to stick with my little brother who was a much safer bet. She spent the rest of the drive looking out the window and jiggling her leg faster and faster.

When we reached my parent's house, I stopped next to her car but asked:

"Do you want me to see if Drew is home?"

"Nah, I'm exhausted. Tell him I'll see him tomorrow," she said. She jumped out of the car and waved. I thought she might have been crying.

I went straight to my room. I lay down trying to sleep. I hated drama. I didn't need it.

Chapter 25

Friday, I awoke early and danced until about three in the afternoon. When I stopped aching with hunger, I went upstairs to find my dad sitting behind the huge oak desk in his office.

"What are you doing home?" I asked, tilting my head in.

"We're having all the partners over for a cookout," he said. "Your brother is in the hot seat tonight."

"That'll be nice for a change," I said knowing the lengths my father would go to for his children. "Is Phoebe coming?"

"No, I guess her judge is making her stay late. I heard you dropped the prenup bomb on her," he said standing up and walking over to me, not allowing his work to distract him.

"I'm sorry, I … it was wrong, but she's terrible to Drew. I just wanted her to jump ship."

"Your instinct isn't off. I've thought about asking Drew to have her sign one, but your mother says it's not supportive," he smiled.

"I know. I already apologized to Drew for lying to her. I won't do it again."

"You are too clever to need it," he said, and hugged me.

I set my head on his shoulder and sighed.

"Let's talk about you, dearest," Dad said.

"I am… I'm still processing," I said.

"You know American is going to take you back, right?"

"Should they?" I asked pulling away.

"Do you really doubt your talent?"

"I .... I don't know, I doubt everything right now."

"That stupid show," Dad said. He surveyed me in the way he did to get the truth out of his clients. Knowing it was pointless to lie to him I said, "They were mean. They set me up to fail from the very beginning. I've never failed so hard before."

"What is failure?"

"I didn't win."

"I don't always win. Would you consider me a failure?"

"No."

"Why not, darling?"

"You ..." I closed my eyes, "because you don't give up, you find another angle."

"The Whole Package was simply an angle you tried, and it didn't work. What can you do next?"

"I don't know. I mean, I always thought if I worked hard enough, I would succeed. But no matter how hard I worked I didn't move up at American. Now I ... I don't see the next step. I don't know how to build an audience."

"Can you move forward blindly?"

"Excuse me?"

"I have a few ideas, but it will take a couple weeks. Can you trust me, and keep working hard?" he asked.

I looked at him wondering what he was planning.

"All I can do is keep pushing myself back in shape," I said. "I've even been choregraphing something… I think it's good."

"You have the talent. You are more talented than Natalia. Noel knows it. You are destined to be the top principal dancer," he said.

"I can't even make it past a soloist," I said, closing my eyes trying not to lash out at my dad for supporting me implicitly.

"That has nothing to do with you. Noel wants something. Once she gets it, then you will be in. It's how the game is played."

"I want to be good enough without bribing Noel," I said knowing by sheer will my dad could do anything he put his mind to.

"You are, honey. This is just how it works," he said.

"Maybe I should audition for New York, or San Francisco."

"Have faith in your old Papa. Give it a few weeks," he said. "At least until American is back on the East Coast."

"Okay."

"Have you blogged lately?" he asked.

"Yeah, all my followers have been really supportive," I said. "I told them there is a documentary of me coming out. One of the cameramen filmed it for a class he's in. I'll try to get a copy and post it. That might be something."

Dad laughed a little.

"What?"

"The young man called me. He tried to tell me he didn't need my permission, since you signed a release. He was still rather hard pressed to get it," Dad said with slight chuckle.

"Yeah, it could be something though," I said, hoping my dad had made Colby sweat it out.

"I'm already looking into it for you," he said. "Just keep choregraphing. Keep trying."

"'Kay, Dad."

A sadness washed over me. I felt like I let him down. Seeing he'd lost my attention he bobbed his head until I had to look at him. He looked worried.

"Are you around for dinner tonight with the partners? It sure would be nice for your brother."

"Yes, of course. I'd better go get dressed."

I left quickly; unsure what else I could say to my dad.

I drifted the rest of the evening away disappearing in the comfort of polite conversation. No one said anything too interesting. Endless talk about claims and counter claims, judges and back-room deals made me drowsy. Drew, who was taking the bar in a week, soaked up everything being said. I smiled for him. I tried to be charming for him. Because that's what siblings do for each other.

Chapter 26

I danced for hours. After a while I danced the piece I was working, over and over. In my tormented mind, I started to believe if I could perfect it, I would find my way onto center stage.

Jaxon called Wednesday a little after noon to see if I would go with him and Mia to the magic act. He must have stopped by Mia's place on his lunch break because I heard her in the background moaning, "Please Erin, please. I wuvvvv magic."

I relented.

I couldn't help thinking Jaxon only wanted to hang out with me because his brother asked him not to. Was I really such a PR nightmare for an upscale sports therapy clinic? Whatever his motivation, I didn't believe it had much to do with him feeling any affection for me. Rather it had more to do with him wanting to live his own life, and not let his brother dictate to him. I could respect that, and Jaxon wasn't that bad when he wasn't acting like a perpetual teenager.

They picked me up a little after six that night.

My mom found out I was having another late night and did not even pretend to be civil about Jaxon. She meant to tell him what she thought of him derailing my training. When she opened the door at his arrival, Mia however, quickly found a place in her heart. Mia took my mom's hand and pulled herself into the house without being invited.

"I'm hungry," Mia pleaded with my mom, pulling her arm.

"Mia, come on, we are going to eat," Jaxon cajoled. Mia pulled Mom deeper into the house and no matter how Jaxon coaxed, she worked her way back to the kitchen. Mom laughed and followed her.

"I'm hungry, so hungry," Mia said scouring the inside of the fridge without an invitation.

"Okay. Okay, Hun, let me feed you," Mom said.

"Thank you, Erin's mom," she said with big grateful eyes.

I sat up on a bar stool at the huge granite island and watched my mom take care of Mia. I patted the seat next to me. I watched my mom prepare Mia a snack. She was so proficient. Her caring instincts were so strong, and she had boundless energy. I had been cocooned my whole life in her care, but lately it felt a little like being smothered.

"Did you get me my ballerinas?" Mia asked.

I drew a blank.

"I didn't take the fairy ever again, so I could have ballerinas," Mia said.

"Oh, not yet, I had to make sure you didn't take the fairies again. But now I'll get them okay," I promised. I almost opened my mouth to pass the task onto my mom. She would do it for me. But then would that give her permission to keep doing everything for me?

Mia insisted on eating her cheesy omelet. Then mom found her a sugary snack cake that I didn't even know we had in the house. At last, Jaxon coaxed her toward the front door with promises that we were going to eat at the show.

"Bye, Erin's mom, bye. I'll come again, don't worry," she waved with a huge grin. Mom couldn't help it; she cracked a smile as she shut the door behind us.

I was almost put under an enchantment by the pleasant sweetness Mia added to the situation until we walked into the magic show venue. The Magic Show was at a bar with a two-drink minimum for every person who entered.

"Mia how much…ur," I felt uncomfortable asking her about alcohol consumption. I knew she could do most things I could do. It was all so foreign to me. When Jaxon said, "You can get a strawberry daiquiri, that's it."

I figured he had the situation well in hand. Mia replied:

"Daddy let me have three. I'm not a drunken."

"Let's go one at a time," I said quietly, and she took my hand.

The tables were in rows with a thick crimson carpeted aisle for the magician to run up and down, working the crowd. The whole room was rich dark oak, gold and crimson. The excitement generated in the place beat through me, but it took over Mia, who bounced along with the beat of it. We sat down and ordered drinks and appetizers. We watched the magician pull quarters from people's ears, signed cards, ripped them up, then restored them. At one point he even changed a ten-dollar bill into a one. The drunk man let him keep it; he could spare a dollar.

Drawn to our table, the man in a white button-down shirt and black jeans came toward us shuffling a deck of cards by flipping them through the air.

"You look like the kind of lady who wants to pick a card," he said into the microphone attached to his face.

"I am, I am," Mia cried taking one from his pile.

"And you," he said to me.

I grinned at Mia and took one – the queen of spades.

"All right, remember your card," he said while he invited us to put our cards back in the deck. Then to the audience he said, "did you know there is a deck of cards worth over six hundred dollars?"

"Is it this one?" Mia asked watching the man's hands way too closely.

"No," he said shaking his head until she looked at him and not the deck, "This one is worth two dollars. I think my tricks would be spectacular with a six-hundred-dollar deck, don't you?"

"Yes," Mia said as the man flipped a card out of the shuffled deck, and it slid across the table.

"It's my card," Mia clapped her hands happily. The man grinned and flipped my card at me. I clapped for him as well.

The first half of the show progressed much like this. I tried to see how the magician did things but couldn't explain anything. We were close to the stage and after her third strawberry daiquiri, Mia was loud and easily captured the attention of the performer, who seemed to play just for her and her childlike amusement.

After a while Mia started to slide down her seat. Jaxon, who drank hard and fast, didn't seem to notice.

"Hey, you better stop drinking if you want to drive home," I said, getting concerned.

"Nah I'm fine," Jaxon said, giving me a sloppy drunk grin.

"It's late. I can't drive all the way to Philly tonight. You've got to stop." I shouted over the crowd but he paid no attention to me. Mia began to shake convulsively.

"Jaxon, we need to get her to an Emergency Room," I said, jumping up and trying to hold her into her padded high-backed seat.

"Do you need help?" the waitress asked coming over.

"Nah, she does this sometimes. We just need to get her back to her place. They know how to take care of her." Jaxon was strong. He pulled Mia up and supported her while walking. I exchanged glances with the waitress. We both doubted Jaxon's reasoning skills at the moment

I didn't know what else to do. Mia looked so weak and shaken so I picked up all our stuff, settled our tab, and followed.

"Jaxon, give me the keys," I said stepping out into the warm night.

"No, you can't drive this car. You drive like a grandma," he said laughing.

"What?" I asked, but he was laughing at his own joke.

"Give me the keys," I snapped.

"You want to come back to my place huh," he asked.

"Give me your keys," I snapped again.

"Geez you're so bossy! Fine," he said slamming them in my hands, but he rolled his eyes at me. Really?

"Mia, get in back," Jaxon snapped pushing his bucket seat forward. Jaxon's two-door sports car did not make it easy to get Mia into the back seat.

"Can you just get back there," I ordered as Jaxon tried to push Mia's rump through the small opening.

"No, Mia likes it back there," he said. She stood back up unable to bend down. Her eyes were rolling back in her head.

"You get back there right now Jaxon," I commanded, scared out of my mind.

"Fine Mom," Jaxon said climbing back as if he had any right to whine.

After getting Mia under the front seat belt and over the bucket seat, she leaned forward and fell back into the recesses of the cramped space. I crawled back and buckled her up. As soon as she was settled, I dropped into the driver's seat.

Jaxon drowsed next to me. I didn't know what to do except get Mia back to her place. The gas pedal reacted with little pressure and it took me a while to keep a steady pace without lurching forward too fast.

After a while, I got the hang of how to ease into turns using the whole lane without braking. I drove to Philadelphia too fast, clutching the steering wheel and watching Mia in the rear-view mirror.

When Mia started to shake for the third time, I yelled, "Jaxon, get up. We need to get her to a hospital."

Jaxon roused, rubbing his face.

"It's not as bad as it seems," Jaxon swore trying to rouse himself. "Her home knows what to do."

He must have been a little worried, or the hour and a half sleep helped sober him. Jaxon made a phone call.

I pulled into the visitors parking lot, relieved to see Jaxon's brother, Chris, in knit gray pants and a t- shirt, come out of the doors of her home with an orderly pushing a wheelchair. Chris was furious. The guy seemed like a prick, but considering Jaxon, I was starting to see why.

"Mia, Mia we're here," I said, scared at the sight of her sluggish drooling.

Chris and the orderly pulled her out of the car, just as I got her seatbelt off. Once she was in the wheelchair I walked quickly with the orderly when Chris said to Jaxon, "This is a new low, even for you."

Jaxon walked swiftly past me and when we reached Mia's room, he opened the door so the orderly could let her in. I felt exceptionally guilty though I couldn't be sure why.

The orderly helped Mia to bed and gave her an IV. She kept my hand, so I brushed her bangs off her sweaty forehead. Jaxon came in. He looked concerned, though I couldn't be sure. His face was still exceptionally red.

"She's a little epileptic, you know, that's all," Jaxon said.

"That's all!" I snapped, glaring at him.

"Did you really let her drink?" Chris said, ignoring me completely to growl at Jaxon.

"Brian's been letting her drink since she was eighteen," Jaxon said.

"He let her have virgin strawberry daiquiris; he tricked her, you imbecile," Chris said.

"How was I supposed to know that?" Jaxon asked, disgruntled.

"You ask me. You ask before you take her out," Chris said.

"I'm on the conservatorship. I don't have to get your permission before I do things with her," Jaxon said.

"Fine, don't ask me, but at least clear it with the nurse. I get you hate me, but, Jaxon, taking it out on Mia is beneath you," Chris snapped. His phone buzzed.

"Oh, good this is the on-call doctor," Chris said relieved moving into the other room.

I wanted to disappear. It was almost midnight. I needed to go to sleep. I needed to be sure Mia was okay. Uh, I needed Chris not to glare at me, as though I knew Mia wasn't supposed to drink.

"I'm sorry Mia," he said slurring her name.

"I love you, Jaxon," she said with a sleepy grin.

Jaxon came up behind me and kissed her forehead where I'd pushed her bangs back. He sat down in the chair on the other side of Mia's bed looking miserable. He leaned back. I thought he was feeling bad until I heard him breathe heavily.

Before I knew it, he was snoring. In the span of two minutes, he fell asleep while his cousin was being treated medically for his stupidity. I stood there wondering what I should do.

"Hey, what has she eaten tonight?" Chris called to me.

"My mom made her an omelet before we left," I said walking into the other room.

"Oh, that's good," Chris said, relieved. He relayed this into the phone. I made a mental note to thank my mom for being so good at taking care of people. Chris got off the phone with Mia's doctor.

"She's going to be okay," he comforted. Tears sprung to my eyes, and I breathed deeply in relief.

"I… I didn't know she shouldn't drink," I said apologetically.

"I know," Chris said. "Are you…? You seem lucid."

"I'm in training," I said, "I don't drink while I'm training."

"Right, so you're his designated driver," he said with a sardonic laugh, rubbing his face.

"I… I don't mind," I said, I'd often been the designated driver in college.

"Training means focus. Letting someone into your life that will derail you isn't wise."

"I'm…I don't know if it matters anymore," I said wondering if Chris saw himself as everyone's big brother, doling out unsolicited advice.

"What does that mean?" Chris asked sharply. He looked past me at Jaxon like he'd done something to hurt me.

"No, no. Not Jaxon…my career. It's – I couldn't look at Chris. Finally, I said, "Jaxon said you are a sport therapist."

"Yeah," he said, looking at me confused.

"In your professional opinion, how far should hard work take you?"

"Excuse me?"

I looked at him. He didn't seem as annoyed, but he looked confused. Well, if he wanted to give the world advice, I may as well take him up on it. I planned on never seeing any of these people again. Well, except maybe Mia. I would be sure she recovered from this. I would learn how to take care of people, like my mom did.

"If someone is the best dancer or player, they should be the lead. Right? If someone can't reach a certain level, no matter how hard they work, when do they call it quits?"

"I'm not sure I understand. Many people have successful careers as understudies, and the like. Do you consider your career over if you can't be the best?"

"I don't know."

"We can't all be the superstar all the time. Every cast member is important to the show," he said.

"Yeah, I know, and I don't mind paying my dues. I just always thought if I worked the hardest, I would be the best. It never occurred to me I couldn't get there."

"You're young. What twenty-five?"

I nodded.

"You have at least ten, if you're careful, fifteen years left in your career. Keep working. I am a firm believer if you focus on what is most important, the rest sluffs off. It's the only way to find your true place," he said. I couldn't even look up at him. I knew my face was red. And he was watching me.

"You sound like my dad," I said trying to laugh it off. I looked back at Mia who was now telling the orderly all about the magic show.

"Listen to her," Chris said, emphatically leaning in toward me.

"But…do you … do you agree with someone basically buying their way into a … a certain role?" I asked, examining the rug under the coffee table.

"Uh…it happens, especially in professions where most people get to about the same level. But if the athlete can't cope with the position, they're eventually dropped. There is a certain point in a career, nothing can make up for talent. Nobody can keep something that doesn't really belong to them."

"What if they have the work ethic to be there?" I asked, knowing I sounded desperate.

"Without specifics I can't be sure what to tell you. No athlete can force themselves to be more than what they are," he said, clearly unsure what we were talking about.

"Yeah, no. I know," I said feeling worse about the situation. I could barely breathe. I knew he was right. I couldn't keep something that wasn't mine. Would I ever be good enough to be the top principal? Chris examined me.

This was possibly the most awkward conversation I'd ever had. I took out my phone to navigate a way home, but mostly so Chris wouldn't see the massive road rash his words put on my hope.

"Erin, can I, are you going to sleep… over?" Chris asked. I glanced up at him. His face drained white and he glanced at me with dread.

"No, I have to get home. Do you have the number of a local cab company?" I asked, my voice a few pitches too high.

"I could… I wouldn't mind driving you back. You can tell me what's going on. I hate to give advice without understanding the situation," he said.

"I'm fine, I'll figure it out. I always do," I said blinking hard.

"Yeah, but that's a long cab ride," Chris said watching me. He couldn't want to drive me home; he was cleaning up his brother's mess. I suspected he did that often.

"No, please stay here with Mia. Make sure she's all right. She needs you. I'll be fine," I said.

"Oh, right," he said. Almost like I'd woken him up. He glanced back at the room where the orderly was coaxing Mia to sleep by rubbing her temples.

"Here, I like these guys," Chris said opening his phone, and with little effort he called the cab company for me. He hung up and said, "They are sending someone now."

"Thanks," I said waving, "Tell Mia I said bye. I'll just wait out front."

Ready to burst from disappointment, I almost ran from the room. I wiped a few tears as I waited on the stone bench for the cab in front of the assisted living home. The tree with the golden whisps hanging off it swayed in the moonlight.

I could hear Chris's voice in my head saying no coach could force an athlete to be something he wasn't. No matter how many hours I worked. No matter how much money my dad had, nothing could get me onto center stage if I didn't belong there. And yet, I loved dancing more than anything else in the world. What did I do now?

I felt like throwing up.

Especially after it took me three hours and three hundred dollars to get home.

Chapter 27

I was not ready to wake when my alarm buzzed four hours after I went to sleep. I lay there talking myself into moving. I was not cooperating. What did it matter? I didn't have anywhere to dance. I may as well sleep and forget about training. The little place inside of me, the place where my dream lay in wait, squirmed. I had friends at New York still. Some of their top principals toured their last few years of dancing.

I was too tired to hope. I wanted to give up. I wanted to accept that some people only ever made the understudy.

No!

American wasn't the only dance company out there. This defeatist attitude had to go. Chris didn't know me. He didn't know what I was capable of.

Every time I came up against someone better than me, I worked harder than them and took their spot. That's how it worked.

Maybe I would never take Natalia's spot, no matter how hard I worked. Fine!

My hard work gave me talent. I had nerves of steel. I had the work ethic. Talent couldn't compensate for work ethic. I forced myself out of bed on four hours of sleep. On fire with the need to see my dreams accomplished, I danced two extra hours, despite throwing up twice and my back spasming.

When I finished, I reached out to a dancer I knew at the New York Ballet who was in the incubator program. I asked if they had any auditions coming up. It was time for me to grow up and be in charge of my own life.

Jaxon called me several times, but I did not answer. I listened to his messages just in case he was going to tell me how Mia was doing. He only wanted to watch *The Whole Package*, then go clubbing. On a Thursday night. Did this man never work?

That morning, my friend from New York emailed back. He'd sounded excited to place me, and told me if something came up it would be fast, and to have an audition piece ready. By Friday at lunch, I had a few versions of my dance perfected, and could audition with it if I had to.

It scared me to put my piece to music. I forced myself not to care. I had to believe that I worked hard enough, and I had indeed created something beautiful worth seeing. Even if nothing in New York panned out, I would find my way back into the world where it mattered.

I ate salmon and veggies in my dad's office researching music on his computer. When I found something promising I downloaded it onto my phone. After an hour, my dad came in.

"Hey. What you up to?"

"Just putting my piece to music."

"Good idea," he said. "Your mom said you won't let her see what you're working on. Why not?"

"I've never choreographed like this before. I'm a little…self-conscious."

"We're going to tape it for your blog so you'll need to get over it," he said tipping his forehead toward me kindly.

"I will," I promised.

"Tonight, Simon and Zack are coming over to help your brother and his study group cram.

"I'm glad they take the bar next week. Seriously, he's so ready," I said.

"You want to eat with us?"

"Oh no. I'm busy," I said quickly. He laughed a little. I did my due diligence the week before with all his partners. I was not sticking around to watch his associate attorneys kiss his hind end while quizzing my little brother. Not to mention Zack came close to proposing marriage to me the first time I met him and had only grown bolder every time since.

"What are you doing tonight?" he asked, concerned. Mom must have told him about Jaxon. I stammered. If I didn't have something, I'd be expected to attend his barbeque.

"I've downloaded hours of music to listen to. Which means I have plenty of time to drive back to Philadelphia. I need to check on Mia. The lady at the front desk won't answer my questions since I'm not family, and I am not calling Jaxon back," I rambled.

"It sounds like someone needs to take care of her," Dad said.

"I promised her I'd get her some ballerina figurines. If I don't follow through, she may keep stealing another lady's fairy figurines and get kicked out of her home," I said. "Do you remember where Mom bought mine for me?"

"You could just give her yours."

"Um, no."

He laughed.

"Here, let me get them, then," he said pulling out his wallet and handing me a smooth stack of bills.

"I wasn't going to buy her the store and I have my own money, Dad," I said trying to hand some back.

"Just keep it. Get some dinner. Makes me feel like you're still my little girl," he said pulling his buzzing phone out. Then he finished, "I've got to take this. Love you, honey."

I went up on my toes and kissed his temple. This made him grin, as it always did. Knowing his associates were coming over pushed my schedule up. I ran upstairs and showered. I quickly dressed. I wore a casual scoop neck wrap-around summer dress that made me feel confident. With any luck I would be in and out of the assisted living home without seeing either of the brothers.

I went to Mom's craft store bought several different ballerinas frozen in different positions. Then, for good measure, I bought her a few of the fairy figurines in the next bin over.

The fairies were so cute I bought a few unicorns for them to ride. Then I bought a fun little suitcase for all her figurines to hang out in.

Lastly, I went to find a wreath for Mia to have on her door. All the other tenants had something nice on their doors. The stickers Mia put on hers made me feel sad, like she didn't have someone in her life who knew about decorating.

I picked out a wreath with flowers, butterflies and a few fairies. I knew she'd love it.

After that, I drove all the way back to Philadelphia. I flipped through song after song, trying to find the perfect music for the dance I started choreographing on the reality show. One benefit of Mom's car, the state-of-the-art sound system vibrated my seat and made me feel the music.

I stopped at a place that sold the best Philly Cheese Steak sandwiches in the world just outside the city. I sat alone eating and listening to music in Mom's car. I knew she'd send it out to be detailed as soon as she smelled it, but I needed to be alone.

I found my song. I listened to it over and over counting the beats to my steps the rest of the way into the city, until I knew every beat by heart. I checked in at the assisted living center for Mia, but was not surprised to find she'd been checked out by her cousin. I walked back toward the apartment and realized a few cars down from mine was a dark red coupe that looked exactly like Phoebe's car. I felt a sick lump in my throat.

Wasn't Phoebe working late tonight since Drew had to study?

I went up to the apartment and heard the television up way too loud. I knocked hard and loudly. Someone knocked back.

"Mia is that you?"

Mia opened the door.

"Erin!" she said, clapping.

"Can I come in please?" I asked.

"Oh uhhh… you can't come in right now," she said.

"I brought you dolls," I said showing her the suitcase.

"Chris went for his run, and I don't let anyone in when he is gone," she said.

"Oh," I said, but looked past her to see a familiar Luis Vuitton purse hanging on a chair. It couldn't be Phoebe's – not the one Drew bought her. Jaxon didn't make enough for her. Right?

It had the same sparkly lips keychain.

"Mia, you need to let me in," I said feeling apprehension crawl through my stomach like an alien life form.

"Erin, he said you won't understand," she said. "Please don't leave me."

I kissed her forehead. Then I pushed past her. I walked up the stairs to Jaxon's bedroom. I took a deep breath and opened the door.

"Erin," Phoebe screeched grabbing for a sheet to cover her.

"What is…" Jaxon asked walking in from his bathroom with only a towel on.

"Whoa," I said turning and leaving the room.

"This is not what it looks like," Phoebe called, then snapped at Jaxon to put something on.

I held tight to the railing as I hurried down the stairs, trying not to vomit.

Chris came into the condo sweaty wearing workout clothes.

"What's going on here?" he shouted turning off the TV, so he didn't have to yell so loudly.

"Jaxon is... with Phoebe," I said trying not to cry.

"Come on, you knew he wasn't a saint. Don't act as if you didn't know how this was going to end."

"End?" I questioned wondering why he was being so callous about my little brother's four-year relationship, "I didn't think it'd end like this."

"How could you not?" he asked.

"You're seriously a jerk," I said. I pushed past him to help Mia pick up all the little figurines she dropped when she opened the suitcase.

"I am speaking in terms of real life. You knew, or at least suspected, Jaxon wasn't your type," Chris said following me. He bent down to help Mia as well.

"This has nothing to do with me," I said glaring at him, unsure what he was talking about. I handed Mia back her suitcase full of figurines.

"Erin, look you don't understand," Phoebe cried, pummeling down the stairs barefoot looking like she'd hastily put back on the button up blouse and pencil skirt she wore to work. Jaxon followed her wearing only his boxer briefs.

"I got a pretty clear picture," I said walking toward the door. She grabbed my arm. Jaxon skidded in next to her.

"Would you put on some clothes!" she snapped. She pushed Jaxon, who checked out his pecks in the reflection of the dark TV to make sure they looked good.

"Come on, this is nothing," he said pulling away from Phoebe and moving to my other side.

"This is not nothing," I said glaring at him.

"Drew and I have been together for so long, I just wanted to…"

"Cheat?" I asked glaring at her.

"It's just sex, it's not…"

"Actually, it's four years of dating down the toilet," I said.

"Come on. You can't tell Drew. This will break his heart," Phoebe said. "I just wanted to try something different."

"I suspect you will be free to try as much different as you like," I snapped.

"Come on Erin, be cool," Jaxon said. "We just wanted to try each other out, and I have to be honest. You and I have way more chemistry."

"Excuse me," Phoebe raged at him. I stepped out of the way. She looked violent. Jaxon didn't notice.

"Come on. We meshed way better," he said winking at me. But he didn't look at me. He looked past me. I turned to see Chris soaking this all in. What?

"You… you've been with her…" Phoebe stammered. She looked hurt, blinking back tears. Maybe it wasn't just sex.

"You and I are nothing, Jaxon," I said. "Stop calling me." I hit Jaxon's hand away because he started rubbing my back, of all things.

"We have –" this time he didn't even look at me.

"You and I will never be anything," I interrupted. Then I turned to her and said, "Phoebe, you have two hours until I get home to tell Drew. He's studying with my dad's associates right now, and since I know you don't want to look like the crazy girlfriend in front of them, you'll try to beat me home."

"It wasn't anything," Phoebe snapped waspishly. "We just got carried away."

"Mia, how many times has Phoebe come over?" I asked.

"Four alone and once with you," she said, crying. She hit Jaxon hard in the stomach saying, "I hate you. Erin won't come back now, Stupid."

"Wait, you're the one who's been coming over and staying the night?" Chris asked Phoebe, confused.

"Jaxon is right. It was nothing. It was cold feet, Erin, I swear it was nothing. It will never happen again," Phoebe said glaring at Jaxon. He went quiet. He forgot about Chris. He examined Phoebe putting on her high heels.

"Erin, you will go away forever," Mia wailed.

"It's okay Mia, I'll call you," I said trying to calm her down. "Maybe Chris can bring you to see me some time, okay?"

"For sure, Mia," Chris said examining me like he missed a step.

"Okay," she said sniffling.

"Erin, please give me a few days to… to prepare him for – I need to tell him how confused I've been…" Phoebe stammered taking a brush out of her bag trying to understand her own feelings while pulling it roughly through her disheveled hair.

"You have two hours, and if you want to tell him in person, I suggest you drive faster than me. I drive like a grandma so that should be easy enough."

I stormed toward the front door forcefully. Jaxon grabbed my arm too hard and pulled me back.

"Erin, please. Let's just talk," he said.

"You're hurting my arm," I cried. He released me and looked apologetic. At the same time Chris grabbed him and yelled,

"Let go of her. This isn't you."

"You don't know me," Jaxon raged. He was furious. He charged Chris. Chris grabbed his face and threw him to the ground.

Jaxon fell over backward, startled. He scrambled back to his feet. The brothers faced each other. I only barely noticed Phoebe throw her brush back into her purse and run out the door gingerly in her high heels with her arms flailing.

Jaxon faced Chris like an angry bull, his nostrils flared, ready to charge.

"No, no! Bad boys," Mia cried, putting her hands between them. Chris moved her behind him. I ran over and grabbed her. Using all my strength as a dancer, I pulled her away from the altercation.

"Are you done?" Chris asked. Jaxon threw his arms up in frustration.

"It's okay Mia. We are stopping now," Chris said, but he didn't sound certain. He kept his hands out just to be sure.

Jaxon sneered. Something bottled up inside of him vented out in rage. I knew that feeling. Something was destroying his peace. Jaxon scoffed at Chris and his blood-shot eyes grew small.

"That's all right, brother, I give her to you. I know how much you like my leftovers," Jaxon said, flourishing his arm toward me.

"Excuse me," I glared.

"The two of you are both so uptight," he continued. "It's just sex, Erin."

"No Jaxon, it's loyalty, it's something more than a selfish egomaniac like you could ever understand or fully appreciate," I said.

"You hear that, Chris? She values loyalty," Jaxon said. "You know Erin, Chris is so pathetic."

"Please don't," Chris said. Jaxon continued,

"He couldn't even meet you. He watched you for weeks on *The Whole Package* but didn't have the nerve to come meet you."

"Jaxon, that's enough," Chris said turning red.

"No, she should know. Chris was supposed to be the judge of *The Whole Package*."

"What?" I stammered.

"Chris was supposed to be the judge, but they decided he was too lame after all. That's the only reason he watched the show in the first place, because he wanted to see why they dumped him."

I looked at Chris. Is that why he hated me? Because I wasn't *The Whole Package*?

"You were supposed to be the judge, not Ethan?" I asked. Chris looked up, examining me in his unnerving way. Finally, he looked away.

"Yeah… I … six months before the show started, they decided to go another direction," he answered flushed looking toward the city out the window.

"Why?" I asked.

"I don't know," he answered glancing at me, and looking away again.

"Took it like a pathetic little girl," Jaxon said. "He watched the show just to see who was better than the great Chris Giles."

"I just wanted to see –" Chris started, but Jaxon interrupted in the same sing-song voice that was giving me a headache. I cut them both off:

"Look I'm sorry you were disappointed, but you should be glad you weren't the judge. Thankful even. You're lucky you didn't let Julian Morrows near you. He convinced me to cut my hair. He convinced me to… I've never made such stupid decisions in my life as I did on that show. I'll never dance as a principal for American because of him. Everything I worked for my whole life just went to crap. Don't be sad he didn't screw you over, too," I said trying not to cry.

"I didn't know you lost your spot," Chris said.

"I had to give it up to leave mid-season," I said.

"I see," he said nodding like the conversation where he dashed my hope made a little more sense.

"It doesn't matter. I didn't mean to make that about me," I said looking at Chris whose eyes had changed from frustration to compassion. He was extremely good looking when he used his compassionate eyes.

"Ethan is a big old mess right now. Be thankful it isn't you," I said.

"Yeah. You couldn't have dealt with it, Chrissy," Jaxon said.

"Look, I don't know what's going on here," I said. "But clearly the two of you need some serious help. I need to go make sure my brother's going to be okay, because that's what siblings do. They look out for each other."

"Not when you can't be perfect like your brother," Jaxon said.

"You know what Jaxon? You are an accomplished Physical Therapist. You pulled good grades in school, you played football in college, just to one-up your brother. Look at how much you personally accomplished because you had an older brother to challenge you."

"I didn't do it for –"

"Oh, yes you did. You are naturally lazy and the only time you show any giddy-up is when you are competing with Chris. You really ought to thank him, and then figure out what you want out of life instead of copying everything he does. Because that's pathetic. Seriously, you ought to at least be the Prima in your personal ballet."

Jaxon's face looked just as surprised as it had when Chris threw him down.

"Wait, Erin, if you – " Chris started, but I turned on him.

"And you, you can judge me from afar for not being nice enough or whatever made me not *The Whole Package* in your eyes. I have no clue what I did to you. All I know is I need to get to my brother before Phoebe starts manipulating him."

I turned from them to Mia who was examining her figurines and said, "Good-bye, Sweetie."

Exasperated, I dodged out the door and jogged to the elevator that graciously opened as soon as I hit the button.

I drove home too fast with Philadelphia in my rear view. Poor Drew, what could I do for him?

Chapter 28

When I arrived home, Mom cleaned in the kitchen. The partner's dinner was catered, but my dad grilled steaks for his associates himself.

"Where's Drew?" I asked Mom.

"Phoebe showed up like something was chasing her, and they left," Mom said.

"She'd better do the right thing," I said.

"Is it bad?" Mom asked.

"Yeah, you know how we all thought she was cheating last year, but couldn't prove it?" I asked.

"Can you prove it?" she asked. She looked discouraged.

"Yeah, her and Jaxon were hooking up," I said.

"Oh, Honey, are you okay?" she asked.

"No. Can you believe Phoebe would do that?"

"Yes, I can, but what about Jaxon. Aren't you two—"

"No, he isn't my type. I just went out with him to bother you," I said.

"It worked. Congratulations," she answered, raising her eyebrows.

"Sorry," I said.

"I love you. Please let me—"

Her phone rang. “It’s Dad. I have to get him some figures from the office.”

“Go ahead,” I said walking with her to the stairs.

“Come get me if Drew comes home,” she said sternly, answering the phone.

I went to the sitting room and waited. Finally, Drew came home. He walked into the large entryway holding Phoebe around the waist. He glared at me as I came forward.

“What?” I asked meeting them in the entryway.

“I can’t believe you,” he snapped.

“You can’t believe me?” I asked wondering what she told him.

“Why can’t you just let me and Phoebe be happy. This is last summer all over again. She did not…cheat with that guy in her building. And now you use poor Phoebe as an excuse to dump Jaxon? Erin, just do the right thing.”

I glared at Phoebe. She looked away uncomfortably whipping her hair behind her. Drew barely glanced at me, but his sapphire blue eyes had a glisten to them. His jawline was hard, enhancing the dimple in his chin.

He knew. He was refusing to believe what he knew. If he couldn’t face it yet, was I brave enough to take it for him? It wasn’t the same as it had been when we were kids. It made me sick to swallow this, but I would if I had to, even if it was just until after he took the bar this next week.

“I’m sorry,” I said to Drew.

He flinched and looked at me. I felt the tears start in my eyes. I did not want to hurt him.

"What happened?" he asked.

"I already told you," Phoebe said grabbing his arm, so he looked away from me, "and if you love me you are going to tell your sister to stay out of our business. Now go get your stuff. You can move in with me until Erin goes back on tour."

She crossed her arms like she was pissed, but fear danced in her eyes. Drew looked at her, he looked at me again.

"I'll take it for you if you want me to," I said quietly. He closed his eyes.

"What happened, Erin?" he asked.

"I walked in on her and Jaxon. She was in his bed. Mia said it wasn't the first time," I said choking over the words.

"That is not true. It isn't fair that you trust your sister's word over mine," Phoebe cried growing desperate. Real tears pulled the mascara from her lashes.

"I've never lied to him, Phoebe. That's why he trusts me to tell him the truth," I said, my jaw clenching. I had only ever tried manipulating him once. I stopped, but what if I hadn't? If I tried to play the games Serena did, it would have still come down to this moment. Only Drew wouldn't have been able to trust me when it mattered most.

"Phoebe, it's time we end this thing," Drew said blinking hard. My heart broke into pieces with his.

"Come on, Drew. Let's talk about this, alone," she said pulling on him desperately.

I saw something I'd never seen before. When Serena wanted to manipulate me on the show, she always pulled me away from the people like Carrie who would have helped me separate truth from lies.

"Drew, in my opinion you are way too emotionally invested in Phoebe to be alone with her right now," I said feeling angry.

"You have no right," Phoebe said glaring at me.

I paused. What right did I have? Human decency, busybody, or my brother's welfare. Where did one person's rights to influence another person's life end? Phoebe was poisoning my brother, like Serena did to me. He didn't deserve that. I started fuming. What right did they have? They weren't looking out for our well-being, just their own. I wanted what was best for my little brother. Phoebe wasn't that.

Phoebe pleaded with Drew to go with her. She slept with another man less than four hours earlier. What was wrong with her? The anger I felt took over.

"Leave him alone!" I growled.

"Excuse me," she said, looking at me startled. I must have looked mad because I took a step forward and she took a step back toward the door.

"I can smell Jaxon's cologne on you. You have some nerve," I said feeling the anger grow inside me.

"I love Drew," she stammered, pleading with him when he leaned in realizing her scent was decidedly masculine.

"You don't know how to love. Drew will not go with you right now. You realize he is taking the bar this week, right? Just leave him alone until it's over."

"You can't tell me what to do," she said.

I glared.

"He is going to take twenty-four hours to himself. You will not contact him in any way until he calls you," I snapped, the tremble in my voice growing as my anger erupted.

"I… look maybe we all just need to calm down," Phoebe said, stepping back again. I clenched my jaw and balled my fists, strong muscles from hours of dancing rippled along my arms. I took another step toward her. She flinched like I was going to hit her. She turned and ran to the door calling, "I'll talk to you tomorrow, Drew."

"Give me your phone," I said. Drew, in shock, like he couldn't understand what happened, handed it over without hesitating.

"What's going on?" Mom asked, rushing into the hallway. "Who's yelling?"

Phoebe didn't even wait a minute until she sent him an angry text about letting his sister talk to her that way.

"What happened here?" Mom asked again.

"Erin…kicked Phoebe out," Drew said trying to decide what happened. I was too busy trying to delete the angry text she sent.

"What did she say?" Drew asked, looking at his phone.

"She's mad at you. She slept with someone else, and she is mad at you. What a trapeze artist."

"What?" Mom said.

"I don't know. I am not in practice of calling names, and clearly, I'm not good at it," I said, glancing outside and relieved to see her headlights leave the curb so Mom couldn't go running after her.

"You are not accustomed to calling names because I don't allow it in my home. Please try to find your compassion in this situation, for your brother, and the woman he loves."

"Drew, yes, but why should I have to…" I stopped. The look on my mother's face indicated I should not call Phoebe names, so I didn't.

"I could have handled that myself," Drew said.

I dropped my head onto his bicep, and he wrapped his arm around me.

"I'm sorry I overstepped," I said quietly. But I wasn't.

Chapter 29

We all walked back into the well-lit kitchen that smelled like lemon disinfectant. Both my brother and mom just kind of watched me like I might explode.

"Erin, that show was pretty hard on you, wasn't it," Drew said.

"Serena was so mean to me," I said looking up trying not to cry.

"Maybe we should—"

A text on my phone interrupted what we should do. It was Jaxon.

"Wow. He's got some nerve," I said glancing at the text. But the words caught my eye.

"This is Chris. It's important, call me," and he gave me his phone number.

I showed Mom and Drew.

"Chris is the older brother?" Mom asked.

"Yeah, he hates me. He wouldn't contact me if it wasn't important. Do you think Mia's okay?" I asked.

Neither seemed sure.

"Should I call him?" I asked.

"Can you be civil?"

I grimaced at her and then saved the new phone number to my contacts. I called Chris.

"Hi, this is Erin," I said uncertainly after he answered.

"Erin! Thank goodness."

"Is Mia okay?"

"Oh, yeah, she's fine. She calmed down after you left," he said.

"Oh good," I said. He didn't answer.

"Then... um… so what's up?" I asked.

"My aunt is the director of the Philadelphia Ballet Company. She's a dancer down for next weekend's opening. The Fairy Queen from *The Dream* sprained an ankle. If you come tomorrow morning before eight, you can… at least try to find a place with them." He paused. "I didn't know you had to give up your spot."

"You got me an audition?" I said, still so confused.

"Yeah, but you have to be in downtown Philadelphia at the theater by eight am tomorrow ready to…audition. It only runs for a little while, but it's something. They start rehearsal at nine. Can you do that?

"Yeah, I can. Uh…I think I have to check with American first."

"My aunt knows Noel Landry. They spoke. Ms. Landry thinks it's a great idea."

"She does," I said, my heart falling. Why was Noel pawning me off on another dance company?

"It's a top principal role," he said.

"Yeah. No, I get it. Thanks, Chris, for doing this, I mean, this is really decent of you," I said trying not to sound confused.

"I…I'm not really…anyway I'll meet you there and introduce you. It never hurts to have an in with someone, right?"

"Yeah, right… I'll be on time, I'll text you when I'm close, okay."

"Sounds good. See you tomorrow,' he said hanging up.

I turned unsure what to say to Mom and Drew who were watching me.

"What is it?"

"He got me an audition for *The Dream* with the Philadelphia Ballet, a principal role," I said.

"This is the older brother," Drew said.

"Yeah, he cleans up after Jaxon. I'm sure Phoebe will get a fruit basket. I guess he really is perfect," I said with a laugh.

"What are you going to do?" Mom asked.

"They've spoken to Noel. She thinks I should," I said.

"When?" mom said confused.

"I drive like a grandma."

Drew laughed. It made me smile. He was going to be okay.

"It can't hurt to audition, right?" I asked.

"You are going to get back into American," Mom said. She didn't mention how much it would cost my dad.

"Noel is pawning me off to Philadelphia."

"That doesn't mean you don't have a place at American still."

"Not as the Fairy Queen," I said to avoid the argument. "I just want to dance, Mom."

"Okay. Well, it's your career, I respect that. It sounds like we need to get you ready."

"I'm going to bed," Drew said turning, resigned, toward the hallway. Mom and I watched him go. My heart hurt so badly for him.

"I've got the stage make-up already packed. We can look up audition protocol online. I'm sure you're in a black leo," Mom said.

"What about my hair?" I asked, fingering my short hair.

"Slick it back into a small ponytail. It'll work for tomorrow," Mom said. "We'll get you a false bun."

"'Kay," I said trying not to cry, but the tears trickled down my face without my permission. I finished my dance, and now I had somewhere to perform it. Mom put an arm around me, apparently remembering I could use some compassion. Maybe she could take care of her own daughter before the shallow fool who cheated on her son.

"Come on, Erin, let's get you to bed so you are well-rested," she said.

Chapter 30

I at least tried to feel bad for interfering with Drew and Phoebe, until the next morning. Drew insisted on driving us because he did not trust anyone related to Jaxon. We looked out for each other. It's what we did.

I sat in the back seat of Drew's truck doing my hair with huge glops of gel. I put on neutral make-up colors and finished my look with fake lashes. Then I used the extra room the truck cab offered to stretch myself into impossible shapes while being choked by the seatbelt. I had to be limber. My back couldn't stiffen up on me at a time like this.

"What if this isn't a real opportunity?" I asked when we were almost there.

"I looked it up, *The Dream* is opening next Thursday. We've only done Balanchine's *A Midsummer Night's Dream* in school. This is Ashton's *The Dream*. Same story though," Mom said. She rambled when nervous.

"Right. I don't doubt *The Dream* is opening, but what if there is no audition?

"Why would you even say that?" Mom asked.

"Okay, I'm going to tell you something, but you can't freak out."

"When you say it like that, I'm already freaking out," Mom said.

"Chris was supposed to be the judge of *The Whole Package*."

"What?"

"He was supposed to be Ethan, but he was dropped six months ago without an explanation. That's weird right?"

"And you think this audition is his revenge for not getting to go on the show?" Drew asked sarcastically.

"I… no. Chris seemed genuinely surprised I was kicked out of American."

"You were not kicked out, Noel never said that. Eavesdropping does not tell the whole story Erin," Mom said.

"But –"

She interrupted, "I don't think you should harp on this right now. Let's go into this audition assertively. Be professional no matter what happens. Rise above the negative."

I nodded but gritted my teeth. I could not handle this lecture again. Rise above the negative. If a person can have a mantra, that was my mother's.

"It's hard not to think about it," I said.

"Close your eyes and go through your audition piece, and I'll wrap your feet. Have you done much en pointe since you got home?" Mom asked.

"Hours. I have the perfect pointe shoes ready to go," I said.

"Well thank goodness for that, but I … we may as well wrap you," Mom said. We both knew my feet would bleed in the next week if I got this part.

"It will be fast footwork. What piece are you thinking?" Mom asked.

"I worked something new. It has the footwork and lines needed. I found a song yesterday, but I've never put them together."

"You're going to perform your own?" Mom asked, surprised. I couldn't blame her. She always saw every piece I worked on before I ever performed it, but I'd been so private about this one.

"It's the most complicated piece I've done so far. If I'm going to win a top principal role, I need to put up my best," I said.

"Well, that will be lovely, Erin," Mom said, biting her top lip.

In her days on the stage, she'd struggled with nerves, but I must have inherited my dad's nerves of steel because I didn't. I loved dancing. I came alive on the stage in a way I couldn't in real life. The anxious anticipation gave me pleasure. I felt like I was finally coming home.

Drew stopped at the front of the theater. It had a simple brownstone exterior, with a row of arched doorways. Chris came quickly out of one of the doors. He wore street clothes – jeans, and a t- shirt, but still looked put together. He came forward to help me out of the truck with my bag and water bottles. His blue-green eyes watched me in an unnerving way. It was to the point of weirdness, almost like he couldn't believe I was real.

"Okay, we have to hurry," he instructed after we dragged my stuff to the front of the theater, and he held the door open for us. Leaning over to Mom, he said, "I'm Chris. You must be Erin's sister."

We both squinted at him.

"Mom, Chris Giles, Chris this is my mother, Megan Peale."

"It's a pleasure," he said taking her hand, but quickly started walking. We hurried past the box office then a quaint bar set up on one side of the lobby. The bottles, lined up with liquid courage, ranged from dark amber all the way to light cream, and somehow, matched the pillars, chandeliers, and even the woven rug of the lobby. It surprised me how ornate and grand the entryway to the theater was, considering how unassuming it looked from the outside.

Mom and I walked a step behind Chris. Mom looked at me significantly.

"What," I mouthed behind his back without making a sound.

"He's cute," she mouthed back.

I glanced at his amazing rear physique, but quickly looked away and rolled my eyes at her. Chris stopped to open another door that led down a long hallway to the side of the main theater. I passed so close to his bulging chest and striking chiseled face, I couldn't even look at him, but noted he smelled right. He wore chamomile and witch hazel aftershave. He took us back into the depths of the theater's basement to a few well-lit practice rooms.

"Here, Erin warms up in here. You have ten, maybe fifteen minutes. Megan, would you come with me and hand in her resume," Chris said.

"Of course," she said.

As I warmed up, a few other dancers came in. One of them wore a huge sweater with boy shorts and the other had a florescent pink leo, bare legs and a shirt tied around her waist. I could not imagine Noel's face if any of her auditions showed up looking like that.

I stretched. Wearing wireless earbuds, I went through my audition number a few times, counting every step and adding in a few to be sure I ended at the same time my song did. I watched the way my arms held their position.

I noticed the other women practicing, but they seemed unwilling to exert themselves in front of me. It was strange. I always saw everyone's audition pieces at American. The warmup could not be understated, yet they seemed reluctant to engage. I practiced my turns. I balanced perfectly and just allowed my body to stop when I finished. The bright pink woman exclaimed a little.

"Was that eight pirouettes?" she asked.

"Uh nine," I said blushing.

"That was impressive," she said.

"Was it?" I asked. I was so used to being the runt in the litter, I couldn't be sure if she was being sarcastic.

"Your dancing is magnificent," she said.

"Thank you," I said, having the strangest urge to cry.

Chris came back after ten minutes.

"You ready, Erin?" he asked.

"Sure," I said prancing over to my bag. I pulled out my shrug to keep my muscles warm and my boots to put over my pointe shoes.

"Hey, Chris," the girl in the fluorescent pink said walking up to him.

"Hey Beth, how are you?"

"I'm good. I haven't seen you in forever," she complained. He nodded to her, but he looked nervously at me. When he didn't respond she said:

"You going to take me out again? We had some good chemistry."

"I'm really busy, sorry," he said watching me put away my earbuds, "Erin, we really need to go, Madam is waiting for you."

"Wait," the woman said. "She can't just audition for the fairy queen, can she? I mean I'm the understudy. I know the show. I've been working for years toward this."

I walked up to Chris and bit my lip. I hated this part.

"She's a guest talent from the American Ballet. You know she's going to be mixed into the pot," Chris said easily. The woman looked disappointed, so he said, "Sorry, Beth."

"I saw her warmup. I get it," she said. She stooped down and picked up her bag. "Good luck."

"Thanks," I said, and I waved to her, thankful she was such a good sport.

"Bye, Chris," the other woman said waving. I followed him pulling at my warmup boots that protected my pointe shoes.

The confrontation of competing for roles never bothered me before but felt excruciating after the reality show. Especially considering this was starting to feel like it might not be a real audition, but a crapshoot on Chris's part.

Chris directed me up to the right wing of the stage. Mom waited for me and took my bag, shrug and booties.

"I need to go plug in your music," Mom said. I handed her my phone showing her my song and disconnecting my earbuds from the Bluetooth.

"Okay. Good luck honey, I'm going to slip in with Drew to watch. I'm so excited to see your piece." She waved at me with a bootie, shaking slightly. I stood waiting with Chris.

"How do you know everyone here?" I asked, trying not to think of the girl cursing me to hurt myself.

"My aunt is the director, and I dated…well, Hailey, the one who hurt her ankle," he said.

"And possibly the whole company," I said glancing up at him coyly.

"My aunt likes setting me up. Hailey was the only serious one. We met when I moved here five years ago," he said. "She married last year, but we're still good friends. She lets Mia sleep over in her guest room when I go out of town and she's lonely."

"That's nice. I've never really stayed friends with any of my ex's," I said, growing distracted as I finished my sentence. The overhead lights flipped on and danced across the dull black Marley flooring. The back lighting projected purple over the outline of trees at midnight in an enchanted forest. The red velvet curtain swayed slightly with anticipation. I shivered a little.

"You okay?" he asked. I'd just drifted off.

"Yeah. Thanks for doing this," I said, looking up at him, refocusing.

"My pleasure," he said and grinned at me. I felt taken back. I'd never really seen him smile; it made his aqua eyes dance like the lights. He didn't seem mad at me anymore. Looking for a way to break the tension between us I said:

"Can you smell that?"

"Body odor," he returned.

"And the musty scent of costumes being pulled out of storage. They're being steamed," I said.

"I smell balm to sooth sore muscles," he said.

"Yes," I answered excitedly, but then looked up at him blushing, wondering if he thought me crazy. He smiled again and said: "It smells like passion and hard work."

"And hairspray," I said, content. I was home. Chris seemed to understand. He looked like he might say something else, but a theatrical female voice called, "Chris are you there?"

"Here, come on out," he said taking my arm and walking me out onto the stage.

"This isn't very professional," I said looking at him.

"Oh, it's more laxed here than at American," he said.

"Clearly," I said grinning up at him. He stood behind me and had my arm in his hand like a security guard. I didn't feel the pressure of the audition at all, but where he held my arm our skin mingled. That made my heart pound.

"This is my friend, Erin Peale," he said.

I slid my leg behind my body lowering myself toward the floor and bowed my head demurely in greeting.

"All right my dear, let us see what you have," said a voice behind the lights.

"Good luck," Chris said moving off the stage.

I stood in the lights, feeling the warmth. I finally made it home. The place I loved the most—center stage.

I forgot everything when my music began.

Painstakingly, slowly, I bent over grazing the ground, looking for my foot. Upon coming back up with oval-shaped arms in fifth position I gently brought my turned-out foot with me. I stretched my leg into a Grand Adage, controlling its progress upward and to the side of me like the rising sun, then I shifted it behind me as the day waned on.

My leg dropped deliberately to perch behind me. All at once a sudden storm cloud blotted out the sun, the music grew dark. I was caught so unaware. My arms moved quickly in tight elegant positions, and led my sweeping feet until my leg swung and I was swallowed into the swirl, like a tornado picked me up into the piqué turn. I turned violently, desperate to keep my body perfectly aligned to control the force against me. My face stayed tilted toward where I had felt the sun. I slid across the stage whirling around in the storm. I stopped turning. My feet pranced tensely, always beating my pointed toes against the neck of my foot. My perfect footwork outran the storm. My legs whipped then ended in a clean arabesque behind my head. It came back to my face, and I launched triumphantly into a complicated pirouette combination.

Finally, the music calmed, the storm abated, but the sun left me, and I was alone. I reached into my reservoir for sorrow. I shouldn't have done it. The melancholy of the lone cello brought out the burden sitting heavy and deep in the well of my soul, keeping me captive there.

I danced slower this time. My body found each piercing position and I held them for three beats. My leg came up in a controlled piqué arabesque and I held it raising it higher and higher behind me. I danced, growing into the self-pity of my life. The sorrow of my situation overwhelmed me, and it came across my face.

All at once, the storm came down again, fiercer this time. I pushed myself off the floor and jumped high leaning diagonally into brisé until I was shoved back by a brisé volé. I repeated this action several times without making any progress. I straightened out with a grouping of jeté only to reach out into the grand jeté, my legs extended in perfect unison behind and in front of me.

No matter how hard I fought it wasn't enough. I could not outrun the storm this time. It was deep – too deep. I was heavy. I did little hops in arabesque trying to leap again. I couldn't get high enough with a series of little jeté much like a graceful skip. No, I was a fighter. Finally, in desperation I turned to the most complicated steps in my repertoire. It started with the very graceful Italian fouetté.

My core muscles were always engaged. They were built up from years of protecting my back and held my body like a rod as my leg whipped into a series of elegant turns. Then I did a simple slide and leapt into a series of en dedans fouettés.

It was my signature turn, my curved spine made it easier for me to transition my extended leg from the back to the side then bring it in, never losing control as I whipped it back out again. With tragic beauty I curled in tightly on the last fouetté. I whipped my pointed toe into my knee, pirouetting nine times in a tight solitary turn. I came to a dramatic stop and slid my back leg until I sunk onto the stage, trapped with no escape.

My music ended. I hadn't fled the deep well. I turned my head off stage, trying to catch my breath and hide my shame, but Chris was still there. I felt a tear course down my face. I wanted to turn away, so he didn't see, but I stopped.

His face showed more than mine. He stared at me, breathing hard, enamored with my performance. Trapped deeply in the well with me, he looked upset, profoundly affected by my sorrow, so I shared it with him.

I turned as I stood, taking air deeply into my lungs to slow down my breathing. I wiped the tear away on my arm.

I plastered the ballerina smile upon my face, and I bowed.

There was applause. I'd never been applauded at an audition. There was more applause than just the director. When the lights on the stage turned off, and the theater lights turned on, I realized the entire dance company was there.

Again, I had to wonder what strings Chris pulled to give me this opportunity.

I suddenly realized they were rehearsing, not auditioning.

Mom and Drew sat off to the side. I didn't allow the surprise to show, but when I looked at Mom to take a bow in her direction, she mouthed, "I know," to share in the weirdness.

"Erin, come on down," a woman in her fifties called from the center of the third row of stadium seating.

I nodded, unsure how. The orchestra pit was a gaping hole, dropped down into the basement, being used as an elevator to set the stage for the show. I could use the stairs, but I wanted to take off my good pointe shoes. I wasn't going to destroy them for anything. I didn't have time to decide. Chris came out and took my arm and we moved to the side of the stage.

"Here, I'll show you how to walk around," he said.

"Okay, uh can I just…" I stooped and pulled at my footless tights.

"Oh, I can just carry you if that's all right," he said.

I stared at him, sure my mouth opened wide. He seemed… repentant?

"Um… it's …" I picked up my foot pointing to my pointe shoes, "they're worn in perfectly. I don't want to roll my ankle on the carpet…I know it's dumb."

"No, I understand," he said holding his arms out to me.

"If you don't mind," I said, and I could feel the blush spread across my sweaty face.

"Come on," he encouraged.

I wrapped my arm around his neck. All at once he hoisted me up, and I jumped into his arms as any self-respectable dancer would. I hit his chest hard.

"Sorry," I said.

His chest heaved. His strong arms pulled me in tightly. Something inside me sparked alive and electric, drawn from him. He held me so close. His intense face came close to mine. His breath warmed my space. His brows creased as his beautiful eyes searched me, eagerly. The sudden intimacy running between us was like a live wire. It scared me. The fear must have shown clearly in my eyes. He looked away and slacked his grip some. He started to laugh as if to cover up his intensity and said:

"It's okay, I didn't realize you were going to help."

"Yeah," I said. I felt strangely vulnerable in his arms, despite my being carried by muscly men all the time. I tried to think of something to say as he carried me down a set of stairs. My mind was blank, and I was sweaty. I stayed rigid, fighting the impulse to release my body weight on him. He smelled good and his arms were strong, secure, and inviting.

Finally, Chris said, "You're really talented. All that stuff you were talking about the other night – I'm not sure what you meant. You're good enough to make it to the top of whatever venue you try for."

I shrugged. I didn't realize he put together the pieces of our conversation enough to know the battle I waged against self-doubt and my dream.

"I'm fighting for it," I finally said, hoping it was enough.

"Good for you," he said, and he gave me a squeeze. My body sprang to life. I pulled myself up on his chest further. Scared of the chemistry palpitating between us I said,

"This theater is exquisite," pretending to be distracted by the massive crimson and gold honeycomb he carried me into. The glowing gorgeous chandelier dripped golden light down.

"Yeah," he said just as awkwardly, "I love empty theaters."

"Because you can smell the… what – its passion and hard work?" I asked with a grin.

"Dreams coming true. It seeps into every seat," he agreed mirroring my grin as he carried me to the seating where my mother stood.

"Thanks," I said as he sat me down next to Mom.

"My pleasure," he said with a mischievous grin. I thought it seemed more natural than the scowl he used speaking to Jaxon.

"Sorry, sweetie, I didn't mean to take your booties," Mom said working the ribbons on my pointe shoes. She called to the crew watching us, "Just give us a minute."

A few hands waved in acknowledgement but the hum in the hive meant the other dreamers were already distracted.

"You okay?" Mom asked, scrutinizing me.

"Yeah. I feel better," I said like my dancing siphoned something dark out of me.

"That was probably the best performance I've ever seen you give," Drew whispered. "It was a little sadder than anything I've seen you do."

He glanced up at Chris who was standing close enough to hear. Chris squinted at me in the way any good therapist would. I wondered if he was analyzing me. Did he see how desperate I was to be center stage?

"I've been working some new stuff," I said quietly.

"It was beautiful," Mom said. She slipped my regular ballet slippers on my battered feet, then she put on my warm-up boots.

"Thanks, Mom," I said. I stood and followed Chris over to the middle section to meet the director.

Chapter 31

"Erin, this is my aunt, Madame Annette Friel," Chris said, pointing. She stood, pulling her clipboard up from the velvet seat next to her. She reached out and shook hands with me.

"Barely his aunt," she said wrapping her clipboard in her arms. "His uncle dumped me for a model after two years of marriage. Chris was four, but it is sweet he still gives me the title."

She grinned and reached up, patting Chris's smiling face with her thin fingers. She was a small, slight woman in a black turtleneck, way too warm for the summer day.

"Erin, it is such a pleasure," Madam said. "You dance beautifully. Your extension was flawless. I expected to see some trace of your movement hinder, but it was undetectable. If anything, you used it to your advantage. Well done!"

"Thank you," I said trying not to look shocked. I'd never been complimented by a creative director. Either it was disgust, or a simple head nod of approval.

"This is our company. We'd love for you to perform Tatiana in *The Dream.* It runs for ten days," she said gesturing around her at a hodge-podge of dancers in warm-up clothes. Beth, who would become my understudy, looked discouraged. Other than that, the other dancers smiled at me.

"We're just starting practice for the day. I'd love for you to work with Ivan. I need to see some lifts."

"Sure," I said, glancing around for the man she spoke of. Ivan stood. He was huge in dance terms and young to be dancing principal. He couldn't be older than twenty-one, and at least six feet tall. If a person passed him in the street, they wouldn't call him bulky or overly muscular by any means, but in the dance world his bulk would be considered hindering to his lines.

"You dance beootifully," Ivan said in a strong Eastern European accent, his brown eyes shining, like he'd enjoyed my performance emotionally. His high cheek bones enhanced his jutting chin. I thought him adorable, though I doubted he would want to be categorized as that.

"Thank you," I said.

"That choreography. Did it come from someone at American?" Madam asked, scrutinizing me.

"Oh, no, it's just something I've been working on," I said, reaching up to smooth my hair.

"Good, I'd like you to do the fouetté sequence for your solo. It was…divine."

"You're going to let me perform my own choreography?"

"Yes, parts of it."

"Thank you."

"We can use some of your piece other places. It has far too many elements for you to perform at once and make it through the entire show."

"Fair enough," I said, knowing I had created it to prove I was a good dancer.

"Don't get me wrong, it was exquisite. You'll have to adapt it to the music, but the emotion is perfect for when you are dancing about the lost mother of the changeling boy with Oberon. And the footwork in the beginning can be part of your solo with the fairy court. Wouldn't it be arresting for you to step twice for every beat while they stepped once?"

"Yes, and thank you for this opportunity."

"Of course, my dear, of course. If you can work some lifts with our Oberon, Ivan, just to size the two of you together."

"Sure. Do you want me en pointe?"

"Better not. We'll just size you up. You're tall, that's helpful," she said nodding.

That is when I noticed a lovely, small woman sitting behind us. She stood and leaned forward whispering to Chris. She hobbled a little holding on to the seat in front of her. Her ankle was bound. Her smooth face and dark eyes had slight indicators she was a touch Asian and her hair, a caramel color, wrapped in a perfect bun. I blushed, realizing I stole her part. My gaze caught her attention, and she stopped whispering to look back at me.

"Sorry about your ankle," I said quickly.

"Oh, it's okay. Sorry you didn't win *The Whole Package*," she said.

I couldn't tell if she was being snide, so I just nodded and followed Ivan back up to the stage, where we began our inevitable adjustments to each other.

Ivan moved with grace and agility for someone so big. He picked me up in a simple fish dive. We held it. His strong arm crushed the leg he held straight up in the air; he feared he would drop me. That didn't make sense. I didn't need him to hold me – I could stay in the pose with the bulk of my weight on his quad and wrap my bent leg around him making his overbearing arm support completely unnecessary.

I expected him to gently release me. Instead, he threw me.

"What the…" I heard as I flew and barely stopped myself from toppling into the pit. Thankfully, I wasn't en pointe.

"Whoa there," I said to him. "You can't just toss me."

"Oh yeah," he said turning red. I could see I intimidated him. But that didn't make sense either. He was the principal dancer, and at such a young age. He must be all talent.

Madam called, "Erin, I've tried to explain the motion he needs to release in, but he needs to feel it. He is a fast learner when he feels the motion. Can you work with him while we run through the lover's scenes?"

"Sure," I said.

We walked back into the warmup room. Chris followed us, as did Mom. Drew stayed in the theater and opened his backpack to study. By the time we entered the practice room Mom looked like she had something not so positive to say to Ivan, but I quickly intervened.

"Here, the trick is to slide into the release, like this," I said showing him. We moved in time. I didn't let him pick me up. I moved with him from the lift to sliding into the release. As we worked, he told me how he joined a Russian Circus as a performance artist when he was fifteen. One of his coworkers was a classically trained ballerina, who injured herself and was not allowed back into the Bolshoi Ballet Company. She said he had a gift and trained him.

When the troupe performed in Philadelphia, his mentor found Madam, now the creative director of the ballet. The two knew each other from their life in dance.

Ivan tried out and the company accepted him as a soloist. He stayed behind his troupe to cultivate his gift.

And gifted he was. He had the fastest muscle memory I'd ever seen. He soaked up everything I taught him and did not revert to his old methods. After only a half hour I let him pick me up again. His strong arm crushed my leg still, but he did not drop me. He slid into the release like I showed him.

"Good. Much better."

"Spasiba," he said shyly as if he had no idea, he was an incredibly handsome muscled young man.

I taught him how to hold me without bruising me. From then on, he cradled me. He allowed me to pull my weight off him by arching my back instead of him trying to support it all. By the end of my tutoring, I could have been a

Fabergé egg and never cracked. We worked on how to move into the lift naturally. I told him to leap and then come toward me. I stopped and had to balance myself the first time he leapt. It shook the floor.

"That was high," I said.

"I dance on bands with troupe. They throw me to the air," he said more with his arms.

"Or the bands really did nothing, and you threw yourself in the air," I answered mimicking his arm movement. He grinned.

An incubator choreographer named Paul came in to work with us on the actual show after a while. Just developing his own creativity, Paul, Hailey's regular partner, had paused his own dance career to help Madam choreograph.

After six hours, Ivan and I had our main pas de deux that ended the show marked out. Paul vaguely followed the choreography of *The Dream*, but he quickly put in more solo time for me and my choreography, cutting the pas de deux short.

In the next week, he would cut much of Oberon's solo whilst Tatiana slept and put in the saddest part of my solo during the turning over of the changeling child. This gave Ivan less to perfect as he was in his first principal role. He wasn't sad about it. Madam wasn't so fussed about accuracy as self-expression.

"I swear you have the memory of a dolphin," Paul said to me. "I teach you something once and it's there," he said, tapping my head. I laughed.

"Why a dolphin?"

"They can memorize the individual noises of every other dolphin they ever meet."

"Umm," I said, feeling Paul might need to be fact-checked when I got home.

Chapter 32

Drew drove home fast. No matter how often I offered to drive so he could study, he said no.

When we arrived home, he disappeared to his room. Dad waited for us in the kitchen with food.

"How did it go?" he asked, smiling at me.

"I got Titania," I said.

"Of course you did," he said, and he hugged me. "I am so proud of you, honey."

"It's not American, but I…" I looked at my dad. He positively beamed at Mom.

"Don't you worry about that, Honey; audiences have to learn to love you somehow. Let's eat, then you can go blog. Your mom recorded your solo to upload. We'll have American eating out of our hands in a week," he said grinning.

"But dad, I … I was good enough for them on my own. I was a star to them," I said.

"Oh, Sweetie, you're a star at American as well," Dad said glancing at Mom who smiled back like they had a secret.

Uhh parents…I had to find my own place. I took a deep breath.

"I've been thinking. What if… maybe I join this dance company, and look into getting my MBA," I said.

"Erin," Dad said, his grin faltered.

"Come on Dad, being in one theater instead of touring the world. I could work toward a career that isn't a one in a million longshot," I said.

"Erin, what is the difference between those who succeed and those who fail?" Dad asked sternly.

"Those who fail quit before they can succeed," I said.

"You are a star, even at American. Don't you doubt that. You have worked so hard to get where you are. Don't give up now. You are so close," he said.

"Well, I am an appreciated star in Philadelphia," I said blushing. For the first time since I left the reality show, I felt talented. No pressure, no cut downs, nothing to put me in my generic place. I was no longer one of many girls Ethan could choose from, one of many dancers Noel could pick. I was gifted and important. Dad looked like he may start in again, so, grabbing a bowl and filling it with tetrazzini, I said, "I'm going to bed. I'm going to need my rest to make this crazy schedule."

"Good idea, Sweetheart," Mom and Dad said together. I rummaged through the fridge for a few cold-water bottles. When I emerged, I noticed Drew came in, lured by the smell of food. Digging into the noodles, he looked angry.

"You okay Drew?" I asked handing him a cold water.

"Yeah… I don't know," he said.

"She's not worth it. She's seriously a bi--"

"Erin," Mom interrupted.

"Come on Mom. You can't possibly be defending her. We need to support Drew right now."

"I am not as concerned about Drew and Phoebe as I am about you."

"Me?" I questioned. I motioned to Drew, who was stabbing the noodles.

"Your anger is out of control," Mom said.

"Mine?"

"Who are you to label Phoebe with such a cold-hearted word? Please don't say anything like that to her. She already feels very worthless about herself."

"You're worried about her?"

"Erin, I'm worried about you. You are engulfed in protection and splendor. All you can see is the littleness in Phoebe. You don't care where she's come from, or what she's endured that would make her behave like she does. You don't want to help her. You simply write her off as horrible and move on. But ask yourself this, who would you be if you hadn't grown up with every advantage coming to you?"

I shrugged, hating this lecture.

"Drew is going to be fine; you are going to be fine. What is going to happen to Phoebe?"

"Who cares?"

"I don't want bad things to happen to her," Drew said. I glared at Mom. What was wrong with her? We needed to talk Drew out of

Phoebe. I turned to Drew and said, "So, you're just going to date her to keep her from herself? That's not fair."

"That's not what I said," Mom answered, exasperated.

"Do you even care if Drew's okay?" I snapped.

"I do," she said. She took a deep breath. With a look that said this conversation wasn't over, she turned from me and walked over to him. She put a hand on his back.

"Drew, honey. Are you all right?"

"I don't know yet," he said honestly. "But I need my phone back, Erin. My study group is probably wondering what happened to me."

"Right," I said, seeing Drew getting me out of any more conversations with my mother. I ran to my room for his phone. I took it to him, but once he opened it, I took it back.

There were a ton of messages from his study group, mostly from someone labeled Smarty. One message showed from Phoebe. It read: "Don't worry about us right now. Let's talk after you take the bar. Good Luck."

This surprised me. I thought his phone would be full of nasty messages from Phoebe. I'd hoped to show Mom who she defended. I handed it back to Drew a little uncomfortable.

"It's us against the world," I said, giving him a hug.

"Us against the world," he answered, but he looked so sad I wished I could cheer him up.

Chapter 33

The next week I stayed near the theater. My dad insisted I get a suite at a local hotel that had a restaurant with an organic menu and a safe underground parking structure so I had access to a car. I did not pay for it, but suspected it was pricy. My suite was on the tenth floor overlooking Old Town. The suite provided two beds so Mom could come stay if needs be

I learned the ballet in only four days before the first performance. The first day of getting my body back into performance shape was my hardest. I came to the hotel and ice-bathed my feet. On Tuesday, we finished for the evening when Chris, with Mia in tow, came into the theater.

"ERRIINN!," she yelled, barreling toward me down the long aisle of seating. Ivan saw her girth and, in total concern, blocked her from reaching me.

"Move," Mia ordered.

"You cannot break Erin. We need her," he said. As they faced off, I realized how guilty Ivan felt for injuring Hailey. Perhaps that is why he protected me so diligently when the plump little mentally disabled lady, whose golden ponytail swung with enthusiasm, tried several times to evade his capture.

"Okay," Mia finally said. She put her hands up in defeat and looking at Ivan with huge grey eyes, promised, "I will be very carrrefullllll."

"Okay," he said moving. I grinned at him, and he smiled back at me. It felt like I had another little brother, only this one danced with me.

"Hello, Mia," I said leaning in for a hug, "I have something for you."

"More dancers?" she asked. "I love the ballerinas you gave me. I'm going to be a ballerina."

"I'll show you later," I said smiling at her. I never gave her the butterfly wreath I bought for her door. I meant to take her back to her room and help her hang it, but seeing Phoebe with Jaxon – I never got around to it. Mom put it in the trunk of my car and called me twice to remind me to give it to Mia.

After I took a cold shower, I still tried to cool down, so I wrapped in a towel, and I fanned myself.

"You ready for next week?" Hailey asked, changing into shredded jeans and a white tank top.

"I think so," I said. "Sorry it couldn't be you."

"Nope. It's my own fault. They tasked me with helping Ivan settle in as a principal. I knew he was throwing me too hard. I thought it was fun and didn't tell Madam or even try to correct it."

I bent over to pull the towel out of my damp hair. “Well, it’s still disappointing,” I said pulling a brush through my matted hair.

“I’ll get over it. I’m glad you were available. Chris said they may not be holding your spot at American, but that doesn’t make sense,” she said.

“When I took leave, I wasn’t supposed to make any dramatic changes to my appearance without permission. It’s more of an unwritten rule that I wasn’t supposed to cut my hair until I made principal,” I called over the blow-dryer while trying to style my hair, still disliking it.

“You aren’t even a principal at American? How is that possible?” she asked, “I’ve danced with Natalia, American’s top principal.”

“I know her.” I grimaced.

“She’s not as good as you.”

“I don’t know.”

When I finished drying my hair, I offered Hailey the blow dryer.

“No thanks. Anyway, doing *The Dream* with us can’t be financially beneficial to you,” Hailey said.

“It’s not bad,” I laughed, embarrassed. My family never talked about money. Hailey waited for me to say more, so I stuttered, “I was making… more before. It’s about half. *The Dream* will cover the hotel room… Probably. I don’t care.”

I cringed having to quote my mother. "I'm so blessed. Dad sponsors me. I just love to dance."

"Sounds good to me," she said.

"You've done a great job with the soloist," I said, feeling uncomfortable. I pulled out my jogging shorts trying to make them look a little classier.

"Here," she said. She rummaged through her duffle and pulled out a rolled-up piece of cloth, "I was supposed to go out with my husband tonight, but one of his jobs in New Jersey burst a pipe so he's up there. You may as well wear it."

She unfurled it to reveal a hunter-blue waterfall maxi dress with the tag still on it.

"Chris has never seen it," she said when I paused.

"Thank you. At least let me buy it from you," I said checking the price tag and handing her over twenty dollars thinking that couldn't be right.

"I'll get you some change," she said.

"Don't bother, I really appreciate this," I said unsure how to get the tag off. Without saying anything Hailey grabbed it and pulled off the tag with her teeth. Then she handed it back. I tried not to stare. I put it on, and it didn't flow as freely as it would have on Hailey's short, small frame, but it came up past my knees in front and made my legs look good. When I finished examining myself, she said, "Here, sit down."

I sat in front of her, and she quickly pulled the hair at my crown up into a few knots making my hair look fuller and extremely cute.

"Thanks," I said.

"All day yesterday I saw you trying to figure out what to do with it. This is a pretty easy style that you could dance in without your hair falling in your face."

"Thanks," I said unsure if I should pay her again. I didn't want to offend her. She didn't wait for me to decide but pulled out her make-up. I examined my reflection. I looked fashionable, and ready to go out. What's more, I liked my hair for the first time since it was cut.

We were both quiet for a few minutes while she sponged the shiny out of her face. I didn't know how to bring up what I wanted to discuss. But then she asked me about money. Is this how friends talked?

Pulling out my own makeup up, I asked, "What's wrong with Chris and Jaxon. Why don't they get along?"

"Oh, that's a long story."

"Oh well." I started to back out of it, but she continued to share so I listened.

"I guess they were always competitive. When Jaxon graduated from high school and went to college, his parents retired and went to Doctors Without Borders."

"Doctors Without Borders, like the release I signed before going on *The Whole Package*?" I asked.

"Yeah, they're on the board. They helped set up the mobile team Ethan will go out on. Chris can treat mental illness, not just sports. He's a clinical psychologist with his Ph.D."

"He wasn't always in sports medicine?"

She shrugged. "Nah, and his mom feels like Uncle Brian manipulated him into it when he was sick. She wants him to leave it to Jaxon and do something to help the world."

"What would he do for Doctors Without Borders," I asked.

"The show was set up to do clinics for post-partum treatment. Chris is…he's very good at mixing meds with talk therapy. I don't know what they'll do now. The Giles made that happen for the show. We were all surprised when the show dropped Chris for another doctor."

"That was bold."

"Yeah, especially since the show reached out to recruit Chris. I think his mom did some quid pro quo," she said.

"Did Jaxon want his mom to recommend him for *The Whole Package*?"

"I don't know. I think it's more his mom wants Chris out of sports medicine and helping them in Doctors Without Borders. She says things like sports medicine is more Jaxon's speed like he couldn't handle doing anything she would consider important," she said.

"Ah, I see."

"She pressured them to put Chris on the show, so he would go out and see how rewarding it is. They never asked Jaxon."

"That's why Jaxon hates Chris."

"Not entirely. Jaxon's never been okay since his long-time college girlfriend dumped him."

"Ouch."

"No, it gets worse. After she dumped Jaxon, she asked Chris out."

"He didn't go!"

"Sort of."

"He went?" I asked, pausing in the act of putting on Drew's gift earrings.

"Yeah, he thought if…he thought they would have dinner and he could talk her into giving Jaxon another chance. Chris says he was at the dangerous phase in his psychology education, the one where he tries to fix everyone's lives whether they wanted it or not."

"I'm not sure he's ever left that phase."

"Maybe not, but Jaxon didn't see it like that. He just figured Chris was moving in on his girlfriend after they broke up."

"That couldn't have ended well."

"Yeah, it didn't help the situation. Plus, within a year Brian was diagnosed, and Jaxon couldn't process that. Jaxon kinda checked out."

"Jaxon said he went into sports medicine first and Chris copied him."

"That is putting an impressive slant on the thing, but I guess it's true."

"Jaxon always wanted to be a PT?"

"Jaxon always wanted to be his Uncle Brian. Jaxon's parents were busy all the time. They weren't really in the picture. Brian flew in just to watch Jaxon's football games, even in high school. He took Jaxon for his first drink, taught him how to work hard and play hard. They were kind of the same, I guess."

"So, the uncle really did mean for Jaxon to have his practice."

"Well, he wanted Jaxon to work with him, but it was more of a fun time kind of thing. Then Brian got sick, and everything shifted. He had Mia to think about."

"Mia isn't Madame's daughter?" I clarified.

"No, Madam was wife No. 1. Mia was wife No. 3's daughter. Right after Mia was born with her disability, she bailed."

"Jerk," I said sadly.

"Well, Brian was no saint. He cheated before Mia was born."

"Did he…did he cheat on Madam?"

"Yeah, just causing more bad blood."

"How so?"

"Madam and Chris's Mom are best friends. Madam married her best friend's older brother. Such a romantic story for a couple years. Until she realized when she went on tour he cheated."

"But if Chris is so close to her, they must have stayed friends? Did they have kids?"

"Nah, they didn't, but Brian always kind of came back to her. Madam knew he wasn't done messing around, so she never went back to him. They were close friends, especially right before he died last year. I always wondered if Brian figured out his priorities a little too late."

"That's sad," I said, lathering lotion over my arms. "So, then the uncle decided Chris would be a better guardian for Mia?"

"It was more of a matter of timing, really. Chris did a Ph.D. His program took two years longer than Jaxon's. Jaxon could have done his Doctor of Physical Therapy in three years and caught up to Chris. They would have been ready for their internships at about the same time. Jaxon played a little harder than he worked, and it took him five years to finish."

"He just stopped trying?" I asked.

"He idolized Brian. We all thought Brian would beat it. He... Chris thinks Jaxon was stalling, waiting for Brian to get better. Brian was a bench-pressing superstar before he got sick. When I was a soloist, he'd come into the theater the day of a performance, his voice booming. He lifted Madam into his arms. We all thought nothing could bring him down. When he got sick, we thought he'd beat it. The last time I saw him he was quiet, weak. Barely standing. He still brought Madam flowers. He always brought her flowers."

Unable to contain my curiosity, I asked, "I know it's not fair to say, but does it seem like Chris really did steal Jaxon's place with his uncle?"

"No. Brian offered Chris an internship if he'd specialize in sports medicine his last year of school. Brian's partner was a clinical psychologist. He was getting ready to retire. Brian grew sicker by then, and it made him comfortable when Chris moved here."

"Just for Mia's sake if nothing else," I decided.

"Yep, anyway, Chris slid right into a yearlong internship, then had a place in the practice. I mean, I guess from Jaxon's perspective he's made a ton of money from year one… but..."

"Like you said, if he was recruited, the uncle did that, not Chris," I said.

"Well, Brian bought his partner out. He meant to give Chris that half and Jaxon his half. Anyway, he and Chris worked well together. They both thrived, Brian had a great relationship with the Eagles."

"And Jaxon partied," I said. "He didn't bother to finish his schooling despite his uncle's failing health and a piece of the practice when he was done?"

"Brian couldn't wait for Jaxon, so he hired another physical therapist to train."

"But he's here. Something must have happened for him?"

"Even though Brian was so sick when Jaxon graduated, in his last few months, he worked all his contacts to build up more clientele. He tried to… I don't know. Tried to fix Jaxon. He spent his time taking Jaxon around to meet all the right people. He was so sick all his friends helped Jaxon for him."

"Did it work?"

"Yeah, for those few months anyway, Jaxon made good money."

"Then what happened?" I asked, confused, pumping my mascara, and looking at her through the mirror.

"Brian died last year. Jaxon never really…committed to the job. He wanted out all together after Brian died. He sold his part of the business to Chris, so they didn't have to work together. Chris thinks Brian's death hit Jaxon hard. He couldn't even go into work without being haunted. Apparently, that's why he drinks so much at night now."

"You don't think that?"

"I think Jaxon is an ingrate who didn't know what he had."

I laughed. I didn't know what to think of Jaxon.

"But that doesn't make sense. If Jaxon sold his half of the practice, how is he here now?"

"Last September Jaxon took off for New York fashion week, certain he could be a model. The other Physical Therapist took all his clients. And that was that."

"What happened?" I didn't pretend to put on makeup.

"Don't know. Jaxon came back a few months ago demanding his job back. He wanted Chris to give him back his half the practice. He claimed the whole practice should have been his anyway. Somehow, he genuinely thinks Chris cheated him."

"Well, if the uncle always meant to give it to Jaxon, maybe—"

"Chris is keeping the practice going. I think Brian sold the majority to Chris there at the end so Chris would always have control. Plus, Chris wiped out his savings to buy Jaxon out when he left."

"It's Chris's practice legally no matter what Jaxon says."

"Yep."

"Why did Jaxon come back then?"

"He must have spent all the money Chris gave him. He bought that stupid car and traveled to all the hot fashion spots for a while. Reading between the lines, I think everyone told him he's too old."

"Twenty-eight isn't over the hill."

"Or he couldn't control his anger and drinking."

"It's too bad he couldn't make it."

"Yeah, in the three months he's been back he's made so much trouble. He's like a ball of anger throwing himself at Chris. It's Mia we are all worried about. Jaxon is named her conservatorship, so Chris can't do anything about that. He teaches her the worst things. He's almost gotten her kicked out of her assisted living home a few times since he's come back. He thinks it's so funny. I don't think anything can be done for him. Why Chris continues to support him is beyond me."

"Yeah, that's weird," I said throwing all my stuff back in my makeup bag. I knew why. Family takes care of each other.

Chapter 34

Chris took us all to a fun little Italian restaurant named after its proprietor. We sat at a table clad in red. Ivan sat near the brick wall on one side of the table and stretched out. He put his bag down so Mia, who was growing infatuated with him, couldn't sit next to him. I maneuvered her to the opposite corner next to Hailey on one side, and I took the chair next to Ivan's bag. To my surprise Chris moved Ivan's bag and sat next to me, though there was a seat open next to Hailey.

Ivan glanced at him and scooted closer to the wall. In this interaction, I realized Ivan was barely more than a teenager. Whereas Chris, only eight or nine years older than him, seemed so mature.

Chris ordered a ton of food family style. Hailey never opened her menu expecting this. Because I held a menu, Chris asked:

"Did I miss anything you wanted, Erin?"

"I don't think you missed anything on the menu," I teased.

Hailey talked, mostly to Mia. Every time Mia talked about Jaxon's farts, or cursed, Hailey patiently told her she couldn't say things like that because she would get in trouble. This approach didn't seem to help because Mia thought the idea of being an outlaw romantic.

After a while I tried to help. Mia harbored an unnatural hero worship for me. Unfortunately, I sounded an awful lot like my mother.

"Mia," I said, "Did you know about the magical well of energy inside of you?"

"No," she said, wide eyed.

"Inside each of us is magic."

"I'm magic?" she asked.

"Yes, but every day you only have a certain amount of magic," I said.

"Yes, sometimes my magic runs out," Mia agreed.

"Do you know why?"

"Um…no."

"When you reach down and draw magic out from inside you, you have to choose where to put it. I'm afraid you have been wasting your magic, my friend," I said.

"Really?" she said looking concerned.

"Don't worry," I said. "Every day we get a new store of magic when we wake up in the morning. And daily you get to choose how you use your magic."

"Okay, okay Erin, I won't waste my magic… but wait. How do I not waste it?"

"First of all, you can share it. I think sharing your magic would be good."

"With who?"

"Maybe you could be very kind to someone, even if you didn't like them very much."

"Oh, I don't think so, Erin."

"You think about it. But remember, you never know if a fairy dressed up as an old hag."

"Oh dear," Mia said.

"I just think we need to look for the best ways to use our magic so we don't get caught by an elder wizard."

"Okay, I'll try."

When I finished my lecture, Mia thought for a few minutes then said, "Chris, I would like to paint again."

Chris grinned at her.

"That would be a great way to use your magic. Your dad always loved your paintings so much."

Mia nodded and took a huge slurp of her pasta.

While Hailey and I worked on Mia, Chris fed me. At first, I thought he wanted us all to carb load. But he was only attentive to me. He passed me some of everything, but then he waited to see me taste it. I felt like a queen at a feast. My attendant at my elbow waiting to serve me.

His curiosity to see what I liked was sweet. Invested as he was, he'd groan when I didn't care for a dish, then looked for something else I was sure to like. He knew what Mia and Hailey wanted, but I was like a new puzzle he needed to solve.

Ivan ate his weight in pasta and said little. He was exhausted.

Hailey started to see that Mia would do anything I asked.

"Mia," Hailey said, "Do you see how Erin uses her fork and spoon, so she doesn't have to slurp her pasta?"

I grinned at Hailey and exaggerated the twirling of the pasta in the spoon. Mia was occupied, twirling. Chris leaned over and said:

"Here, Erin. You didn't try the sautéed shrimp."

I took it from him and dished some up. I tasted it, then mixed it with my pasta, and out of the corner of my eye, I saw Chris do the same. I glanced at him.

"That cuts down the garlic."

When I looked over and caught him looking at me, he smiled.

His behavior toward me altered so drastically from the first time we met I thought maybe he was drunk.

"Um, bread?" he asked, handing me the basket.

"Thanks," I said laughing a little. I reached out and took the last piece, brushing my fingers against his holding the basket. I looked up at him. He kept the breadbasket where it was, so our fingers stayed connected and said, "My pleasure."

"Uh…" I stammered and disconnected. I brought the bread curled in my hand to my mouth, but the breath in my chest retreated. I set it back on the edge of my plate.

"Uh, yeah, thanks," I said again, to cover up my sudden blank mind. It felt like the electric charge between the two of us sparked again. I wanted to hold his hand. He left it on the table next to me. I could brush it again with ease. I considered a way to do it the rest of the meal but didn't. Apparently, my magic well was overdrawn.

After we ate, Mia left with Hailey. Ivan caught the bus, and Chris drove me to my hotel. He parked on the street and opened my door for me. Chris turned, leaning against the car. I turned my back to the car as well and he put his shoulder against mine. The life swirled around inside me; his touch felt like the high I got from dancing on stage.

"I love this time of night," Chris said.

Trying not to stare at his serious, soulful face watching me I answered, "It's like … like the heat gives up for a little while and the cool breeze doesn't have to try as hard."

"I like that," he said. His face was so expressive. I could analyze every line that appeared when he listened to me. He radiated empathy. I could see him as the man who took his brother in after being so foolish. The guardian of a handicapped cousin with no one else in the world. His ex-girlfriend rooted for him to find happiness. And now it seemed he was adding me to his list of people by getting me a principal role in a ballet.

"Why are you being so nice to me?" I asked.

"I… I don't want you to think I'm a jerk," he said looking at me.

"Done," I said grinning.

"I want to be your friend," he said twitching a little.

"Okay," I said. "But I don't want to be around Jaxon."

"That's fair. How's your brother doing?"

"I don't know," I said. "I hope he recovers."

"He will," Chris said. "He's got good support. When I saw him, he was studying pretty hard. Distraction is good."

"Yeah," I said. "I don't think they'll ever be friends like you and Hailey."

"It's hard not to be friends with Hailey," he said.

"That's very mature."

"It helps to be a psychologist."

"Right."

"Seriously though, the No.1 reason athletes lose their game is because of a bad breakup. May as well make it amicable if you can."

"Well, she's great, and I am sorry it didn't work out," I said unsure what else to say.

"Not me. I want a relationship like hers and Nate."

He looked sidelong at me, his mouth closed in a half smile, like he had a secret. I had no idea what to say. We were quiet for another minute. Chris said, "I think you did him some good. Jaxon, I mean."

"Really?" I asked disbelieving, resting my head against his car feeling a wave of exhaustion hit me.

"Yeah, since you called him out, he's been coming into work on time. He isn't hungover as much."

"Progress indeed."

"He's had a rough couple of years. He did not react well learning his hero had cancer."

"Not to mention you stealing his girlfriend."

"Oh, Hailey! What did she tell you?"

"She is very open."

"I was hoping to get to know you better before you found out all my terrible secrets."

He took a deep breath and shook his head. I bumped him and said:

"We all have them."

We were quiet again just leaning back and taking in the night sky.

I asked, "Is Jaxon still seeing Phoebe?"

"Not that I've seen. Jaxon stays in his room most of the time. We keep really different hours. I see him more at work than home," he said and stifled a yawn. I nodded, realizing I was keeping him and started rummaging through my duffle for my wallet.

"Hey, thanks for dinner."

"Anytime."

"Really," I said pausing to lift my eyebrows at him.

"Yep," he said. He had no fear of my over running him with requests. I laughed and pulled out my wallet.

"Good night, Chris. I really don't think you're a jerk anymore."

"Thanks, Erin."

"Hey, thanks again for tonight."

"Sure, let's do it again tomorrow night," he said.

"Yeah, that'd be nice. I'll tell Ivan, and Hailey," I said laughing.

"Maybe tomorrow night it could be just you and me," he said examining me.

I stopped. Was Chris into me?

"You're asking me out?"

"Yeah," he said his face erupting in a grin as he stepped toward me.

"You hated me a week ago."

"I never hated you."

"Yeah, you did," I said, laughing.

"I hated that Jaxon met you. I hated that he… We watched you on *The Whole Package*. Mia played like I was the judge and asked who I picked. He knew I picked you, and he…"

"That's why he came and met me," I said, "That makes sense. He never had that much to say to me. We didn't click at all and yet he kept coming around."

"Yeah, we have this history."

"Right. Hailey told me about his girlfriend."

"Oh, yeah. Well, you understand why he went to…"

"Turnabout and all that."

"Yeah. I didn't even realize I was in sour grapes mode until you called me a jerk. I'm sorry I was being such a jerk," he said.

"It's okay."

"Jaxon exaggerated his relationship with you to make me jealous, and I reacted," Chris said.

I shyly examined the gorgeous man in front of me. He had a crush on me. Before he even met me, he had a crush on me. I found that adorable.

"You want to go out tomorrow night?" he asked.

"Will that cause problems between you and Jaxon?"

"No more than we already have. Besides, he must know I'm going to try," he said grinning again.

"Okay," I said grinning back.

Chris leaned in and kissed my cheek. My heart dropped into my stomach as he waved and turned to leave. I wanted to sit and watch him but forced myself to turn and walk into the hotel. I could not suppress the grin I wore to bed.

Chris and I had dinner again, but it was an early night. I almost fell asleep at the table. I couldn't physically do more. He promised we would go out and do something fun once the show ended, then took me back to my hotel. He walked me to my room, and leaned in, giving me a soft tantalizing kiss goodnight, and I thought maybe I believed in my mom's magic well again. That must be what tingled inside me.

Chapter 35

Drew drove all the way to Philadelphia the night before my first performance. He came to my hotel suite and sat in a wintery cobalt blue love seat that looked out over Independence Hall. Though the Hall was lit up, I couldn't be sure if he saw it or his own refection in the window. He seemed far away and reserved. At first, he sat so quietly I couldn't understand why he came. Except to make me dislike Phoebe even more if possible.

"How was taking the bar?" I asked.

"I can't even wrap my head around it right now. It's over. Hopefully, I passed," he said. He went quiet again. I couldn't tell if he was decompressing, or what.

"You okay?" I asked, watching him sit there.

"Oh, right, I have to show you something," he said. I sat next to him, and he pulled out his phone. A message from Phoebe was on it. She wrote that she missed him so much, and she was done sowing her wild oats. Now they could be together.

"That's some pretty impressive self-talk," I said.

"A few hours after I left the convention center, she started sending those texts. I don't even know what to text back," he said.

"You may want to block her," I said pulling the throw pillow out from behind me to hug.

"I don't know. We have so much history to throw it all away. Should I just…"

"Drew, have you ever cheated on her?" I asked.

"Lately I've been so busy studying. Sometimes she… you know she gets nervous when I can't give her enough attention. She lashes out."

"Did you cheat?" I asked again.

"I made friends with this girl in my study group. Phoebe said she could feel me drifting. I probably was." He stared out the window again.

"Did you call this girl from your study group for anything besides studying?" I asked.

"No, no. I just really like her," Drew said turning from his reflection in the window to look at me.

"But you were still faithful to Phoebe."

"Well yeah, but I understand being curious about other people."

"Right, so date. Find a girl who will be faithful to you. Someone you get along with. You're so young, especially compared to her. Phoebe was always trying to dress you and make you into Jaxon. You don't want to be Jaxon," I said.

"No, that's for sure," he said. He looked so worn down.

"Take out the girl from your study group, I'm sure you can find her number."

"Just because I took the bar doesn't mean I deleted her out of my phone."

"There you go," I said excitedly.

"Yeah, maybe I should," he said perking up a little.

"What's her name?

"Isla, she's so warm and yet ambitious. She's becoming an attorney to fix her family's charitable foundation. She's so feisty when she talks about it," Drew said.

"All righty then," I said smiling at him.

"All right."

"In fact, Chris, Jaxon's perfect brother, is taking me out tomorrow night after the show. Why don't you ask Isla to the show then we'll all have dinner after," I said.

"Okay, yeah, that's a good idea."

I watched him think about this. I thought I might hint I really needed a good night's sleep, but then Drew shook his head.

"That isn't why I came," he said opening his phone again.

"What?" I asked.

"Have you seen this?" he asked scrolling through YouTube. He found something and held his phone out turning it up so I could see and hear a video.

Music played and it showed me. It was an artistically created short of me dancing in the elimination room on *The Whole Package*. It showed blips of contestants yelling at me, the chaos of the reality show, then me dancing. I remember the shot of Serena interrupting my dancing to howl at me for something I hadn't done. Serena's voice was blurred out as if nothing could touch me while I danced. I found Colby's take on my morning exercise strangely arresting.

"Did you know they were filming you?" Drew asked after it ended.

"Yeah, he did it for his degree, his videography class or something. I told dad about it."

"Oh, so at least he had permission," Drew said.

"I didn't realize he'd put it on YouTube, but it's well done. Look it's gotten over… Wow is that a million views?"

"And climbing. We looked at your contract. You don't have any way of having it pulled offline," Drew said. "The network would have to do that. Dad and I will look into it if you want."

"I don't see any harm in it. Do you?" I asked.

"No," he paused. "Dad," and I could tell they were disagreeing, "thinks it's great publicity. He's sharing it on your blog, and your professional social media. Does it embarrass you? Serena really goes after you a few times. I thought she was so nice."

"Nah, she wasn't. But I feel sorry for her in a lot of ways. She grew up in the system. She's…," I stopped. Drew didn't seem to notice. Phoebe was in the system for two years after her father was sent to prison. It made me extremely uncomfortable to think about.

"Why did she keep yelling at you?" he asked.

"She accused me of stealing one of her breakfast shakes. Tess did. She thought it was funny to provoke her. Serena knew I didn't do it, but she was trying to get me to tell on Tess, so she had proof to give Julian. But at the end there, right before she stomped off, I pointed out that Julian had cameras everywhere and already knew. "See – that's when she glowers at me and stomps away," I said.

"Are you all right, Erin?"

"I don't know, but I love *The Dream*. I love this performance. I can't wait for you to see it. Bring Isla with you tomorrow night. I can't wait to meet her," I said.

"I don't know. I'll think about it."

"Okay."

"If you really don't care, I will make sure everyone who views this knows about your performance. Dad's so old school. Here, open up your computer."

"Kay," I said giving him access. He pulled out the "just in case," credit card and started opening windows on my laptop. When he finished, he had created a pop-up ad. Everyone who watched Colby's video would see a link for tickets to *The Dream*. It instantly started getting likes.

"Thanks, Drew," I said, watching it climb.

“Sure,” he grinned.

“You want to sleep in the spare bed?”

“Nah.”

“You drove all this way.”

“I know. I can’t be at home right now. I’m kind of buzzing, post-test nervous energy and all that. I’m going to get food, and you really need to go to sleep,” he said.

I nodded but couldn’t help watching the likes for my video climb.

“I guess this is what it means when something goes viral.”

“Yeah.”

We watched it blow up for another fifteen minutes. He left in better spirits. I hoped for him with all my heart.

Chapter 36

The Dream opened on a hot and muggy evening. I warmed up with Ivan. He made so much progress in only a week I wanted to get him an audition for American. His leaps alone were so high, it made the floor shake when he landed. We sat in the warmup room full of mirrors stretching with the other dancers, all in costume.

My hair slicked back in a little bob of a bun; the prop mistress dug a long wig into my scalp. I cleared my throat trying not to groan. She nodded to me and then crowned me the fairy queen with a ring of flowers. A loose curling ponytail fell halfway down the gauze covering my back. The hair fell over my shoulder as I stretched, and I almost looked like myself again. I missed the feeling of my hair. I never realized how much of my identity was tied to it.

"Erin, these came for you," said Hailey, who worked as Madam's assistant until she healed. I stood and she handed me a box of crimson roses cradled in baby's breath. I smiled thinking they may be from Chris. In the two days since I'd seen him, I started imagining what would have happened if I didn't let him leave when he kissed me. I felt extremely eager to go out with him again.

"Who are they from?" Hailey asked, and her smile told me she thought they were from Chris as well.

I dug through the tissue paper and opened the card. I almost dropped the roses.

"What is it?" Hailey asked.

"To the girl who knows how to be the Prima in her own life. Good luck. Jaxon."

"No way," Hailey said pulling the card from my hand.

"Did I miss something?" I asked.

"I don't know," she said, "but everything he does is a hundred percent selfish. Don't let him in your head."

"Okay, okay." I handed her back the flowers. "I can't think about this now. Give these to … Ivan."

Ivan looked up and laughed. Hailey took them and said she would take care of them. I doubted I would see them again. I went over the steps in my solo a few times, it being the most complicated of the show.

"Hey, Erin," Hailey said coming back in the warmup room.

"What's up?" I asked, standing with my leg lying flat against the wall.

"Your brother wanted to see you. Said it was urgent."

"Where is he?" I asked.

"Stagehand wouldn't let him back, and the auditorium is filling," she said.

"Oh, he probably wanted to confirm or decline for after the show. I'm not going to worry about it now, I'll connect with him after."

"Okay."

"On second thought, maybe I'll just check my phone," I said shoving on my warmup boots, I quickly went to the dressing room I shared with Hailey. I didn't have a message from Drew, but Mom left a text saying,

"Noel called; she's coming to see you tonight. I know you will be amazing! Love you!"

I didn't know what to think of this, any more than I knew what to think of Jaxon, so I just didn't. I made it back to the warmup room, wishing I hadn't left. I moved to the barre, clearing my head of all thought. I rested my stomach on my leg and examined the tulle on my costume.

Iridescent like a dragonfly's wings, the tulle glimmered from a shamrock color to violet. Small flecks of silver woven into my costume would glitter in the stage lights. I raised my hand in a soft elegant arm movement to see the shimmer of the glitter that covered me in magic. I closed my eyes and saw myself as the fairy queen taking every step perfectly. Chris, with his intense eyes, would be watching me.

A few minutes before the curtain went up, Madam scooted in to give us all a pep talk. Her words were positive and glowing.

And when my turn to take center stage came, I glowed.

I entered stage left as Tatiana with my little Indian changeling boy, my godson, to applause. My performance echoed generations of dancers immortalized by the fairy queen defending the child in the magic of the enchanted forest. The gnarly old tree built on the stage held my little hollow bed and glimmered with flecks of fairy dust. The stage was backlit by the glow of the moon. The outline of distant trees made up the forest.

I mingled my own choreography with Ashton's, the original choreographer, and felt something more than satisfaction at the reception of my solo. Usually, it is Tatiana who is humbled through trickery. With my solo, I mourned as I gave the changeling boy to Oberon, the king of the Fairies. After the tricks he pulled on me, I liked that he had to see my sorrow as I allowed my godson to be his attendant. I gave up the boy's childhood to a fulfilling future.

Every audience has a spirit. This unseen energy surges. In thousands of quivering surges of awe and enjoyment, sorrow and delight the audience encourages the performer to tell their story. The spirit of this audience connected with me and I with them. The swells of emotion drew in and out like the ocean current until the audience and I were one. I danced for the love of dancing just as Madam suggested, and the audience gave me as much of themselves as I gave them of me. We had the perfect opening night.

I loved finishing the show well. The exuberance I felt after performing sent me into a state of euphoria, as if I flew inside of myself, or I somehow made my own glow. I was warmed from the inside out. Chasing this feeling always pushed me forward.

After the show ended, we went out to the lobby to sign autographs in our costumes. Apparently, it brought in money for the show. I stood next to Ivan thronged by admirers for over half an hour. Showered with attention I still noticed Chris hanging back. He wore slacks with an open neck button down shirt. There was nothing so attractive as a man I really liked holding a single white lily for me.

I glanced at him often and that feeling of flying inside myself only increased. I'd only ever felt the feeling on stage, so it confused me. How did Chris make me glow from the inside?

It would have been my perfect night except for two incidents. As the crowd began to die down, I realized my parents were waiting for me over near the bar. I excused myself and went to kiss my dad. I stopped mid-stride. My breath went out of me as if I'd been sucker punched.

Drew stood with an arm around Phoebe sitting on a bar stool. I stammered; unsure I could talk.

"Hey, look we are starting over," Drew said happily, squeezing Phoebe.

"I just realized how much he means to me," Phoebe said playing with his collar and looking into Drew's eyes.

"Um hum," I said looking to my parents. My dad's eyes blazed, and his jaw twitched. Mom's smile was genuine, she put a supportive hand on Phoebe's shoulder. Phoebe smiled at her. This infuriated me.

I hated Phoebe. I hated her for ruining my night. My first night in a principal role, and she sat making kissy face at my brother. She made my parents' pride in my performance secondary to their concern for Drew. I felt like she took something from me.

"Hey," Chris said lightly, touching my arm from behind. I leaned back into his warm electric touch.

"Hey," I said, "uh… this is my dad, Andrew. You know Mom."

Chris put a hand to Dad, and they shook, then he leaned in, and Mom kissed his cheek.

"It's so good to see you again, Megan."

"You know Drew and Phoebe," I said gagging over her name. Chris started in surprise. He gave a noncommittal head nod to Drew and glanced at me, to see if I was okay, instead of Phoebe. Phoebe pretended not to notice and leaned over to whisper something that made Drew smile. Clearly, she didn't need to acknowledge the brother of the man she cheated with. I watched her dumbfounded. Dad tried to turn me away from staring. He said:

"I need you to focus, Honey."

I was in a daze unsure what to think or say. Dad patted my shoulder blade.

"Erin, focus, Noel Landry is here. You just missed her. She went to congratulate, Madam…"

"Friel," I filled in for Dad still staring at Phoebe and Drew.

"Right," Dad said, glancing at Phoebe over his shoulder. He finished, "Perhaps you can go look for Noel, allow her to congratulate you away from –"

"Erin, I can't wait to go out tonight, we are going to be best friends. I want you to be my maid of honor," Phoebe said loudly, talking over my dad trying to salvage my career.

"No," I said stubbornly. I turned back to my dad, to hear what I should do about Noel, but he and everyone else stopped.

"But…" she stammered. Phoebe was so used to receiving a full fellowship from my family as soon as she graced our space again. I couldn't do it. I wouldn't pretend she wasn't ruining my brother's life.

"Erin, look, I told you." Drew started to defend her. Trying to fight the tears in my eyes I interrupted:

"Drew, you know I love you, but I can't…I can't watch this unfold again. I can't be around you right now. You're right Dad. I'd rather talk to Noel away from the group. I'll go find her."

I felt the tears start and so I ran across the lobby, through a heavy door, and down the hall where only dancers were allowed, knowing none of them could follow me. I didn't know where else to go, so I headed back to the stage. The one place it was safe to show my sorrow. Before I could make it to the stage, I felt someone grab my hand. I turned to find Chris. I forgot no one would stop him from following me.

He didn't say anything, he just pulled me through a door where it was quiet and dark. He curled me into a hug. I buried my face in his neck. He smelled so good, and I didn't hate him. I shook and hated all the users, all the people who hurt me, and Drew. Oh Drew. What was the matter with him?

"I'm sorry…I don't know why I'm being such a baby," I sobbed growing embarrassed.

"Get it all out Erin. You can't face the Creative Director of the American Ballet like this," he whispered, stroking my neck with his thumb.

"I feel so…" I started. I didn't finish. I felt so betrayed by Phoebe but also by Drew and Mom. I felt so close to Chris. I wouldn't want anyone else holding me.

Chapter 37

After I calmed down, I realized Chris pulled me down into the orchestra pit. The pit, on a hydraulic lift, wasn't as high as the audience seating, but neither was it deep into the recesses under the stage as before.

My head sat at about the level of the audience's front row. Chairs in the pit were set up in a pecking order, each chair indicated how many hours of time someone took to master their music. The pit smelled like that effort; the conductor did not allow perfume, nor cologne.

I leaned into Chris again, so I didn't smell the pit stench. Chris and I stood close to a huge drum set. He loosened his hold with his arm, and his hand ran across my misshapen back, covered only by delicate gauze until it found my rib cage. His other hand brushed my face with his fingertips, almost like he might want to kiss me. I closed my eyes, trusting him, wanting him to. His warm breath mingled in my space.

My eyes flipped open. I flinched, pulling away.

"You put on a fine show," Noel said, her theatrical condescending voice amplified by the perfect acoustics of the stage almost directly above us.

"Yes, our humble little corner of the performing arts did quite well tonight," Madam Friel said sarcastically. The Philadelphia Ballet wasn't exactly the middle of nowhere, fly-all-your-principal-dancers-from-big-city's-second-casts-for-the-nutcracker-small.

The two vastly different voices – voices that taught me – conversed about the show. But the voices didn't belong together. I pushed Chris back into the shadows. He looked very confused.

"Erin…" Chris started, but I threw a finger to my mouth and said, "Shhh."

He mouthed, "What?" bewildered, but I pushed him back further against the wall so we wouldn't be seen and pointed upward. I listened hard. The next thing I heard was Noel say, "Erin is classically trained. I told you from the beginning you can push her back in shape, but you can't expect her to be satisfied with this little show of yours. She is meant to grace the stages of royalty and true critics alike."

"If that is so, why isn't she touring with you this fall?" Madam asked.

"Who said she isn't?" Noel asked.

"I didn't press her as you asked me not to, but she told my assistant she lost her place with you over a haircut," Madam said.

"I never said that. I don't even know why she thinks that," Noel said.

My mom was right. Eavesdropping wasn't the best way to get information. I still listened when Madam said, "Noel, what is it you are after from the girl?"

"I'm letting her sweat it out. She knew the rules and she broke them. It's as simple as that."

"Perhaps," Madam said, "or perhaps it has something to do with the substantial donation her father has already given to make this show a success."

"Well, his donations can't hurt," Noel said.

"Come now, what are you really after? Erin should be the principal dancer. She's better than Natalia, who by the by, needs to retire," Madam said.

"Erin is young, when she gets there, she will have her chance," Noel snapped.

"In terms of her dance career, twenty-five isn't that young, especially considering her back. But I suppose Natalia fills the seats," Madam said, as if that's really what Noel meant.

"Natalia has a very loyal following," Noel agreed.

"But that doesn't explain why Erin isn't in a principal role. Your audiences should be learning to love her."

"Natalia threatened to quit if I promote Erin," Noel said, "I can't seem to get Erin transitioned and Natalia out. If she had only won that stupid show, Erin would have brought in her own crowd. The other board members would have no choice but bring her up. As it is, I can only promote her this fall if I can get her father to sponsor this little Russian dancer the board has their eye on."

"Oh please!" Madam exclaimed, "Your board members are all silent and trust you implicitly. You cannot pretend there is any opinion that matters but yours."

"Yes. Well, I have Natalia, then Erin will take her place, and then I need a little Russian Dancer to be ready when Erin retires…or if she injures herself…It leaves us so vulnerable. I must protect the company first," Noel said peevishly.

"That does make more sense," Madam said. "Natalia needs to retire, but refuses. Erin should be in a principal role if she's to take her place. That is a tough spot."

"Oh, Erin will take her place," Noel said. "You cannot be so naive as to believe that you can keep her. I appreciate you pushing her back into shape. But understand, I made her. I have guided her career for years. She is mine. Your little show was impressive, her solo was beautifully choregraphed, and could have graced my stage – "

"She did that herself," Madam said.

"Really," Noel answered. "It gave the show more depth for Oberon to have to see the pain it caused Tatiana to hand over the boy."

"I agree. Siphons out some of the misogynism," Madam said.

"I knew she had it in her eventually, but I didn't realize she was so far advanced. Perhaps next summer I will put her in my incubator program instead of sending her on vacation. If you break her in this little endeavor of yours…"

Though I held my breath, I could not hear anything else being said. I let my breath out and realized I was clinging to Chris' collar, and he was still holding me. I let go of him moving back a little.

"I'm good," I stammered with little breath.

"You're okay now," he said confused, still reaching for me.

"No, I mean, I'm good enough," I stammered yanking out the hair piece and shaking it as if it were the hair Julian cut from my head.

"She doesn't want me to know I'm good enough, all so she can get my father's monetary support of another dancer?" I asked Chris to confirm what I heard. My last bout of eavesdropping hadn't gone so well for me.

"That's what it sounded like," Chris said searching my eyes.

"I'm a good dancer," I said looking up into the stage rafters, the tears welling around my eyes.

"Maybe the best I've ever seen," he said pushing the wispy stray hairs out of my face, "I can't really understand how you would doubt it."

"I lost something on *The Whole Package*…I did not realize how quickly I could lose my…magic," I said laughing a little.

"Your dancing was powerful tonight," Chris said grinning at me.

"My dad said I was good enough, but there was a game being played. I didn't believe him. I thought he bought my way onto American, and he was trying to do it again. But he didn't. I work harder than the other dancers, and… I am good enough," I said emphatically.

"Yeah, there's always an underlying game being played in professional sports," Chris said.

We were quiet for a minute.

"Do you want to…" Chris didn't know what to say. He examined my face. I thought maybe he wanted to kiss me still, but my head had deserted the pit and was following Noel through the theater.

"I need your help."

"Anything," he said grinning down at me.

"I am going to go get dressed. Turns out I don't need to go look for Noel, she will come to me. After I speak to her, I need you to get me out of here. I can't deal with Drew right now. My mom's going to go full court press on me. I need…I need to think," I implored, looking at him.

"Okay I can do that," he said. I went up on my toes and kissed his cheek hoping he knew I wasn't rejecting him. He grinned at me, easily placated, then turned to the door, and let me go.

Chapter 38

I ran to the locker room, squeezed out of my costume and showered.

I changed into my favorite shimmering black cocktail gown. I looked at myself in the mirror. The sparkling boat-neck top without sleeves and mid-length gauzy skirt may as well have been a costume I could wear on stage. Serena would tell me I should at least try not to always look like a ballerina. Before the reality show I loved my style. I – was this just me and I needed to be okay with myself somehow?

I put on the earrings Drew gave me and examined myself. That girl in the mirror, what happened to her? She used to be confident and eager to fight for what she wanted most. The girl I once was, knew how talented she was. How did I get her back?

"Chris is waiting for you," Hailey said startling me.

"Oh right, Thanks," I said grinning at her, and I hurried out of the women's locker room.

"Are you ready?" I asked Chris. He stammered and couldn't stop looking at me. He liked the way I looked. Then I liked the way I looked. How did I like the way I looked without needing him to approve of it? Or did he just like me, and whatever style I liked he liked? I shook my head. I would think about this later. I had to be the strongest version of myself right now.

Chris asked, "You okay?" as we walked up the long hallway that spanned the theater.

"I don't know."

"We could slip out a side door, leave before they see us," he invited, looking at me again.

"Nope, I'm facing Noel right now. I like how I look. I just killed my performance and now, I'm going to…"

I stopped. I turned to Chris.

"What am I going to do?"

"What do you want?" he asked, tilting his head to look at me. I wanted him; he was… no. What did I want?

"I don't know." I felt so backward.

"May I make a suggestion?"

"Sure, shrink."

"Embrace your success before you go out there. Don't be the person who sees their dreams coming to fruition and run away. Do not downplay what you've done here. Now, with that in mind, what do you want?" he asked.

"I want Noel to eat her stupid head nods when I dance sufficiently," I said. "I want her to acknowledge I did a good job tonight."

"I bet you I can make her acknowledge your performance," he said quickly. He looked suspicious.

"How?"

"Do we have a bet?"

"What's on the line?"

"I get to order your dinner for you, and you have to eat whatever I order."

"Okay, but you can't lie. Just by your powers as a therapist, you have to get her to acknowledge I was good."

"That's all you want?"

"For now, but I have dreams," I said leaning in and smelling him.

"You want your place back at American?"

"I want the prima ballerina assoluta title," I said feeling the tears grow in my eyes. I wanted it so badly.

"Even I know that's a title bestowed upon you. Do you know anyone from the Royal Theater in London or the Kirov perhaps?"

"Not yet."

"Well, if a queen gives you the title, it's yours."

"I won't get the title until I tour as the top principal for American. Tonight was so much fun, but I owe it to myself – to that little girl who pushed through agonizing dance classes, to the teenager who gave up sit-down dinners to stretch and strength train, to the woman who degraded herself on a reality show for a little bit of fame. I owe it to them to keep pushing."

Chris grinned at me.

"What?"

"I work with a lot of professional athletes. There is something similar in the drive you show. It's contagious. I admire all your hard work," he said.

"I don't know it's just…" I flushed, unable to say what it meant to me to see my dream within my grasp.

"Let's start with tonight then. Our goal is to get Noel to acknowledge you're an amazing dancer," Chris said with a grin when I couldn't finish.

"I like it when you smile at me," I said out of nowhere.

"Good, let's smile together and I'll hold your hand. Is that all right?" he asked, reaching his hand out to me in the most adorable way. I took it.

"I don't want Drew to feel bad, but I can't stand Phoebe," I said as we walked slowly along the high traffic maroon carpet. Now that I knew Noel would wait for me.

"That's fine. You're setting a boundary," he said squeezing my hand he held.

"I love my brother," I said. "I can't stand to see her hurt him."

"Okay, so you see your brother without his girlfriend. That's okay."

"Mom doesn't want me to be mean to her, but sometimes I can't help it," I said glancing up at him.

"Why don't you honor your mom by not degrading Phoebe, and honor yourself by not being around her," Chris suggested.

"How do you stay so calm with Jaxon?" I asked.

"It's not the same. I taught Jaxon how to ride a bike so he could keep up with me and the neighborhood boys. I read to him at night to help him sleep when my parents worked late."

"Yeah, being a part of where he's coming from helps," I said.

"Could you try to see where Phoebe's coming from and forgive her?"

"Easier said than done, but I will try."

"At least try to be kind to her, so she doesn't change who you are. You are a truly kind person," he said.

"Am I?" I asked, unsure I even knew myself anymore.

"You're so quick to take care of Mia. I see through people fast when they interact with her. The worst thing Phoebe could take from you is that kindness" he said.

"She had a rough childhood. I get it, but I don't want to watch her hurt my brother anymore," I said.

"There's a difference between forgiving someone, letting go of the pain they caused you, versus inviting them to continue to do it in your life," Chris said.

"I guess." I reached up, touching my earrings, "but for me, I think it's harder to forgive someone who hurt my little brother than myself."

"That is because you're sweet," Chris said, his gorgeous face breaking out in a grin. I loved having someone to strategize with. I hoped Chris wanted to be my boyfriend.

Chapter 39

Stragglers drank and talked about politics. My parents and Noel sat with drinks, while Madam stood aloof, waiting. Thankfully, Drew and Pheobe were nowhere to be seen so I could do this, one step at a time.

"Erin, you…" Mom stammered seeing I'd taken the time to change.

"Hey," I said kissing her to cut her off before she could lecture me.

"You were amazing, darling girl," Dad said moving between Chris and I to kiss me. Chris let go of my hand. Dad looked at me with a probing look. He was trying to read me. I winked at him. He looked baffled.

"Noel," I said condescendingly offering her my hand, "So good of you to come to our performance. I know PDC is a bit smaller than you're used to, but I hope you enjoyed the show."

"It was not what I'm accustomed to, nor is it, I would think, up to your standards," she said snidely.

"Sometimes we must accept our level in this life. I am thankful Madam accepted me," I said bowing piously to her. "After all, I must dance, despite my limitations."

"Well, I did tell your father you may come teach some of my younger dancers this fall," Noel said.

"Thank you, that would be an honor, but here I am helping my partner, Ivan. He is making great progress, I think," I said looking to Madam.

"He is moving along by leaps and bounds," Madam replied. She used her hand dramatically to gesture a leap.

"Yes, his talent may be wasted here along with yours," Noel said.

"Wasted here? I am teaching and dancing a principal role. I can see you mean to check up on me, and I thank you for it. I will always be proud I danced with you at American for as long as I did," I smiled and curtsied to her as if her most respectful student. I glanced at Dad. He worked hard to repress a smile.

"Perhaps you and your new partner can come do a few master classes with us next week. If he can find a sponsor," she said looking to my father.

"I would be honored to support him. He is only twenty, and has a long career ahead of him," Dad said.

"He really may have untapped raw talent," Noel said looking interested at a banner with Ivan and myself on it.

"Oh, he does," I said. "He doesn't have to work half as hard as I do to pick up his steps. Did you see how high his jumps were? He can jump over many of the shorter dancers."

"Also, it may interest you to know Erin is a YouTube star," Dad said, "Some footage of her dancing on the reality show has gone viral."

"I suppose since you're building a fan base and your fouetté has improved so drastically," she said standing, "I will see both of you at the theater in New York the Monday morning after your show ends. You know what time we start. On time is late, and the tardy may as well not show up."

"Thank you, Noel," I said, bowing my head.

Noel turned to leave. I was satisfied. My father hadn't dropped a dime for my replacement, and I'd gotten both myself and Ivan into fall training. Chris was not satisfied.

"Ms. Landry," he said. She turned, looking at him as if he had no right to say her name.

"I'm Chris Giles. Madam is my aunt," he gestured.

"Yes," she said, lifting her eyebrow at him.

"The reviewer Mark Talbot from the Washington Post – he's an old friend. As a personal favor I asked him to come see the show. Even now he's writing up his piece on the performance. He and I argued that Erin's solo this evening may have been good enough to be incorporated into *The Dream* by other companies to give the ballet depth. You are the professional here. What is your opinion?" Chris asked.

Noel clenched her jaw. I needed the publicity, but she needed me to be humble. I could see her internal battle.

"It was very well done. It is one of the finest solo performances I have ever seen. Talbot may quote me on that," Noel said, disgruntled.

"Thank you," I said, curtsying again. She waved me off and quickly left. When she was out of sight I smirked at Chris. He lifted his hand for a fist bump, and I realized he was super awkward. I laughed and lifted my fist to him.

"That was surreal, but we agreed, no lying," I said.

"I did not lie, I'm texting Mark right now," Chris said pulling out his phone and turning from our group.

"What's going on?" Dad asked, watching us.

"Chris bet me he could get Noel to admit how good my performance was. I didn't know he had a reviewer in his pocket," I said.

"I can't even figure out what happened," Dad said.

"One minute she is extorting us and now this? Did she mean for Erin to –" Mom stammered trying to figure it out.

"She wants you to sponsor a Russian ballerina for Erin to train," Madame informed.

"Why didn't she say something?" Dad asked.

"I supposed there is no grace in outright saying something. One must finagle," Madam said. Dad relaxed a little and smiled as if he understood this. I was starting to learn. Chris put his phone back in his pocket and rejoined the group.

"Thank you for inviting your friend," Dad said, reaching a hand to Chris.

"My pleasure," Chris said looking Dad in the eye and giving his hand a firm shake.

"Now that matter is cleared up, on to the next," Mom said eyeing me, "Drew and Phoebe are getting us a table at Rittenhouse and I expect you to be civil."

"I can't," I said, turning to plead with Dad, "I saw her climbing out of another man's bed. I can't even stomach her. The sight of her literally makes me sick."

My parents looked at each other.

"Erin did already agree to spend this evening with me," Chris said politely.

"Oh well, if you already have plans, Erin, we will give your brother your regrets," Dad said firmly to Mom, then nodded to Chris.

"Fine," Mom relinquished, as she only did for Dad when he pushed her to give me a break.

"We'll see you later," Dad said, and he kissed me. He seemed to find something in Chris he liked because he gave him a friendly head nod, and turned to close out his tab.

"Erin, shall we?" Chris asked holding his elbow out to me.

"Thanks," I whispered, and took the arm Chris offered.

"Erin, darling," Madam said standing from her bar stool to stop me.

"Yes," I said trying not to cry.

"You were incredibly good tonight," she said, glancing at Mom, annoyed.

"Oh, I guess," I said feeling drained.

"I'm proud of you. Let all this sluff off. Take your moment in the sun. Be proud of yourself and enjoy your success. Tonight, you were a star," she said kissing my cheek.

Mom looked chagrined trying to agree with her when she realized the euphoria I lost. The glow I should be basking in over the first lead role I ever danced as a professional dancer was gone. I tried my best to smile for the folks, but quickly moved away with Chris who took my hand and told me I really was amazing.

Chapter 40

"What are we doing tonight?" I asked as we walked the block to where he parked.

"Oh right," Chris said pulling out his phone. He called The Rittenhouse and canceled his reservation.

"Well, that would have been awkward," I said.

"Yeah," he said, laughing. His eyes crinkled at the edges when he laughed, and it made him look more human. Sometimes when I looked at him, and remembered he had a crush on me, it felt impossible, but when his eyes crinkled like that everything felt right.

"We can just go back to my hotel. They have a great little restaurant," I offered, nibbling my lip.

"I actually have an idea if you are game," he said.

"Okay but I have to be asleep in two hours tops," I said following him to his car. He drove to a grocery store and bought French cheeses and fresh herbs that he smelled before he put them in a bag. Then we drove to his condo.

"Won't this be weird with Jaxon?"

"It's Thursday night. Ladies drink for half price at his favorite club. He won't be home."

"He didn't want to hang out with Mia and watch *The Whole Package* tonight?"

"He would if I still watched it. He just liked to make sure I remembered being dumped."

We climbed out of the car, and I asked, "If he's so bitter why does he live with you? Did you buy the condo from your uncle together?"

"No, it comes with the conservatorship for Mia. Jaxon just… he has nowhere else to go. I would move out, but I'm uncomfortable getting too far from her. Especially with him so close."

"Jaxon is highly educated and has a job. He must have other places to go," I said pulling myself out of the car. The parking garage shared the same plaza as the nursing home, the condo and a healthcare clinic.

Through a fountain in the center of the plaza, I could see Mia's building. I felt guilty for walking past without stopping by. I wanted to be alone with Chris. He didn't seem inclined to go get her, as he glanced at her building.

As we walked, Chris said, "Jaxon can't hold onto his money. He has a sickness. My parents just gave him whatever he wanted when he wanted it, and he thinks that's real life. Plus, he … you were right when you said he doesn't really know who he is. My parents have this mission to save the world, but kind of forgot about their own kid."

"So, you try to help him," I said stepping into his building.

"Yeah, but he hates me so I can't do much," he said stepping into the elevator that an older couple had just stepped out of.

I grabbed the handrail as the elevator shot upward, reminding me my legs needed to be stretched. When we stepped out of the elevator, I asked:

"Your parents want him to succeed though, right?"

"We both pulled good grades, we were both all-state football stars. We both got scholarships to UB. They paid for both our graduate degrees. What is success really? It's what their parents did for them."

"They didn't notice your competitive tension?" I asked as Chris unlocked the condo, juggling his bag of groceries he wouldn't let me hold for him.

"They created it," he said.

"Do you mind if I stretch?"

"No, please do," he said.

I used a bar stool as leverage to stretch while Chris unloaded his groceries on the bar.

"What do you mean by they created the tension between you too?" I asked.

"The first vivid memory I have is the summer before Jaxon started kindergarten. My mom wanted Jaxon to read after she read statistics on illiteracy within the school systems. He wouldn't sit still, even though she bribed him with a bike. Finally, annoyed, she said something like Chris could read when he went to kindergarten, and you will be so embarrassed if you can't. It worked. Jaxon applied himself and he could read before kindergarten."

"I see, but he could read, I mean that's good right," I asked.

"If only it stopped there. After that, every time she wanted him to do something, and she couldn't bribe him, she used the-Chris-does-it card. He'd hate me for a while, but then my parents would get busy at work. It didn't take long for him to become my little buddy again. All through elementary school, I took him everywhere I went –friend's houses, football practice. I hated leaving him with the nanny."

"You guys were friends growing up?"

"Until Jaxon fell behind or got in trouble. Then my parents got involved in our lives again. Jaxon hated me for doing everything before him, or for not getting in trouble. Back then all I had to do was ignore him for a day and he'd come running back to go wherever I was going."

"That had to be hard."

"It wasn't all the time. We had a lot of fun. In middle school and high school, we trained together. We had all the same friends. We were brothers," Chris said, putting a pan on the stove. He made a rue, then threw in his cheeses with some white wine. Finally, after thinking, he said: "I doubt either of us would be as good at football as we were if we hadn't worked out with each other."

"Is that why you decided to be a psychologist?" I asked, putting the stool behind us, and propping my leg up.

"I am what you would call a fixer. I didn't have much direction for it until junior year in high school. I injured my ankle and started to think maybe I didn't want to play football anymore. My dad had me into a therapist so fast," he said.

"Did you really want to keep playing, or did he talk you into it?" I asked.

"I was tired of football being my whole life. I enjoyed it, but my life felt lacking. Junior year I learned how to budget my time better."

"The therapist helped then?" I asked.

"Yeah. I was always expected to get good grades. I studied and played football. Jim, the therapist, was my first real mentor. My parents are good people. They really were just trying their best. They have a mission to save the world.

"Jim taught me how to arrange everything so football was only a part of my life, not my whole life. It was something new."

"Yeah, it might have been nice to have someone help me have more of a balance," I said, switching legs.

"I wanted Jaxon to meet with him, but my dad couldn't understand why. Jaxon wasn't injured."

"Not that he could see, anyway."

"Well, and it was like building a house of resentment. Jaxon had the foundation to hate me, but it wasn't this bad until Rhonda left him and asked me out. That's when things between us just snapped. I kept trying to get him to be my friend again, but, well, you've seen how we are now."

"Hailey said he started partying instead of finishing his degree."

"That was more when Brian was diagnosed. Jaxon didn't really spiral after Rhonda left him. He just hated my guts. Rhonda was really bossy, always telling him what to do. When she left and he hated me, he only had Brian to look to for direction. When Brian took a turn for the worse Jaxon just kind of checked out."

"Did you like Rhonda?" I asked, feeling a little jealous.

"Rhonda and I were friends first. I talked about asking her out a few times. Jaxon asked her out first to one up me."

"Like how he came and met me?"

"Yeah, but they ended up dating for a long time through college. Jaxon knew how to have fun and I didn't. But when they graduated, Rhonda didn't explain; she dumped him. She told mutual friends of ours that she didn't want the copy anymore but the real thing, which got back to Jaxon. Just after he found out I went out with her," he said.

"Ouch."

"Yeah, it was like throwing gasoline on fire. It brought up so many old wounds. I hadn't heard what she said. I just went out with her thinking I could fix them, I was… overly self-assured at the time, certain I could fix people. Anyway, Jaxon and I have never had an easy time since," Chris said.

"Did your parents do anything?"

"My parents were out of the country by then. They literally counted down the days until Jaxon graduated high school so they could leave.

They came home for Christmas that year after Brian was diagnosed. That's all we talked about. I don't think they even know what happened to us in college," he said.

"Do you want something to drink?" Chris asked.

"I have to do water," I said, already feeling parched.

"Okay here," he said. He took a bottle of water from the fridge for me. I drained it, and then smashed the thin plastic bottle against my head like we did amongst ourselves during the show. Chris laughed, a little astonished.

"It's good to stay hydrated," he said and reached me another one.

"I'm not doing it again."

"Come on, that was hot," he said. I rolled my eyes at him.

"Is that something the locals taught you?"

"Uh no. I brought that from American with me," I said. He looked at me unconvinced and I wondered if he would text Hailey later to ask.

After the cheese melted, Chris lit a fondue pot and dumped it in. I spooned the broiled veggies into a serving bowl and followed to his veranda. Pricks of lights danced against the dark river. I sat next to him, but dug in, half starved.

"Did you always want to live in Philadelphia?" I asked looking out at the skyline.

"No, I didn't get along with my Uncle Brian. I didn't like the way Jaxon acted after they spent time together."

"Are you glad you specialized in sports psychology? I mean it feels like your life was almost hijacked. For you to move here all for Brian's sake?"

"I came for Jaxon," he said.

"What?"

"He lost it," Chris said, "This was all supposed to be his future and he went spiraling. I figured I could come here and take care of things until Brian got better. Anyone who met Brian never would have thought anything would kill him."

"So, you came here just to help out?" I asked.

"I wasn't sure what I wanted to do. I figured maybe Jaxon and I could reconcile if I protected his future," Chris said.

"If you and Brian didn't get along, why did he recruit you in the first place?"

"Well, the practice was started by my grandpa and his partner. Brian got grandpa's half. After he got sick, he bought out his partner for me."

"Okay, so it's a family thing," I said.

"Yeah. When Brian was first diagnosed, he realized he needed my help keeping it in the family. That's when he started recruiting me. Before that I was just the older brother, who could only teach Jaxon to be a wet rag."

"It's interesting how quickly wet rag changes to responsible, when everything is on the line."

"Brian made sure when Jaxon finally finished, he could take his place at the practice. We agreed on this," he said.

"But Brian didn't get better."

"Nope, and neither did Jaxon. If anything, he's angrier. Especially with me for keeping the practice intact. I would give anything to see him be the responsible, creative kid that would thrive."

I nodded, nibbling on cauliflower, as I moved into Chris' strong bicep. He adjusted, putting his arm around me so I could snuggle into his chest, pull my sore feet up and watch the gas fireplace.

"Did Madam re-marry after him?" I asked.

"No, she kept her maiden name for publicity reasons when she married. He's the worst thing to ever happen to her, and she's the best thing that happened to him."

I sat thinking about that as Chris said, "Near the end of Brian's life, Mis came down with the flu. He couldn't be with her. His immune system was compromised. Madam sat with her for hours. She cooked for him when his treatment got bad. Just before he died, he told me to find the love of my life and never let go. It's the only advice on love I've ever gotten," Chris said.

He glanced down, embracing me in his arm. The look on his face reminded me of the intensity in his eyes when he picked me up. I felt my face go red, but I leaned into it this time. I pulled closer to his face.

"If you want more advice hang out with my mom," I said

"Yeah, like what?" he asked, glancing at my eyes and my lips in turn, trying to tuck his adoration for me away. He couldn't manage, and he stared at me, waiting to hear what I had to say.

Soaking up the sweet devotion seeping out of his eyes, I said, "Love is inclusive. Apparently loving Dad makes her love me and Drew. Loving me and Drew makes her love my dad more. She told me when I fall in love, it needs to be with someone who makes me want to be kind to everyone. When I want everyone to feel cocooned by love like I am, then I'm doing it right."

"Does it work?" Chris asked.

"I don't know if I really understand her logic," I said laughing.

"It's nice though," Chris said. "The idea of pulling people into a loving situation, making them a part of your family instead of falling in love and shutting everyone else out."

"I guess," I said laying my head back down on his chest, "Maybe my mom would have thrived in the sixties."

He laughed. "Thanks for listening, I didn't realize how much I needed to talk about this. Everything comes at you and it's almost…reactive, you know?"

"Yeah," I said.

"Most women find out I'm a psychologist and want a therapy session, not a date."

"It's not just you, I've had first dates like that," I teased.

"I've been on some doozies," he said. "But then, there's you. We're having a conversation about me and my family."

"You already saw me and mine," I said.

Chris laughed.

"Still," he said picking up my hand from his knee where I rested it, "you are refreshing."

He lifted my hand and kissed it. I loved the way his aqua eyes danced as he watched me. My body ached, my eyes were so heavy, but I didn't care with him so close.

The warm night air tucked around me like a shawl. The fireplace made a line of flames licking the Philadelphia skyline. I watched them dance for me.

"You falling asleep?" he asked when I hadn't said anything for a while.

"Yep."

"Come on, let's get you back to your hotel so you're ready for tomorrow."

I let him pull me up, but I leaned on him the entire way to the elevator. I felt him stiffen when the elevator stopped before he had a chance to push the button. The door opened and Jaxon started at the sight of me leaning against Chris.

Chapter 41

"Hey, Erin," Jaxon said, but he glared at Chris.

"Hey, Jaxon," I said standing up straighter, feeling the anxious tension from Chris.

"Did you get the flowers I sent?" he asked.

"Yes, thank you."

"You didn't mention that," Chris said, taken aback.

"Oh right, they came right as I was going on. Hailey did something with them," I said.

"Probably put them in the garbage," Jaxon said with a laugh. "Hailey isn't my biggest fan."

"I'm not sure what happened to them, I'm sorry," I said biting my lip. I started to walk past him, but Jaxon said, "I'm a guest DJ tomorrow morning during rush hour, that's why I'm home so early."

"Good for you," I said.

"It's a sports station. I'm talking about personal injury and stretching, but the station manager says I might be able to run a techno show on Thursday nights on one of the main stations if I can get a following."

"Good for you."

"I am kind of finding myself," he said. "I'd love to talk to you about it sometime."

"Sure."

"I'm just taking her to her hotel so she can rest up for tomorrow," Chris said defensively.

"But I'm proud of you, you know, for chasing something you really want," I said.

"Thanks Erin," he said. He leaned in and kissed my cheek. There was something completely vulnerable in his action and it surprised me. I could almost see the version of Jaxon that Chris wanted back.

"Good luck tomorrow."

Chris and I got into the elevator, but Jaxon watched us. He looked like a little boy unsure what to do next. I waved again as the door closed.

"That was weird."

"He sent you flowers?"

"Yeah, sorry. I meant to tell you, but everything happened so fast after the show," I said.

"No, yeah, I get it. I told you he seems different lately… I… would love to see this be a turning point for him. He was the sweetest kid."

"Maybe he sent me flowers to say thanks. The card said something about knowing how to be the Prima in my own ballet. Maybe he's just figuring things out."

"I don't know, but my uncle always said you never send flowers unless you mean it."

"Hopefully, he doesn't mean it because I'm not into him," I said looking up at Chris.

Chris looked at my face, really examining me.

"I want to kiss you."

"I'd let you," I answered, barely breathing.

"Here's the thing. It's not just Jaxon who's competitive. I engage, I pushed myself to always be better than him. We push each other. Him giving you flowers… it makes me feel desperate, like if I don't hurry and kiss you…"

I heard his rambling. It sounded like he might talk himself out of kissing me. I reached up as the elevator jerked to a stop and pulled him down. I covered his mouth with mine. He cupped my rib cage in his large hands and pulled me up to him.

The doors opened and I heard someone clear their throat.

Chris looked up.

"Sorry, Mr. Smith," he said almost carrying me out of the elevator.

"You should drive me back to my hotel."

He wrapped his arm around my waist, and we walked toward the car. As we passed Mia's nursing home, he pulled me under the large weeping tree, and in the cover of the golden whisps of willows kissed me again. I savored the way his mouth fit mine. His strong arms pulled me up against him tightly and his body wrapped around me like a glove. We were perfect in each other's arms. We fit – almost too perfectly.

"Come on, you've got a show tomorrow," Chris finally said, pulling away. I moaned unwilling to leave our perfect spot.

"Come on," he said and kissed my neck.

"Fine," I agreed knowing I needed to go to bed but hating it.

He held my waist as we walked to his car. I watched him drive wishing there were some way to get closer to him; desire threatened to eat me alive. He didn't feel real. I'd dated attractive men before, but nothing like him. Not just physically, but he felt so perfect – made just for me. When we pulled up to the hotel, I asked him to walk me to my suite, hoping he would give into my coaxing. He didn't need much encouragement.

When we reached my floor, a lump sat outside the door. It stood as we got closer. It turned out to be Drew.

"Hey," I said confused. "What are you doing?"

"I need to talk to you," he said.

"Um, okay," I said glancing at Chris wondering how I could get rid of Drew. Chris shifted to leave us alone.

"You may as well come in. We need your expertise," I teased pulling him back.

"You need to get to bed," he said grinning at me, but also glancing at Drew.

Disappointment trickled over me, and I went up on my toes to kiss him good night. He held me for just a second too long, like it hurt him to let me go.

I grinned and as he turned to walk away. I asked,

"I'll see you tomorrow night?"

"Yes, you will," he said.

Chapter 42

I watched him walk away until Drew cleared his throat.

"Sorry," I said. He laughed at me. I opened my door, and Drew came in.

I closed the door, and said:

"Did you lose Phoebe again?"

"Erin, she drove home with Mom and Dad," he said.

"It was a fair question," I said sarcastically.

"I need you to be in my corner," Drew said.

"I'm trying. I just can't swallow that fast. If you knew last night you were getting back together with her, you should have told me."

"I…I was so amped up when I left last night, I went back to that club she took us to."

"You went looking for her?" I asked.

"Not really… She was there. It was fate," he said.

"You knew she was likely to be there. That's not fate," I grumbled.

"Well, we … we reconnected. We talked for hours. This is the last time, I swear. We are so much better now. She's so sorry for what she did. She knows she made a mistake, but she was so nervous about getting married. She self-destructed."

"She everywhere destructed," I said.

"Please, Erin. She needs us. Look I need to tell you something, but you can't get mad," he said.

"Does that ever work?"

"Last week, after she… made you go to bed, Mom went to Phoebe's apartment."

"What?"

"Mom got her in to see a therapist every day last week while I studied, and you rehearsed. Phoebe is talking to someone about her dad."

"Oh," I said taken back. Mom had been strangely distant since I started *The Dream*. Usually, she would sew my shoes and hang around the theater.

"She's working through what happened to her. We're going to go together next week."

"Okay," I said. What else could I say?

"Can we go out tomorrow night, double date with you and Chris?" Drew said. I closed my eyes. I did not want my little brother going out with me and Chris.

"Let me finish my show. I don't think I can process this right now. Let me finish the show, and we'll double date, and I will try so hard to give her another chance. I will try to see her the way you and Mom do."

"Thanks, Erin, you're the best," he said squeezing me with his arm.

"I really am," I said putting my head against his arm finishing our little homemade hug. "You want to crash on the extra bed?"

"Yeah, I'm so tired. I haven't really slept for a few days," he said. He laid down and we talked for a while. He told me all about Phoebe facing things she always wanted to avoid. I didn't mention it'd only been one week. Every time I closed my eyes, I saw Phoebe bolting up right in Jaxon's bed.

The next morning Hailey had to call me twice to let me know I was late for warm up. I slipped out while Drew was still asleep.

Chapter 43

On Friday night I danced, knowing Chris watched me; it felt mostly like I was showing off for him. After the show he took me to the restaurant at the Rittenhouse. He ordered and the table quickly became a myriad of colors and tastes. Everything served was in season and at its most flavorful. Every sense came alive to Chris. I felt I danced off stage.

We walked to my hotel after we ate. I tried not to look sleepy. When we stopped at the door to my suite, I drew him to me. I reached up, gliding his lips across mine. Despite my tenderly bestowing all my affection upon him, he pulled away.

"You are exhausted." he announced.

"No, I swear I'm not that tired."

"I just… I don't want to rush this. Being with you, it's not something I want to do quickly, just to do. When it happens, naturally, it will be something we savor," he said, rubbing his thumbs against my hips. Then he kissed me slowly.

"Fine," I agreed when he pulled away. I reluctantly kissed him one last time, then went into my room alone. He was right about one thing. I was exhausted. It took everything in me to change and take off my makeup. I climbed in bed and conked.

I danced all day Saturday. Matinee days were always the hardest. I could have let Beth dance the principal role, but after Colby's YouTube video blew up and Drew shared my performance dates, tickets sold. The theatre was packed with people who came to see me. I knew I had to create my own fan base so I relished my role. I met with patrons all afternoon and ordered a whole lot of pasta for my pre-show dinner.

By the end of the night, only the idea of seeing Chris made me capable of meeting the crowd after. I wished I could just take off with him.

The first sign that something was off was Madam. She looked concerned. I followed her stare and realized that the large bouquet of flowers moving in my direction was Jaxon.

Ahh, Jaxon.

I looked everywhere for Chris but couldn't see him. I looked at Madam and she gave me a head nod toward the doors. I took this to mean I should leave. I saw Hailey intercept Jaxon. I used the distraction to escape. I showered and dressed. I waited, my feet throbbing, thinking Chris would come but he didn't. Hailey met me in our dressing room.

"What's going on?" I asked.

"Jaxon's still waiting for you, but Madam doesn't want him to make a scene, so if you could wait a few minutes, she'd really appreciate it," Hailey said, looking away.

"Where's Chris?"

"He's an idiot."

"What?"

"I didn't tell you between shows because I didn't want you to lose focus; in fact, how are you? Sore?"

"What is going on?"

"Jaxon used his…oh this is so stupid," Hailey said.

"What?" I asked dying; the dread on her face sinking my life force.

"Jaxon told Chris they could start over as brothers if Chris would back off and not date you," Hailey said.

"Did Chris tell him to shove it?"

"You have to understand. Chris has felt so guilty since Rhonda. He isn't thinking straight," Hailey said.

"He didn't tell Jaxon to shove it?" I asked trying to suck in air, but I couldn't. Chris was dumping me. For his brother?

"What?" I stammered, feeling my eyes swim with tears.

"I'm sorry," Hailey said, her eyes started to tear up as well.

"Is this really happening?" I asked, but her face was the answer.

"There's another thing I'm supposed to tell you," Hailey said blowing out a breath.

"What?" I asked.

"Jaxon's trying to be his old self again. He's making a real effort because of some things you said to him. Chris is hoping you'll keep encouraging him to be present in his life again. For some reason he really listens to you," Hailey said.

"Why would I do that?" I asked, feeling the rage build inside me.

"That's what I said, but Chris just… I don't even know," Hailey said.

"He used me as a bargaining chip."

"Don't blame Chris. He's been trying to fix Jaxon since they were boys. Chris can't even help it."

"So, I'm supposed to go out and let Jaxon charm me, or what role am I supposed to play?" I asked.

"Personally, I'd flip him off and leave," Hailey said angrily.

"Yep," I said tying my tennis shoe and grabbing my bag.

Hailey followed me. "Erin, Chris is a nice guy, too nice really," she said. "What big brother backs off so his little brother has a chance at the woman of his dreams?"

"I'm not the woman of Jaxon's dreams. I'm the woman of Chris's dreams. Jaxon doesn't have a dream, so he takes his brother's," I said. "He needs a therapist to give him life hints, not a girlfriend."

"Yeah, but if you think about it, Uncle Brian loved Madam. Do you think Jaxon is so screwed up he sees you as the dancer he's supposed to love?" Hailey asked, trying to calm me down.

"Again, all good questions for a therapist."

"Sorry, Erin," Hailey said. "When it comes to Jaxon, Chris is so screwed up."

"Yeah," I answered entering the lobby, Madam sat talking to Jaxon. She flinched a little when she saw me. I could see the fear in her eyes. She loved Jaxon. She was afraid I was going to hurt him.

"Oh, good Erin," Jaxon said standing up, "I got you these."

"No thanks," I said, "give them to Madam, congratulations for her sold-out show. It's what your uncle would have wanted."

"Yeah, of course," he said, starting, obviously surprised. Without hesitating he handed her the flowers. Madam smiled at me. Jaxon continued, "Look Erin, I just wanted to say thanks. I really appreciate you… I know I've been mixed up, but I'm going to get my life back in order. Tomorrow night I get to be a guest DJ for WPRK, will you listen to me?"

I did not want to listen to him DJ. I wanted to hit him. I wanted to rage at him.

"Jaxon, I feel like maybe you should get your crap together without me."

"I don't know how," Jaxon said studying my face. "Please give me another chance. I swear I haven't seen Phoebe since she stormed out –"

"I know. She's dating my little brother again," I said. Jaxon flinched like I shocked him. My anger sucked up my post-show high and I sank, feeling dead. Why did these people get second and third and fourth chances, when I didn't get a first chance with Chris?

"See, there's no reason we can't try each other out," Jaxon said.

I couldn't even respond to this at first.

"Jaxon, I don't see us working out," I said feeling like I might vomit.

"Not now, but I'll sweep you off your feet," he said grinning at me.

"That would be tricky. I have amazing balance," I said.

He flinched, and Madam laughed to show him I was teasing him. I could see how much he meant to Madam. The way she rested a hand on his arm, he was the son she and Brian never had.

Only because she meant so much to me, I said politely, "Look, I am really impressed you're looking at yourself. I know how hard that is. I'm proud of you. But having said that, we are not each other's type."

"Not right now, not with the way I've been since college. When you get to know the real me, I promise we'll be perfect for each other."

"Well, I look forward to that day, but now, I need to go to bed. Good night, and good luck to you," I said. Madam smiled at me, relieved.

I sat in my car and texted Chris, "Is this a joke?"

His text back to me was long and full of apology. He just felt like if he could repair his relationship with his brother he had to. He admitted to me that he did flirt with Rhonda, Jaxon's girlfriend, and he always regretted it. He deeply regretted having to cut off our fresh exciting relationship but giving me up was the penance he must make for what he did back then.

I drove back to the hotel. I felt mean and angry about it all, so I turned off my phone, asked for a wakeup call from the front desk and went to sleep.

Chapter 44

I listened to Jaxon's radio performance, after my own the next night. All the techno wasn't my thing. I ended up watching TV and sort of listening. I texted him thanks for the shout out, and congrats on doing such a good job. Again – for Madam's sake.

Jaxon came to every performance of *The Dream* for the next week. He brought me flowers every night. Hailey and Madam looked on in worry and I noticed that the face they watched us with was the same face I gave my little brother and Phoebe.

Is this how Phoebe did it? She waited for Drew to get vulnerable and lonely, then she showered him with attention and affection.

Every night my solo grew darker and darker. Before the closing night performance Madam pulled me aside and said:

"I have noticed you seem heavy. Your leaps are not so bounding as they were opening night."

"How do I get past all the personal stuff and just perform?" I asked, so sick of it all.

"Hailey told me you are being kind to Jaxon for my sake. I appreciate it, I really do."

"It's fine. Ivan and I will be in New York next week. You don't feel betrayed we are leaving do you?" I asked.

"Oh, heavens no. I have lifted two stars into the sky. Nothing could make me happier," she said.

"Thanks," I said.

"Erin, be careful with Jaxon. I appreciate you being kind to him, but he will break you if he has the chance. He's stuck. He isn't right for anyone until he gets unstuck," she said simply.

"Then why did Chris just leave me? Why is he letting him in his head?"

"His misplaced honor thinks if he lets Jaxon break you, he can swoop in and fix you and Jaxon. It is the curse of the fixers," she said.

"He thinks he can just swoop in and I'll give him another chance?"

"That's the gist of it."

"That's hilarious."

"You love him, you will let him swoop in when the time comes because you love him. Brian came back to me the last few years. I waited so long for him. Only when he was dying did he realize what he wanted in life. Hopefully, Chris will not take so long."

"You were married to Brian. I've only known Chris for a couple weeks."

"You have the heart of an artist. We love a little faster and fall a little harder than most. It is all in your dance. Your solo has grown sadder, and your love scenes are unbelievable. When you expected Chris, your solo was charming, and your love scenes were intense."

"Am I ruining the show?"

"No dear, you dance so beautifully your audience is enthralled no matter what."

"What can I do?"

"On the stage, you are not Erin. You are Tatiana. Your joy is hers, her sorrow is yours. Do not think of anything accept the part you are playing."

"I am Tatiana."

"What I wish for you on this final night is your best. Not for me or anyone else. Simply so you know you left this performance with your best," she said.

"I will try," I said, determined to give everything.

"I came to a crossroad like this in my life many years ago. Brian… he left me for another woman. I sulked for a month or so. Then I refused it. I refused to let my divorce ruin my career. I danced harder and with more energy than I ever had before. Sometimes it was more like the avenging angel than the Sugar Plum Fairy, but still I danced.

"Be sad if you must but use dancing as your outlet. Do not give up what you love just to sulk. It almost ruined me. Thankfully, I had a mentor who would not allow it, just as I encourage you now."

She kissed my hand.

"Thank you."

She nodded, then left me to put on my costume. I thought about what she said. When the blonde curls of the wig tightened into my scalp, I welcomed the pain. As the crown of flowers was placed on my head, I transformed into the Fairy Queen; I gave up myself. I was a powerful fairy queen, beholden to one, and I would defy him when he asked for the changeling child.

When the lights rose on the stage I followed through. I waged war with Oberon, truly angry. I loved Bottom, desperately, though he wore a donkey's head. My body danced to each statement without any hint of my own confusion. I did not have to be Erin.

Only my solo was mine, and I could not help the sorrow I felt coming through. When I gave up the changeling boy, I gave up my heart. I left it on the stage. I could not give it to Queen Tatianna if I tried. I danced it in exquisite sorrow, and I knew it was the best I could do.

And when it ended, Tatianna reconciled with the Fairy King, passionately and without restraint.

Usually at the curtain call Ivan and I bowed together then separately, then together again. This time when I came forward, the audience of three thousand came to their feet as if orchestrated. Ivan stayed back. I bowed overwhelmed with pride and gratitude to the audience who took my performance and gave me back their adoration.

It hit me: these people paid money to come, to see me. They loved me for making them feel something with my talent. I loved them too.

I should have left after my performance. I should never have willingly gone out into the lobby where everything brewing left me in the center of a perfect storm.

My performance high lasted about thirty seconds outside the door.

The first sight I had was Chris. Perfect, gorgeous Chris, whom I later found out always used his season ticket on closing night. He stood ten feet of crowd away from me. He kissed Madam, who looked to be arguing with him. Both stopped when Madam spotted me. Her face grew concerned. Chris turned to see what she looked at and we locked eyes. Confusion colored my face, and the longing that crossed his took me by total surprise. He opened his mouth like he could talk to me, despite the busy lobby and the ten yards between us.

"Sorry," he whispered through the air. It hit me in the chest, harder than I expected.

Chris looked like he might come speak to me, but Jaxon appeared yet again with a larger bouquet of flowers. Chris said something to Madam, and then waved to me. He tucked his head down embarrassed and walked away. I did not wave back but turned from him and set my face in the perfect ballerina smile, albeit a little too fierce to ring true.

I greeted my new fans, the fans I needed to dance with American. The fans that would boost me into a principal role, that would send me back on tour and away. I had a dream. I was done with the distractions that would take me away from my dream. I knew what I wanted. What I had always wanted.

"Wow, I swear every night you get better," Jaxon said kissing my cheek and giving me flowers.

"Thank you so much," I said taking the flowers and waving to a fan who called out to me. I consumed myself with my fans and ignored him. Madam approached and I gave her my undivided attention.

"Erin, I am proud," Madam said.

"Erin," I heard a voice call, and I blanched white as a sheet. Drew approached me with flowers in one hand and Phoebe in the other. Jaxon turned around just as Phoebe started to say something. She made a whimpering sound. One of my fans asked me to sign something. And I didn't hear what Drew asked, but it must have been something like, "What are you doing here?" because Jaxon responded:

"I messed up. I'm sure Phoebe told you we were a stupid mistake."

"The stupidest," Phoebe said angrily. Jaxon nodded, but he clenched his jaw and his eyes turned to avoid hers.

"Look, can we just start over?" Jaxon said. "Let's all go out for dinner."

"Not a chance," Drew said looking at me to agree with him. I stared back. Phoebe was just as culpable as Jaxon. How come I had to be okay with her? I felt the anger grow within me. I smiled my perfect smile, but I was on fire. I said waving to a fan:

"Sure, why not."

"I can think of a lot of reasons," Drew said examining me.

"No really. If it was just a mistake, and Phoebe's better now, why not have dinner together?" I asked.

"That's the spirit," Jaxon said. As if I were serious.

"I'll go change after I'm done here," I said pointing them over to the bar. The mean-spirited pixie still swayed me. Wasn't it only fair they all face each other? Maybe then Drew would remember his girlfriend really did cheat on him.

After greeting my fans, I showered and changed. As I tied my shoes, Hailey came in. She looked upset.

"You, okay?"

"Are you going out with Jaxon? I thought the plan was to ignore him until he went away."

"Oh no," I responded. "Didn't you hear? Chris sold me to his brother. I am to be traded for a few sheep and a jackass. That is really is the way it goes."

"Come on Erin. I can see you're pissed. Last night Chris even agreed it would be best if you just ignored Jaxon until he – "

"Are you talking to him about me?"

"He just wants to make sure everything – "

"Does Chris really think he gets to dictate how this goes?" I snapped. "He bowed out."

"It wasn't like that. Look, it will probably be best for everyone if you drift out of their lives. I know that's stupid but getting involved with Jaxon is stupider."

I looked at Hailey feeling so betrayed. She was Chris's friend. Her loyalties would always be to Chris. Had she ever been my friend? Finally, I took a deep breath and sent Chris a message through her.

"I'm not getting involved with Jaxon. I'm forcing my brother to accept that sitting across the table from a cheater isn't fun. You can tell Chris not to worry. After tonight, I'm leaving, and I won't look back."

"I still don't think it's a good idea," Hailey said. She handed me a bunch of flowers she collected for me.

"Thanks," I said flatly. I noticed the one white lily. I took it out and gave it back.

"I think this one is yours."

"He said you were perfect… It was the best performance you –"

"Chris came every night?"

"He's such a romantic. Giving you up as penance when he clearly loves you is the stupidest thing ever."

"You can't love someone after a couple weeks," I said, determined to believe it.

What other choice did I have?

I walked out of the locker room trying not to cry. Anger felt better than hurt.

Drew and Phoebe sat at the bar looking grim. Well, good. They both dressed in cocktail attire. Drew wore his blue suit with a blue and white striped shirt open at the collar. Phoebe wore a matching blue dress. It was loose and innocent looking. It looked like something I would wear. I don't know why, but this made my anger flare.

Jaxon wore a buttoned-up vest, his dress shirt rolled a few times at the sleeve. I came out wearing jean shorts and a t-shirt. That is the effort I made. Jaxon acted like I'd dressed up for him, exclaiming how good I looked. I just nodded. Phoebe and Drew were silent.

"My Uncle Brian's favorite Italian restaurant is pretty close to here if you want to go," Jaxon said. I knew he meant to take us to the place Chris had already taken me.

I quickly said, "No, I couldn't eat Italian. Dad's favorite place for Philly Cheese Steak sandwiches is just outside the city. Let's go there."

"Oh right, I love that place," Drew said. I waited for Phoebe to refuse to go back to that hole in the wall, but she said nothing.

"I walked over from the hotel as a warm-up this morning," I said.

"We can follow you, Drew," Jaxon said.

"I'll drive everyone," Drew said.

As we walked out, Jaxon said, "So I understand you're taking the bar soon, the multi-state one?"

Phoebe flinched and glared at Jaxon.

"I just took it," Drew said, pulling Phoebe in closer. The action pushed Phoebe's hair to the side, and I realized we were both wearing the earrings Drew gave us. This made my anger pulse stronger.

"Phoebe, you finally got the diamond earrings Drew's been promising you. Drew, are you out of the doghouse?"

Phoebe glanced at me and self-consciously reached for her sparkling ears.

"They're nice. You have good taste," Jaxon said to Drew.

Drew glared at him. Phoebe, sounding uncomfortable said, "His Mom helped him. She is so cool."

I glared. Mom was such a traitor.

Nobody said anything else. We all climbed into Drew's truck. We drove for a while and Phoebe kept glancing at Jaxon in the rear view, as if she couldn't believe he was there. Finally, she took a deep breath and broke the silence, proving she could be civil.

"I've been trying a new plank in my work out; it's supposed to be better for my back," she said. "Do you ever do those with any of your clients, Jaxon?"

"Yeah, for sure," he started.

I interrupted. "Phoebe always has perfect bikini abs… oh right, everyone already knows that." I shook my head like I forgot.

Drew glared at me through the rear-view mirror, and Phoebe went red. I took a deep breath trying to calm down, but I had brought the stubborn pixie off the stage with me.

We climbed out of Drew's truck at the restaurant and moved as one group with all the tension of trying to avoid a mine field. We stopped at the walk-up window that served as the base of the restaurant. We ordered and found an orange-red metal table to sit at along the sidewalk.

"Here. Wait a sec, Erin. I got this," Phoebe said taking out wipes and cleaning all the sticky streaks off the table.

"Thanks," I choked out wishing she would yell at me or prove she wasn't this act she was pretending to be. We sat at the table for a while waiting for our order and when the silence became too awkward, I broke it.

"You've been DJ-ing," I said to Jaxon pretending everything was normal.

"Yeah, I love it."

"That's cool," Phoebe said, snuggling into Drew like he could protect her.

"Jaxon, Hailey said you went to New York for a while. Were you trying to be a model or something?" I asked.

He nodded, taking a sip of his drink before he answered.

"Yeah, I actually landed a few commercials. It's pretty cutthroat so I came back."

"Didn't you say you got on a soap opera?" Phoebe asked.

"Just as a background character," he said with half a laugh, "I tried for something I felt passionate about. I should have stuck it out a while longer, though. I worked at a gym where a lot of stars go. Lincoln Turner asked me to be his personal trainer. I didn't do it. It felt like a waste of my degree. If I had it to do over, I would humble myself and take the money he was throwing at me to keep him in shape. Who knows where that could have led to?"

"Yeah. Lincoln was just a landscaper when he made it big," Phoebe said.

"Right," I said. "It's like if you want to meet a lawyer, work in the courthouse. You want to meet an actor work in a gym." Phoebe flinched. She met Drew when he was a paralegal and had to get some paperwork from her on a case.

"Or you start on the career path a social worker can help you get into," Drew snapped. I bit my lip. Phoebe had taken the limited knowledge she had. Because of her father, she knew the court system and made a career out of it. It was something I once admired her for.

What was the matter with me?

Phoebe blinked a lot and looked anywhere except at me. I tried to brush her pain off as the shallow slogs of someone who wasn't worth my time. It was harder to do as she forced herself not to cry. Jaxon, taking compassion on her, said,

"Drew, I really appreciate you giving me another chance. It's me that was stupid. Me," and he looked at Phoebe sincerely to let her know all this mess was his fault.

"I'm not pretending I didn't do this," Phoebe said.

They were being so generous to each other. They were so connected. I wanted to scream…to claw out at everyone at the table for being so stupid, so careless with their love when I didn't even… I hated them all.

I tried to take a deep breath. This anger, it … it wanted to consume me like a living creature ready to pull me down into a burning furious inferno.

What was I doing?

I thought it would feel good to … to give Phoebe and Jaxon their comeuppance. The crueler I was, the more it fueled the anger. I couldn't seem to calm down.

"I'm going to use the bathroom," I said cutting Jaxon off mid-sentence and running away from the table.

I went into the single person bathroom decorated by someone who wanted their little business to thrive. It smelled like cinnamon, and the walls were covered in amber wooden carvings of turtles. I leaned against the pedestal sink and looked at myself in the mirror. My eyes were pricked with red veins. My body was exhausted. I wanted to fall over. I looked pretty enough, almost like the villain who uses her good looks to get what she wants.

But the eyes couldn't hide my real character. I could hear Mom's voice in my head telling me to examine why I was being so cruel. Anger built on itself, using up all my energy. I would have nothing left to be present in my own life if I billowed with flames of anger all the time, obsessively recalling all Phoebe did to Drew.

All Mom's hippy live-and-let-live that I wanted to discard was proven this one night when I made no effort to rein myself in. I closed my eyes and swore I was just trying to save Drew. The image of Drew pulling Phoebe in like he would protect her rolled through my head. He was trying to protect Phoebe from me. If anything, I was pushing him toward her. I was losing him.

But shouldn't Phoebe have to face what she did?

"What gives you the right to be her judge, Erin?" Mom's voice was in my head so clearly, she could have been standing next to me.

No matter what Phoebe did, Mom was right about one thing. This isn't who I wanted to be.

Why was I being so cruel to Phoebe? It wasn't for Drew's sake. I was humiliating him. I saw it in his eyes.

What was the matter with me?

In my heart of hearts, I knew.

I wanted Jaxon to tell Chris how mean I was being to Phoebe. I wanted him to know I wasn't taking his advice. I wanted him to know I wasn't okay, and it was his fault.

"Ahhh," I said to myself, "I'm going to need an exorcist to get my mother out of my head."

I washed my hands, and left the bathroom. The woman waiting for the bathroom gave me a weird look. Was I going crazy? I walked slowly along the building that was lit up like Las Vegas to attract customers. I sat down at the table in time to hear Jaxon ask politely:

"Drew, how did you feel about taking the bar?"

"I feel fairly good about it. I'm doing some paralegal stuff for my dad while I wait for my scores to come in."

"He's such a smarty. He passed for sure," Phoebe said leaning into him. The action felt so forced. Jaxon looked down sadly, unable to even look at them. Didn't they see how drawn to each other they were? On some level Drew knew. He wouldn't be so annoyed if he didn't know. What did I do? How did I…. I glanced at Drew. He looked so miserable. My first loyalties were to my brother.

"Phoebe, you must be planning your wedding by now. Do you want to tell us about it?"

"Oh yeah," she said squinting at car lights passing. "December 14th. Mark the date."

"That's soon," Jaxon said watching her.

"The sooner the better," Drew said.

"Right," Phoebe agreed, but she turned a few shades green in the yellow lights glaring down on us. She looked like she may be sick. I had been so busy thinking up the perfect insults, I hadn't realized Phoebe was really struggling in her relationship with Drew. She chose to be with Drew. But Jaxon made her crazy.

The calmer I grew, the more I saw what was really happening. It felt like we were in a Three Stooges movie. Except instead of physical slapsticks, it was verbal. Drew, smack; Phoebe, whap; Jaxon, augh!

The performance was so forced I waited for someone to fall out of his seat or poke me in the eyes.

Chapter 45

We drove Jaxon back to the theater. Drew parked under a yellowish cone of light beneath a streetlamp. Jaxon turned to me and asked:

"Erin, can I walk you to your hotel?"

I stammered unsure what he thought was going to happen. Phoebe, turned in her seat, stared intensely at Jaxon, and through tears answered for me:

"Please Jaxon, please leave Erin alone. You can have any woman you want. I need you to go away. This is my family. They love me unconditionally, and I need that. I'm fighting for this: this is my fight. Please."

She was serious. I knew she was. Guilt stabbed at my heart. Jaxon, of all people, took compassion on her.

"I…I need…" he started. I watched him stammer, caught between the strange ideal of loving a ballet dancer, and giving Phoebe what she wanted.

"Please," she pleaded, the tears in her eyes welled and fell.

"You deserve to be happy, Phoebe, after all your dad did to you. You deserve a real family," Jaxon said. Both Drew and I stared at Jaxon. Phoebe was very private about her early life, and her father, who was in prison. I glanced at Drew, and he was no longer mad, but sad. Neither of us realized Phoebe and Jaxon ever had enough of a relationship for her to confide in him that deeply.

"Sorry, Erin," Jaxon said turning to me. "I think maybe we have too much baggage for this to work out."

"I understand," I said watching him as he climbed out of Drew's truck. I almost respected him until he turned back and said:

"Please Erin. Chris has never… he's all I have." He looked down like it hurt him to admit it. "He's my family. We have to work together; we have to be able to … he gave you up for me. I know that makes you angry. I know it doesn't even make sense. I hear myself saying it out loud and I know it's stupid. I just … I need my big brother back. I need him to lose someone he loves so he can understand."

He opened the door and slid down out of the truck.

"Are you kidding?" I whispered.

"Uh," Jaxon murmured with the door in his hand he looked back at me. I slid across the seat and followed him out of the truck. I shoved him in the arm and stammered, "Are you kidding?"

"No, he's never loved anyone or anything until you," Jaxon said crossing his bulging arms stubbornly, looking out at the cone of light across the street where his pretty car was parked.

"He became a psychologist the day your father wouldn't let you go see his therapist in high school," I said.

"Yeah, so he could shrink me," Jaxon said.

"And he didn't like Brian," I said.

"Right, he said he was a bad influence on me," Jaxon said.

"Yet, he took a job from him. He's here to protect your future, you idiot! He is in a career he never meant to take. All because he knew you'd end up here. You weren't finishing school. Brian needed you, and you didn't finish, so Chris came instead. He's followed you around his whole life, to be sure you're always okay."

This time Jaxon was quiet.

"He knows what it's like to lose someone he loves," I said. "He lost you, Jaxon. Every decision he's made in the last five years is to get you back, because you are the one who is deepest in his heart."

"I… I guess I never thought of it that way," Jaxon said.

"But you know it's true because you can get him to do anything you want. He gave you money to leave, he took you in when you came back. And now he dumped me for you. Chris never stopped being your big brother, and you never stopped being the child who expects him to pick up the pieces of your life."

"I don't expect him to –"

"Who do you think you're talking to? He dumped me because you asked him to."

"I need him."

"Yes, you do, but so do I."

"You… you're going to – "

"No Jaxon, Chris chose you. What can I do but respect that?"

"Really?"

"Really?" echoed in my head. If I really loved Chris, would I support his crazy like Drew supported Phoebe's? Did I step back and let Chris make this sacrifice?

I noticed Drew followed me out of the truck. He stood between Jaxon and I, but his stance showed he was defending Jaxon from me. I was the angry, and possibly violent, one.

I took a deep breath and tried to calm down.

"Yes, really but I need a favor from you."

"I'd do anything for you Erin," he said glancing at me, and I realized he had the same aqua eyes that Chris had. They were vulnerable.

"Only because you hear what I say, not because you're in love with me. I chose Chris because he is my sort of person. I did not choose him to hurt you. You see that, right?" I asked.

"I…I mean, yeah, but…" he stammered.

"Your uncle would have, I suspect, told you to find your Madam, your dancer."

"Yeah, right before he died."

"He didn't mean it literally, Jaxon," I said wondering if his uncle was somewhere in the great beyond doing a face palm. "He chose Madam because she is his sort of person. You chose Phoebe because she's your sort of person. She's not even available, but she is your type," I said.

He nodded this time glancing at Phoebe who now stood behind Drew.

"This is where we start over. Your favor to me is to find someone you are really attracted to. From all I've heard, the girl who left you in college – she was Chris's sort of person. Except she sounds like a total jerk. Who comes between brothers like that?"

"She was very self-centered," Jaxon admitted.

"Yes, and that's why it ended between the two of you. It had little to do with Chris, but rather than admitting you made a wrong choice in girlfriends, you blame Chris. That's childish and needs to stop. You find your own happiness, and if it doesn't work out, try again until it does. That is how we succeed."

Jaxon watched me like he was soaking up my advice. Why he cared so much about what I said was weird, but he did.

"You may be right," he finally said looking wistfully at Phoebe.

"Look, just do me a favor, find someone like Phoebe to love— just not Pheobe."

"No, she's marrying Drew," he said.

"Exactly, and stay away from the next girl Chris is attracted too and you'll be fine," I said glancing at Phoebe, standing just outside the circle of light. She watched Jaxon. She ugly cried. She wrapped her arms around herself and looked so uncertain, almost afraid of what I said.

Jaxon took one last long look at Phoebe and taking a small step toward her. He said, "I may never see you again, but you really were… my perfect woman. I'm sorry for… for saying we were a stupid mistake. I was lucky for the time you gave me. You're really lucky, Drew."

He turned and jogged to where his car was parked. We all stood there and watched him until he climbed in and drove away. I did, because I knew Phoebe needed to see him go, and I didn't want it to hurt Drew's feelings.

That's who I wanted to be.

Chapter 46

After we all climbed back into the truck, Drew drove away too fast.

"What were you thinking Erin?" Drew snapped.

"Excuse me,' I asked, feeling the anger grow in me again.

"You get out of the truck like you're going to fight him? I can't even believe you—"

"Had sex with him," I shouted back. "Oh wait. That wasn't me, was it?"

With tears streaming down her face, Phoebe said, "She's right Drew, she didn't do this, I did. I'm sorry, Erin. I put you in a bad position."

"It's not any of her business, Phoebe," Drew said.

"Isn't it?" I asked, livid.

"If I'm good with Phoebe, you should be too," said Drew.

"No Drew," Phoebe said caressing his arm, "my therapist said her witness of my betrayal had to be traumatic. Not to mention she invited me to hang out with her and I … I went after her date. This is on me; I am screwed up. Please be patient with her."

"Phoebe you're trying. Erin is attacking a man on the street. What would you have done if he hit you?" Drew asked.

"He's not violent. He wouldn't have hit me," I said.

"Oh please, that guy would hit a woman," Drew said angrily.

"No," I said remembering how even with Chris he wasn't the one to strike. "He's not dangerous; he's just lost." And Chris was the only one in the world trying to find him.

"Well, maybe, but you may have hit him. Erin, what's wrong with you?" Drew asked.

"I… I don't know," I said feeling the pricking in my eyes. It felt so unfair that all this was now my fault.

"This isn't like you," Drew said. I took a deep breath. I couldn't be sure who I was anymore.

"I really hope not. I feel so… I'm so furious," I said.

My admitting this stopped Drew. He glanced in the mirror at me.

"Did…did Jaxon really ask Chris to back off and he did?" Drew asked.

"Yep."

"I'm sorry Erin. I saw how much you liked him," Drew said, kinder.

We all went quiet. I didn't want to look up at the front seat. In the reflection of her window, I could see the tears on Phoebe's face. I turned from it all and waited for the short drive from the theater to my hotel to end. Drew stopped in front of the hotel. He looked at me in the rear-view mirror, but all I could see was Phoebe swiping her face. I did that to her.

I swallowed hard – hard.

"Phoebe, I'm sorry. I shouldn't have been such a jerk to you tonight."

She turned in her seat, surprised.

"No, I get it, he's your little brother. You've been taking his screw-ups since he was little. You just can't figure out how to take me," she said with a little laugh.

"I have been…" I stopped. Chris took Jaxon's screw-ups, and I took Drews. We both were the protectors of our little brothers. It was time for me to take my own screw-ups just like I told Jaxon to do.

"Phoebe, I'm…I'm livid at Chris and I took it out on you. It wasn't fair. Please forgive me," I said.

"No, no. What did you say that wasn't true? I deserve it."

"Do you?"

"Of course, I do," she said, and I could hear the loathing she had for herself as she assured, "I'm going to be so good from now on."

"What does good even mean, Phoebe?"

She couldn't answer, but the way she told Drew to be patient with me had to be what her therapist was telling her to do for herself.

"You will be okay with me again. I want us to be friends. I really do," she said.

"I'll try, okay? But I think being good would include being kinder to yourself than I was. It wasn't good for me to be cruel to you. Tonight you didn't do anything wrong. Tonight was all me being mad about Chris."

"Thanks Erin," she said reaching out to me. I took her hand and squeezed it. Tears rolled down my face. I smiled at her. She seemed a lot more like the Phoebe whom Drew introduced to me four years earlier. Like she'd stopped trying to…elevate herself to some warped sense of who she thought she was supposed to be. I liked her better, just being herself. I opened the door. I felt better climbing out of the truck. Drew climbed out as well.

"Do you want us to wait while you get your stuff? We can caravan home," he said glancing at Phoebe.

"My body is stiff. I haven't stretched. I'm exhausted. I gave everything to the stage. I'm sorry I was so mean tonight, I really am. But remember, I have nothing left in my well after I perform," I said.

"I'm sorry. I should have given you another day. I just wanted you to love Phoebe."

"Can I try again in the morning?"

Drew put an arm around me. I dropped my head to it, but couldn't suppress the sob.

"I'll see you tomorrow," I said running away.

Chapter 47

Once on my floor, I limped down the hall toward my hotel room but stopped. There in front of my door sat Chris, his white lily limp in his hands and a vacant stare toward the opposite side of the hallway.

"Chris," I said. He started and stood up stretching, like he'd been there for a while and was stiff.

"What are you doing here?" I asked.

"You didn't take my flower," he said handing it to me.

"I can't," I said nodding and backing away. "It hurts me."

He closed his eyes and stammered, "I am so sorry."

"Are you?"

"He needs to feel like we're even. I love you, Erin. If I give that up, in his mind we're even."

"Because you stole the woman he loved," I said.

"I'm sorry Erin, I can see you don't understand. For the first time in years, I have his attention. He's at a crossroads. He's engaging in his life for the first time since Brian died."

"Whatever, Chris," I said, walking past him toward my suite.

"Did you have fun with Jaxon tonight?"

"Jaxon dumped me because Phoebe asked him to."

"He swore if I bowed out," Chris stammered, "you would date him. He… he thinks being with you can –"

"You are a therapist; you know that one person cannot fix another person's damage. No matter what support he gets, ultimately, he has to do the work. Did you tell him that?"

"I tried. He just kept asking me to bow out, so I … I did, but I…" he took a deep breath. "I didn't know how hard it would be."

"Look I … I don't want to come between you and your brother. This is a stupid game the two of you play, and it will always end badly."

"That's fair."

"In that spirit, what are you doing here, Chris?"

"I don't know. I shouldn't be here, I just can't… please don't… don't hate me," Chris said finally looking me with ruddy passion, drilling into me intensely.

I grabbed his face and kissed him. I kissed him with anger and love and all the passionate emotion I usually only had access to on the stage. Chris unleashed my passion for dancing and bound it to himself. I loved him and hated him for it all at once.

Chris had me around the waist and pulled me in so tightly I could feel his heart beating through his chest. He kissed me without restraint, pushing me against my door. I wanted more.

"Please, I… please I have to go," he said, pulling away.

"Are you kidding me? Can you feel that? You're going to give that up for your little brother?" I asked, shoving him like I had Jaxon.

"I have to. He's my family."

"I could be your family." I realized I begged.

"I…I can't abandon him right now."

"But you can me?"

"What if it was Drew? What if you watched Drew spiral out of control for years, with no way to help him? What if out of nowhere an angel steps into your life and Drew, for the first time in years, starts to realize he is out of control and wants to change? What would you do to save him?"

"I…I don't know."

"I don't believe I will ever feel like this again," he said covering his face with his hand. I pulled it away angrily, forcing Chris to look into my eyes.

"Jaxon dumped me. You are giving me up for a brother who blames you for everything. Wouldn't it be better just to let him suck it up for a change?"

"He doesn't. He self-destructs."

"But I love you, and you love me," I cried.

"I don't know what to do. Let me figure out my relationship with Jaxon first. Then maybe I can…" Chris drifted off, searching me. He leaned in like he might kiss me again, but I leaned away. He said, "Please take this." And reached out the smashed lily to me.

"No, you can give me your lily when you mean it as a token of your love," I snapped angrily. I took out my room key card. "And if you meet me in a deserted hall again, I can promise you it will go pretty much like this until you come to your senses."

I opened my door, stepped into my suite and tried to slam it, but the hotel door had something mechanical on it that wouldn't allow it to be slammed. It was sadly anti-climatic.

I spent the weekend in the bathtub. Trying to heal and remembering my dream. I couldn't help but think Chris wasn't entirely lost to me. He loved me. Maybe when Jaxon calmed down and found a girlfriend, Chris would come looking for me again.

In the meantime, I had a dream to see to. And like Madam said, I wasn't losing it over a man or anyone else.

Chapter 48

My first morning back at American I relished the feeling I had of belonging. The dance studio overlooked New York and I loved seeing the city as I stretched. I never felt good enough to be among the other reflections in the room full of mirrors before. Usually, I watched my extensions and controlled my arms at the barre with great anxiety. Instead, I invited Ivan to be my barre buddy and smiled trying to help him relax.

"Erin! Good! There you are," Noel said coming in near the end of the master class. She avoided Natalia's glare.

"Ivan," she said, addressing him so he would stop leaping into the air, "you will be under the instruction of Master Keith and given an intensive introduction to our company over the next few weeks."

"Thank you," he said with so much reverence she smiled only very slightly and I knew she liked him.

"Erin, your father agreed to get his citizenship issues taken care of?"

"Yes."

"Good," she said nodding to Ivan who grinned and bowed with another thank you.

"Erin, at the end of the week, you'll have a young Russian dancer named Svetlana come to class. You are to be her mentor," Noel said.

"Okay," I said.

Natalia, in a set of high flying grand jeté', smirked at me without losing the beat.

“Also, I’m having a little trouble with one of my afternoon classes. It’s a pointe class Master Keith usually helps with. I need you to teach it so he can focus on Ivan,” Noel said.

“I’d love to.” I said rubbing a droplet of sweat from my forehead with my wrist.

She nodded her head and moved out of the way so the ballet mistress could have her class back. I didn’t mind her abrupt nod this time. I knew she thought me good.

I reported to the class I would teach for ten days. It was a pointe class for girls who would try out for the dance company’s apprentice program. Most of them were members of the studio company hoping to move up into the professional dance world. These young women just graduated from high school or would be graduating within the next year. Unless they were chosen to apprentice, then they would likely finish online.

I came in and introduced myself, smiling at the girls. I hoped they would see me as a mentor, someone they could confide in. I meant for them all to make so much progress Noel and the Ballet Masters and Mistresses would not be able to choose between them.

This outlook dimmed quickly.

“Okay ladies let’s start at the barre,” I said. I spent so much time turning out feet and repositioning free arms, I felt more like a gardener reworking topiary. Fixing posture and technique were only the start of it.

Determined to give praise where it was due, I quickly gave out compliments as I worked my little garden. I did not realize it would come back to bite me.

"Good stance, Camilla," I said to one student who quickly outshined the others. The dancer behind Camilla glared at her as she turned to work the other side. The object of my praise tried to ignore the censure, but I could see it bothered her. The glaring dancer then turned to me and, kissing up, said, "Erin, I just wanted to say you were so good in *The Dream*. I went closing night with my boyfriend. It was amazing."

"Thank you," I said patting her shoulder indicating she should drop it. She didn't but looked smug like I'd been patting her shoulder in praise.

"All right ladies, good work today. I need you to do some core training so we can be more successful in this class. It'll improve your balance drastically," I said handing out a paper detailing the strength training.

"Oh, I core train every night," the glaring dancer said shoving the paper haphazardly into her duffle bag.

"Right, that's good but –" I said.

"I do a hundred of these…every night," she said, getting down and showing me some V-ups.

"That's great, but I need you to add some side and back training—"

"Look, I can do a million of these," another girl said getting down on all fours. "With your back like it is, I bet you'd really benefit from this exercise."

"Right," I said trying not to sound annoyed. "Here's the thing. There are muscles that are really hard to gain access to, but when strengthened it's like wearing a corset," I reached around my mid-section to demonstrate.

"My dance instructor called those the game changers," said Camilla scratching her overly long nose.

"And they will change your balance if you can do some exercises every night," I said cutting off two other young ladies who wanted to comment. I tersely demonstrated all the exercises. Then I dismissed them, but I was the first to leave.

I tried giving out more compliments over the next few days, but every time I did, I completely lost control of the class again. The interruption in class became much the same as a five-year-olds wanting to show me every little thing they did. Not to mention how many times they tried to correct me, and my way of teaching.

Finally, instead of letting thc dancers stick to me with their verbal cling, I stopped and nodded to indicate when a dancer was doing well, and moved on. Camilla got more nods than the rest, but the other girls didn't seem to notice. I begrudgingly admitted it was the only way to keep a class moving.

Camilla was the only one doing the core exercises I asked all the girls to do. I knew this because only she flinched at the barre from sore muscles when they should have. After her muscles soothed, Camilla's balance improved drastically in the days I worked with her. There was no doubt who would be advanced when the time came.

Teaching this class, I realized how I'd become better than many of the dancers at school. My success lay in the little things and pushing past the failures. In the end nothing could take the place of being willing to learn and working hard.

When I went to my own classes, I cherished every head nod a master or mistress bestowed on me. I even started to smile when I realized I was getting more nods than most. Why had I spent so much of my energy resenting those precious nods?

Chapter 49

Ivan did all the little things I taught him. He soaked up everything he was taught in the company. He thrived. Feeling challenged, he progressed quickly. Every female dancer fawned over him. Even Natalia congratulated him on his positive reviews for *The Dream*. I did not get such a warm welcome from her.

Over the next week she feigned friendship with me like usual, but this time I saw when she tried to trip me up in front of the other dancers, and especially Noel.

"Erin, what's your plan to take off all that extra weight you put on?" Natalia asked after our last master class one afternoon, and the master teacher was walking by.

"I'm actually down after *The Dream*," I said. I could feel myself physically leaning away from her.

"Really, I would never have guessed. It looked like Ivan was having trouble getting you up at the end."

"No, no problems," Ivan said. Lately he grew protective of me and tried to keep me away from Natalia as much as possible. I started to walk away with him, but turned and said:

"Nati, let me know if Stephan needs to practice with me so you can take a break. You really seemed tired by the end of class."

I waved to someone across the room so I could appear nonchalant and pretend not to notice the scowl on her face. I kept pace with Ivan to the exit so she couldn't answer back. Another trick I learned at Serena's school of catty behavior.

I would have felt smug if I hadn't wasted the whole evening obsessing over what else I should have said to her. Sadly, the beauty of my dream began to fade. Hadn't I already trod this embittered road growing negativity until my anger couldn't be unrooted for anything? Several times in the last month in fact.

I thought about the last few days. I lived on an emotional tidal wave of frustration trying to find my place in the company. Every time I climbed up, Natalia pushed me back down. The frustration grew into anger quickly. It was the same anger I spent so much energy trying to diffuse since I'd walked into the hotel and Julian Marrows manipulated me into chopping my hair. The same anger after Chris left me vented at Pheobe. I was angry. How did I release the anger without lashing out?

Julian hijacking my life made me rage, but obsessing until it took up all my time and energy made me so low. Now it happened all over again with Natalia. How did I manage her vindictive nature without getting angry and hurt all the time?

I couldn't be snarky and content. Mom's stupid speech about having a limited well of energy to draw on revolved in my head. I had to choose how to use it. I had to leave the negative behind so I could thrive. But how?

Svetlana made her appearance the Thursday I had to leave early for *The Whole Package* reunion show. She was put in master classes with the soloist and principles. She had dark eyes and hair with a perfect triangle nose and high European cheeks. Her talent intimidated me.

She did not need me to help her. She picked up the dances with ease and moved like a human contortionist. For some reason I felt my dreams slipping through my fingers when I watched her dance. Fear struck me hard and fast, and I couldn't pretend I hated her. I was afraid of her.

Noel introduced us after class, but then scurried away, and I thought even she wanted to avoid Natalia's wrath.

"Erin it is such a pleasure," she said in a British accent. I would soon find only her name was Russian.

"I believe you are rooming with me until you can find a place of your own," I said.

"Thank you," she said nodding, but grew distracted when Ivan walked up to us.

"Ivan did you meet Svetlana?" I asked when their glancing at each other grew uncomfortable.

"Privyet," he said shyly.

"If you speak much more to me in my native tongue, I will have to open the App I use to speak to my grandmother," she said.

"Oh, sorry," he said in his thick accent.

"That's better," she said. "I moved to England as a child and attended The Royal School of Ballet where my father teaches. I prefer to be called Lana if you don't mind."

"That's a great school."

"I actually saw you take the gold medal in the international dance competition a few years ago," Lana said to me.

"Really? You weren't competing?" That was ten years earlier in my high school days, and she couldn't be more than twenty.

"No, my father took me, but it made an impression," she said. I nodded. Was she calling me old? I couldn't tell if she was really complimenting me or telling me to get out of her way. I no longer felt like I was chasing Natalia for the lead role but running from Lana.

I left practice early, discouraged. Obligated to appear on the reunion show for *The Whole Package*, I took a cab the couple miles over to the theater.

When I made it to the theater, I was taken into the taping area. My designer, Von, met me.

"Go get your hair done and then we will talk. I made three dresses for you to try on."

"Okay," I said, surprised. He talked to me more in that sentence than the whole show. I walked further into the backstage area where rolling mirrors were set up in a line.

"Erin, you look so cute," I heard a familiar voice call. "Didn't you have to grow your hair back out for your dance company? It looks like you cut it shorter!"

I nodded. I let Phoebe take me to her place and had side bangs cut over the weekend I spent at home. Carrie sat next to Serena. Serena, who first pulled me down into the negative hole where I now lived. I would not look pathetic in front of Serena. I would find the positive, the social media edit of positive if I had to. I lifted my chin confidently. I totally ignored Serena and kissed Carrie's cheek.

We talked about my dance, and how I choreographed. It was hard to explain how one ballet company could borrow a dancer from another. So I didn't.

"Where can I see you perform?" Carrie asked.

"I just finished a show at the Philadelphia Ballet. I'm working on material for Sleeping Beauty that will run in D.C. for a week; that's the only East Coast theater on the schedule. Then the Nutcracker in December."

"Did you enjoy Philadelphia as much as your last place?" she asked.

"More," I said. Noel had Lana now. I was considering going back so I could avoid Natalia and be around warm people. Mostly, I wanted to go so Chris couldn't continue to ignore me.

"Good for you! There's something about how you choose to react," Carrie said.

"Yeah," I said, glancing at Serena. She smirked at me and I flared. But then I stopped myself. This felt important, but I couldn't put my finger on why.

"I worried about you after the show. I'm so glad it worked out okay," Carrie said.

"The publicity actually helped me in more ways than one," I told, but I couldn't even be sure why I said the next part, except that maybe if I put it out into the world, karma would make it happen, or maybe the way Serena still looked so snide, I had to prove I thrived.

"How so?" Carrie invited, ignoring Serena clicking her tongue.

"I started dating this guy. He's amazing. He's a sports psychologist; we have so much in common. He watched the show –"

"Um…" Carrie gave me a skeptical look and I laughed. I laughed out everything mean sitting on my chest. I defended.

"No, he watched because he was supposed to be Ethan."

"What?" Carrie asked. She got serious fast.

"He met with Julian and everything. Then six months before the show started, he went in to sign his contract. They dumped him. Said he wasn't right for the show," I said watching her. The way her face grew in concentration, I felt like she knew something I didn't.

"Really," she said, perplexed.

"Yeah, he was curious to see who took his place. Then after he saw me, he kept watching," I said unable to contain the blush that spread across my face.

"You guys have a lot in common?" she asked.

"Everything," I said. She didn't seem surprised.

"That's interesting," she said. I wanted to ask her what was interesting, but Von called me, waving his arms like he may have one last chance to get discovered if I looked amazing. Disappointed I didn't get more out of her I said, "Oh, gotta go! The benefit of short hair."

She gave me a pained sort of look and waved. I waved back. I sighed as I walked away. Was it delusional to act like Chris would eventually be my boyfriend? It didn't matter I would likely never see Carrie again. This thought made me sad. She changed me. Is it possible to feel connected to someone, and yet know they would never really be a part of your life? Are those the people I should fight for, or is there a point when you move on?

I dressed in a generic spaghetti strap Prussian blue cocktail gown that matched my eyes. I moved to a backstage area and was told to be quiet. It was a boxed-in space, behind the stage area where I was supposed to stand around and wait for my turn to go on stage. Instead of feeling set aside, feeding my anger, I found a little space for myself. I climbed up on a wooden box so I could sit and watch the performance before me as the murmuring audience would on the front side of the set.

Serena badgered everyone who stood near her. How didn't I notice her noxious stench right from the start? It felt so familiar the way people scattered from her when she walked toward them. It was the same way the dancers looked when Natalia came around. I physically winced when Serena walked over and sat on my box next to me.

"You are going to eat your words in a few minutes," she whispered, giving me a haughty side glance.

"Excuse me?" I asked, leaning to stretch my back out. I must have said it too loud because Julian's blonde assistant glared at me, even though they weren't filming yet.

"You said Julian wasn't looking out for me," she whispered.

"Oh, he isn't. Why would you think he is?" I asked in the same murmur the audience was using.

"He just invited me to be the host of *The Whole Package* next season. Lance is going to try for Carrie," she gushed.

"Carrie is going back on *The Whole Package*?" I asked.

"Yep, and I'm hosting," she said smugly.

I laughed. Again, the blonde lady scowled at me.

"What's so funny?" she asked quietly squinting at me.

"You have no idea what real success looks like, do you?" I asked.

"Being the host of a—"

"No," I interrupted, "allowing your success to rise and fall with a man like Julian is so unwise. If you want to be famous, go after it. You could easily get an agent. You could model or try out for roles as an actress. Anything but this."

"You have to have allies," she said so quietly I almost couldn't hear her.

"Julian is only taking care of himself. When he goes down, which he will, because he's set himself up to fail, you fail with him."

"He is remarkably successful," she said.

"Think about it. He basically stole Dr. Corbon's show. He didn't put in the work and hasn't ever had an original idea. You and I could cast every contestant before the show even started. It's a tired formula. Considering the studio let Colby put that video online last week, it does not bode well for this show," I said.

"Yeah, thanks for that. I have to work extra hard to redeem myself in the eyes of the viewer. I need to talk to Julian about that," she said.

"You knew Colby was filming. I did not do that to you," I hissed.

She rolled her eyes getting down off the box.

"Make your own success, Serena," I said. "That way no one can take it from you."

A man yelled, "Quiet on Set!"

Serena started to say something, but I hissed, "Shhhhh," and she stomped away to the loud clapping sound of the slate.

The show started and everyone moved to Samanatha Prowers voice, like they put on a silent film. Julian watched the screen and the contestant he was feeding onto the stage with his head like a spinning dancer trying not to get dizzy. At the first commercial break, Serena walked up to him. She whispered something to him. He glanced at her annoyed, then turned to find me.

They way his eyes scrutinized me felt…predatory. He needed something from me. When we first met, he needed something from me. But a year later when I went on his show he didn't anymore. What did that mean?

I wanted to find Carrie. How did she know Chris and I had everything in common? I looked for her but couldn't find her anywhere backstage.

I watched as Julian made his way to me, his blonde assistant, and Serena on his heels. Instead of stepping toward him into the chaos I stayed still and let him come to me. I breathed deeply.

"Ah, Erin. I needed to speak to you," Julian whispered.

"Yes?"

"You won't have as long an interview as the other girls," he hissed quietly. "Serena needs a chance to redeem herself after sounding so catty on the morning show. You and Serena are such good friends. You don't mind, do you?"

I took a deep breath.

"The less I am associated with this show the better."

"That's ungrateful. I single-handedly launched you," he said, surprised.

"You can't honestly believe that," I said forgetting to whisper, "You did nothing but scramble up my life and force me to put it back together."

He stared at me slack jawed. Apparently, he believed he helped me simply by letting me deign to be on his show.

"Where's Colby?" I asked, thinking I'd like to tell him thanks for the free publicity.

"He finished his schooling and didn't bother keeping his commitment to the show by finishing the season. He took a job with the studio. But I guess you know firsthand, loyalty isn't his strong suit," Julian said in a disgruntled whisper.

"I don't know about that. He seems to have done right by me after all," I said.

He glared at me.

"Where are Carrie and Veronica?" I asked, as I hadn't expected Ethan to be put back here with us.

Julian looked around like something just went very wrong.

"Where did Carric go?" hc hissed at his assistant, who threw her blonde head into a frenzy looking for his star.

They moved away and I took another deep breath refusing to give in to the feeling of being less than Carrie. I did not need chaos in my life.

Chapter 50

For her interview, Serena walked out onto the stage like she owned it. She answered all the questions like she'd been prepared. She talked about having to really face her parent's death and she'd been really struggling on the show. The audience forgave her everything by the time she took her seat in order of when she left. We had to sit on stage for the rest of the show in case the hostess had any follow up questions.

I went out on the stage and did my interview. The hostess used the screen above her to play some of Colby's short film that showed up on social media. She seemed enchanted by it.

"I wish I'd caught your show. You dance so well," Samantha said, watching me. Then with something like a devilish grin she said, "I really wish we could show our audience parts of the documentary coming out at the Lincoln Theater, but we simply don't have time."

"I'm sorry? What?" I asked.

"Colby Miller's documentary, *A Spin on Reality*. It's premiering at the New York Film festival," she said like I should understand.

I drew a blank and Samantha squinted at me, but then quickly said, "I heard you've been accepted into the prestigious American Ballet."

"Yes, I'm training to debut in the upcoming production of Sleeping Beauty," I said still trying to understand what was happening.

She congratulated me. I smiled and said thanks again. Neither of us mentioned American was the company Julian got me kicked out of in the first place.

After that, my interview ended. The audience clapped politely for me. And we went to a commercial. Serena's segment took up most of the block of time.

When the camera operator nodded that we were clear, Samantha whispered, "You haven't even seen the documentary?"

"I saw a reel on YouTube. The studio owns everything. They don't have to get my permission to use the footage," I said.

"Right. Well, Colby turned it into a whole documentary and it's playing at a few theaters, most notably Lincoln."

"Like a whole documentary of me dancing?"

"Sort of. Dr. Corbon gave Colby everything he needed to get into the grime of the show," she said.

"Doesn't that hurt the show?"

"She already lost the show. Julian stole it from her. The studio head, Richard Blanchard calls it raw and engaging, but Julian thinks it's defamatory."

"Julian said he had complete control over whatever was filmed on the show," I said, a little confused.

"No, Dr. Corbon and the studio does. Colby received permission from the studio head Richard Blanchard to air it. I guess some high-priced attorney got involved and, like I said, Richard loved it. I almost laughed. I had a guess which high-priced attorney got involved.

"Colby really did you justice," she said. "I only meant to watch it for a few minutes but ended up watching the whole thing. I'll have my assistant email you a copy if you want."

"I'd like that, thanks," I said. She waved over a man with a head set on and told him to get me the film. He nodded then asked, "Erin, can I show you where to sit?"

"Is that code for move it?" I asked with a laugh.

"Sorry," he said. I nodded and stood up.

"Here, if you enter your email, I can just forward the link to you," he said as we walked down stage. I sat down and typed my email into his tablet. He tapped it a few times after I handed it back.

"Okay, it's sent," he said walking away. I didn't get the chance to say thanks.

The stage was set up in a large V-shape of chairs, like geese flying south for the winter, the hostess being the lead goose. Her extremely efficient assistant had taken me back to a part of the formation where I could glide through the rest of the show. At this point I realized I had no idea what happened after Mia and I watched Carrie walk off the show.

This audience also had an aura. They had been polite for me, but these were not my people. This was Carrie's kingdom, and the buzz of anticipation built up in the air.

When Carrie came out the audience erupted.

Carrie was charming. It fascinated me to watch her work the hostess instead of the other way around. They did a little dance for each other. It was filled with tension, almost like an argument but they stayed cordial. I found value in this. Even though it wasn't purely positive, it was expressive. Like each instrument could be a separate animal in Prokofiev's *Peter and the Wolf*, each expression could be beautiful in its own way. Even if the instrument didn't always harmonize, it did have a place in the song. This was important.

Carrie's interview ended and she sat across from me in the V shape, and next to Serena. From that point on Carrie and Serena put on a show just for me. Carrie smiled; Serena worked overtime to be snide to her. Serena spoke to Carrie, Carrie nodded tolerantly and then waved to a young girl in the crowd.

Carrie glowed and Serena smoldered.

Since I left the show, I had done both.

I preferred to glow. Yet, it was so easy to fall into the angry place where I smoldered. I had used Serena's antics only that morning against Natalia. I couldn't do it anymore. It made me into someone I didn't like.

Veronica ended up winning the million dollars. That was not surprising since she won so many of the competitions. The surprise was when they made it look like Veronica had somehow stolen Ethan from Carrie. When Ethan finally came out on the stage, he stared at Carrie. I could easily see that whatever happened between them was unresolve

The strange thing was Carrie. Carried joked around with Veronica, and Tess. She soothed Sandra's hurt feelings. She didn't wallow in the bitter feelings Veronica must inspire sitting next to Ethan. Nobody watching could deny that Carrie and Ethan would eventually be together, nobody except Veronica. She glanced at Ethan with hope that broke my heart for her. Despite everything, Carrie was kind to her, and it felt classy.

Then the most amazing thing happened.

Samantha announced Carrie was doing *The Whole Package* again, only this time as the judge. The audience erupted again. Carrie lost her composure for the first time. I read her surprise.

Once she got the crowd's attention, she explained some mistake was made. She was not coming back in the fall to take on the role of the judge. Did that mean Serena was out of a job already?

What's more, Carrie's responses reminded me of my mom. She held to her truth, no matter how she was picked on or pecked at. I felt inspired and vowed to try and do the same.

The reunion show ended as abruptly as my time in the Manor House. It seemed like they went over time and had to just stop.

I went to the back room where all our personal items were being kept. I needed to talk to Carrie. I figured she wouldn't be available for quite some time, so I sat at a mirror to try out a few hair styles with my side bangs.

What did Carrie know about Chris? Did she know why they dropped him? She seemed very curious about him. I needed to know why. Everything dimmed next to Chris. Would I be doomed to wait for him, like Madam did his uncle? Would he ever come back to me? Would the intense desire now turned into agony ever extinguish so I could push him into the background of my life?

A movement across the room caught my attention. Carrie had slipped in. I thought she would be thronged by admirers. I moved to intercept her. She grabbed her stuff from the other side of the room and ran out like the audience chased her, which they probably did.

I quickly pulled all my stuff together and followed her at a trot, hoping I could intercept her on the street. I wasn't the only one looking for her. The host hurried into the hallway, and spotted Carrie. She jogged quickly down the outer ring of the theater. Lance called after her. Of course, he wanted to ask her out, so I ducked into a theater entryway that would soon be filled with the audience after they talked to Ethan. I scooted in to hear their conversation. Apparently, I had to keep working on this life lesson. I heard Carrie say:

"Can I ask you something?"

"Sure, let's go get a drink," Lance said.

"Oh, I can't. I work tomorrow," Carrie said. "I'm just wondering, was Erin supposed to win, you know, before Adam brought me in?"

I stopped. What? I did not breathe waiting to hear what Lance said.

"How'd you figure that out?"

"She's dating the perfect guy, and he was supposed to be the judge," Carrie said.

"Yeah, she was supposed to win," Lance said. I couldn't breathe. What?

"So then… Is he a nice guy? Should I warn her?" Carrie asked. Carrie was looking out for me?

"He's fine. They're actually very compatible," Lance said.

"Then why don't the couples from this show last? Aren't the guys …"

"No, no… I mean Ethan was a rock. He was the first judge in the show's history not to sleep with anyone."

"He didn't…um?"

"No, but usually Julian can get the judge to sleep with the final two women if not more."

"Julian manipulates them to sleep with the contestants?"

"Yeah, and it works. Every time!"

"Eww," Carrie said.

"Makes good television," Lance said, "Most of the judges really are decent in normal situations and wouldn't otherwise sleep with that many different women in such a short amount of time."

"Julian's a real peach," Carrie said.

"That's why Dr. Corbon bailed. So many girls were being… well anyway, no. Erin's fine. He's a nice enough guy, and without the baggage of having slept with half a dozen women at the same time he was sleeping with Erin. They should be fine," Lance said.

"Well, that's both a relief and disturbing," Carrie said.

I smiled. Carrie valued me enough to look out for me. A commotion broke out in the theater. I heard someone scream from behind me. I couldn't hear anything else that was said. A moment later, Lance ran past, but didn't notice me.

I stood in the doorway shell-shocked for some time. Without knowing how, I walked to the subway. Numbly I swiped my card and went through the turn style. I was supposed to win. That's why Chris was dropped. Ethan was compatible with Carrie.

I spent so much time watching, learning what made a contestant the best. I adjusted my personality to fit in with it. Is that what happened to Phoebe? She wanted to fit into our world, and misguided, she read too many magazine quizzes or worse, watched high-bred sarcastic reality show characters? Thankfully she had my mom to get her into therapy.

When Julian made it clear I had to cut my hair, was he trying to make me quit the show? Why couldn't he have just said something? There were so many better ways to handle that situation. But then hadn't I kept reminding Phoebe of all her mistakes when I was trying to make her quit Drew?

Why was it so easy to see the missteps in everyone else and not myself?

After everything else, it turns out there was no such thing as the whole package. Julian created an image I wasted so much time trying to become. Just like Phoebe, I couldn't be anything except me. And that had to be enough.

By the time I made it to my apartment I left the reality show behind me. I didn't want anything to do with the show that would have ruined Chris. I also felt surprisingly calm. Anger was no longer building inside me. I let go of the experience. I left the Manor House, emotionally as well as physically. My new goal was to use the same calm with Natalia.

Chapter 51

"Hey Erin," Lana said as I walked into my apartment. I jumped and screeched a little.

"Sorry. Ivan let me in before he headed to his night job," she said, taken back.

"Hey. No, I'm sorry. He was supposed to. I had a previous engagement and couldn't…"

"*The Whole Package*," she said.

"Ugggh," I groaned walking past her and hanging my backpack on its hook. Three beds in one studio apartment was snug. One bathroom was going to be a nightmare. No, I changed the way I was thinking. I had someone to talk to while Ivan worked odd jobs to support himself.

"You did great. You talked about your dancing as much as you could. You've got to get publicity somehow," she said, nodding to the muted TV on the news.

"Yeah, I just wish I'd found some other way. Speaking of which, this guy on the show made a documentary of me. You want to watch it?"

"Yes," she said. I took out my phone and ordered Chinese food. Then I worked the Bluetooth to connect my phone up to the TV.

"Did you find the remote?" I asked hopefully.

"Nah, I had to do it old school," she said, but it didn't bother her. Well then it wouldn't bother me.

I ducked down to the TV to change the source. While I worked, I wondered what I was doing. Would I be this woman's friend? She may very well kick me out of a job one day. She seemed nice, but then so had Serena at first. How did Carrie do it? Befriend Veronica knowing she was kissing the man she loved?

Lashing out, being angry – those feelings were like an addiction I would no longer feed. How did I stop being so afraid of Lana stealing my world?

Is this how Natalia felt watching me dance my way through the ranks at American? Was she just as threatened as I felt? Is this how Jaxon felt always chasing Chris? Did they allow this fear to choke them? The fear made me entirely irrational. My first instinct was to push her out of my apartment, and never look back.

But if I deserved the principal roles, shouldn't I get them? I paused my busy hands and stilled my breathing. If Lana deserved the roles, shouldn't she get them?

I took a deep breath. If she could take the lead roles from me, she should. But she would have to take them. I wasn't going to give them to her.

However, that didn't mean we couldn't be friends, did it?

I smiled in my best imitation of Carrie and pulled out from the TV.

"Okay, you are going to have to tell me if I look … or just lie to me and tell me it's great," I said. I played the thing on my phone, and it appeared on the screen of the TV.

"I'm sure it'll be fine, your technique is flawless," she said, her accent forcing the aw sound, making me laugh.

"That was believable. You may stay and watch with me. I was only ever in my soft slippers, so I can't imagine it will be too exciting," I said turning up the volume by hand, then moving over to curl up on the sofa.

We watched and I didn't know what to think. It was poetic in a way. I danced. Colby showed me working through the creative process to choreograph my piece. I wasn't en pointe, making my steps less refined. I was often interrupted, and it was frustrating to watch. Serena snapped at me. I danced. Veronica needed my help hooking on a bracelet. Then I danced. Tess wanted me to taste her breakfast before Carrie came in from her run to be sure it was good. Again, I danced.

"Aren't they supposed to narrate or something?" I asked.

"Nah, sometimes they just put the viewer into a world they've never been before," Lana answered.

"Do you want to watch it in fast forward. I'm not sure this is all that interesting," I said.

"Are you kidding? It's fascinating," she said.

"I'm just…dancing," I said.

"No, he caught you creating," she answered. "Look at your face as you try to figure it out. Plus, the longer it goes, the faster it's moving. It's intriguing."

I laughed. After a half hour, I went to the door to get the food. As I walked back Lana was tilting her head with my leg tilt.

"What?" I asked.

"Wait for it," she said. Instead of contestants interrupting my dancing, images from the show disrupted the process. In between the dancing I was clapping at the fourth of July parade in my dance clothes. Serena pushed me into Ethan. I looked up at the cliff like I might cry. Veronica took a Weiner dog from me as I went into a fit of sneezing. I ballroom danced, going into a turn. I spun back into my workout. My face grew more determined. My workout grew into my solo. I grew dark. I didn't realize how dark I'd become at the end. Something bad happened to me. And now, I had to overcome it. Is that why I felt so angry?

We ate broccoli and beef and watched my transformation. The beginning of the documentary showed me smiling and excited. Through my dancing and extra footage of the show I became older, more mature. The last scene showed me plummeting toward the water. I screamed and kicked water into my face. The scene closed to black, but I still screeched. Then it switched over and I danced the entire version of my solo that I choreographed there. When I sunk to the floor at the finale, the documentary ended.

"I don't even know how I should feel about that," I said looking over at Lana.

"I think that guy," she read off the credits, "Colby Miller, is a little in love with you."

"He was with Tess," I said.

"I doubt he was the only one," she said.

"The feel of it though...Samantha Prowers said Dr. Corbon helped him. The tempo has elements of the whole package when it first started. I think Dr. Corbon must have helped him quite a bit," I said smiling, because I thought perhaps, she was a fan of mine. I'd always been a fan of hers.

"Still, it's romantic," she said, and I could feel her youth in the need for romance.

"I know who I want," I said.

"It…or… are you and Ivan a couple?" she asked, looking toward the twin size bed he crammed onto until he could find a place to live.

"No, and no thanks. He's like my little brother," I said. "However, he was looking at you, a lot."

"Well, I definitely didn't get the gay vibe from him," she said, grinning.

"Natalia's partner Stephan is, but he also seems very interested in you," I said.

"Maybe he wants to change partners," she laughed. "He dances with the dragon."

I glanced at her. How had she determined in one day what it took me six years and a reality show to figure out?

I'd admired Natalia near to worship at one time; it blinded me.

"Well, Natalia for sure rules the roost," I said.

"For now," she said. "But I have plans."

"You're not planning on doing a Tonya Harding are you?" I asked. She threw a pillow, and I dodged it.

"Oh, I'm all about the hard work, old lady," Lana said. I laughed, stooped down and threw the pillow back at her.

"With age comes experience, little girl. I suppose we will have to see what we can do with you."

"I will soak up your wisdom," she said putting her hands together and bowing to me like a karate student.

"I will only share my wisdom if you answer 'Yes, prima ballerina assoluta,' after everything I say. You have the accent so it should snowball from there."

"Yes, prima ballerina assoluta," she said with great sarcasm.

"Perfect," I said grinning.

We talked for a while before bed, and I thought maybe we would become incredibly good friends. Our life experience made us so similar.

The next morning, we went into the studio together. Lana was stopped to be questioned about her father by a ballet mistress who knew him. I dropped my stuff by the wall.

Natalia smirked at me, thinking I must be struggling when I walked over to my barre. Did she think I couldn't face my own mortality? I rolled my eyes at her. She flinched.

Ivan stood next to me at the barre.

“Lana, come be barre buddies with us,” I said. and she dropped her stuff and skipped over. Lana came in and said, “Is there room next to you guys?”

The other dancers knew Natalia had singled me out as if I were a rotten piece of meat and stayed away. I smiled at her and said:

“Of course. Got to get some experience under your belt, little girl.”

She grinned and said, “Whatever, Grandma.”

We both laughed.

Natalia glowered at us. However, Noel, who was just behind Lana, gave me her slight head nod of approval.

Chapter 52

As our first show loomed near, I decided I was tired of waiting for Chris. I had to see him. He haunted me. Every time a knock came at my door, or I received a text, my heart jumped. When it wasn't him, disappointment seeped over me.

I had to know if it was really over between us. I had to let go somehow. I couldn't live within the giant shadow of longing, shivering, hoping he'd finally come for me – someday. Madam was a saint. I wouldn't live that way.

We finished early on Tuesday, so I put on my favorite flowing midi-striped summer dress. It hung on me comfortably. I knew Chris would like it because he liked me for me. I took the train to Philadelphia. I picked up takeout and made it to his office building right at closing time.

I walked in suddenly terrified of confronting Chris again. A fit looking middle-aged office manager scanned me as I walked off the elevator and into the classy office. She must have just gotten off vacation because her sunburned face gave way only where a pair of sunglasses should be. She wore her hair in a high bun on the top of her head. She scanned me. She hadn't decided whether she liked me or not.

"You must be Erin," she said as I approached her desk.

"Yes," I said wondering how she figured that out.

"Jaxon's not here," she said.

"I was hoping… I wanted to see…"

"I know, everyone wants Chris. It must be hard on Jaxon. Chris's session ends in five minutes," she said pointing to a few high back chairs.

"Thanks," I said. She eyed the bag of takeout I brought.

"Chris has made so many sacrifices for his family," she said. "He deserves happiness, but it is so hard when they both want the same thing."

I chanted to myself, "stay positive," then answered, "I suppose that I am the thing to which you are referring. Unfortunately, I also have an opinion in the matter."

I gave a happy little laugh after my statement, just as Carrie did. It worked. The woman thawed and said, "I suppose. Jaxon's not a bad kid."

"No," I agreed.

"A lot of women come through here looking at the brothers. Jaxon looks back, but not many of them can turn Chris's head. You did," she admitted.

"Not enough," I said sadly.

The woman drilled her eyes into mine.

"Maybe more than you know," she said, "He's sad these days. Still, they are finally working together like brothers. Jaxon is doing so much better. He and Chris are so civil, but it's tenuous. Please don't ruin that."

Before I could answer, Chris came out, walking a beefy football player in an expensive suit to the door.

"Hey!" He lit up when he saw me.

"Hey," I said glancing at the receptionist, feeling uncertain.

"What is this?" Chris pointed to the take-out.

"This is to thank you," I said.

"Come on back," he said helping me pick up the packages.

"There is plenty, you come too," I said to the receptionist suddenly afraid of being alone with Chris. I couldn't be sure what was right anymore.

"No, no. You kids enjoy," she said taking a deep, concerned breath.

I followed Chris into his office. It was set up as a small sitting room. Everything was glossy.

"What did you get?" he asked pointing to the leather love seat next to an armchair.

"Pork buns. The stage manager told me about this place, but I never got a chance to get some during the run of *The Dream*. I thought it would tickle your foodie tongue," I said setting everything on a round coffee table.

"I love pork buns," he said.

"I had a feeling," I said with a shy grin looking over at him. I could see he waged the same war in his head I did in mine. I smiled at him, and he sat next to me on the love seat.

"You did great on the reunion show," he said.

"Thanks to you. Seriously if I hadn't been in *The Dream*, what would we even have talked about? I would have been pathetic, with no life. I would never have made it through that interview."

"Hence the thank-you pork buns," he said, watching me. I grinned and handed him a paper plate.

"Thanks, Erin," he said.

"Of course, your receptionist said everything is going really well around here," I said.

"Yeah, it's professional. Pleasant, you know?"

"Yeah. You've been looking for a way to get along with Jaxon since college, haven't you?" I asked.

"Pretty much. He resents me so badly," he said looking up from his food.

"Badly enough to go through the effort of meeting the ballerina you were supposed to connect with on a reality show?" I asked.

"Yeah, that badly," he said setting down his plate and glancing at me.

"And after all of this, you will be loyal to your brother, and not your ballerina," I said trying to push the tears back.

"I have to," he said in agony.

"I just… I had to know for sure. It's the only way I can let you go," I said.

"I'm sorry Erin," Chris said, watching me.

"Okay," I said. I stood. "Enjoy your dinner, Chris. Thanks for everything. I really mean it."

"Erin?" he asked.

"Yeah," I said watching the frosted glass door, afraid of what I might say or do if I didn't walk out of it.

"Can you at least eat with me, just this once. Pretend there is no impediment between us. We are just old friends eating together."

I looked down at him and he looked just as miserable as I felt.

"No," I said picking up the extra, extremely large plastic bag I'd hauled all the way from New York with me. "I can't even fathom how Madam did the back and forth. I need a clean break, Chris."

I turned and left. I dropped the plastic bag on the receptionist's desk and said "It's all yours."

I didn't wait for her to respond. I shifted and ran down the stairs.

Chapter 53

It was still fairly early so instead of heading right back to the city; I caught a cab over to the assisted living home. I took the fairy wreath to Mia that had been in my car.

When she opened the door, she almost destroyed the wreath in her happiness to see me.

"How are you?" I asked.

"I am not in trouble anymore. I have my own dolls and my friend even moved in to play with me," she said.

"I am so proud of you. I got you a present for being such a refined lady," I said.

"What?" she asked. I took the wreath out of the box.

"Everyone else has decorations on their doors, I thought we could put one on your door."

"No, no, no," Mia said shaking her head and looking down.

"What is it sweetie?" I asked. "You don't like the fairies?"

"No, I love it, so, so, so much," she said looking at her kitchenette counter. It was full of canvases drying. They were really good.

Finally, she took the wreath. She cried a little as she pushed on the fairy wings, so they flew.

"Yes, I want this on my door," she said wiping her eyes. I grinned and we skipped to the front desk to ask for help hanging it. The maintenance man came to help us. He seemed glad to be hanging the wreath. Mia was very particular on how she wanted it hung and was only content when an orderly came to get her for a movie night she'd been looking forward to. I kissed her goodbye and promised to come back to visit.

"That was mighty nice of you," the maintenance man said when she left.

"It wasn't anything," I said.

"No, it was. She hasn't let anyone put anything on her door since her dad died," he said.

"Why not?" I asked.

"It was their special thing. Once a week he sent her fresh flowers. He always said you only send flowers to the special ladies in your life. I hung flowers once a week for her on a hook that used to be there. After her dad died, she refused to put anything on her door. Until now."

"Oh, I didn't know that," I said.

"I'm glad you came back. The last couple weeks you are all she talks about."

I smiled at him, too sad to admit I couldn't come back. I called myself a cab and walked out of the home feeling quiet and somber. It wasn't until the cab pulled up and parked in the visitor parking lot that I realized Phoebe's car was three slots down from it. I sat there staring at it. I didn't know what to do.

Drew knew who she was. He didn't seem to let it bother him. Still, for Chris to be sacrificing me, for his brother… it all felt wrong.

I took a picture of Pheobe's car. I felt like I needed to since she bold-faced lied the last time I told Drew what happened. As I walked toward the cab, Chris came toward the assisted living home in his workout clothes. He saw me, and looked over at Phoebe's car, then back at me.

"How long?" I asked.

"It's only the third time. Jaxon isn't even encouraging her because she leaves bawling. He doesn't know what to do for her. He just holds her and tries to make her feel better. I tried to talk to her last time, but she feels so guilty. She's so…" he stammered.

"Why didn't you tell me?"

"I couldn't, I just …It hurt you so badly last time, I didn't want to do that to you on top of everything else," he said.

"You've done all of this for your brother. But who cares what happens to mine? Is that it? It's always about you and your brother," I snapped.

"It's not…" Chris couldn't figure out what to say.

"I wish I never met you or Jaxon," I said, hurt far more by his betrayal than Phoebe's. "How did it go again? I'm the best thing that happened to you, and you are the worst thing that happened to me?"

Chris stared at me open-mouthed. Perhaps he never thought his uncle's sin could be his own.

"You enjoy your relationship with your brother, Chris." I snapped, climbing into the cab. "I hope it's worth it."

I slammed the door.

"Please just go," I instructed. The cabbie didn't hesitate. Chris tried to get my attention, but I couldn't even stomach looking at him.

"Can you take me all the way to New York?"

"It'll be a hundred."

"Fine," I said sitting back. Why did I come here? I was finally putting myself back together. I couldn't put myself together and help Drew. Could I just pretend I didn't see it?

The cabbie drove fast to the city, and I felt like I might throw up. What was I supposed to do? Finally, I sent the picture to Drew, and said, "I love you. I don't think she is capable of committing to you until she deals with herself. I'm so sorry, Drew."

I left it at that. I couldn't get more involved. It was too easy to lash out and take my hurt and anger out on their situation. That wasn't fair to anyone.

Eventually, I noticed the brush and the wispy trees along the turnpike had shriveled and died. It was yellow brown sepia; it was all the color of decay.

Chapter 54

By opening night of Sleeping Beauty, I could, without conceit, say I deserved my spot among the principal dancers. In rehearsal I waited on the other dancers to get their parts right; they never waited on me. If there was something I needed to work on, I did not hesitate, and was never given any instruction twice. I lived only in the world where I flourished – I lived there in something of a frenzy.

I danced as the understudy for Princess Aurora, Ivan, as Prince Desire. This meant we would dance those roles in the matinees. We also played our own roles, mine as Princess Florine, and Ivan played Blue Bird. Lana was my understudy.

Hailey called me several times, but I knew she was calling for him. I didn't answer. I pushed his memory away until I forgot him. If I remembered him, the sadness washed over me until I fought to refocus on my debut. I barely spoke to my family, choosing to give Lana and many of the other dancers my time and the minuscule space left in my life.

By opening night, every matinee sold out in which I performed Aurora.

We were at the theater in D.C. warming up at the barre for our master's class at 9:30 AM of opening night. I joked around with Lana. Ivan was hanging out with us, looking shy.

"Erin, Natalia, I need to speak to you in my office," Noel said.

I looked over at Natalia. She glared at me.

I put on my boots over my dance pants. They were different colors of black, and my sweater was closer to the black of my boots than my pants. I pranced a little to her office, just to keep my muscles warm.

What was so important that she would interrupt our final master's class on a performance day?

Noel took us to the small theater office she was using while we performed. She gestured toward the sofa, but neither Natalia nor I chose to sit. She leaned against her desk, her flouncy silk sleeves draping over the desk. She glanced over at the entryway, and said:

"Shut the door, Erin."

I reached over and shoved it shut.

"What's going on? I must get my stretching in," Natalia snapped.

Noel tapped her desk twice. Then, trying to look stern, she said, "I need Erin to dance Aurora tonight."

"What?" Natalia screeched and it echoed.

"The *Wall Street Journal* would like to do a full page spread on Erin. The documentary she starred in is being picked up by three different streaming companies after it airs on public broadcasting. Our dance company will likely be able to gain a whole new avenue of donors. We cannot ignore this opportunity. The board is reprinting the programs as we speak to cast both you and Erin as Aroura."

"No!" Natalia huffed.

"Natalia, you must be reasonable about this," Noel coaxed.

"I have given you years," shouted Natalia. "I have given up my life for this dance company. I could have married and had kids, but no. I stay here and danced."

I watched her pitching her fit. At her mention of children, I realized she hadn't been the same since her long-time boyfriend left her two years previous. I wondered if she regretted not retiring then. She wasn't moving as fluidly as she once had. She was thirty-six. She had to know her career was coming to an end.

"Look. Tonight, Erin has to be Aroura. There is no argument, but if you—"

"No! I've already told you. I'm the top principal or I'm not at all," Natalia threatened. "You know I can do guest appearances and make far more money than I am here."

"Perhaps it is time for you to do so. Erin will play Aurora tonight. It would be irresponsible of me to pass up on an opportunity like this," Noel said firmly.

"Fine, I quit," Natalia said. She paused, waiting for Noel to convince her to stay.

"I accept your resignation," Noel said folding her arms. Natalia walked through the door and slammed it behind her.

"What…what about Stephan?" I asked. Noel crossed behind her desk and picked up her phone. Distracted she said, “He’s her fourth partner in six years, he’s so young…”

“Are you calling Natalia to try and stop her?” I asked.

Noel looked up at me as if I must be losing my head, “No, I’m calling my assistant, Jaycee. Now go warm up.”

“Am I dancing with… Stephan?” I asked.

“No. Ivan isn’t ready for the grand Pas de Deux’ in the secondary role, which is more difficult than the primary role. I’ve been sick over letting him try. Master Keith insisted, but I am far more comfortable with him in the less-difficult primary role of Désiré.

She continued: “I suppose you noticed I had Stephan dancing the difficult role of Blue Bird with Lana lately? They will dance beautifully together. Now get going before I nix you too,” she said, but her gloomy expression appeared to have cleared into that of a busy but very satisfied creative director. She said into her phone: “Natalia quit, run the alternate program.”

Then she hung up.

“Noel,” I said.

“Yes,” she said. Her thin, painted-on brows lifting in annoyance.

“When I need to retire, will you just tell me,” I said.

“You are reasonable Erin. You will know when it is time to go. You will see the changing of the tide and embrace new opportunities before I have to send Lana on a reality show, then find ways to promote a documentary she starred in to get you to see your time is past."

"Oh… you did all that?"

"How do you think Julian Morrows saw your blog? We have crossed paths many times. He swore you would win, and will never be given comp tickets again," she said glaring at her computer screen as she typed something in.

"I was supposed to win before he met Carrie?" I said.

"Yes, well 'supposed to' doesn't count for anything. At least I still know a few people from the network, and your father is a bulldog when he needs to be… it is all working out now."

"I guess I did just as much for Colby's documentary as he did for my career," I said.

"Unless you are not ready to perform tonight. Then you are lugging stage equipment instead of dancing," she said nodding to the door.

"Thank you for this opportunity," I said bowing my head.

"Yes, yes." She waved me away, but her face smiled. Walking back into the studio, it reminded me of the day Serena left the reality show. It was almost as if I could breathe a little deeper.

By the time I finished warming up, Noel came in to announce to the group I was playing Aurora. Some of the other principal dancers looked annoyed, but no one said anything. I won the understudy fair, and there were so many good roles in this ballet everyone had a chance to shine. Stephan did not seem at all displeased to take the role of Blue Bird. He enjoyed dancing with Lana and wasn't fused that Natalia left.

Only one of the Dance Masters appeared overly upset at Natalia leaving, but I often suspected the man who'd been in his prime when Natalia started with the company was a little in love with her.

That night I came to something of a professional high. I danced with a fury, giving myself over to the role. I slept when the time came. Ivan's kiss, though tender and theatrically done, did not stir me awake. I forced my own eyes open.

I threw myself into my dream, shutting the door on the man who festered inside my heart since he picked me up and carried me to meet Madam. Every night my passion in the role grew. I had nowhere else for it to go so it went into my dance.

Chapter 55

Over the next few months, I worked. I danced in a frenzy to prove my excellence. I was better than Lana, but she kept me on my toes. She pushed me, and I pulled her. We were good for each other.

It wasn't just her, either. The other principal dancers all became my friends who loved me like family. I grew comfortable with the me who was ridiculously dedicated to my craft, standoffish until I was comfortable, feisty when I knew what I wanted, sad when I remembered his face, and a fighter to the bitter end.

Critics also loved me. Audiences gave me their energy, and I gave them my heart. We moved together and I did not bother breathing for months. By the time I came back to New York for our final performance of *The Sleeping Beauty* after touring the world, I was at the top of my profession. I'd gotten the attention I needed to be a star everywhere, like I was in Philadelphia.

We returned from the Philippines the week before Thanksgiving. We did one final performance for donors and honorary guests in New York before we were given a week off before the craziness that was the Nutcracker started. In master class that morning, we started working on rolling my foot work to prepare for my role as the sugar plum fairy. All this occupied me, and I forgot my parents would have been given tickets. That is why I exclaimed when I found Mom in my dressing room sitting at my makeup chair, looking in the mirror and putting on lipstick after my final curtain call.

"Hey, Mom," I said.

"You danced very… well tonight," she said blotting her distinctive raisin-colored lips with a tissue, then putting her tube of lipstick back in her purse.

"Praise indeed. Is Dad here?" I asked.

"He gave our tickets to clients. I had to reach out to Noel to get another," she said. I nodded, taking off my earrings and reaching over her to put them in a dish on the counter.

"Can I take you to dinner?" Mom asked, squinting at me.

"I'd like that. Do I need to change?" I asked, flouncing my tutu so it bounced.

"Please," she said.

"Okay, I'll be back," I said. I showered and put on a dress I used for a publicity shoot. Mom dried my hair, and I did a little light makeup. After I was ready, we walked back out into the lobby that was being emptied of theater goers. We blended right in. Mom stared up at a huge banner advertising Stephan and me as the Nutcracker and Sugar Plum Fairy.

"Do you enjoy dancing with him?"

"Very much. He's on a whole other level dancing. He's so kind, such a patient man when teaching. There are few people in this world I love more than him."

"Good. Well, you look beautiful," she said.

"Thanks, Mom."

"Are you growing your hair back out?" she asked, as it was past my shoulders again.

"I haven't had a minute to worry about it," I said.

"Have you been dating someone new?" she asked looking at the bracelet on my arm.

"Nah, Lana bought this for me at a market in London. She showed me all her haunts."

"That's lovely of her. I thought maybe…well your father said the man who made the documentary called and asked for your number."

"He took me to dinner when we were in Costa Mesa. He's with the studio in Southern California. He took the struggling artist thing too seriously. I don't think he would have made it without Dad. He doesn't really inspire people to want to help him."

"But you do," she said. "Noel said her dance company is like a family now."

"Yeah, the whole company is…more relaxed since Natalia left. I guess we are kind of like a big family now," I said, smiling.

"Noel mentioned you have been kind to Lana, and it helped the whole company heal. It seems to me if you hadn't had such a bad experience with Serena, you may never have realized just how much one person can infect the whole group."

"Yeah, and I decided I wasn't going to be that person. It would have been easy to see Lana as a threat and fight everything about her. Instead, I have a good friend. I am grateful for her."

"Hailey was so good for you. I love her for showing you that dancers don't have to always be at odds," Mom said. I felt so guilty for never calling her back. I couldn't handle talking about Chris and I felt that's where Mom was steering the conversation.

"Mom, you know it was you who showed me it's better to be positive," I said doing up the top button of my coat as we neared the door.

"I thought you couldn't hear me."

"Hearing and acknowledging are not the same," I teased.

She pulled me into a side hug. I hugged her back, and then stepped through the door opened for us by another patron.

"Hey, aren't you…" he asked looking at me, then looking at the banner.

"Her sister," I said, unwilling to engage when I wasn't on stage.

"Ah, tell her well done," he said.

"Thank you, I will," I said grinning and stepping away into New York. It had grown chilly by the middle of November. I loved the crisp fall air that smelled like snow and the nutcracker.

"I'm parked over here in valet," Mom said turning toward an underground garage. I followed her automatically.

"Noel also said you are working yourself into the ground," Mom said once we were free of the crowd.

"I'm really progressing," I said.

"That's great, but she's worried you might do yourself injury if you don't rest more," she said.

"I'm being careful mom, I swear, but there is so much to learn," I said.

"Are you progressing or avoiding?" she asked.

"Huh?"

"Have you seen Chris lately?" she asked bluntly since I wouldn't let her lead us into the subject. She stared at me instead of handing the valet ticket to the parking attendant, who'd just come out of her cube made of windows. Mom didn't flinch. I didn't allow myself to remember Chris if I could help it. In my mind, he visited me at night, but for the most part I could blot him out.

"He… he did what was best for his family. That wasn't me," I said, turning away to focus on the woman in a navy-blue jacket that made a rubbing noise when she walked. After Mom handed the woman the slip, she went back to her office for our key.

"Is that really what happened?" Mom asked.

"I asked him to make me his family. He chose Jaxon. It hurt so bad I'm not sure I even care about dating anymore. It ends and then you have to recover and still focus on the performance. I love my career, the little family I've made for myself. I'm happy."

"Are you?"

"I am…content," I said, wishing the woman were a little quicker with the car.

"In the past you have always used your dance to express yourself. Your performance tonight was incredible, passionate, full of life. You gave all of yourself to your audience, and now you are dried out inside. Is there anything left for you?"

"That is me."

"No, it's what you do. Where have you gone, Darling?"

"I… I don't know," I admitted. "I'm a little lost when I'm not on the stage. It's the only place where things make sense."

Mom took my hand. "We will find you," she said.

"I don't want you to." I pulled away.

"Why not?"

"Because right now, I can control the things I can, and I let go of the things I can't. Isn't that what you taught me to do, Mom?"

"Don't get me wrong, I'm very proud of how you are handling your life," Mom said kissing my cheek.

Just then the valet brought our car. Mom tipped the attendant while climbing in. Mom didn't say where we were going, but I knew she'd take us to our favorite restaurant. It was the place we always went when we made it back to New York after we traveled together in high school. It was our place. After we drove out of the garage and mingled sufficiently into traffic Mom said, "Erin, I need you to try again with Phoebe."

"Mom, I apologized to her… I didn't sway Drew to dump her when I saw her cheating again. Staying out of his business is all I can do. When I get too involved, I get angry and I don't like who I am…I can't like her. I…I think I feel sorry for her. It's the best I can do."

"Negativity is addictive, I agree, but you can't simply cut everyone out of your life so you never feel it."

"What else can I do?"

"At some point, you will fight with Lana, and Ivan, or Stephan. What will you do then?"

"I… I am trying really hard to get along."

"The truest test of a person's character is accepting the flaws in others and loving them anyway."

"I don't know how… you love people so unconditionally. I don't know how to do that. Not with someone like Phoebe."

"You have to love her. Drew needs our help. Please."

"Okay, I will try. For you…for Drew, I will try," I said, clenching my jaw.

"Phoebe has talked Drew into a Christmas wedding."

"I don't get how they are still together. Let alone getting married," I said feeling the frustration grow inside me.

"Phoebe swears she has a problem with fidelity," Mom said. "She doesn't know how to control it. She thinks as soon as she's married, then she can commit to Drew, and it won't be a problem anymore."

"What does her therapist think of that?"

"Phoebe stopped seeing her, so I would assume she told her that's not how it works."

"Come on, Mom. You can't possibly think staying positive and supporting their relationship is the way to go."

"Being positive doesn't mean being stupid, dear. Turning a blind eye isn't the same as being kind. You can treat someone with kindness even while disagreeing with their behavior. We don't love that Phoebe cheats on Drew. We know their relationship is doomed. That doesn't mean we call Phoebe names and degrade her," Mom said, braking for a red light.

"What…What can we do?"

"We are having our give-thanks-for-the-clients at the house this Saturday night. I hoped you would come."

"I meant to, I just forgot to RSVP. I'm not staying in the city next week for anything," I said. It was a full week before the holiday and the Thanksgiving Day parade could already be seen floating down the streets.

"Perhaps you could bring a date."

"Huh?" I squinted at her.

"To the party," she said, turning the car despite the glowing yellow light.

"A date?" I asked as someone from the other direction honked because she wasn't all the way out of the intersection.

"An old friend perhaps."

Fear struck my heart. What did she expect me to do?

"What old friend?"

"Phoebe isn't happy with Drew, just as Drew isn't happy with Phoebe. Drew is with her out of loyalty. He is sweet and can't leave her to the world. Phoebe is with Drew because she is afraid of looking at her life without him. It is time we helped the matter along a little."

"Okay."

"If you are not dating this documentary man, perhaps you could bring Jaxon."

"Really?"

"Since you sent your text showing her car at Jaxon's, Phoebe claimed to have a problem with fidelity. She says being with him was an act of self-sabotage, but I don't think so. She hasn't been the same since. I believe she cut all ties with him."

"Why do you say that?"

"She's pretending to be happy, but she's not. She looks like she might cry sometimes," Mom said.

"We are going to meddle," I said to Mom who tried to look innocent as she pulled up to the curb near the valet stand.

"This thing has gone on too long. Phoebe desperately talks about having children, hoping to be pregnant by their honeymoon. She thinks diving in head first will keep her from wanting Jaxon. Drew doesn't know what to do."

"Could you imagine a child in the mix?"

"People do strange things to prove they are all in, even when a relationship is falling apart. That's why I thought maybe if you weren't already taken, you could perhaps invite Jaxon," she said.

My mouth dropped. That is not what I was expecting.

Mom pulled herself out of the car and politely handed her keys to the valet. I followed her, taking the valet slip. She always manages to lose them. We made our way through the swarm on Madison Avenue and walked through the restaurant door being held open for us.

Mom used her smile and amazing interpersonal skills to get us into the restaurant quickly without a reservation. We were seated without pausing.

"You know, you should invite Drew's study group to the give-thanks," I said. "Drew said they all passed the bar but one guy. That's something to celebrate," I said.

"I did feel there was someone in his group he took a shining to," she said, pulling out her phone. "I'd better have Drew do it now, or they won't be able to respond by Saturday."

"Yeah, who knows if she'll come. Knowing Drew, I'm sure he brought up Phoebe often enough, so she'd know he was taken," I said.

"I can't believe I forgot them," Mom said, still texting. "We could help them out in their careers just introducing them to some of your father's associates. Drew wouldn't begrudge them a leg up."

"No, of course not," I said, perusing the menu while she texted.

We talked about my December. We would be in Southern California for our performance of the nutcracker season. Because it was the money maker for the year, most theaters had their home ballets performing twice a day for the entire season.

We would go a few places for two or three nights, but only in the U.S. so it wasn't so hard on our bodies. This in turn gave the local companies a break. We would work with their casts of youth, giving them a chance to up their performance as Noel called it. Our tour nights were always sold out.

When we finished eating, we went to my apartment.

Mom helped me pack. Lana took Ivan home to meet her parents. They left for the airport directly after the performance to spend the weeklong holiday with her parents in London.

"We can leave tonight," I said to Mom, who insisted I lend her pajamas and she would sleep in Lana's bed.

"No, no. This will be snug," she said.

"But we could miss the traffic tonight," I said.

"Oh, it's fine. You look so tired. We'll sleep late," she said.

I watched her, sensing she was up to something. I didn't bother saying anything else, and went to stretch.

Mom not only slept over but lounged in bed for an hour on social media in the morning. As we loaded up her car at ten, I realized Mom came to get me.

"Were you worried I wasn't coming home?" I asked.

"I … you haven't come home since you left, you barely pick up your phone. The only communication you've had with your brother is the congratulations text you sent at the beginning of the month after he passed the bar. We weren't sure what was going on."

"Oh, I've just been busy. Sorry." I realized her plotting with me might have been just as much about getting me home as it was saving Drew. She once told me her family always came first and she would do whatever it took to keep us together.

"Drew is miserable without you," she said.

"I'm… I never said we had a problem. I love him, more than ever. I just can't be calm around her," I said.

"At first, you were her friend," Mom reminded, climbing into the car.

"Blood is thicker than water," I said opening a game I liked to play on my phone to zone out. Mom let out a loud sigh to be sure I knew she thought me ridiculous. Then she navigated her way through the city.

We drove almost all the way to Philadelphia on the I-95 before I realized Mom wasn't thinking I could text Jaxon. She meant to drop by.

"Mom, what are you doing?" I asked as she exited the Interstate.

"We're going to talk to Jaxon," she said. "We discussed it last night.

"Are you crazy?" I asked.

"No, you said it was a good idea," she said. "The party is tomorrow night. Besides, I would like to talk to the young man about Phoebe. Despite your dislike of her, I have grown rather attached to her, and want to be sure we are not setting her up for heartache. I am sure she is smitten with him but cannot be sure what he is thinking."

"I… are you sure?" I asked, seized with terror. What if I saw Chris. I couldn't even think of his name without the massive spasm of ache in my heart. How was I supposed to face him?

Mom pulled up at their office building. I watched her and realized she set me up. She waited until they would be at work, and most likely in the same place before we set out on this mission of ours. Chris was usually available Fridays, unless the Eagles were out of town for Monday night. Sometimes he went with them if someone was struggling with their game. However, with Thanksgiving coming up, they'd play next Thursday instead.

I looked over at Mom. She meant for me to face Chris.

"Let's go," she said.

"I can't," I said, petrified, looking up at the building through the windshield.

"Of course, you can. You get up on stage every night to audiences of thousands."

"No, I … I really don't know if I can…. I can't see him," I said.

"Jaxon is not that intimidating," Mom laughed as if she didn't know exactly who I meant. She quickly got out of the car before I could balk and back out.

I watched her walk away then come back and wave me on. What was I supposed to do? Chris made it clear he didn't choose me. I tried not to blame him, I tried to understand. That didn't mean I wanted to stroll into his office building so he could reiterate he chose his brother over me – again.

Mom knocked on my window. I was that little girl again. I knew she wanted me to keep trying instead of giving up. This wasn't something I could throw myself at until I succeeded. He didn't want me. She knocked again, and reluctantly I climbed out of the car. I realized it would take him rejecting me in front of my mother before she let it go.

I wondered what I was doing as I walked into the elevator and hit the floor. Mom exited the elevator first and walked up to the receptionist. Before Mom could make her request, the woman stood, surprised, and said:

"Erin, it has been too long."

"Yeah. Hey, is Jaxon around?" I asked.

"Jaxon?" she said, surprised.

"Yeah, that's the one I should ask for, right?" I said trying to laugh. I looked at her, biting my lip and feeling vulnerable. She smiled at me and, looking more professional, said:

"Let me call back. He doesn't have a client right now."

"Is Chris here? I'd love to say hello to the young man," Mom said.

"No, sadly not. He's out on a call," she said, glancing at me as I sighed in relief.

"Oh well. Be sure to send my hello," Mom said and though her face didn't change, I could feel her disappointment just by the drop in energy surrounding her.

"Of course," the woman said. She looked at me to see if I wanted to send a message. I did not.

"Erin, Megan! Hey, welcome," Jaxon said, coming into the reception area, hospitable and warm as if I hadn't chewed him out the last time I saw him. Mom took his hand in a warm embrace. I watched them and could see Jaxon looked different. He looked softer and more grown up since I last saw him.

"Here. Come back to my office," he said motioning us to follow him.

We walked through what looked like a small gym, then into his office. It was smaller than Chris's and it was set up with a desk and a chair. He had trophies on shelves behind him.

"How are you?" he asked me.

"I'm doing really well. Next week I'm touring as the Sugar Plum Fairy in the Nutcracker. It's a dream come true, really," I said clenching my jaw. "How's DJ-ing? Are you making a name for yourself?"

"I am, actually. I've started doing Saturday and Sunday nights at a club here in town. I'm getting guest jobs, too."

"Congrats," I said.

"Well, it's not worth my time hardly, except I enjoy doing it. It makes this job better too. I'm happier with work, all around," he said.

"Good for you," I said. There was a pause. I didn't know what else to say.

"What can I do for you two?" he asked.

Mom started to say, "We wanted to invite you to a holiday party. Every year we kick off the holiday season with a huge –"

"Do you love Phoebe?" I interrupted.

I sat still. Mom's eyes grew and she turned with her mouth open to say something about finesse, but nothing came out.

I preferred the straightforward approach to life like my father. I was in a hurry to leave.

"I … I probably do," he said looking down. "I really miss her."

"Why don't you tell her that?" I asked.

"It wouldn't do any good she's so set on marrying Drew. She says he's her family."

"She hasn't had a lot of luck in the family area. It makes sense she adopted us and finds it extremely hard to give that up," Mom said.

"Even so, she can't marry simply to…" I stopped. What did Phoebe think she could do?

"You are very blessed to have all you do, Miss," Mom snapped at me with big eyes, like she expected me to bash on Phoebe. I took a deep breath.

"I know that, Mother. This has nothing to do with me … I don't know what to say. I get I'm blessed. But she can't force herself to love Drew if she doesn't."

"You don't think she loves him?" Jaxon asked hopefully.

"When we left that first night, when I met… Mia, and you said you wanted to date me, do you remember?"

"Yeah."

"She looked like she was about to cry the whole way home."

"I'm such a jerk. I was taunting Chris. I was so wrapped up in this stupid competition I didn't notice what was happening between me and Phoebe."

"We are having a party tomorrow evening," Mom said. "It is our tradition to start the holiday season on the Saturday before Thanksgiving by inviting all those who have helped us over the year into our home. We would like to invite your family," Mom said.

My jaw dropped. I didn't recover in time and Jaxon said, "Do you think if I bring Phoebe flowers –"

"Try something more original," I said. "There must be something, an inside joke that you can play on."

"I'm DJ-ing at The Zone in two weeks. I've done it twice already, hoping to see her. Do you think if I got her a flier, she'd come?"

"Couldn't hurt. Good for you Jaxon. You're getting your crap together," I said, standing. Now that I saw it was Mom's intention to get Chris at her thankful party, I had to get her out before she reiterated the invitation was for both brothers.

"Look, we have to go, but please come tomorrow night," I said.

Before I could reach the door, he asked, "Chris, too?"

"I'm sure he's too busy," I said quickly.

"He's not the same since he gave you up. I needed him too. That's how I knew he was serious about starting over, but I wish I'd never asked him to."

"You cannot pretend Chris didn't help your career along tremendously," Mom quickly said to me.

"He won't come. He's avoided me like the plague since… for months."

"He saw you in Sleeping Beauty twice," Jaxon said.

"He… he came to D.C.?"

"He also flew to Los Angles," Jaxon said, "just for the weekend. He didn't think I knew, but the receptionist makes sure I know what a jerk I was."

I looked at Mom, with no words left.

"Be sure Chris knows he's invited," she said.

I walked out before I could hear any more. Mom was seriously a busybody. I moved as quickly as I could back through the gym and into the reception area. I looked back to see if Mom was following me, but she was taking her sweet time.

I walked past the receptionist who called out, "Oh, Erin! Can I get you something to drink?"

"What?" I asked, slowing in front of her desk.

"A snack, something to drink. I have candy left over from Halloween," she said reaching in her desk. The woman was stalling.

"I'm in training. I can't eat sugar," I said.

My suspicion was confirmed when Chris came from the door to the stairwell, out of breath.

"Erin, hey," he said, gasping for air.

"Hey," I whispered, unable to get any breath behind it. He looked perfect; his dark suit made him look like he belonged on the red carpet. His whole body leaned toward me. His aqua eyes searched me.

"It's so good to see you," he said inching his way toward me. I turned to look for Mom, but she was loitering in Jaxon's office.

"Can we talk in my office?" Chris asked, reaching out and putting a hand on my shoulder.

"I… I'm not sure that's a great idea," I said backing up. "I've got to get going. We have so much to do."

"Can I walk you to your car?" Chris asked, his hand hanging mid-air, still reaching for me. I wanted so badly to kiss him.

I turned to see Mom with Jaxon. Finally making her appearance. I hit the down button for the elevator.

"Chris, I was so hoping to see you," Mom said, speed walking over and hugging him.

"It's so good to see you again," he said leaning into her hug.

"I was just telling Jaxon about our thankful party," Mom said. She pulled the invitation out of her purse. She did not hand it to Jaxon. Mom often chaperoned my out-of-town dance competitions in high school. She would loudly tell me which boys she thought were cute. That humiliation was nothing compared to this.

"Tomorrow night at the house we are having everyone who helped us out over the last year for a lavish dinner and entertainment from some local bands."

"That sounds great," Chris said. He watched me as if he were trying to read my mind. I didn't bother giving him a chance.

"Mom, that might be awkward. I invited Colby," I said. I glanced at the receptionist thinking she would support my standoffish behavior. She looked disappointed.

"Who is Colby?" Chris asked.

"He's the one who did the documentary on me. He really helped push my career along."

"Oh, that's great," he said looking out the window to see what I found so interesting.

After Mom nudged me, I said, "Yeah, but it is a thankful party. I owe you one. If it wouldn't be awkward, then…"

Chris stepped in. He came into my space. His smell wafted over me. His blue green eyes stared intensely at me. He leaned in even closer, lightly touching my arm. He kissed my temple. I stared at him with my mouth open, my eyes watering.

"It was the greatest pleasure of my life to help you," he said.

My mouth moved, but I could not respond. Anger started in. What was he doing? He chose not to date me. I felt the rage start up my throat. He reached out with his other hand to touch my face.

"No, no," I snapped pushing his hand away before it shot electricity through me. "You don't get to do this to me again."

"Erin, I—"

"You need to tell my mom you have no interest in dating me. She needs to give you up. That's the only reason we're here. You need to break her heart like you did mine so she will leave you alone."

Every other pain, every cruel person I'd endured had done nothing to me compared with the agony Chris caused me.

"I didn't mean to…" He stammered and looked from me to mom, unsure what to say.

"Are you kidding?" I said, feeling the rage start up my throat as I backed away from him. The elevator opened.

"Great! We will see you boys tomorrow night," Mom said. She pushed me into the elevator and hit the button trying to get it to close.

"Erin, I deserve your anger, I know I do," Chris said confused why Mom wasn't letting him hash it out with me.

Mom waved and pushed the button to close the elevator doors with one hand and kept the other hand on my arm keeping me in the elevator. We moved quickly through the parking garage and into the car.

"What… what do you think you're doing?" I cried at her when she fit the key into the ignition.

"Calm down. Yelling is not necessary," She scolded. She drove quickly from the parking lot.

"How could you!" I whispered with what air I had.

"Erin, we agreed on –"

"Oh, cut the crap Mom! You did that on purpose. He broke me, and you took me back, you humiliated me in front of him. I have fought for months… months to breathe when I think of him. And you shove him in my face…Why would you do that?"

"I know you think I'm cruel, but sweetie, he is the nicest guy you've ever dated."

"I fell in love with him, Mom. I was vulnerable and open to him. I asked him to make me his family. I gave him my heart… He said no."

"For his brother, for his family, Erin."

"Right, but he still dumped me. And I had to live through it. Now, now you would have me…what? What do you think is going to happen here? I'm not just pretending everything is all right, like Drew. I'm not pretending I'm not in love with him like Phoebe. He dumped me, Mom."

"I think he's sorry," she said.

"I'm going to die now," I said. I pulled my legs to my chest and wept into my folded arms.

When we arrived home, I stomped into the kitchen from the garage. I felt spent and angry at the same time. Drew sat at the table alone. He texted someone.

"Hey, it's so good to see you," he said giving me a head hug. "Just a sec, let me finish this."

"Phoebe?" I asked.

"Nah, my study group. Mom wants them to come tomorrow night," he said. I watched him. It sucked being blindsided. I get that Mom wanted us to face our problems, but her hit-and-run methods were too extreme. I didn't want to ruin Drew's night. He got a text and his face lit up. His smile was sincere and bright. It had to be her.

"Drew."

"Yeah," he said looking up from his phone like I'd caught him doing something wrong.

"Mom invited Jaxon and Chris."

He went white.

"I'm sorry. Mom felt like they helped me so much with my career…" I started but trailed off.

"Mom's been really worried about us lately," he said.

"She said Phoebe won't go back to the therapist."

"She kept telling Phoebe to push back the wedding. Phoebe won't. She's sure it will fix her."

"What are you going to do?"

"I don't know. She's so… How do you know those things about someone and not feel like you have to take care of them?"

"I don't have any idea," I said, "but Jaxon… I think Jaxon's in love with her. I know you don't want to hear that, but what if he could make her happier than you could?"

"I… I don't know."

"Just stand back and watch them tomorrow night. See what you think. You're smart."

"Okay."

"Phoebe doesn't make you happy, not like whoever sent you that text just now," I said. He twitched and flipped his phone in his hand a few times.

"Phoebe is going to be so pissed when she finds out Isla is coming."

"Yeah, and come to think of it, I bet Mom is counting on her lashing out and flirting with Jaxon to hurt you because of it."

"Come on, Mom isn't that devious," Drew laughed. I didn't say anything else, but I thought she just might be. The subject of our conversation walked into the kitchen from the garage.

"Erin, I know you didn't have time to get anything for tomorrow, so I picked this up before your show," Mom said opening a garment bag and showing a dark red chiffon gown. It didn't have tulle, but it was layered at the bottom and flowed beautifully. It was perfect for me. One thing showed up for sure: My meddling in other people's lives was inherited.

"Mom, I have plenty of dresses upstairs," I said.

"I know but I want you to feel glamorous," she said, shrugging innocently.

"Did you get me anything?" Drew asked.

"Oh, my Drewy. I had your blue suit dry cleaned and you have a new tie next to it," she said.

Before she could dote on him, I cut in. "You believe in having a positive attitude, right, Mom?"

"I do."

"You also believe to get what you want, you have to work hard and push until you get it. Right, Mom?"

"I do."

"What is it that you are after, Mom?" I asked looking at her seriously.

"I want my kids to be happy," she said and to my surprise she had tears in her eyes. Drew hugged her.

"How do you know what will make us happy?" I asked. I didn't even know what made me happy.

"I've been your protecter since birth, Erin. I've championed every healthy desire you've had."

I stopped. Maybe, just maybe my mom knew me better than I knew myself. When I didn't answer she said: "I just want you to find your happiness. I don't want you to regret anything."

"But Mom, I don't know how to find my happiness because I've always had you finding it for me. You can't always be with me. I have to learn for myself."

"I don't know how to do that."

"Mom, you are the best mom in the world."

"Now you sound like my five-year-old Erin," she laughed.

"It's time for me to take over," I said. "The hardest lessons I've had to learn come with regret and pain. Strength comes from the storms we weathered, not the storms we avoided."

"Yes, but I can always point out the blue skies, instead of letting you wallow in sleet and icy wind that cuts through you. Especially if your sun is simply a few humble steps away, Erin."

I looked at her.

"Mom, don't you think maybe it's time for you to find your own sun? Maybe you ought to work on your career again. That would leave us a little room to make our mistakes," I said as kindly as possible.

"I'll try, I will. But promise me one thing, Erin. If there comes a day to embrace your happiness, please don't run from it. Fight for it like you would your dancing."

"I'll try Mom, but I need it to be mine, because I can't embrace something that is yours."

"Okay," she said, resigned.

I sat wondering if it really would only take a few steps toward the sun to find my joy. I watched Drew, wondering how he didn't see Phoebe made him miserable. I was so quick to plan out a lifestyle change for him. Yet, he couldn't embrace my plan for him any more than I could embrace my mother's plan for me.

A few hours before the party started, Mom took Phoebe and me to the hairdresser so we would be out of the caterer's way. Mom went in the back room to get waxed and left us sitting there awkwardly.

"How've you been?" I asked.

"Oh, same old, you know," Phoebe said, glancing at me while the hairdresser curled her hair.

"Is that judge still being creepy to you?"

"Uh, my therapist helped me switch judges a month ago. I'm with a woman now. It's so much better. I guess I wasn't the first court reporter to feel really uncomfortable around him."

"Good for you."

"Yeah, work is so much better now," she said, smiling. Her smile was different. It wasn't saucy or competitive. It was natural. She didn't say much, she wasn't as jittery to fill the silence as she had been before.

"Look at this," she said, handing me a gossip magazine. Carrie and Veronica were on the cover together with Ethan and some other guy.

"I knew Carrie would end up with Ethan. Oh, I'm glad they're still friends. I kind of learned about friendship watching them," I said.

"Do you think we could be friends?" Phoebe asked.

"Yeah, sure, why not," I said giving in. She smiled her calm, real smile again, and despite my irritation with my mother, I was glad she'd been kind enough to get Phoebe some help. It then occurred to me; Phoebe looked a little too calm.

"Phoebe, did Drew tell you Jaxon and Chris are coming?"

"What?" she asked, her peace destroyed.

"Mom's meddling."

She nodded like she understood but didn't say anything else. I reached out and put a warm hand on her trembling arm.

"It's going to be okay; we'll get through this together. That's what friends do."

"Thanks, Erin," she said tears rimming her eyes.

"Mom said you stopped therapy. Do you think you might want to go back to your therapist?"

"I…have to let Drew go before I can," she said shaking.

"No, she doesn't control your life. She can give you well-meaning instructions, help where it is needed, but she's not your legal guardian."

"I think she's right about me using Drew as a crutch."

"Well, you don't have to do anything tonight. Take some time," I said. "I just wanted to give you a heads up about Jaxon."

"Thanks, Erin."

When we left the spa, Phoebe went to her apartment to get dressed and Mom and I came straight home to get dressed. I put on the dress Mom bought me. In all fairness she bought me dresses she knew I'd like, instead of dressing me like her miniature. Still, I would try to be more prepared, like texting her back and telling her I already had a dress.

I waited in Mom's sitting room for the guests to arrive. This sitting room was decorated in what she called Island sunset. The purple and gray room had a huge picture of the sun setting over Maui cut into three tiers. It felt symbolic, like on some level mom knew she was done raising her children.

"Something wrong, Erin?" Dad asked, sitting down next to me on the love seat against the far wall with a view of the door where his guests would soon be coming in.

"Nah, I wanted to say thanks for all you did to save my career."

"I didn't do much."

"Right."

"Really, Erin," he said. "You did the work. No matter how much contriving I did to get you in the spotlight, it wouldn't have meant anything if you didn't know what to do once you were there. Enjoy your success, but also recognize how many people it takes to get someone center stage."

"Like Mom," I said, grinning.

"She doesn't mean to overstep."

"I know she can't help it. And I am trying to pay it forward with the other dancers. Like you always do for your associates."

"That's my girl," he said. We sat there quiet for a minute, then I asked:

"Dad, do you get mad sometimes? Not just mad, like… Noel called you a bulldog. Sometimes I get angry and just start lashing out at people. Am I a bulldog?" I asked.

Dad laughed.

"I have a passionate disposition; you get that from me. It is important to have something to pour your passion into. I found my stage when I was a bit younger than you are now. I think a bulldog has little to do with anger, though. It is more a term for someone who can get things done," he said.

"You do get things done," I said. I thought of all he must have done to get that documentary into the right hands.

"We all have our strengths."

"How did you get over your anger. How did you focus?"

"I met your mother," he said with a grin. I laughed and nodded.

"You know anger has its place, though."

"Not according to Mom," I said.

"There is such thing as a righteous anger. Drew told me you got angry at Jaxon. You told him to grow up."

"Everything he did was so juvenile but I think it helped him," I said. "I went to their office yesterday. It's peaceful. They seem to be getting along."

"Right, so that anger may have been necessary, or he wouldn't have heard you. In a perfect world people would be able to talk to each other calmly, but that isn't this world, and sometimes anger is justified," Dad said.

"But I was mean angry to Phoebe," I said looking up at him.

"Cruelty and anger are not the same things. Drew said you were very mean to Phoebe," he said wincing.

"I was lashing out. It wasn't fair."

"Doing further damage to someone who is already injured is not appropriate. People like Phoebe need to be helped, not yelled at, but that's why they find people like Drew and your mother who are protectors, not bulldogs," he said with a laugh.

I laughed as well.

"Mom says yelling at people isn't necessary," I said.

"She has her own limitations. Being such a gentle soul, she fears anger," Dad said, like this perplexed him, as he could brush anger off.

"Yeah, I was yelling at Chris yesterday. He deserved it. Mom couldn't get out of there fast enough," I said.

"He deserved it," Dad agreed nodding at me. I smiled.

"That's what Chris even said as Mom pulled me away." This made Dad smile for some reason.

"What?"

"I like that. He knew he deserved it."

I looked at him wryly. He said quickly as if he knew Mom would want him to: "Most of the time yelling falls under mean… Most of the people you meet are struggling under some weight or other. Anger directed spitefully toward someone drowning can just finish pushing them under," he said.

"Then what do you do with it?" I asked.

"Anger is better used as fuel to launch us into action, to right wrongs. Sometimes just seeing the problem, getting angry enough to push and fight for those who cannot fight for themselves; that's when it's useful to be a bulldog."

"Like when you saved all that low-income housing, though it lost your firm millions of dollars."

"Just like that."

"I wish I was like that," I said taking a deep breath.

"You are more than you know and I love you very much," Dad said kissing my head.

"I love you too, Dad."

"Like I said though. I'm not ashamed to admit your mother helped me become who I am. The people you let into your life, especially who you date, affect you," he said. He glanced at me to be sure I understood.

"Chris dumped me."

"So you said the last time we spoke," he said.

I nodded and we sat comfortably together without speaking. Even when his biggest clients came in, he didn't leave my side. We didn't say much else, Dad and I didn't need to say much to each other.

"Excuse me, Andrew. May I borrow Erin?" Phoebe asked when she arrived.

"Of course," he said standing and helping me up, as he always did.

"Thanks," she said and motioned for me to follow her.

"Everything okay?" I asked as she led me out to the backyard strung in lights and warmed by space heaters.

"I just need you to clear some things up for me," Phoebe said as we walked, and she smiled at all my parent's important guests.

"What's up?" I asked, nodding to someone who waved to me. She stopped next to the waterfall spilling from the hot tub into the pool, making noise, as the music blared.

"Is Jaxon here?" she asked smiling, but her eyes looked terrified glancing around.

"Not yet."

"Are you sure he's coming?"

"He sounded like it. If it makes you feel better, I think the whole family is coming. If I have to endure seeing Chris, you can see Jaxon," I said, jiggling her crossed arm playfully. Her face looked like my insides felt.

"Did you… did he want to… you talk to him?" she stammered, her eyes glassing over.

"I did."

"And?" she said. She nervously adjusted her little black dress and looked down to be sure she wasn't creasing.

"Do you really want to know what he said? It will disturb your peace. It will possibly come between you and Drew. Are you ready for that?"

She closed her eyes. Without opening them she asked:

"Would you take this from me, Erin? Like you take Drew's mistakes. Will you take Jaxon away?"

"Was he a mistake?" I asked, "or was he just bad timing?"

She opened her eyes, blinking hard as she shrugged because she couldn't seem to say anything.

"Are you sure Jaxon didn't find a way into your heart? Would it really be such a bad thing to be in love with the man?"

"I…I don't know anymore. I can't … I don't want to marry my father. I don't want to do that to my children."

"Is Jaxon so much like your father?"

"He parties, he's aimless. He never holds down a job," she said.

"Jaxon's working two jobs. He's really making progress on the DJ scene, but he didn't quit. He's still working as a physical therapist."

"Oh, his taste in music is flawless. I knew he could make good on that if he tried," she said. She pressed a finger to the side of her eye, dabbing her eyeliner so it didn't spread.

"Do you want to hear?"

"Okay," she said taking my arm, like I could make her stronger. She really was terrified at the idea of loving Jaxon.

"Jaxon said he made a mistake letting you go. He loves you and he's going to try to steal you away from Drew."

"Uh…" Phoebe opened her mouth, but nothing else came out.

"I think you need to decide where your heart lives. It's only fair to Drew, yourself, and Jaxon."

"Will you stay with me tonight, please, Erin? I can't do this by myself. I know you've been pissed at me. Rightfully so, but I've always thought of you as a sister. You think of me at least as a friend, right?"

"Of course," I said putting an arm around her. Drew came out to the deck where we were standing like he was looking for us. I saw a pretty, light-haired woman watching him through the window and wondered if that was Isla.

"Drew," Phoebe said. "Can we talk?"

"I have a feeling you're going to give me back my ring," he said glancing at the rock she was pulling up and down her finger as if she waged a war inside. Part of her tried to keep the ring on, but she couldn't seem to.

"I'm sorry, I love you, I do, but…"

"Not like you love him," he said, nodding.

"I'm so sorry Drew. You deserve better than me," she said dropping the ring in his hand.

"Not better, Phoebe," I said. "Just more compatible."

Phoebe looked at me surprised. She examined me to see if I believed this. I smiled at her wishing I hadn't been so quick to tear her down. Finally, she said, "I think I might be more compatible with him. We like a lot of the same things."

"I knew you clicked with him. That doesn't make you less of a person, Phoebe," Drew said.

"You knew," she said quietly.

"I've known for a while, but I didn't want to let you down," he said.

"That's because you are an amazing guy. The girl who gets you is going to be so lucky," she said. She wiped a tear daintily while also managing her eye makeup. I meant to walk away so they could talk, but Phoebe almost leaned against me while they hashed things out. I knew she couldn't do it alone so I held her up a little. It felt right.

Chapter 56

I heard Mia before I saw her. She called for me, pushing her way through the crowd, and out the back door onto the portico. People's expressions ranged from slightly amused to astounded, but Mia didn't care.

"Erin!" she called. I didn't see anything but her tackling me.

"Hey, pretty lady! We match," I said to stop her, holding her hands out and examining her wine dress with a lace collar. She had a wreath of big fall flowers in her hair, and she looked adorable.

"I weared this to my Daddy's last wedding," she said.

"You look beautiful."

"Hey," Jaxon said from behind Mia. He was directing his "hey" to Phoebe.

"Hey," Phoebe said, glancing at Drew.

"I'm needed inside," Drew said, his eyes drawn to the window at a pretty woman mingling.

"So… how are… what's going on?" Jaxon asked, looking around, surprised Drew would leave him alone with Phoebe.

"Drew and I just broke up. It's really awkward for me to be here," she said, watching Jaxon.

"I could get you out of here," Jaxon said moving to her instantly and playing with her bare fingers.

"Yeah?" she questioned.

"Um, Erin, do you mind hanging with Mia if I bail?" Jaxon asked.

"Oh, is…did Chris not make it?" I asked.

"He said you didn't seem to want to see him. He didn't want to make you uncomfortable. Especially since you had a date," Jaxon said, jumbled, not even looking at me.

"I…" I stammered.

"She lied," Phoebe said helping me out. "She didn't have a date. That was nice of Chris though."

"Yeah, he's a nice guy," Jaxon said. He brushed at a curly hair pulled over Phoebe's shoulder. Realizing a minute too late it was weird, he dropped his hand to his side. Phoebe took hold of his hand. He leaned into her and gave her mouth a quick peck.

"I will deserve you, I promise," Jaxon said.

"I know," Phoebe answered, kissing him back, a little longer this time.

"All right. Just go. Mia can sleep here tonight. I'll drop her off at her home tomorrow," I said.

"Yeah! A sleep-over," Mia said.

"Chris can come get her," Jaxon said.

"No, really. It's fine. I'll drop her off," I said, not wanting Mom to figure out a way to trap Chris in our house until he agreed to propose to me simply for his freedom. She needed to get back into sales. She had way too much energy and her powers of persuasion might be getting a touch aggressive.

Phoebe and Jaxon went out the back gate and did not look back. Mia and Zack, Dad's underling, followed me around. Finally, I snuck away with Mia and a ton of junk food to my bedroom. I found her one of Drew's tee-shirts and basketball shorts to wear as PJ's and we did each other's nails. She told me how sad Chris had been since I left. Apparently, I needed to come back so he could be happy again.

I tried to explain to her that's not what happened, but Mia said it was. I dropped Mia off at her home the next morning because she looked sick from our late night. I sat with her until an orderly brought her a lunch. Chris didn't come. I kissed Mia goodbye when the orderly insisted she lay down for a nap.

I walked out into the hall and found Chris leaning against the wall with a white lily.

"What are you doing here?"

He stood up.

"Ah," he stammered looking nervous. His aqua eyes lit up a little. I moved closer to him unable to stop myself.

"I was just hoping… well, that you'd keep your promise," he said pushing off the wall.

"What promise?"

"You know about meeting you in abandoned hallways, and how I could expect things to go," he said looking at me slyly.

"Oh yeah," I said disbelieving his nerve. "Have you been waiting here for me?"

"I've even scared away a few residents so I could assure it would be abandoned," he said grinning. I laughed sardonically.

"How did you do –"

I didn't finish my statement. He grabbed me around my rib cage, pulled me in and kissed me. I dropped my coat and threw my arms around his neck. I did, after all, promise. The passion built between us. I couldn't even think, I couldn't breathe. I just felt him against me and needed more. I finally pulled away when I heard a door rattling, and the slow movements of a wheelchair-bound tenant trying to get into their entry way.

I breathed like I just ran a marathon. My body was alive, but I wanted to cry. Chris watched me, torn between grabbing me again and just helping the tenant to wherever he was going. Finally, he looked to heaven for strength and walked over to the door while I bent down to pick up the coat.

"Hi, there," he said. "Do you need some help?"

"No, I can do it," a gruff voice replied.

"Right. Here, just let me get the door around your…" Chris said, reappearing with the man and setting him free into the hall. The man grumbled a thanks and wheeled as quickly away as possible, not noticing his scarf was hooked to the back of his chair and trailing along behind him.

I hugged my coat as I followed the man down the hall.

"Wait, Erin! Where are you going?" Chris called.

"Isn't this how it goes Chris? You light me on fire, then leave?" I asked, already in tears.

"Erin I'm sorry. I had to fix things with Jaxon," he pleaded throwing his arms around me and kissing my temple, trying to get me to turn to him.

"I know, I get it. I'd never ask you to lose your brother. But now, you have to fix things with me.

I turned and walked away.

Chris tried to follow me, but the man in the wheelchair couldn't get his scarf out of the wheel. I left Chris trying to resolve it. As I drove away, I was sure I had just made the stupidest mistake of my life.

Shouldn't people just have everyone they love in their lives?

I exited the freeway a few times and even drove around the block a few more times, but I couldn't figure out how to go back to Chris. Maybe I needed to be in a wheelchair. Then it wouldn't matter how demanding my pride was.

I drove to my parents where cars still lined the street. My parents always provided hotel rooms and insisted the drinkers take a taxi and enjoy the hotel until they sobered up. Sometimes cars would line our road for a few days after the thankful party. I parked in the garage and thought I may want to go back to bed. Mia kept me up late.

I walked into the kitchen and froze. Chris sat in a stool at the bar eating leftovers from the party, chatting with Dad.

"What is happening here?" I asked.

"Are you okay?" Chris asked, standing up. "It took you a long time to get home."

"I drive like a grandma."

"I like that about you," he said, his face erupting in a smile.

"I…" I flushed. "Are you just?" I asked, looking at my dad.

"We're snacking," Dad said, shrugging. "Here, Chris, this is smoked salmon and quail eggs. The bread is a variation of sourdough. I don't know what the seasoning is, but it's really good."

Chris took it and bit down. He could have been on a food show, taste testing, his expression was so satisfied.

"That is good. It might be ground anchovies and olive oil," Chris said eating the whole thing.

"Here, Erin. Pull up a chair and try some," Dad said.

"Okay," I said feeling the whole thing was surreal. I noticed the white lily on the counter in a vase. I sat next to Chris, and he adjusted his stool, so he was closer to me, and our shoulders touched. I felt his whole body relax into mine. The simple action purged my heart of anger somehow. It wasn't anything except he wanted to be touching me.

Mom came rushing into the kitchen and stopped when she found us sitting at the bar eating.

"Erin! Is everything okay?" Mom asked.

"Yeah."

"Is your phone dead?"

"No," I said pulling it out of my purse. I had several missed calls. How long had Chris been here? Mom sat next to me as Dad got up and found another container full of leftovers.

"These are Erin's favorite. The crisp is actually a vintage white cheddar, the mushrooms are wild, and the green olives are a nutty Italian variety, salty enough to give the mushroom the right flavor."

"These mushrooms are so good," Chris said.

"A place in Paris has the most divine mushroom sauce," Mom answered happily.

Dad and Chris talked. Mom and I ate, and it was pleasant. Drew came in after a while and sat down.

"Missed you last night, Chris," he said.

"Yeah, I should have come," he said glancing at me. Turning back to Drew, he asked, "You okay?"

"Yeah, it's weird, like a chapter of my life ended. It was hard to let go, but now that it's over, I feel better. I finally see a different future for myself."

"Like as a prosecutor," I said.

"I think I might, for a few years anyway," he said, glancing at Dad.

"I thought about being a public servant for a while," Dad said calmly. "Your opportunities at my law firm will always be available. It wouldn't hurt to fight the good fight for a few years."

I always knew deep down Drew wanted to better the world instead of arranging business deals. It was the same reason he couldn't just leave Phoebe until he knew she'd be okay. We ate for a while longer, until finally I declared I would put nothing else in my mouth.

"All right then," Mom said. "It is time."

Drew and I stood up, expecting this, but Chris sat on his stool and looked confused.

"Chris, we always pick out a Christmas tree the day after our party. Would you like to join us?"

"Yeah, thanks," Chris said, glancing at me.

"I'll go get my boots on," I said, walking out into the garage. I sat down on the step to put them on. Chris came and sat next to me.

"Is it cool if I just hang out?" he implored.

"I like you here. You fit," I said. I leaned into him, and he kissed me, just a quick peck on the lips. I went back to tying my snow boots, certain this was my perfect moment, sitting on the cement steps, with Chris.

"I want you in my life," Chris said. "Even if you can only be my friend right now, I'm going to make things right between us."

"Are yuh?"

"I don't give up on the people I love. Even if it takes the next ten years, I'm going to put in the work to fix us. I'm going to become your family."

"I think that is the definition of family – the ones you never give up on."

"And I have serious staying power," he said.

"Yes, you do," I said with a laugh. I laid my head on his shoulder, wondering why this felt like romance to me.

It did not take Chris long to become my family. In fact, we did not exclude anyone from our family. Phoebe and Jaxon came to Thanksgiving, with Mia. Drew had a date, and though it was a little awkward at first, we made it through. I never saw Mom more pleased than welcoming all those sitting around the table supporting each other. She was better than I, and always would be, but I liked her concept of finding life through the people I shared it with. Love multiplies when it is done right.

Over the holiday season, Chris became my groupie, flying out to find me after Monday night football.

Jaxon started taking on more responsibility at the practice and increased his clientele until he could afford a nice apartment for himself and Phoebe. By Christmas, my mother added Lana, Ivan, Stephan, and half the dance company, to her table. The more we added, the closer Chris and I became. We bonded under the weight of not only our love, but everyone else's.

Chris had a knack for promotion, and my name was soon everywhere in the ballet world. I was soon called a Prima Ballerina, and I was proud of that accomplishment.

But I knew it was not mine alone. It came from the ones I loved unselfishly lifting me up. My desires matured solid and unmoving the day I married Chris and our passion for each other fueled our dreams into reality for the rest of our lives.